ANGELA CLARKE

Follow Me

The Social Media Murders

avon

AVON
1 London Bridge Street,
London SE1 9GF

A Paperback Original 2015

1

Copyright © Angela Clarke 2015

Angela Clarke asserts the moral right to
be identified as the author of this work

A catalogue record for this book is
available from the British Library

ISBN-13: 978-0-00-816543-7

Set in Minion by Born Group using Atomik ePublisher from Easypress

Printed and bound in Great Britain by
Clays Ltd, St Ives plc

MIX
Paper from
responsible sources
FSC
www.fsc.org
FSC C007454

For the authentically badass Amy Jones

Chapter 1

FML – Fuck My Life

05:35
Saturday 31 October

From where she stood in the doorway of the bedroom of 39 Blackbird Road, London, E14, Freddie could see blood. A lot of blood. The plastic overall she was wearing rustled in time with her clipped, panicked breaths. The blue walls were splattered with red, as if a food fight had taken place with thin, runny Lidl ketchup. But it wasn't tomato sauce. She could taste it: metallic. It was coating her tongue. Sweat stuck clumps of her thick frizzy hair to her forehead, loosened her glasses on her nose, and opened her pores to the gore. She was absorbing it.

Dread pinpricked her skin. The source was to her right, shielded by the open room door. There was still time to leave. To turn back. To run. She could be home in thirty; pretend none of this had happened. Heavy footsteps fell on the stairs behind her. More people were coming. She had to decide.

Seize the story. It was now or never. Opportunity follows struggle.

Fear makes you braver. Despite deriding the inspirational quotes that appear over photos of sunsets and the ocean on Facebook, Freddie was disappointed to discover that when she reached her own life crossroads her brain filled with nothing but clichés.

To shut herself up, she stepped forward. Reassuring herself: *it was just like the movies. You've seen it all before.* (The time she'd had to lie down after watching a beheading video online didn't count. This was different. She was prepared.) She turned.

The floor undulated under Freddie's feet. The body of what had once been a man was slumped over a desk, his neck cut like deli salami, blood pooling round his bare feet. A computer, its worm-hole screensaver winding over the monitor seemed to propel blood toward her. The last thing she heard before the dark red obliterated everything was her childhood friend Nasreen Cudmore's voice.

'Freddie Venton, what the hell are you doing here?'

Fifteen hours earlier
14:32
Friday 30 October

Sat on the windowsill, trying to block out the late lunch drinkers in the Queen Elizabeth pub below, Freddie pressed her phone to her ear. How, in Dalston, in the middle of the country's capital, could this be the only place to get signal in her room? Her new flatmate – what was his name, short guy, wore glasses, worked in ad sales, always out drinking after work. Pete? P – something. Edged into her room, en route to the kitchen, mouthing, 'Sorry'. Must be his day off.

She nodded. Three people in one pokey two-bed flat had seemed a great money-saving plan. But that was five flatmates ago, when she'd actually known the two girls she shared with. Now she slept in the lounge, the sofa claimed as a bed, and all and sundry crossed her room to get their breakfast cereal. Privacy and mobile reception were for other people.

Freddie gurned at her reflection in the seventies mirror above the faux thirties fireplace opposite. Her brown hair, cut by a mate with kitchen scissors, sprang away from her shoulders like she'd been shocked. Flashes of red hair chalk zigzagged toward her DIY fringe. Her legs, stubbornly plump despite working on her feet and taking more than the recommended 10,000 steps a day, poked out from beneath her nightshirt (a T-shirt that had belonged to a long-forgotten one-night stand). Unless she squished herself in with her hands or a belt, she never looked like she had a waist. Her torso, like her mum's, was square, with the addition of breasts that practically needed scaffolding to restrain them. She wiggled her black plastic rectangular-framed glasses. *Not traditionally beautiful.*

The line in her ear clicked, and the noise of the busy newsroom came through. 'Freddie.' Sandra, the deputy editor of *The Family Paper* online, sounded tense and tired. Business as usual. 'Is there a problem with this week's copy?'

'No. No problem.' Freddie pushed her back into the cold glass, willing the signal to hold. 'It's just I've been writing the Typical Student column for three years now...'

'Time flies when you're having fun.'

Freddie thought of the two years she'd spent on the dole, clawing her way into glass collecting jobs, churning out pitches, unpaid articles and free features during the day – a blur of coffee, cigarettes and unpaid bills since she graduated. 'Yes, it is fun. And popular. Didn't I get over 90,000 hits last week?'

Sandra didn't deign to confirm or deny this figure.

'Well I was wondering if, given the column's popularity, I might get paid for writing it?'

There was silence on the other end. Only the sound of the UK's busiest and most hated newsroom could be heard. The clamorous grind and grunt as the newspaper was conceived in a hail of profanities all journalists told you was the best-paid gig. The one that Freddie had written one hundred and fifty-six eight-hundred-word columns for, and been paid precisely nothing by.

'Sandra?'

'We don't have the budget. If you could get the column into the print edition then you'd be paid,' Sandra sighed. Freddie noticed it was more from annoyance than shame.

'How do I do that?' *Surely you could do that for me, you lazy cow.* 'I'll think about it. I'll send you some emails.'

Unlikely.

'Didn't we try this before?' Sandra sounded on the verge of dozing off.

We? There's no we in this, Sandra. You go off with your monthly pay packet, and I sit in my lounge bedroom trying to work out how I'm going to afford to eat this month. 'Yes.'

'What did they say?'

'The student focus was too young for the main paper.' *Snotty baby-boomers.*

'The online readers enjoy your stories of debauched students, Freddie. They really go for it.'

They really go for hating on it. Last week she'd written about getting wasted the night before an exam. Total fabrication. Her and her mates had sat in night after night working in fear, as they watched the collapsing economy swallow everything around it like a dead star: paid internships, graduate schemes, jobs, benefits. She might as well have spent her time downing pints of vodka. 'I graduated two summers ago, I'm not even at university anymore.'

'It's up to you, it's all good experience.'

Experience. Everything was good experience: writing articles for free for a national newspaper, landing a job in Espress-oh's coffee chain to pay her bills, pitching, publishing, pumping out all her words for no reward. When was this experience supposed to pay off? When would she have *enough* experience? 'I'll send the copy over now.'

'Let's do drinks soon.'

They wouldn't. That was what people with paid jobs said to get rid of you. They didn't need contacts. They didn't need any

4

more drags on their time. When they were done, they wanted to go home and wank off in front of their latest box set. Drinks were for those who needed a way in. Drinks were fucking fictional.

Freddie left the phone on the windowsill. She should sleep. What had she managed? Her shift finished at 6.00am. She'd brainstormed ideas on the way home on the Ginger Line. 9.30am first commission came in. There were three in total today, all wanted them filed within a couple of hours, all under a thousand words, only one of them was paid. Thirty pounds from a privately funded online satire site. Gotta love the rich kids. Awash with their parents' money, they didn't have enough business sense to demand that their contributors work for *experience*.

She clicked refresh on her Mac mail. No new emails. Then she clicked refresh again. Then she did the same on Twitter, Facebook, WhatsApp and Snapchat. Round and round. Waiting. For what? Something. Something big.

She placed her glasses on the coffee table, closed her eyes, and pulled her duvet up. She'd been awake for nineteen, nearly twenty hours. Her flatmate, Pete, whatever, moved quietly through the room, only ruining it when he spilt hot tea on his thumb and swore. She liked him. Good egg. The tug of sleep came easily.

Her head was shaking. No, vibrating. Her hand had the phone and she was answering before her brain caught up.

'Freddie, it's Neil here. Neil Sanderson.'

Neil Sanderson. *The Post*. Broadsheet. She'd met him at the industry awards she'd blagged a ticket to. Built the relationship on Twitter.

'Neil, hi,' she gulped from a cold coffee as she climbed up onto the windowsill. Work brain, work.

'I've taken a look at the stuff you've sent me and it's great.'
Fuck!

'The writing is sound, the points salient and well argued,' he continued.
Fuck, fuck!

'But I can't use it.'

Fuck. 'Why?'

'The thing is, Freddie, you're a great writer, but that's not enough these days. The world's full of great writers and the Internet's only made it easier to find them. You need that extra something to stand out.'

'Like what?' She wasn't sure she had much left to give.

'Did you see Olivia Williams' piece on being kidnapped by Somali pirates? Laura McBethan's blog on surviving the Air Asiana plane crash? Or Gaz Wagon's real-time microblogging from the London riots? All excellent reporting. All game changers. All propelled to stardom now.'

'So I need to get kidnapped, or embroil myself in a riot? I'll get right onto it.'

Neil laughed. 'Are you working class?'

She thought of her parents, her mum a dedicated junior school teacher, and her dad a local council worker (retired early, following one too many dazed and confused moments at work), in their leafy suburban home. 'Er, no.'

'Shame, that's quite in at the moment. Not landed gentry?'

What was this, an UsVsTh3m online game – What Social Class Are You?

Neil continued, 'Because of Made in Chelsea, people are obsessed with the posh.'

'I'm middle class.'

'Middle class like Kate Middleton?'

'Nobody is middle class like Kate Middleton.' My career's over at the age of twenty-three, condemned by my parents' traditional jobs and the good fortune not to have been caught in a natural disaster, thought Freddie.

'And you're not black…'

Did he even remember meeting her? 'I don't see how that's relevant.'

'Just looking for a unique angle.'

6

'Being black is a unique angle?'

'Pieces written about the ethnic experience are very popular with readers.'

'I'll tell my Asian mates who lived in the same street as me, went to the same school, studied at the same university, and get paid the same as me, to give you a call to share their *ethnic experience*.'

Neil laughed. 'Okay, then you'll have to try the old-fashioned way. Keep getting your name in print, and with a bit of luck you'll land a contract.'

She felt all the air go out of her. 'How'd you do it?'

'Wrote small pieces for a local newspaper and worked my way up till I was on the nationals. I was an apprenticeship lad.'

An apprenticeship: so scarce it'd be easier to book onto a plane that was going to crash. There was silence for a moment.

'You could always consider another career, I pay my accountant a fortune?' Neil sounded like he was only half joking.

'Thanks. I mean, for the advice and that.'

'Anytime, good luck.' He sounded sad. Or guilty. 'You've just got to seize the story, Freddie. Push yourself into uncomfortable situations. Keep your eyes and ears open.' He was trying to be encouraging.

'Sure,' she tried to sound upbeat. 'Something'll turn up.'

After the phone call, Freddie lay looking at the nicotine-stained ceiling. Replaying Neil's words over in her head. *You've just got to seize the story.* If she called her mum she'd only have to fend off her soft pleading to give up this 'London madness' and return to Pendrick, the commuter market town she'd left behind. Her mum didn't understand she wanted to do more than try for a job at Pendrick's local council. She wanted to make a difference. Bear witness. Maybe one day be a war correspondent. She sighed. It was half past four and already getting dark. The night was winning the fight.

Chapter 2

YOLO – You Only Live Once

20:05
Friday 30 October

No tattoos or unnatural piercings are to be visible. Freddie rolled the sleeves of her black shirt up, stopping just below the feet of her Jane and the Dragon tattoo. *Partners are free to wear any black collared shirt and pants they choose, with many proud employees purchasing those bearing Espress-oh's logo from the company store.* She tucked the ends of her H&M shirt into her trousers. *All partners are supplied with Espress-oh's world-famous apron and hat to wear with pride.* Freddie tightened the yellow apron strings round her waist. As if dealing with douches who wanted extra caramel syrup wasn't enough, they made you dress like a freaking banana.

'Turn that frown upside down!' Dan, the manager of Espress-oh's St Pancras branch, appeared in the hallway they called the staffroom. His fake-tanned skin an alarming orange next to his yellow Espress-oh's uniform. He resembled a Picasso fruit bowl.

Freddie punched down the overstuffed bin bags that were shoved under the tiny kitchen surface. *Ten Signs You Hate Your Boss (mental note: look for amusing gifs to accompany pitch).* She lifted the bag she knew contained the expired best-before-date produce. 'Bin's full, Dan,' she said. 'I'll just pop this one in the wheelie outside.'

'Quick, quick, customers to bring joy to,' Dan said without looking up from his stocktake clipboard.

All Espress-oh's food waste is to be incinerated. Clutching the bag, Freddie left through the staff-only station exit and stood in the underground area that housed the bins and a healthy population of rats. She let her eyes adapt to the dim light and whistled. There was slight movement from the far corner. 'Kath, that you?' she called.

An elderly woman in the remains of a tattered skirt and layered jumpers, her hair matted and grey down her shoulders, edged into the light. She smiled a yellowing grin at Freddie. 'Nice evening for it.'

'Bit colder than when we met in July, hey? Do you remember?' Kathy was getting increasingly confused, and Freddie had read with senility cases it was important to reiterate reality.

'Course I do,' said Kathy. 'Me and Pat asked for one of your cigarettes.'

'That's right,' said Freddie. 'I was on my break. And what did you tell me about the old days?' She glanced over her shoulder to check no one was following her out.

'Oh! All the fun we used to have! The girls and I. This was our patch,' Kathy smiled.

'That's right' said Freddie. *Until the regeneration tidied up the safe spots where you and the other ex-sex workers slept rough, and turned them into crowdfunded hipster coffee shops.* She couldn't write about Kath and the others and risk alerting the private security guards to their whereabouts, but she could *recycle* food that was destined for the bin. 'Here you go.' She held the bag out. There was a nasty cut on Kathy's hand. 'What's that?'

9

'Just some drunk kids. They took my sleeping bag.' Kathy rooted through the packets. 'Any of those funny cheese and grape ones today? They're my favourites.'

'Did you get the sleeping bag back?' Freddie tried to get her to concentrate.

'Nah,' she hooked out a sandwich and put it in her pocket.

It was bitterly cold out: what was Kathy sleeping under? 'Did you report it to the police?'

Kathy laughed. 'They don't care 'bout likes of me, dearie. No bother, though. I'm just A-okay.' She squeezed Freddie's arm, and Freddie felt how thin her fingers were. 'I'll make sure the other girls get their share.' She bundled the bag up.

Kathy shuffled back toward the fire escape door Freddie propped open on her way into work. Freddie resolved to find a sleeping bag on Amazon and bring it in for her. She'd roped in her sympathetic work colleague, Milena, and they took it in turns to make these illicit drops. 'Me or Milena will see you tomorrow,' Freddie said. 'If Dan's out the way, I'll try and get you some hot drinks, yeah?'

The old lady held up her hand to signal goodbye.

'Here, Kathy, hang on,' she jogged over to press the last of her fags into the old lady's hand.

'Pat'll be pleased,' she said.

'Yes,' nodded Freddie, though she knew Pat had been found dead of exposure at the end of September. The authorities weren't interested: the NHS and homeless charities she'd spoken to were too stretched to come here and hunt out one elderly, senile woman. Kathy had far outlived the average age a homeless person was expected to reach. She was a tough old bird. 'Try and keep warm, yeah?' Freddie turned and headed back toward work. *A Terrible Waste: how food destined for the bin could save lives.*

Out on the floor she nodded at Milena, whose pony-tailed long dark hair and high Bulgarian cheekbones incredulously worked with Espress-oh's uniform. Would she agree to an interview? *An*

Immigrant Truth: two jobs, business school, and sharing a room with three others – how London betrayed its silent workforce.

'Freddie?' Dan had fixed her in his sights. He hadn't seen anything had he?

She watched as he dug his hand into the dusty beans that formed an interactive display along the till.

'Never forget, these are magic beans.'

Nope. He just wanted to share some more inane motivational drivel. Behind him, as the customers inspected the soggy sandwiches, Milena smacked the palm of her hand repeatedly against her forehead.

20:19 *Nine hours and forty-one minutes to go. How Childhood Fairy Tales Set Generation Y Up To Fail.*

04:43
Saturday 31 October

Eight Times People Actually Died of Boredom. A WhatsApp chat alert flashed on Freddie's phone, which was under the till out of the sight of customers.

A white speech bubble from Milena, who was outside taking a fag break, read: 'Dan is', and then there was a series of smiling poo emojis.

Freddie typed back: 'Espress-woes.'

'Are you in charge?'

Shoving her phone into her pocket, she looked up to find a drunk in a pinstripe suit, swaying in front of her. His eyes pink.

'Look!' He prodded at the fruit toast he'd placed on the counter. 'This slice has no raisins. This one all the raisins.'

She waited…

'Is not right,' he stabbed again, catching the edge of the paper plate and flipping one of the half-eaten slices onto the Almond Biscottis they were pushing this month.

You've got to be kidding? As she reached out to retrieve the toast, his hand – cold and damp – grabbed hers and she was pulled across the counter toward him.

11

'Or yous could give me your number?' His stale beer breath buffeted her face.

She scanned the cafe for help. A Japanese couple, heads down, earphones in, oblivious. The gossipy women who'd been here for hours had left. Dan was in the stockroom. She was on her own.

'Giz a kiss,' the drunk lunged.

Shame burned up her body and then ignited into anger. Wrenching her hand free, she sent the fruit toast flying toward him. 'Get lost!'

Alerted by the disturbing sound of an employee raising their voice, Dan bustled into the cafe, oozing toward the drunk. 'Sir, I'm so sorry. There's obviously been a misunderstanding. I'm sure Freddie here can help.'

What the… 'Are you suggesting I prostitute myself for a piece of sodding fruit toast?'

Milena swung through the glass door – had she seen?

'Our Freddie, ever the joker!' Dan laughed like a screaming kettle.

'Sir, I make you some new toast, please, have a seat. I bring it over.' Milena's megawatt smile blindsided the pink-eyed man.

'Sure,' he swayed.

'The customer is always right,' Dan glared at Freddie.

How the hell was this her fault? 'But he…'

'I don't care, Freddie. You need to see the positives in all customers. Visualise them as your close personal friend.'

'That's what I was sodding worried about!'

'Espress-oh partners don't use language they wouldn't feel comfortable saying in front of their mothers,' Dan stage whispered.

Flinging her arm in the direction of the drunk who was now face down asleep on the counter, a puddle of drool spreading toward the discarded fruit toast, Freddie screamed: 'If my mum was here she'd tell that dirty bastard to fuck off!'

'Enough! Take your break! Now!'

Furious, she smacked her palms hard against the glass door and powered toward the train platforms. A few hardy souls were bundled, with suitcases, on the cold metal benches, waiting for the first Eurostar. All this money regenerating the station and they forgot to put doors on? Yet another deterrent to Kathy and her homeless mates. Barely more appealing than metal spikes. She was heading to the taxi rank where she could bum a cigarette off a cabbie, when she saw her: Nasreen Cudmore.

They'd played together virtually every day since they were six, until…she couldn't deal with thinking about that now. Eight years ago. Must be.

Nasreen looked the same. No, different. There was no puppy fat, and she was tall too, like her dad. Five foot eight, at least. She'd cut that ridiculous waist-length black hair. It now hung in a sleek curtain to her shoulders. Perfect against her milky coffee skin. With both pride and pain, Freddie acknowledged Nasreen Cudmore had grown into a beautiful woman.

What the hell was she doing here at this time in the morning? Wearing a hoodie and jeans, Nasreen was stood with a group. All dressed casually. Most looked to be in their twenties or thirties. One guy, slightly older, early forties, broad shoulders, Bruce Willis buzz cut, was wearing a blue down puffa jacket zipped up over a tight white T-shirt. Friends' night out? One of those godawful-sounding corporate away-days?

Freddie remembered seeing Fiona Cogswell at a pop-up Shoreditch tequila bar. Among the inane drivel about what every Pendrick High alumnus was now doing – mostly out of work management consultants, or pursuing worthless PhDs until the economy recovered – there'd been one lime wedge of interest: Nasreen Cudmore had joined the police.

She looked again at Nasreen's group: men, all with regulation-neat haircuts. Police. Undercover? A bust? *Seize the story.* Neil's advice echoed in her head. Behind her, Dan was waiting for a grovelling apology. A plan formulated in Freddie's mind.

Thrusting her cap into her back pocket, she approached her old school friend. 'Nasreen! Oh my God! It is you!'

Nasreen startled, turned toward her, taking in the yellow apron and the red hair. 'F…Freddie?'

Feeling awkward and teenage again, Freddie kept smiling. Up close she could see a new hardness in Nasreen's face.

'Cudmore?' The older guy with the puffa body interrupted. He clearly didn't want Freddie here. She was onto something.

'Sorry, can't stop.' Nasreen looked embarrassed.

Oh no you don't. 'Are you on Facebook, or Twitter?'

'Er…no.'

Because you're a policewoman. 'Gmail? Google Plus – you on Google Plus?'

'Yes. I think.' Nasreen looked over her shoulder as the body-warmer guy grunted.

'Awesome: what's your email? Give me your phone so I can type mine in?' She had one shot to get this right.

Nasreen, looking increasingly peeved, handed over her iPhone.

'Here, you write yours in mine.' Freddie pulled her phone from her back pocket, knocking her cap to the floor. Passing her phone to Nasreen, she turned to retrieve her baseball cap. At the same time, she opened up Nasreen's Google+ app, clicking through: Menu > Settings > Location Sharing On. Years of following exes round the Internet was paying off. She clicked into contacts as she turned back: adding her name, number and email. She pressed call.

Her phone, which was in Nasreen's hand, vibrated.

'Now I've got your number.' She beamed at Nas as she held the phone out to swap.

'Great,' Nasreen mustered a weak smile.

'Who was that?' the body warmer asked Nasreen as Freddie walked away.

'No one. Just someone I used to know…'

Sorrow settled under Freddie's hat as she pulled it on. She was nothing to Nasreen anymore. Perhaps that made it easier? Unlocking her own phone, she opened Google+. Little thumbnails of her friends appeared on the map. There was Milena, pinpointed in St Pancras station, and there, squashed up against her, was a new blank profile picture: Nasreen Cudmore.

Gotcha!

Chapter 3

#FF – Follow Friday

04:59
Saturday 31 October

Freddie slowed her pace and rubbed her eyes, hoping her mascara would smudge. Could you think yourself pale? One arm across her stomach, she half fell through Espress-oh's door.

Dan and Milena looked up.

'You okay?' Milena put down the hot panini tongs.

'I know why I lost my temper. Not feeling great.' In the corner of her eye she saw Nasreen and her colleagues exit the station and head to an arriving police van. Dan's face was a hesitant scowl. 'Pretty sure it's just my period, but I've been sick, everywhere...' *Three...two...*

'Sick!' Dan bowled toward her.

'You don't think it's like that norovirus case you told us about from the Kuala Lumpur branch?' she slurred into his panicked face.

Dan was surprisingly efficient when under pressure. He had her, and her coat, out the cafe in under a minute.

16

'Not sure I can walk.' Freddie bent double, as Dan tried to stuff her apron under her jacket. He kept glancing round, as if a health and safety inspector might leap out from behind one of the trees lining the station approach. Beads of sweat ran in orange rivulets over his forehead.

'I'll get you a taxi!' he stage whispered.

'I'm broke.'

'Here!' Dan pulled notes from his wallet and thrust them at her. 'We have to get you away from here. I mean home.' He stuck his arm out as a black cab drove toward them and scooped her into the back. 'Dalston, she lives in Dalston.'

Dan, thankful disaster had been averted, watched as the taxi disappeared past the lights. Freddie saw him take his sanitizer bottle from his pocket and squirt his hands. *You could never be too safe.*

Inside the cab, Freddie pulled her phone from her pocket and followed the flashing Nasreen Cudmore as she leapfrogged across London. 'Actually, mate, looks like we're heading toward The City, no, past that, Canary Wharf. Can you take me there? Cheers.'

Bright coloured lights danced across the Thames, as the night sky airbrushed out the churning grey filth of the river. Freddie didn't look up. She kept her eyes on the faceless silhouette that represented Nas. It had stopped. Had she lost connection? They wound past the glowing phallic towers of Canary Wharf. Cranes, anchors, and industrial cogs – ghostly reminders of the docks' past – punctuated the new gated developments covering the area. They were almost upon the symbol. Freddie looked up as the flats gave way to rows of dockers' cottages. 'Think it's the next right, mate.'

She needn't have worried. The taxi turned into a street of Victorian houses ablaze with activity. A police van, that had presumably carried Nas and her team, was parked behind a police car blocking the road.

'Can't go any further than this, love,' said the cabbie.

'This is fine. Cheers.' She passed Dan's banknotes through the window. There was no sign of Nas, or any of her plain-clothes

17

colleagues. 'What road's this, mate?' Freddie pocketed the change. That'd get her a drink in the pub later.

'Blackbird Road.' The cabbie turned to reverse back the way they'd come.

A white tarpaulin canopy was erected over the entrance of one of the houses. Incident tape flapped in the breeze. People were stood in dressing gowns, and in coats over pyjamas, phones up taking photos.

Residents of a quiet Docklands street were shocked to discover that... What was this? Break-in? Domestic? A uniformed policeman, early fifties, balding, guarded the door. A white van was parked opposite. Freddie watched as a man plucked a plastic boiler suit from the back and pulled it over his trousers and shirt. Forensics.

'What the...?' the door policeman shouted.

Freddie looked up to see a sandy-haired, skinny policeman, a few years older than her, stumble out of the property and spew all over the path.

'Heavy night?' shouted a voice.

The growing crowd of onlookers laughed. *Are Millennials Just Not Cut Out For Work?* The forensics guy tutted, before ducking under the police tape, sidestepping the puking copper, and walking into the house. No badge, no questions, no problem.

Seize the story. Push yourself into uncomfortable situations.

Freddie walked with purpose to the white van and peered inside. Voila! She took a plastic-wrapped boiler suit from a box in the back and pulled it over her clothes. *Disposable Jumpsuits: the Ideal Freelance Uniform?*

'You stay out here and I'll get something to clean this up,' the older cop said as he hauled the pale young lad to his feet. He disappeared inside as Freddie reached the gate. She just needed to get past PC Spew.

His pale blue eyes focused on her as she ducked under the tape. She felt him take in the rustling plastic boiler suit and stop...on her dyed red hair. Shit. Bloody hair chalk. She kept going. Imagining she was walking into a nightclub, like she had for years as an underage teenager. *Behind The Incident Tape: Inside an Active Crime Scene.*

'Evening, ma'am,' PC Spew said.

'Evening.' She stopped in front of him. Nerves rippled through her body. 'Cold night for it?'

'Yes, ma'am.' He looked like he might be about to say something else, and then he nodded and stood aside. 'You must be on the new computer team, ma'am. It's upstairs.'

'Thank you.' She avoided his gaze. The door closed behind her and she was alone in a small laminated-floor hallway. In front of her a patterned glass door made a collage of the people behind it. The sound of a kettle boiling. The stir of a teaspoon in a cup. Someone crying? Must be the kitchen. Black coats hung on hooks at the bottom of the stairs. It was like the man said: what she wanted was upstairs. *In the early hours of Friday morning a dawn raid was carried out…*

There was movement above. She figured she didn't have long. In and out. That was the plan.

Chapter 4

BFF – Best Friends Forever

05:36
Saturday 31 October

Dropping down to the ground from the back of the police van, Nasreen tucked the flask of tea into her hoodie pocket and headed back. Sent for the DCI's tea again. This wasn't what she'd had in mind when she'd requested to be assigned to Detective Chief Inspector Moast's team. She wanted to prove herself on a major investigation, not fetch beverages. Perhaps there'd be a chance to make a real difference on this case. It was a particularly grim one. The body of Alun Mardling, slumped over his computer with his throat cut, had been found by his mother at around 4.30am, when she had returned from her night shift at St Thomas' Hospital. Mrs Lucy Mardling had a job cleaning surgical instruments, but Nasreen couldn't imagine any amount of blood and tissue would prepare you for this.

Closing her eyes, she was back in the hallway with DCI Moast, breathless from suiting up before the others. She replayed the scene in her mind.

'Sergeant Nasreen Cudmore, this is Dr Jim Fisher.' DCI Moast, his blue puffa jacket and jeans covered by his protective full body suit, signalled at the pathologist. 'Nasreen is new to the team. Fresh blood.'

She nodded as Dr Fisher stood back to let them enter the room. At just over six foot, he was taller than Nasreen and the DCI, with smiling crinkly eyes behind thin wire glasses, and thick grey hair she could glimpse under his hood.

'Glad to see you've finally got someone who knows what correct practice is, Ed.' The doctor pointed at the disposable face mask Nasreen was wearing. She blushed. She didn't want to get the DCI in trouble.

'I've got my shoes and my bonce covered, Jim, what more do you want?' The DCI's grizzled jaw broke into a white grin. With his hood up over his cropped hair, he resembled a cotton bud. 'You bods are finished anyway,' he continued. 'I just want to see the body in situ.' They stepped into the small bedroom at the front of the house. 'My, my, this is a mess isn't it? You going to be all right with this, Sergeant Cudmore?'

Nasreen steeled herself to assess the scene. 'Yes, sir. I've worked homicides before.'

'Righto.' DCI Moast pulled his notebook from his pocket. 'The victim is Alun Mardling, aged forty-eight, a local bank manager at Canary Wharf.'

With her own suit hood up, Nasreen had to turn her head to take in the small room. The blue seventies-style curtains were drawn. The orange glow of the street lamp outside could be seen through them. A dusty lampshade with faded red and yellow cars on it hung from above. There was a desk, a chair and a computer, at which the body was slumped. The victim's blood was splattered up and over the wall. Nasreen felt her gut contract and tears threaten at the back of her eyes. She reminded herself to stay clinical. Break it down into small manageable sections. The best thing she could do for the victim and his mother was help find who did this.

Blood was everywhere. Doused. Splashed. Flung. The room contained a slim pine wardrobe, with what she presumed was Mardling's work suit hung on the outside. There was a matching compact pine bedside table, with Top Gear magazines and a box of tissues piled on it, and barely enough room for them to stand in here. Everything was covered in sprays of livid red. 'Single bed, almost like this was a child's room, sir?' She looked at the faded blue checked duvet that was crumpled across the mattress. 'No photos or pictures.' She looked at the drab walls.

'Apparently Mrs Mardling's son, Alun here, moved back in with his mum after his marriage fell apart,' DCI Moast said. 'He was based in Manchester before that.'

'Recently?' asked Nasreen. This was a sad bachelor room.

'About four years ago,' said Moast.

'Doesn't look like he's moved on much, does it?' Dr Fisher said from the doorway.

The victim was dressed in a T-shirt and shorts, his head and body slumped forward over his computer. His blood looked as if it had been dashed against the desk and the walls, indicating it had come out in high-velocity gushes. It was concentrated on the computer, desk and wall Mardling had been facing. 'Was he attacked from behind?' Nasreen asked.

'Correct,' said Dr Fisher. 'His neck was cut with a sharp implement, probably a knife. I'll know more when we're back at the lab.'

'So far we've found no murder weapon,' said DCI Moast. 'I've got the lads outside searching.'

Nasreen had seen something similar once after a gang hit. 'The blood spatter is fairly aggressive,' she said. 'Like spurts. Did the perp cut the carotid artery, doctor?'

'Very good, Sergeant.' Dr Fisher pointed at the sliced neck. 'He would have lost consciousness pretty instantly and bled out in minutes.'

What a horrible, violent end to a life. 'Well, at least it was quick,' said Nasreen. 'Do you think the perp knew what he was doing?'

'It looks like a precision cut,' said the doctor. 'So either he knew his anatomy, or he got lucky.'

DCI Moast nodded and wrote something in his notebook.

'And presumably the perp's clothes would be covered too?' said Nasreen.

'I've told the lads to look for discarded clothing as well,' said the DCI.

'She's a sharp one this one: I'd keep hold of her if I were you, Ed.' Dr Fisher winked at Nasreen.

'She's too young for you, Jim,' Moast said. Nasreen felt herself blush again. And then she'd been sent to fetch the DCI's tea.

Had she spoken out of turn? Did the DCI think she couldn't cope with the rigours of a ghoulish crime scene? No, she was sure DCI Moast made all his sergeants run round after him. Perhaps he drank sweet tea to help combat shock, keep his mind clear? They all did what they had to to cope with a crime scene like this. She understood sacrifices needed to be made. She'd better text Claire and cancel their planned cinema trip tomorrow. Claire had ditched her plenty of times to work late in her bid to make partner at her law firm. That's why their friendship worked so well: they both knew the job came first.

Members of the public were gathering outside the crime scene tape, peering up at the terraced house. What was PC Thomas doing on the door? Where was PC Folland? This wasn't protocol.

'Mind your step, ma'am.' Spindly Jamie's usually pale face looked positively drained.

The toe of her boot nudged a puddle of sick on the floor. 'Oh, Jamie. And inside the cordon.'

'I couldn't help it. It just…Do you think there'll be a disciplinary, ma'am?' He looked stricken.

She still wasn't used to being called ma'am. It made her feel old. She'd paused too long now. 'I bet Dr Fisher loves you!'

Jamie's mouth turned down.

Drat, she'd meant that to be light-hearted. She tried to give him a reassuring smile. 'I best go find the guv.'

'Yes, ma'am.' Jamie held the door for her.

Inside she gathered her thoughts. She needed to speak to the victim's mother – she was with the relationship officers now. The SOCOs were out back looking for evidence of how the perpetrator gained access. DCI Moast favoured the alley that ran along the back of the houses. It wouldn't be hard to vault the fence and enter through the garden. A robbery gone wrong? Perhaps. The perpetrator could have assumed everyone was asleep, come across Alun Mardling and, in the panic, killed him. There were no immediate signs of anything missing. Little sign of struggle. No evidence of forced entry. But she felt there was something disturbing about the way the man's throat had been cut: too...sacrificial. The flask felt warm in her pocket – DCI Moast could wait a minute while she took another quick look at the body.

Nasreen took the stairs two at a time. She could hear people moving around, one of the forensics team must still be here. She reached the bedroom door and froze. But she wasn't staring at the blood, she was staring at the person in front of it.

Was she a scene of crime officer? No. Ridiculous. She was just at Espress-oh's. How'd she...? Where'd she...?

'Freddie Venton, what the hell are you doing here?'

Freddie – and it was definitely Freddie with that bizarre red streaked hair and dark kohl circles round her eyes – dipped her chin, then her eyes rolled back and she crumpled.

Instinctively Nasreen rushed forwards, arms open, but someone got there first. She shuddered to a halt, before she ploughed into the uniformed back, the crown on the epaulette. It couldn't be...'Superintendent, sir!' She stood straight. Heels together. Hands by her side. Palms sweating.

Superintendent Gray, his salt-and-pepper trimmed eyebrows meeting at the exertion, turned to face her. The rag doll Freddie in his hands. 'Sergeant, do you know this officer?'

'I...er...sir...I...' How was this happening? What was he doing here? He must have responded to the call-out. Like them. *Staff shortages.*

'Spit it out, Sergeant.' Superintendent Gray's hands, smooth from deskwork, with neat clipped nails, gripped Freddie's shoulders.

'We studied together.' The words were out before she could stop them. Her cheeks burned red. She'd lied to the Superintendent. Her training kicked in. Counter the epinephrine. Frame the situation. Respond. 'I'll take her outside, sir, get her some air.'

'Nas?' Freddie's voice was hoarse.

The Superintendent looked down at Freddie, his hair parting was ruler-straight. 'Freddie, the Superintendent and I know it's your first active crime scene. I'll take you outside for some air.' She tried to convey the severity of the situation with her eyes. *Play along.* Good grief, the girl was using the Superintendent's arm to push herself up.

Nasreen had gotten onto the Fast Track Programme. She'd put up with her colleagues' inappropriate cracks. She'd faced down gang members, and once a man wielding a machete, she was damned if Freddie Venton was going to be her undoing. 'I really think you…'

Freddie pulled her arm away from Nas. She felt shaky, but there was no way she was leaving. She had to stay and get the story. Even with *that* there in the room. 'Odd, isn't it…' Freddie's words came out in a gasp. Fear ripped through her body like the knife through the dead man. She looked away from the gore. *Must bear witness.* Glimpses of a T-shirt and boxer shorts made it through the red. The thing – once a living breathing man – looked like it was dressed for bed. A hand still lay on the computer mouse. 'Odd, isn't it…that…this…happened at the computer?'

'Plenty of people spend their free time on the computer.' Nasreen seemed to have a problem controlling her eyebrows.

Freddie focused on them going up and down. Up and down. Her breathing slowed. She gestured toward the desk, and then dropped her arm when she saw it shaking. *Focus on something else.* 'Was he looking at porn?' *Porn Addiction: A Very Modem Problem.*

'You noticed his hand then?' said the uniformed cop who'd caught her.

Freddie located the shoulder – carefully avoiding the neck area. *Think about something else.* His other arm was lowered, elbow bent, his hand was…'It's in his boxers! Oh my God! He was knocking one out – what a way to go!'

The copper gave a little chuckle.

Think about something else. 'It's not kiddie porn is it?' *Paedophile Butchered in Revenge Attack.*

Nasreen tersely replied, 'There's nothing to suggest…'

'Let's take a look.' The uniformed copper pulled a latex glove from his pocket and picked his way toward the desk.

Freddie ignored the expression of incredulity on Nasreen's face and looked straight ahead at the screen. Taking a pen from his pocket, the copper gently nudged the mouse. The monitor hissed with static and blinked into life. Not porn. Not a video. But a background of skull and crossbones images, overlaid with text boxes. Familiarity soothed Freddie.

The uniformed copper peered at the computer. 'Is that Twitter? That site where people talk about what they had for lunch?' he said.

Freddie clung to the normality of it. 'It's a microblogging site, good for keeping abreast of the zeitgeist, gathering ideas, and building work contacts.' *Don't stop.* Her mind and mouth babbled in panic: 'I wonder why he was spanking the monkey while looking at Twitter? I've heard of people checking their phones during sex, but this is like dissing yourself.'

'What do all these @ signs mean?' The uniformed copper was still peering at the screen.

If she could keep him talking for a few more minutes, she might get more info for her pitch. Freddie stepped forward.

Nasreen audibly inhaled. 'Be careful not to touch the victim or disturb any of the evidence.'

'I'm sure Miss Venton knows what she's doing, Sergeant,' the copper snapped.

Freddie was thankful his tone obliterated the word victim that seemed to hang in the air.

"Twitter is a social media site. Each user has a "Twitter Handle", which is unique to them. They all start with an @ symbol. Mine is @ReadyFreddieGo. They're also called "@names".'

'I see,' said the copper.

In order to read the tweets on the computer, Freddie had to lean over the body. She could hear it dripping. She focused on the screen: Alun Mardling. That is...*was*...his name. 'So this is the account of Alun Mardling. His Twitter Handle is @MaddeningAlun23.' She turned away from the computer and the body to look at the copper. 'You can follow people, other users, from your Twitter account. Their tweets – what they've posted online – appear in what's called your "timeline" in real time.' The copper's brow furrowed. 'For example, if I've followed Nasreen on Twitter and she tweets to say she is at Espress-oh's in St Pancras, it will appear on my "timeline" when she tweets it.' Nas scowled at her. Freddie pushed on. This was allowing her head to clear and her stomach to settle. 'I can re-post Nasreen's tweet, or share it, so it is seen by my followers in their timeline by doing what's called "retweeting".'

'Do you invite people to follow you and accept invitations like they do on LinkedIn?' The copper looked thoughtful.

'No,' said Freddie, focusing on him and not the body. 'You can follow anyone on Twitter and you can also send anyone a message by using their @name. By looking up an account, say Alun Mardling's @name, I would be able to read what he's posted without following him. I would also be able to talk to him by using his @name in a tweet. This would then appear on his notifications.'

'So anyone can talk to anyone else on Twitter?' Nas asked.

'Exactly, that's what makes it popular. Like, I could directly communicate with my favourite author Margaret Atwood, or a pop star like Taylor Swift. Most famous people and journalists are authenticated by Twitter with a blue tick that shows on their account bio.' She pulled her phone out of her pocket and looked up Taylor Swift's account. 'See the blue tick here?' Nas and the copper nodded. 'You can also see how many people they are following, and how many people are following them.'

'Wait.' Nas pointed at Freddie's phone. 'Over sixty-one *million* people follow Taylor Swift?'

'Yup,' said Freddie.

'Staggering,' the copper said. 'Doesn't she get inundated with these @name messages?'

'Almost certainly,' said Freddie. 'Though you can block people who are causing trouble.'

'And everyone can see the @name messages you send to other people?' The copper ran his gloved finger over her mobile screen.

'Correct,' said Freddie. 'But if you follow another user and they follow you back, then you can send a "Direct Message", which is private.'

Fury bubbled through Nasreen. For the last two years she'd tried to find a way in with Superintendent Gray. She'd managed six words: Good morning, sir, and good evening, sir. And now here he and Freddie were, acting like Starsky and Hutch. It was well known the Superintendent didn't like social media websites. He'd had to let a good officer go last year after he revealed sensitive information about a case on Facebook after a pint or two. It'd been picked up by the press. These websites could not be trusted. She watched as the Superintendent and Freddie turned back to look at the vic's computer. Freddie'd disturb the evidence. DCI Moast was downstairs, oblivious to the fact his case was being destroyed by an Espress-oh's waitress. Forget anything that had been between them in the past, she had to stop this before it went too far. She had to say something.

'He's a troll!' Freddie suddenly stabbed toward the screen with her finger.

'What?' Nasreen recognised excitement in Freddie's voice, for a second they were back, joyfully awaiting the start of her eighth birthday party.

'Trolling – hurling abuse at someone over the Internet. You must have heard of it?'

'Keep up, Sergeant.' Superintendent Gray didn't turn around. 'There was a training course last year. Growing concern for the force: online harassment. Everyone was scheduled to attend.'

'I was there, I attended, sir, I know what a troll is. Of course…'

'Jesus!' Freddie still had her finger dangerously close to the screen. 'He really bloody loves it. It's all at Paige Klinger.'

'The model? The one with the lips?' Nasreen leant forward so her face was alongside Freddie's. She smelt vaguely of stale cigarettes.

Nasreen scrutinised the tweets: a jumble of @ signs and hashtags. 'What does it say?'

'Here,' Freddie pointed at one of the boxes. 'This @PaigeKlinger is him talking to her.' Freddie ran her finger underneath the words:

Alun Mardling @MaddeningAlun23 • 1s
@PaigeKlinger u deserv fuckin wiv a barbed wire dildo u stuck up whore. in front of ur famly ho.

Superintendent Gray pushed air out through his teeth. 'Is that English?'

'Barely,' Freddie said. 'Plus I guess he was typing one-handed.'

Nasreen followed her sightline to the blood drying on the vic's hand.

'The bloody wanker,' Freddie said.

Nasreen ignored Freddie. 'This is pretty strong, sir. Threats of rape. Murder. Why hasn't she come forward?'

'Happens all the time,' Freddie said.

'Sir, if he's threatened her and her family like this, I would say that's pretty good motive.'

'Hmmm,' Superintendent Gray folded his arms. 'Nasty business.'

29

Freddie's mind was in overdrive. Everything was taking on vivid colours. She could see the article she was going to write already. She could imagine the pay cheque. 'It's definitely murder, right? Not suicide?'

'No weapon. Indicates someone took it with them. Foul play.' Nasreen was still looking at the tweets.

'Great!' *Man Who Trolled Paige Klinger Murdered.*

'Great?' The copper turned to look her in the face. 'What did you say your name was again, officer?'

Police declined to give a statement. Time to leave. 'I'm feeling woozy again.' Freddie took a step back away from the body. And then realised she wasn't lying.

'She doesn't look good, sir.' Nasreen grabbed hold of Freddie's arm. 'Better get her outside. Right now. Looks like she might be sick.' This time Freddie let herself be pulled from the room.

Nasreen's heart was beating hard. Please let DCI Moast and the others be outside. No sign of anyone. She glanced back to see Superintendent Gray still looking at the computer. With her free hand she grabbed Freddie's SOCO suit hood and pulled it up over her hair.

'Hey, watch it!' Freddie tried to squirm away from her.

Nasreen silenced her with a stare. Did she want to get arrested? Was this all some elaborate plan to ruin her career? Vengeance for what happened eight years ago? That would be ridiculous, but then this was Freddie Venton. She dragged her across the entrance hall and opened the front door.

PC Jamie Thomas turned to face them. His skin taking on the blue tinge of the sky. 'You all right there, ma'am,' he indicated at Freddie, who was now leaning against her, seemingly in a bid to trip her up.

'Just going out for some air. Seen DCI Moast?'

Jamie shook his head as he spoke, 'He hasn't been this way for twenty minutes or so.'

He was a nice guy, she felt dreadful lying to him. 'Okay, thanks.' Nasreen pushed Freddie in front of her, circumnavigating the vomit on the path.

'Do you think the team'll go for a drink after this, Nasreen?' Jamie called after her. 'I could do with something to steady my nerves.'

'Not for me. Thanks, Jamie,' she kept her voice upbeat. Then put her face close to Freddie's as they passed under the incident tape. 'Don't say a word,' she hissed.

There were still civilians standing outside watching the scene. Where were the constables who were supposed to be interviewing the neighbours? Curtains were twitching. Early-morning commuters in suits were appearing. They were close to Canary Wharf – when did the financial markets open? Soon there would be more people staring. Five doors down, Nasreen spotted an alley and took it.

As the walls of the houses either side rose up around them, Freddie shook herself free.

'Oh my God! All the blood and…Let me get my breath…God! I can't believe that.' Freddie leant forward spitting phlegm onto the ground. 'Thought I was going to hurl like that bloke on the door.'

'What the hell are you doing here, Freddie? I haven't seen you in eight years – we haven't spoken – and suddenly you're at St Pancras station and now at a crime scene? Don't tell me that's a coincidence.' This couldn't be happening. She checked no one had followed them.

'That copper on the door. The one who spewed. I'm guessing he could get in a lot of trouble for letting me in.'

Nasreen looked at Freddie Venton, the girl she'd idolised as a child, the girl she'd wished was her sister for years, as she struggled to free her arm from her stolen SOCO suit. 'Do you have any idea what you've done? What I've just done. You could've cost PC Thomas his job. You've contaminated the crime scene. What do you think you're playing at?'

Freddie didn't look up. 'You sound like your mum that time she busted us for eating all the chocolate digestives.'

31

'This is serious. What are you doing here? I could lose my job. You've put me in a very difficult position.'

'Don't flatter yourself, I would've got out of there without your help.'

Nasreen exhaled. 'That's not what I meant. I could arrest you for breaking and entering, contaminating a crime scene, impersonating a forensics officer!' This was unbelievable.

'Oh yeah.' Freddie rolled the SOCO suit down her legs and over her shoes. The colour back and fiery in her cheeks. 'Then why don't you?'

Nasreen thought of Freddie's mum, Lorna Venton, was she still in her neat little house trying to keep it together while her husband was off drinking? Was Freddie's alcoholic father still alive? How would the gentle woman, who used to give her an ice lolly if she grazed her knee, cope if her daughter was arrested as well? 'I won't. But only to spare your mum the shame.'

Freddie turned to look behind her, her attention already shifted. 'Is the DLR that way?'

'What?'

'The Docklands Light Railway, or is public transport too good for you now you're a copper, Nas?'

All those years mourning the loss of their friendship, but instead of the warm-hearted fearless girl she remembered, here was an entitled loud-mouthed stranger. What an idiot she'd been. Nasreen's cheeks flamed. 'The station's that way.'

'See you later, *Sergeant Cudmore*.' Freddie gave a fake salute.

Nasreen closed her eyes. It was like a bad dream. When she opened them Freddie was gone. She headed back to 39 Blackbird Road. DCI Moast's flask of tea cold in her pocket. She never wanted to see Freddie Venton ever again.

Chapter 5

OMG – Oh My God

06:06
Saturday 31 October

'Neil, it's Freddie Venton here. Give me a call as soon as you get this. I booked myself onto that Asiana flight.' Freddie heard the screech and rumble of an approaching DLR and picked up pace. It was the first dead body she'd seen. And it turned out adrenaline was more effective than espresso. She easily caught the 6:08.

A ride on the DLR would normally mean sitting in the front, driverless carriage and pretending to steer, but there wasn't time for that today. Away from the body she was fine. *She was fine.* The Citymapper app on her phone confirmed she could pick up the 277 bus at Westferry. She pulled up Alun Mardling's Twitter account: what else could she find out about him? She read his bio:

ALUN MARDLING
@MaddeningAlun23

This is my cage for when
I've been naughty and they've
closed my other account down.
Saying it like it is.
London.

Dick.
167 followers. Hardly any followers at all, at least that was something. They were still all shitbags.

What kind of idiots follow this kind of abusive drivel? Freddie
clicked onto his followers list. More skulls and crossbones. *Original.*
More old white dudes giving the bird. *Oh yeah, subversive.* She
scanned the names: Stephen Anderson (@Stalker77), Vernon Jones
(@MenzRites), Dave Injustice (@TruthNBalls). *A twat clique. A twique.*
She clicked through their tweets discussing 16-year-old Paige Klinger.

From @Stalker77 (37-year-old schoolteacher, head of department, married, one daughter aged 2, real name: Andrew):

@TheDestroyer76 u told that skanky ho. Stuck up rich girls get
on my fucking dick. Whining on. Rape is least of her worries.

From @TheDestroyer76 (suburban bank manager, divorced, 42,
sits on local hospice board, real name: Richard):

@Stalker77 left-wing cock sucking slut should work for a
fucking living. Death to whores!!!!!

From @BurnyMe (19-year-old Economics student, single, real name:
Emily):

@Stalker77 @TheDestroyer12 Fuckin cunts don't deserve rape.
Burn the mother fuckerz flesh of.

Nice guys, real friendly. Kind you'd take home to your mum.

She scrolled through the rest of Alun Mardling's followers: more of the same. Then something caught her eye. The train jolted, the phone shook in her hand, air caught in her throat. She must have made a mistake. She refocused on the screen. Looked again at the list of followers: at one particular follower. Freddie felt her stomach fall away. With a shaking hand, she clicked on the follower's profile picture. The screen went black, a white line scrolling painfully slowly across it. *Come on. Come on.* The photo appeared. Enlarged. She let out a yelp, clamping her hand to her mouth. It was Alun Mardling. Or what was left of him. His neck cut, his head lolling forward onto the keyboard. Blood.

How'd the picture get online? Who'd taken it? The account had no followers. It was only following one person: Alun Mardling. The name of the account was Apollyon. @Apollyon. The bio said:

Trick or treat? Everywhere.

'No.' She was going to be sick.

The man in a suit opposite looked at her, rustling his paper. Instinctively she clutched the phone to her chest. She had to get help. Nasreen. She had to get hold of Nasreen.

'This train is for Bank. The next station is Westferry,' the prerecorded electronic female voice boomed into the carriage.

Freddie lurched up as the train came to a stop, hitting the door button with her free hand. Don't vomit. Saliva pooled in her mouth. Recent calls > Nasreen > Call. Voicemail.

'Nas, it's Freddie. There's a…' She looked up at the commuters bottlenecking in front of her, a small child, in a duffel coat and knitted bobble hat, clung to her mum's hand. She couldn't say the words in front of an innocent kid. '…Something on Twitter. It's urgent. Call me.'

She looked at the profile picture of @Apollyon again. It was definitely Mardling. Definitely the crime scene. She stumbled down the stairs and steadied herself against the ticket machine. *Keep swallowing. Keep breathing.* There, next to Mardling's hand, on his Ikea desk, was a knife. Dripping with blood.

What had Nas said? *No weapon. Someone took it with them.*

She had to get hold of her. She tried again: her phone went straight to voicemail. She nearly screamed. She took a screenshot of the image and texted it to Nas, typing: Call me.

The murderer could be anyone. Once, at the Southbank centre, she'd tweeted and watched her post appear on the phone of the stranger sat in front of her. All the people she let into her world. You could feel like you knew them, but you didn't. It was so easy for people to catfish – to pretend to be someone else online. @Apollyon could be anyone. What if the killer had been in the same carriage as her? What if they'd seen her open their tweet? A man came toward her. His face ghostly, his eyes two black holes in his face. She flinched. He passed and continued up the stairs. She was acting crazy. Why would the murderer be here on the train? She pulled her coat tight and walked with her head down.

Besides, she didn't know what a real criminal would look like. Her head was full of pap shots of penitent American celebs in orange jumpsuits. Justin Bieber's grinning mugshot that launched a thousand gifs. Lindsay Lohan up for a DUI. Britney's meltdown. But they weren't serious felons. The 277 came toward her. She ran for it. Jumping on between the hissing open doors, Freddie swiped her Oyster card and scanned the other passengers. A woman in a hijab, a tiny child with curly dark hair in a buggy in front of her. An old man with a walking stick. A woman wearing large pink Sony headphones, staring out the window. Could any of these people be killers? Surely not. Normal people don't go around slitting people's throats.

What about the model Paige Klinger? Could she have butchered Alun Mardling? She Googled Apollyon. *Greek for the destroyer. In Hebrew, Abaddon, meaning the land of the dead. Apollyon appears in the Bible as a place of destruction.* Not your average idiot troll name. Who murders someone and posts a photo of it online? The bus climbed toward Dalston, swung over canals, past shops, their shutters opening like eyes. What did it mean? Freddie watched as the dark blue clouds of the night transitioned into apocalyptic shades of orange, pink and red. *The destroyer. The avenging angel. Troll hunter. The Revelation.* This was one hell of a story.

Nasreen, still at the crime scene, police helicopter buzzing overhead, the search party combing for evidence, looked at the missed call on her phone: Freddie. She didn't want to hear her apology, or justification, or whatever it was she wanted. If she could forget the whole thing – focus on the job in hand – then perhaps she'd get away with the security breach that happened this morning. No more Freddie. No more games. Without listening to it, Sergeant Nasreen Cudmore deleted the voicemail message.

Chapter 6

DTF – Down to Fuck?

06:57
Saturday 31 October

The front door banged behind Freddie, making her jump. She was buzzing. High on adrenaline. She could hear her flatmate Anton getting ready to leave for his job in The City. Freddie found it ironic that someone who worked in HR could be so void of communication skills. Unless you were talking about cycling he wasn't interested. Least he paid his rent on time, and he'd sourced the new guy, who was apparently a friend of his cousins, when their last flatmate moved out. Anton was dredging his throat of phlegm in the bathroom. A ritual cleansing necessitated by the flat's wall mould. Freddie had grown accustomed to it. Her snot was no longer grey. Spores and pollution colonised her respiratory system. Emphysema or lung cancer, or some other mincemeat maker of her lungs, would no doubt kill her.

Death felt close. She'd leant over Alun Mardling's stiffening body. The world had a new intensity. Riffling through her bedding, she located her Mac. Freddie, adrenaline setting the tempo of her heart, her fingers firing Gatling gun words across the page, typed:

The blood-splattered body of a man was discovered in the early hours of this morning in the East End. Bent over a computer, his lifeless hand still gripping the mouse, the victim had been trolling at the time he was slaughtered. A growing number of cases of online abuse, often of a threatening, violent and graphic sexual nature, have been brought to light recently. Social media sites, like Twitter and Facebook, have been criticised for their lack of response to complaints of misogynistic language, threats of rape and violence, and online bullying. Campaigners have called for an end to the rape culture that is prevalent online. As police seem ill-informed, ill-equipped and ill-inclined to deal with this growing epidemic of online abuse, has someone decided to take the law into their own hands? Is there a Troll hunter out there?

Maybe slaughtered was too much? Slayed? Butchered? Exterminated?

Unconfirmed reports suggest the murder suspect has tweeted a photo of the crime scene. As the popularity of social media sites like Twitter grow, and society struggles to fashion new moral structures to keep pace with increasing technology developments, have we reached a threshold: is this the first #murder?

Freddie was finishing editing when her phone rang.

'Freddie, it's Neil Sanderson, what have you got? Some It girl have a fight in the coffee shop you work in?'

'Try trolling, Paige Klinger, revenge and a tweeting murderer.' Freddie heard the pleasing clunk of Neil's coffee mug as he put it down on his desk. 'An Internet troll who was hurling online abuse at the model Paige Klinger has been murdered. And a photo of the dead bloke has turned up on Twitter. It looks like whoever took it was the same sicko who bumped this guy off.'

'Is this verified? Have you got quotes from witnesses?'

'Better than that,' said Freddie. 'I was there. Saw it with my own eyes. The tweets. The body. The lot.'

Neil exhaled. 'Attagirl. How long till it's ready?'

'Emailing it over now.'

There was a momentary silence in which Freddie guessed (correctly) that Neil impatiently clicked refresh on his inbox. 'Got it. I'll call you back.'

Freddie hung up. The flat was silent. Anton and Pete had both left for work, the kitchen tap dripped into a sink of dishes. She thought of Alun Mardling's blood dripping onto the floor and shuddered. She was back in that room: the rustling of the plastic overalls, the taste of metal and the unnerved look in Nasreen's eyes. She rubbed at her face. She was stained. She stood under the hot shower until the water ran red from her hair chalk, and then clear. Only then did she feel like she'd washed all the blood off.

She towelled her hair while she read an email from Neil:

Great story. Well done. Will be in touch with edits.

She was going to get paid. Properly. She'd be in print: it might be in the hundreds. She could take a chunk out of her phone bill, the electricity bill – she still owed her flatmates for the council tax. There was a hole in her Converse trainers – she should look for a new pair of those in Oxfam. Anything left over could reduce her overdraft, stop its slow, steady growth. Multiplying with each basic need, as her pitiful two-pound boxes of cereal and forty-nine pence pints of milk fed the overdraft fees. Burgeoning. Would there be enough left for a few drinks? The warning letters, the overdue bills, the exceeded limits, the stopped cards, swam through Freddie's mind making her feel at once angry and sick. Perhaps she could wring a few more stories out of this? A few more big paydays and the river of debt might slow, subside, trickle.

She tried to relax her shoulders. Her right index finger drummed against her phone. A siren sounded outside and she flinched. She needed a release. Her phone said it was 09:02. Vacate Bar on Kingsland would be serving. She scrolled through her messages:

there he was. Ajay, a local Tinder find. Didn't he work night shifts? They'd messaged enough during the day. Struggling to do up her size 12 skinny jeans, she typed with her thumb:

'Rough night. Fancy a drink? 15mins in Vacate?'

Freddie pulled the plaid shirt she'd pinched from her dad's wardrobe over her head and adjusted her glasses. She poked her moon-shaped face. Her skin looked sallow. When was the last time she'd eaten vegetables? Her hair, having dried naturally, was almost spherical, in a brown halo round her head. Scraping the remnants from a tub of hair wax, she attempted to flatten it. *Mission unsuccessful.* Coat, mobile, wallet, keys.

Her phone beeped. Ajay replied:

'C u in 20.'

Freddie paused at the top of the stairs, undid one more button on her shirt, reached into her bra and hoisted her breasts up and together. No harm in maximising her best asset. Clattering down the shared stairs and out onto the private pathway that ran alongside the Queen Elizabeth pub, which was under their flat. The Elizabeth's garden – a concrete square strung with half-broken fairy lights – was empty. It didn't open till 11am. Freddie punched the code into the security gate at the end of the path and walked the back roads to Vacate.

The wet pavement was pockmarked with chewing gum. Takeaway cartons blew into her shins. Her fellow Londoners walked with their heads down, bent against the weather or looking at their phones. Cyclists streamed past. Everything and everyone was on the move. She passed the industrial Dalston Department Store. The pop-up boutiques and restaurants. The try-hards. The wannabes. The sky was grey and oppressive, like a Tupperware lid pressing down onto the tops of the buildings.

Vacate was mostly empty; there was a group of bearded men and childlike girls in polyester housecoats discussing their latest free-form art installation. Freddie caught snippets of their conversation. 'I'm really pumped over this.' 'Daryl's PR is *sick*.' 'Is this muesli hand-milled?' *How did they afford to live?*

Crossing the stripped floorboards, navigating the reclaimed crates that doubled as chairs, Freddie reached the concrete bar. A man with a beard shaped into a squirrel stood polishing baked-bean cans – which were used for glasses. Freddie rolled her eyes. 'I'll have a beer please, mate?'

'Any particular brand – we've got some excellent local-brewed, microbiotic, carbon-neutral ales?'

'Just a beer. In a bottle. The cheapest one. Thanks.' When she blinked she could see Alun Mardling's body, except now it was in tweet form. A digital image. Her brain was so used to seeing images framed by her phone, it stored it in her memory alongside Beyoncé memes and artful Instagrams of avocado on toast. She couldn't shake it. @Apollyon.

'Freddie?'

The lad looked close enough to Ajay's profile picture: dark hair, which hung in a long asymmetric fringe over his face, kicking out on the ends like he'd used hair straighteners. 'Ajay?'

'Sup?' He kept flicking his head to keep his hair out of his eyes. Like a shampoo advert gif.

'Nice jumper.' She signalled at his 80s knit decorated with elephants and paisley. Didn't matter. She'd seen what was underneath. 'Fancy a beer?'

'Sure, why not,' he shrugged.

They took their drinks to a small round vinyl-topped table. 'Thanks for coming out.'

Flick. 'No problem.'

'It's good to meet in person after…' Freddie thought about the last Snapchat video he'd sent of him masturbating his hard cock. 'Er…talking so much.'

Flick. 'Sure.'

'You work in a bar, right?'

Flick. 'Yeah. Worked last night. Only had a couple of hours' kip when you messaged.' *Flick*. 'Couldn't pass up the chance to see you.' *Flick*.

Freddie laughed.

Flick. 'What was up with your night?'

'You wouldn't believe me if I told ya.' She pulled a strip from her bottle's label.

Flick. 'I can imagine. We get all kinds of nutters in the bar I work in.'

She nodded.

Flick. 'I'm the manager actually. Spend most of my time out back.' *Flick*. 'Working on rotas and shit.'

'Mmmm.' She tried to shake the image of her boss Dan from her mind.

Flick. 'You should come by sometime. I'll shout you a couple of…'

'I'm not looking for a relationship right now, just to be up front with you,' she interrupted him. She didn't need some boy expecting her to spend all their time together. She needed to focus on work.

Flick. 'That's cool, I'm easy.'

'Ajay?' Blinked stills of Dan and Alun Mardling vied for her attention. She had to shake this off. She gulped from her bottle.

Flick. 'Yeah?' His beer hovered by his lips. His dark eyes looked straight at her.

'You ever done it in a disabled toilet?'

His face cracked into a huge smile. *Flick*.

'Meet me there in a minute. Knock twice.' She downed the rest of her drink. Just before she reached the hallway she looked back and winked at Ajay. *Cheesy, Freddie, cheesy.* Whatever. She wasn't looking for *The One*. There wasn't enough time for a relationship. But why shouldn't she have a release? Some fun?

The disabled toilet was thankfully clean. The smell of bleach gave a sort of swimming pool vibe. A long mirror ran down one wall at right angles to the sink. She practised a couple of poses. Duck face. Leaning over the sink, she could turn back and see the reflection of him behind.

Two knocks sounded on the door. She opened it a crack.

Flick. Ajay squeezed through the door and they both fell against the inside giggling.

'Shusshhhh!' She placed a finger against his lips.

He pulled her into him, his hair falling over both their faces. She pulled his T-shirt up and ran her hands over his smooth chest. He was fiddling with her jeans. She yanked them and her knickers down as he turned her and lifted her up onto the sink. She inhaled sharply as she saw her reflection in the mirror. *Heck, this could work too.* Her shirt was open and Ajay was kissing down, over her breasts, her stomach. He pulled her jeans down further. Kissing up from her knees, the inside of her thighs. She watched his head get closer.

Flick.

She clamped her hand over her mouth to stifle the moan.

Chapter 7

IDK – I Don't Know

19:26
Saturday 31 October

Alun Mardling's face, his eyes wide and bloodshot, loomed. His hand, bloody and cold, reached for hers. There was a thud. Freddie jolted. It was dark. She was sweat-soaked. Fabric was wrapped around her, a shroud. Her eyes struggled to focus. Where was she? Freddie could hear Mardling's blood dripping onto the floor. No! No, it was the kitchen tap. She was home. Alone. Another boom shook through her skull. Ajay? They'd left the bar. There'd been a bottle of wine in the park. Some cans. How'd she got home? She groped for her glasses. Her head reverberated with another bang. The door. Someone was hammering on the door. Ajay? Her flatmates? She stumbled out of bed, grabbed the nearest thing: her H&M Espress-oh's shirt, still half-buttoned, she pulled it over her head. Dizzying herself with the effort.

Her eyes were stuck at the corners, she followed the crystallised salt tracks with her fingers. Peeling her Sellotaped tongue from the roof of her mouth, she managed: 'Coming!' The word was wet, sodden, heavy, though her mouth was dry. Everywhere was darkness. Another thud landed on her like a punch. How much sleep? Still drunk. Boom: her mind shook with fragments of memory. She tried to rub the image of Mardling's body from her eyes with her fingers. *Would a murderer knock?*

'Freddie Venton!' a male voice shouted from the other side. Bailiffs? Like before. She tried to formulate her thoughts, sort them into order. What was she to say? The Mac was P-something's. A flatmate's. They couldn't take it.

'Freddie Venton, open up!' The noise crashed like thunder over her head. Stumbling, she got a hand on the lock, pulled.

Light from the hallway sent her reeling back.

Nas was there, in a black trouser suit, white shirt. Her dark hair swept up away from her face. Chocolate eyes flashing in creamy whites. She had chunky boots on. Next to her: the blue puffa jacket guy who'd been with her at St Pancras. Up close, Freddie could see his blonde hair was silvering, thinning, probably why he had it shaved to a bristly number one. Unfortunately his close-cropped hair accentuated the square shape of his head. He looked like a Lego man. He was in pale pink shirtsleeves, jeans, glowing white trainers: ready to pounce. She could see their mouths open and close like fish. The air pressed upon her, heavy, as if she were underwater, words bubbled toward her. Don't. Be. Sick.

'Venton…you…connection…harm…defence.' Their fish words didn't fit together.

'Nas?'

What was puffa saying? Concentrate on breathing. Don't. Be. Sick. In. Out. In.

Nas's hands gripped her shoulders. Anchoring her. 'Freddie? Do you understand? You have to come with us?' Freddie nodded. Her brain shrank away from her skull, dehydrated, a husk. Nasreen's face came into focus. She looked older. Colder. Distant. 'Put some trousers on,' Nasreen said.

46

Freddie looked down. She was wearing her Little Mermaid pants. Tufts of mousey pubic hair curled round the edges.

What was going on? They walked in close formation down the stairs. In silence. Each step an earthquake in Freddie's body. She needed a Coke. A bacon sandwich. Her stomach tidal-waved. No, no food yet. In. Out. In. Out.

Outside was a waiting police car. Nasreen held open the back door for her. Nasreen's patronising hand guided the top of her head. At the edges of her consciousness something flickered. A warning. Freddie leant her head against the cool glass of the window, closed her eyes and willed herself not to vom. She was thankful they travelled in silence.

They were at Jubilee police station, the aging 1970s jewel in the Tower Hamlets policing borough, a clusterfuck of concrete and white metal-framed windows. She recognised it from the TV news. Nas held the door for her again. Freddie took some steadying gulps of air. The street lights hurt her eyes. The puffa guy strode off. Nas looked pissed.

Freddie's mouth moistened enough to speak. The words disjointed. 'This about the dead dude?'

'Sergeant Byrne will check you in.'

They were stood inside the entrance hall of the station – it looked nothing like *Heartbeat*, the ancient cop show her mum was always re-watching. Scratched wooden-framed glass doors, which reminded Freddie of her old school maths classrooms, were at each end of the room. The geometric pattern of green shatterproof glass filled every available pane, blocking out all hope of natural light. Posters warning of car theft and pickpockets barely clung to the walls. Fluorescent strip lighting finished off the effect: everything had a cold blue tinge to it. It was as comforting as being inside an ice cube. Sergeant Byrne, a fat man in his fifties, leant against the desk like he couldn't support his own weight.

Booked in? What was this?

'Please empty all your pockets into the tray,' the Duty Sergeant's voice was heavy with contempt. Either that or he had a nasty sinus infection, Freddie thought.

Nas stood wordless.

The contents of Freddie's hastily pulled on jeans pockets and jacket were documented and placed in individual plastic bags: 'One iPhone, one wallet; contents: a Hackney library card, a Visa debit card, two Visa credit cards, one receipt from Vacate bar, fifty-seven pence in loose change. One set of keys. Two unopened banana-flavoured condoms.'

'It's easier to get into the airport than in here!' Freddie said. No one laughed.

The copper pulled a small white powdery triangle out of her pocket and held it up to her.

'It's a Smint,' her eyes were too gritty to roll. 'No one has time to do drugs.'

He sniffed it. 'One fluffy mint.' The Sergeant dropped it into a bag and plunged his hand back into her jacket pocket.

'You can chuck that if you want,' Freddie nodded at the empty sanitary towel wrapper he pulled out. He dropped the wrapper into its own sealed plastic bag and placed it on top of her other belongings in the tray.

'Remove the laces from your shoes.' He took a sip from a vending machine plastic cup of coffee he had under the desk.

Her synapses crackled, her neurotransmitters jump-started. 'What? This is a fucking joke, right? I'm being punked?'

'Mind your language.' He spoke like her dad. *Why Is a Young Woman Swearing So Offensive to Men?*

'Dude, these are DMs, it'll take me half an hour.'

'Now,' he said. His small piggy eyes disappearing into the fat of his face.

Freddie looked at Nasreen who was staring straight ahead. Her stomach settled into a hollow feeling of dread. What had Nas and that guy said to her when they picked her up from her flat? She flopped onto a plastic bench that was bolted to the ground. *100 Everyday Objects That Can Kill You.*

'There,' she slapped the laces onto the counter. 'I'll never get them back the way they were. Happy?'

'This way, Miss Venton.' Nasreen pushed a button to release the interconnecting door.

Miss Venton? 'When can I have my phone back? I need to let my boss know I'll be late.' Freddie followed Nasreen's silent back; her boots flapping round her ankles with each step. 'Seriously, Nas, what the hell is going on? I'm sorry 'bout what I said earlier. About you sounding like your mum, and that.' She limped behind Nas as they passed offices with blinds pulled down and closed blue-painted MDF doors. 'I didn't mean any harm. I was just doing my job.'

Nasreen stopped and spun round, her nostrils flaring. Then she turned and set off again even faster.

'This isn't funny anymore,' Freddie called after her as she wrenched her lace-less Dr Martens off and tucked them under her arm. Her feet, damp from sweat, left tiny prints on the mottled grey wipe-clean floor.

Nasreen stopped and held open a door. 'In here, Miss Venton.'

Freddie peered into the room: a table, three chairs. An empty interview room. 'How long is this going to take?'

Nasreen closed the door on her. She went to get her phone from her pocket before she remembered it wasn't there. Behind her a wall clock ticked toward ten to nine at night. What time had they left the flat? What time had she got home? She struggled to piece together the last sixteen hours. Everything had twisted after she'd seen the dead body. It must be shock. She shivered in the empty room. Ten to nine. She'd be fired for sure.

Three hundred people had applied for her job. She'd spun Dan the corporate line he loved, but she knew it was down to Milena that she'd got it. Milena had a little boy. Probably two, she guessed from photos. He was back in Bulgaria, with Milena's mother. A shortlisted eight had worked an unpaid ten-hour test shift as part of the interview process. On the night of Freddie's trial, Milena's son was rushed to hospital. Milena was distraught and out of phone credit. Skype and FaceTime wouldn't connect. Freddie lent Milena her phone, trying not to think about how expensive an international call would be. Her little boy was going to be okay. And so was Freddie: Milena recommended her as the best candidate. She wouldn't be so lucky again. How would she pay her rent now? 'This isn't funny, guys.' Her voice sounded small. If anyone heard her they didn't reply.

Was she locked in? She stormed over to the door and forcefully tried the handle. It swung open with ease, sending her off balance. The back of the policeman outside turned to face her. It was the kid who'd been sick at 39 Blackbird Road. 'Are you chief of door guarding? That your sole bleedin' job?' His forehead crinkled. The freckles spattered across his nose made him look quite cute. He had that whole little boy lost thing going on that made some women go gaga. Not her type, though. 'Sorry, mate. Just wondered how long I was going to be in here for?'

He shrugged and pressed his lips together, making them even thinner. 'I can get you a drink if you like?'

'Suppose a double vodka and Coke is out?' His lips disappeared completely.

'Coffee?' She remembered the piss-poor excuse for caffeine the Duty Sergeant had been drinking. 'I'm having the shittiest hangover.'

'Yes, Miss. If you take a seat I'll bring you one.'

She scraped one of the chairs at the table back, her eyelids fluttering at the noise. She hadn't showered since she'd had sex. She sniffed the underarm of her shirt: funky.

The door opened and the freckled copper came in with a beige plastic cup. 'Sorry – the milk's off.' He placed the cup and a pile of sugar sachets on the table.

'Cheers.' She tore open four sachets and emptied the lot into the liquid. He gave her half a smile and then retreated, closing the door behind him.

The sides of the cup were too hot to touch. She got up and paced. The gnawing feeling in her stomach wouldn't go away. She thought of Nas's cold stare. Her tongue niggled against something stuck between her front two teeth. It better not be a pubic hair. Working the gap with her fingernail, she sat back down at the table. The coffee was still too hot. It was gone 9pm now. She rested her head on her arms and closed her eyes. Too tired to think straight.

The door handle clicked and she straightened up. How long had she been asleep for?

'Not boring you are we?' The puffa jacket man from earlier entered, with Nas trotting behind him.

'Hey what's the idea, keeping me waiting in here?' Her mouth was made of carpet again – she took a gulp of the now cold coffee. Rancid.

Nas and the puffa jacket guy took the two seats opposite her. What did he say his name was? Moist? Toast?

Nas pressed a button on the device on the table.

'Interview with Freddie Venton, Thirty-first of October, commencing eleven zero nine pm.' The man spoke. 'Officers present: DCI Edwin Moast.'

That was it!

'And Sergeant Nasreen Cudmore.'

This was bullshit. 'Can I get a fresh coffee?' Freddie asked.

Moast exchanged a look with Nasreen. 'Miss Venton, I don't think you appreciate the seriousness of...'

'What is it with all the "Miss" stuff? I'm not a bloody school-teacher. Besides, it's Ms Venton.'

'*Miss* Venton...I don't think...'

'Ms. As I said. I prefer Ms.' You waste my time and I'll waste yours, bucko, Freddie thought.

'Freddie.' Nas leant toward her, looking concerned.

As the last of the alcohol passed out of her bloodstream, as the few hours of sleep worked their magic on Freddie's twenty-three-year-old body, she felt bruised but alert. Moast's earlier words drifted back. Slotting into place. *You do not have to say anything. However, it may harm your defence if you do not mention when questioned something which you later rely on in court…* She started to shake. Her stomach twisted away from her sides. *No. They can't think…*

'This is serious,' Nas said.

Black dots spread like ink droplets in water across Freddie's vision, obscuring Nasreen's face. She focused on her voice. On the sickening words.

'Freddie, you are accused of the murder of Alun Mardling.'

Chapter 8

FFS – For Fuck's Sake

23:13
Saturday 31 October

For a blissful second Freddie thought she was in bed. Then the concerned face of Nasreen came into focus, haloed by a yellow ceiling stain.

'Take your time, don't rush up,' she said.

'Is she okay? Jesus this is all I need: the paperwork!' Moast's square head came between her and the overhead strip lighting. His cropped blonde hair glowing.

'I'm okay.' Freddie pushed against the floor. *Sticky*.

'Someone should take a look at you,' Nas said.

'No.' The shock of the accusation sharpened everything. Freddie took in the dirty white box of a room. The pitted table. The grey plastic chairs. 'You can't really think I'm a murderer?'

'Where were you between 1am and 5am this morning, Miss Venton?' Moast was leaning on the table, his knuckles white from the pressure.

'Sir, I really think we should give her a minute.'

She looked up at Moast. 'I'm fine. Let's get this sorted,' Freddie adopted her customer service voice: the one she used when she was at a job interview or trying to get a doctor's appointment. *How Changing Your Tone Can Change Your Life.*

'Miss Venton says she's fine. And I for one am really looking forward to how she's going to explain all this!' Moast said.

'Explain what? There's nothing to explain.' Freddie stood, a little shakily, opposite him. She wouldn't sit first, Lego man.

'Answer the question: where were you between 1am and 5am today?' he said.

'I was working the night shift at Espress-oh's.' She had to keep calm. 'Except for when I was talking to Nasreen in St Pancras station. You were there.'

'Sit down!' he barked.

She sat. Her cheeks burning. 'This is harassment!'

'Freddie, look, I don't know who you've got yourself involved with, life has clearly not gone the way you planned it,' Nasreen nodded at her Espress-oh's shirt.

'I'm a journalist!' She had to make them understand.

Moast scoffed, 'You just told us you work at Espress-oh's? Now you're claiming you're a journalist?'

'I am a bloody journalist,' Freddie said.

'Don't take that tone with me, Missy,' he snarled. 'You're giving it all that about calling you *Ms*. What kind of a name is Freddie for a girl, anyway? Do you have a problem with men? Did you want to silence Alun Mardling?'

Freddie looked from Moast to Nas. 'I didn't even know who he was till this morning.' Freddie tried to remember what she'd said in her voicemail.

'Freddie, you're entitled to legal advice. Are you sure you don't want a lawyer present?' Nas said. Moast glared at her.

'I don't need a lawyer, I've done nothing wrong!' said Freddie.

'We spoke to your manager.' Moast pulled a notepad from his

back pocket and flicked through it. 'A Mr Daniel Peterson. He says you have some anger issues?'

Freddie's mum always warned her daughter: *one day that temper of yours will get you into real trouble.* Pleading with her to think before she spoke. Unfortunately, the mention of her gossiping boss and the stone-cold reality of being arrested for murder meant Freddie returned to type. 'The lying cunt!'

'He said that you seemed very – and I quote – *"agitated"*.'

'A word with four syllables! I'm surprised he managed it.' Freddie could just imagine how much Dan relished dishing the dirt on her.

'Mr Peterson said you left early.'

This was getting ridiculous. 'I did: to follow you guys. Tell him why I was there, Nas! Tell him about the paper!'

'You didn't say anything about any paper, Freddie.' Nasreen looked at her hands. *How My Best Friend Became My Best Frenemy.*

'The suspected murder weapon is visible in the photo you sent Sergeant Cudmore.' Moast slapped an enlarged version of the screenshot onto the table.

Winded from the blood, Freddie turned away.

'The knife is no longer at the scene, because you took it with you after taking this photo,' he said

'No. You've got it all wrong.' She had to make them listen. This was insane.

'Did it make you feel good cutting him?'

Her stomach turned. 'Stop it! Listen! I know about the murder weapon. I mean, about it being in the photo. That's why when I saw it on Twitter I sent it to Nas.'

'On Twitter? The photo was on Twitter?' Nas cut in.

'Lies!' Moast slammed his hand down on the table. The cup of cold coffee spluttered. 'Mr Peterson said you take antidepressants.'

'What the hell! That's private. They're for anxiety!' *Horrible Bosses: The Reality.*

'I think you're a fantasist, *Ms* Venton.' Moast leant toward her. 'Built this whole thing up in your head. Mardling came to your cafe. You took a dislike to him. Found him and killed him. This Twitter rubbish is a distraction. You screwed up: you got cocky, sent this photo to Sergeant Cudmore. And now we've got you.'

'Wait…wait…' Freddie tried to sort things in her head. 'You've had me in here all this time, and you haven't been looking for the sick freak who put that up online?'

'Stop it with the lies, Venton.' Moast stood, slamming his chair into the wall. Nas and Freddie jumped. *Bully-boy tactics.* There was a knock at the door, which broke the tension in the room. Freddie heard Nas exhale.

Moast stormed across and swung the door open to reveal the nervous-looking copper who'd been sick at the crime scene. 'I'm trying to conduct an interview in here, PC Thomas!' Freddie's heartbeat roared through her body.

'Sorry, guv,' the copper stuttered. 'I need a word.' He glanced at Freddie. 'It's about the case.'

'Interview suspended at eleven forty-seven pm. Cudmore, outside. Now!' Moast's voice shook the room.

Nas clicked the tape recorder off and jumped up and all three of them disappeared behind the slamming door. Freddie looked at the dent the door handle had made in the wall and realised she was gripping her chair so hard her nails were cutting into the plastic underside. She didn't realise she was so easily intimidated. This guy was a prick.

There was the noise of squeaking footsteps and a very audible 'Fuck' from outside. The door opened and Freddie tried to see out into the hallway, but only caught sight of another grubby, once white wall. Nasreen and Moast came back in, he running his hand over his cropped hair, she carrying a newspaper.

'Give me that.' He took the paper from Nasreen. 'Interview with Freddie Venton, Thirty-first of October, continuing at eleven fifty-two pm.' Moast tapped the tape recorder. 'It seems you weren't lying about being a journalist.'

The Post, still folded, thudded onto the table between them. Emblazoned across the front was: '#Murder: Troll Hunter Death Link to Twitter.'

'The splash!' Freddie reached for it.

Moast pulled it away. 'This changes nothing. You're not off the hook.'

'You think I bumped off some guy *for the story*?' *Seriously, where did this guy get off?*

'Do you deny you entered an active crime scene under false pretences?' Moast stabbed at the newspaper, threatening to tear a hole in it.

'No, but…'

'And while you were there you impersonated a policeman?' Stab, stab, stab.

'I never said I was a copper, I just showed up in one of those CSI suits and your bloke let me in.' She couldn't keep her eyes from the newspaper. This should have been one of the happiest moments of her life. 'Don't you think the public have the right to know if there's a crazed killer going around bumping off trolls and posting pictures of it online?'

'What picture?' Moast's finger stayed ground into the paper.

'The one you've been waving in my face for the last hour!'

Nas dropped into a chair and shuffled forwards. Dipping her chin like Princess Diana, looking up through her dark lashes. 'Tell me about the photo you sent me, Freddie? You're saying you didn't take it?'

'That's what I've been trying to tell you: some freakazoid has set up an account under the name of Apollyon…'

'Apol-what?' Moast interrupted.

Freddie kept eye contact with Nas. *Believe me.* '…and posted the photo of that guy's body online. Nas, you must find this twisted freak.'

Nas looked up at Moast. 'Sir, I think we should at least take a look.'

Moast slumped into the chair and pushed his hand up over his face. 'Okay. So you're saying that there's someone who has put this photo on Twitter.'

'Yes,' nodded Freddie. *Finally.*

Moast looked at Nas. Something passed between them.

Nas leant forward and pressed a button on the tape recorder: 'Interview suspended at twelve oh one am. 1st November.'

'Pinch punch first of the month,' Freddie said. What a way to start November.

Moast leant toward Nas, speaking quietly, 'Do you have a phone with Twitter?'

'No, sir. Of course not. The guv actively discourages us from using social media.'

'Me either. It's blocked on all the station machines. And we won't be able to get anyone from computer services in until the morning and the paperwork's been completed. I've seen my nephew's Facebook. It can't be that different.'

'In case you two forgot, I'm still here. Being held under false pretences.' Freddie waved at them.

Moast glared at her.

Freddie held up her hands in surrender. 'Just trying to help. If you give me my phone, I can show you Twitter and the account straight away.'

'It's worth a shot, sir. She did alert us to the photo, and having seen this site at the crime scene I'm not confident I could navigate it,' said Nas. *Thank you*, thought Freddie.

Moast exhaled. 'Fine, get PC Thomas to fetch it from the Duty Sergeant.'

When Nas opened the door, Freddie heard voices. Chatter. Laughter. A guy in uniform walked past clutching a copy of *The Post*. Her copy of *The Post*. 'Don't suppose I could...' she pointed at the newspaper.

Moast slapped a hand on it and pulled it toward him.

'Fine. Just asking.' This was ridiculous. They'd arrested and falsely accused her of murder, almost certainly got her fired from Espress-oh's, and now they wouldn't even let her look at her first ever front page national scoop. 'Can I get something to eat or is that not allowed either?'

Moast ignored her as Nas came back carrying Freddie's phone in a plastic bag. Relief flooded through Freddie as she took hold of her phone. She was in control again. She could call someone.

Text. Read the news. Work out precisely where she was. *Could You Last Twenty-Four Hours Without Your Mobile?* Nas coughed.

'Can I take it out – the touch screen won't work through this?' Freddie said.

Moast nodded.

Unlocking her phone, Freddie stopped: that was odd. The front flickered with Twitter updates. Had something she posted gone viral? An angry red spot denoting eleven missed calls pulsed on her phone icon. '19% battery – guys, you could've plugged it in.'

'Just show us the Twitter,' Moast said.

Five thousand six hundred and fifty-seven notifications – must be a glitch. She searched for Apollyon's account. The thumbnail image of the body was easier to bear. Wait…that can't be right: 'He has over 10,000 followers already?'

They huddled round the phone like smokers round a match. 'Is that unusual?' Nas asked.

'Yes, unless he's famous or gone viral. This morning he had no followers, what happened?' She pulled the newspaper from under Moast's arm. 'I'm sure I didn't.' She speed-read her copy. Virtually word for word hers. 'I didn't mention @Apollyon at all…how'd all these people find out about him?'

'You keep saying "he",' Nas said.

'Yeah, yeah, gender neutrality, et cetera, et cetera. Slip of the tongue.' She hit notifications. The screen blurred: there were tens of them. Hundreds. Thousands.

'PC Cudmore is insinuating you know who this Apollyon is?' Moast peered over her phone.

'You idiots.' She looked up.

'What?'

It was right there, the same tweet from the Jubilee Police, retweeted, shared over and over:

We can neither confirm nor deny that @Apollyon is the #Murderer or the #TrollHunter as mentioned in @ReadyFreddieGo's article.

'You tweeted it! Here: see, this is a message from the Jubilee Police. You tagged @Apollyon, and me, and hashtagged murderer and troll hunter. You just told the world @Apollyon is the one who posted the gruesome photo online. It means everyone knows he's the one I referred to as the troll hunter. It means you just called him The Hashtag Murderer. Whoever wrote this tweet has told the world this guy exists. It's gone mental. The cat's out of the bag. The genie's out of the bloody bottle. Who wrote this?'

Moast looked flustered. 'Sergeant?'

'We outsource our PR accounts. There was a social media advisor at that training course, Jackie Whitley,' Nas said. 'She's something big in PR, described herself as a thought leader. I remember that. They run all station campaigns and accounts, sir.' Nas bit her bottom lip.

'Nobody cares about this kind of nonsense. It's not important,' Moast said.

'Not important? Mate, you're trending.' Freddie couldn't believe they'd be so stupid. 'It's showing up as one of the most talked about things on Twitter right now.'

'A load of stupid kids pissing around online…' Moast tapped his fingers on the table.

'Try fifteen million users in the UK. You don't get it. This is big. Look here – this is Mari Blagg from the *Guardian*, this is Charlie Webdale from the Indy. This is going to be all over the nationals – they want to talk to me.' Freddie couldn't keep the excitement from her voice. *Sorry, dead dude.*

'Press? Why do they want to talk to you – it's my case. I should contact them. Send a message to all the journalists saying I will host a press conference.' Moast's chest puffed up. 'I'm investigating the Hashtag Murderer.'

The word murderer reverberated through Freddie. An unease flowered in her stomach and spread through her body. 'You haven't only told the world that @Apollyon is the hashtag Murderer,' she swallowed.

Nas heard the apprehension in her voice. She placed a hand on Moast's arm, a gentle silencer. 'Freddie – what is it?'

'You've also told @Apollyon the world knows he's the hashtag Murderer.' She could be wrong. @Apollyon might not care – but then why post the photo? Why the dark connotation of his name? They obviously wanted to be noticed. She took in Moast's puffed chest – why the bravado? *Reach. Klout. Impact.* People fed off that. Notoriety. People acted up for attention. The performance was part of the game; she shivered. What would someone who'd killed Mardling like that – so brutally – do if they knew people were watching? They'd already posted a photo of a dead man. What else would they be capable of? Dread pooled in her gut: 'You've given the murderer an audience.'

Chapter 9

STBY – Sucks To Be You

Freddie had been sat in the interview room alone for two hours now. Her phone had died. The pale-faced PC had brought her another scalding coffee and something that was supposed to be an egg and bacon bap. *23 Things You Eat That Can Kill You.*

Rocking back on her chair legs, she wondered how long they'd drag this out for. Everyone had jumped up after she'd said about @Apollyon having an audience and she was asked to wait here. Asked or told? She was too tired to be angry. She just wanted to go home.

The door opened and the burble of noise and movement bled into the room. Nasreen stood in the doorway.

'Follow me, Miss Venton.' She turned and Freddie jumped up.

Miss Venton? I thought we were past all that nonsense? 'So, Nas, bet you never thought we'd meet like this, hey? How you been?'

Nasreen ignored her and clicked down the hallway. Freddie noted she'd changed out of her flat boots into black high heels. Let her hair down.

'Wait here.' Nasreen tapped briskly on a door.

'Come!' said a male voice inside.

Nasreen smoothed her hair and tugged at her shirt's hem to straighten it. She wanted to look smart. Correct. Her suit was her armour. Except this situation was a hundred times worse than a job interview. Being summoned to the guv's office like this was bad news. She knew he'd been informed after the Twitter situation broke, journalists were already inundating the station with calls. DCI Moast was shouting about containment. It was a PR disaster. The guv shouldn't even be here – he'd come in on his night off to 'limit the damage'. She'd never been called to see him before. Never. She'd already been hauled over the coals for not outing Freddie immediately by DCI Moast. *Inappropriate conduct. Endangering the investigation.* She hated being told off. Her cheeks burned. She felt guilt and shame and wanted to fix it. She'd been a well-behaved child, only really getting in trouble if she went along with one of Freddie's more crazy schemes. Finding a pot of paint outside a pub and painting one of the building's walls pink. Grounded. Going further from home than she was allowed because Freddie had seen a kitten with an injured leg they had to help. No television for a week. It was always Freddie who'd led her astray. And now this? If Nasreen was to be suspended, she wanted to hold it together. She would not cry. No matter how much it hurt. No matter how upset or angry she was. Not in front of her colleagues. She wouldn't lose their respect as well as everything else.

Freddie's story about being a journalist was true, so why on earth was she wasting her time at Espress-oh's if she worked for *The Post*? That just showed how different they were. Anything they'd had before – any common ground they'd shared in the past – was gone.

She probably did it for free paninis. In a few short hours Freddie had seemingly taken a wrecking ball to Nasreen's life. Her career. Everything she valued. Nasreen felt the wrench of despair as she thought of Freddie confessing to entering the crime scene under false pretences. Why hadn't she raised the alarm when she'd seen Freddie at Blackbird Road? She was complicit in Freddie's offence. And now the suspect, the real one on Twitter, had hours on them and it was Nasreen's fault they'd missed the Golden Hour. The crucial period immediately after a crime when material is readily available to the investigating team. They'd lost it to interviewing Freddie. A false lead. A distraction. A confusion. DCI Moast had talked about creating slow time – trying to regroup, but Nasreen knew her deception about Freddie had lost them valuable ground. At best, Nasreen would be demoted. She tried to make that a reassuring thought, but anxiety overpowered her. How was she going to keep up the mortgage repayments on her home? What would her parents say if she was fired? She'd let everyone down. And all because seventeen years ago she'd gone for fish fingers at Freddie Venton's house.

In front of Freddie, Nasreen opened the door. It was an office, and sat at a large MDF desk was the grey-haired copper who'd caught her when she'd fainted at the crime scene. In front of him a plaque read: Superintendent Gray. *Oh shit.*

'Sergeant Cudmore. And we haven't been formally introduced, Ms Venton.' The Superintendent held his hand out.

Freddie shook it firmly. Taking in the certificates of excellence on the wall. The plant on top of the metal grey filing cabinet. This guy was a big deal. 'How much trouble am I in?' How was she going to explain this to her mum? Nasreen emitted a high-pitched squeak.

'Interfering with police work, wasting police time…'

'You're the ones who wrongly arrested me – you wasted your own time.' Freddie watched as a look passed over Superintendent

Gray's face. A shadow shifted underneath his skin. Was it anger? Disappointment? Freddie settled on disgust.

'I meant your performance at the crime scene.' The Superintendent sat down, stiff and upright.

Freddie took it as her cue to do likewise and flopped onto a chair in front of his desk. 'Yeah, sorry about that.' Nasreen was still standing, hands clasped behind her back. 'Journalistic intuition.'

'I read your piece in *The Post*, Ms Venton,' Gray said. 'Thank you for leaving Sergeant Cudmore and her colleagues out of it.' Another small squeak leaked from Nasreen. Freddie gave her a look: *man up*.

Superintendent Gray continued, 'The way you identified those tweets, made the link to the trolling, and then found @Apollyon was quite…extraordinary'.

Not if you know how to use Twitter, Freddie thought. Nasreen's shoes creaked against the floor.

'The Gremlin Taskforce are our specialists who tackle social media related investigations; there are three of them. Their brief is focused on educating young people about the risks of online bullying,' Gray said. Freddie glanced at the photo frame on his desk: wife, two kids. How very white picket fence. 'They do a lot of work in schools.' The Superintendent sighed, 'I'm sure you're aware, Ms Venton, that the government have slashed our funding. 17,000 police officers have been cut from the force over the last five years, and we're all under pressure to keep costs low. After a number of demand-intensive cases recently, I don't have the budget at my disposal to bring in Gremlin officers on this. So I would like to ask you to work with us, Ms Venton.'

'What?' squeaked Nasreen.

'What?' Freddie sat up and looked at him. 'Are you crazy?' She couldn't imagine anything worse than working with these establishment dinosaurs.

'I would like you to act as our Social Media Adviser.'

'That sounds like one of those idiot Twitter accounts that promise to get you ten thousand new followers, despite only having twenty-seven themselves. No thanks.'

Superintendent Gray looked at the woman in front of him. Scruffy, nonchalant, slapdash, but she had an insight into the online community his officers lacked. From what he'd seen at the crime scene, he inferred Twitter was the same as a religion or race, with its codes of conduct and language. Far quicker to use a translator than risk unintentionally upsetting the natives and closing off communication. She could bridge the gap. 'I have looked into your record, Ms Venton.'

'What record?' Freddie said.

Superintendent Gray opened a file on his desk and began to leaf through. 'I see you provided a witness statement that disparaged the attending officer, for a theft charge involving a Mr Robert Venton.'

'That was a misunderstanding, my dad had just had one too many and accidentally stole a box of melons. Melons. They must have been worth five quid at the most. But your lot came in heavy-handed, it was unfair.'

'You describe the police officer involved as "part of a corrupt hegemony". I've also read the blog post you wrote about the London riots, entitled "Boil the Kettled", during which you describe the police as, and I quote, "brutal fascist overlords who meted out unjust abuse and violence to innocent children".'

Sergeant Cudmore turned to stare at the girl.

'Thousands were unlawfully detained. Women were forced to pee on the side of the street,' Freddie said.

Superintendent Gray interlaced his fingers in front of him, glancing at the file resting in his in-tray: a ticking bomb. Notice arrived from the lawyers last week. A former officer who was of African descent had filed a sexual harassment case against a boisterous team of officers. Superintendent Gray knew the press would have a field day with the accusations of sexism and racism. He could see it now: acres of bleeding-heart liberal editorial on how institutionalised the force was, how out of touch they were. He'd been looking for the best way to counter, and now here was this mouthy woman with media contacts and a history of questioning police behaviour. And a seemingly large online presence. If she was presented as onside: a former objector to the force – young, female, alternative, left wing – who'd been 'won over' by her work with their boys, then it would take the sting out of the sexual harassment claims. People would believe her because she'd been so open with her condemnation in the past. He looked at Sergeant Cudmore, nice-looking girl, polite like most Asians: she'd look perfect standing alongside Miss Venton. That would tick the race box. The optimum public relations campaign to distract from the lawsuit. A female-dominated mixed-race press conference: pleasing. The case would be tied up quickly, once the IT bods had traced the perpetrator. In the meantime Freddie Venton would simply need to be satisfactorily controlled.

'Ms Venton, I'm offering you a way out: join our team as a Social Media Advisor on this case, and you can avoid prosecution. It helps nobody if you're charged with trespassing, breaking and entering, impersonating a police officer, and wasting police time.'

Freddie couldn't speak. She couldn't go to prison. Couldn't do that to mum. Dad's most recent *accident* – falling backwards off a bar stool – had left him unconscious. She'd rushed home to hold mum's hand in A&E and distract her from the pitying looks from the nurses. She couldn't leave her on her own to deal with all that crap.

'We will of course compensate you for your time, and it will only be for the duration of this case,' the Superintendent said.

Freddie shook her head, trying to order her thoughts. What about her career? After working so hard to get into print in the nationals, serving her time on the free or pathetically paid online sites and publications, she deserved this. Her moment of glory. A real shot at making it as a journalist. One that actually paid the bills. Finally she might be able to write about things she cared about, instead of gif-littered quick-read pieces. Now was the time to solidify her career, not dick around with the police. The flood of wannabe journalists would soon render her byline a distant and then forgotten memory. She had to capitalise on this now.

'Funding is tight,' Gray continued. 'But I'm sure we can reach the same wage as you were earning at Espress-oh's.'

'Sir, I really don't think…' Nas said. Freddie had forgotten she was still there.

'You have no grounds to think anything, Sergeant Cudmore. As I'm sure you're aware you've breached protocol and jeopardised this case with your actions.'

'Yes, sir,' Nasreen's head hung forwards.

'You will work with DCI Moast to detain this Hashtag Murderer swiftly, and you and Ms Venton will deliver updates to the media.'

Freddie caught the word media. What about all the interview and article requests on her mobile? A chance to keep hold of her dream job materialised. 'Can I still write?' Nasreen looked at her open-mouthed.

'As long as you don't reveal active details of the case, then we would be delighted for you to interact with the media,' Gray said.

Yes! Freddie internally air-punched. She could work with this. Build relationships up. As soon as this was over she'd be back. Picking up where she left off, and who knew, maybe she'd get something truly juicy out of working with the police. *The Secret Policewoman. #longread*

'Sir, surely a non-police officer shouldn't be commenting on cases to the press?' Nasreen said.

'Ms Venton here is the press, Cudmore,' Gray said. 'And we will make sure she's briefed fully by our public relations team on what can and cannot be talked about.'

'Don't worry, Cudmore,' Freddie smirked. 'I know how to do my job.'

'Yes,' said Gray. 'And Ms Venton won't wish to bring the force into disrepute, because that may alter the way we view those possible charges.'

Freddie saw Nasreen's chin jut forward.

'Sergeant Cudmore will be responsible for ensuring you don't endanger the investigation or bring our officers into disrepute. You two will add a fresh note to the image of the Met.' Superintendent Gray stood, his jacketed form looming over the desk, and extended his hand to Freddie.

'This is blackmail, you know that, right?' Freddie stared into his cold grey eyes.

'You can take it or leave it, Ms Venton. I look forward to working with you.'

Nasreen was deep breathing in the ladies' loos. Ever since her parents had pulled her out of school and out of Freddie's life, she'd been trying to forget her old friend. At first she'd been distraught, arguing with her parents, but as an adult she knew they were right. Freddie Venton was bad news. She was unpredictable, irresponsible, and, she thought bitterly, capable of ruining people's lives. Her guts turned into knotted snakes. Now they were working with each other? Worse than that, she was answerable for Freddie's actions. Her career hung from a thread and Freddie was tugging it. Would she ever be allowed to forget the past? Could she ever compensate for what she and Freddie had done? Nasreen tried to ignore the thought that this was somehow punishment for their actions eight years ago. She had to stay focused, keep Freddie on the straight and narrow. No more tricks, no more lies, no more games. Somehow, and she didn't quite know how, Nasreen had been given another shot. She hadn't been suspended. She was still here. Her dream job. Her purpose. This was her last chance: she would prove to the guv, to DCI Moast, to the team, that she could be trusted. She'd failed once, when she hadn't immediately confessed to knowing Freddie was trespassing the crime scene. That wouldn't happen again. She couldn't let Freddie trip up. One false step from her and Nasreen knew they'd both be out. Fired. That couldn't happen. She would fight it every step of the way. The knotted snakes took up home: a heavy writhing nest in her stomach.

In his office, Superintendent Gray was applying lavender hand cream. He always did this when he was pleased, leading his officers to refer to good days as *lavender days*. *Lavender days* were when you asked for a raise or time off. As Superintendent Gray massaged his cuticles, he congratulated himself on a job well done. This would see off any nonsense about sexism or racism. The Hashtag Murderer case was just what he needed to deflect attention. The press would be looking the other way: cases involving social media gave them scope to get worked up about the growing corruption of young people. This Hashtag Murderer case really couldn't have come at a better time.

Freddie let herself into her flat and plugged her phone in. It buzzed to life. It was just gone 4am, on Sunday 1st November. She'd spent nearly forty-eight hours in the same shirt. She needed a shower, and she needed sleep, but first she wanted to reply to the interview and article requests. She reasoned, with a couple of shots of espresso inside of her, she could get some pieces written and filed before she had a kip and had to get back to the station. No point turning down money. And she was looking forward to cultivating these new contacts. This Mickey Mouse job wouldn't last long, but it didn't matter. Freddie's journalist career was launched.

Scrolling through her phone, Freddie found her manager Dan's number and pressed call. She smiled while she listened to his inane answerphone message: 'You've reached Dan, Espress-oh's Branch Manager at St Pancras Station, London. I can't come to the phone right now as I'm whipping up delicious coffee for our customers, so please leave a message after the tone. Have a great day!' She was going to enjoy this.

She waited for the beep. 'Hey Dan, it's Freddie. Thanks so much for telling the police I had anger management issues and take antidepressants. Your little smear campaign didn't work though, they've hired me as a Social Media Adviser. Yes, that's right. I'm working with the police now. And if I hear that you let Milena, or any other member of staff, be touched inappropriately by a customer, like you did me on Friday night, I'll get my new mates

70

in uniform to come by for a chat. Management won't like that, will they? Oh yeah, and in case you hadn't guessed, this is my formal resignation. See ya!'

That'd put the wind up him. She fired off a quick WhatsApp message to Milena, filling her in and letting her know she'd have to do the illicit food drops to Kathy and the other homeless women on her own. She'd get that sleeping bag and swing by to see them as soon as she could. Job done. Freddie was sorry for the woman sobbing in the kitchen of the murder scene, the mother, but Alun Mardling's death had worked out well for her.

Online, servers and elements flashed, gathering speed through cables and fibre optics, transmitting through radio waves and wireless, 3G, 4G, mobiles, tablets and computer screens hummed with posts, statuses, messages, words. Thousands of them, spilling across the world like blood. Seeping into lives, filling the dark corners, becoming consciousness, becoming truth and meaning, and real. @Apollyon started to type.

Chapter 10

FWIW – For What It's Worth

08:45
Sunday 1 November
1 FOLLOWING   16,877 FOLLOWERS

The alarm on her phone woke Freddie. Unconsciously she put her glasses on and held the glowing screen toward her face, checking her email, texts, WhatsApp. Blinking away the sleep, she looked at Twitter.

She sat bolt upright. Her mouth dry.

She tried to swear but all that came out was a croak. Her fingers shook as she scrambled onto the windowsill to make the call.

'Nas, it's me,' Freddie said quickly. 'You guys need to see this. Now. I'm coming in.' She grabbed yesterday's jeans, sniffed a jumper from the floor before pulling it on, and squashed a beanie over her hair. All the while her mobile vibrated as more and more people retweeted and shared the same message on Twitter:

Apollyon @Apollyon • 57m

Freddie felt like she'd only left the Jubilee a few minutes before. Everything happened so fast. Nas sent the pale sandy-haired uniformed copper Jamie – PC Spew – to collect her from the front desk. Freddie was wearing her new lanyard that proclaimed she was Social Media Adviser, and she, Jamie and Nas were sat in the assigned incident room with some other uniformed officers. The once white room, like most of the station, looked like it needed a good clean or a new coat of paint. Windowless and smelling of stale fags and musty men (Freddie'd only seen two other female cops apart from Nas, and neither of them seemed to be on this case), the room was set up like a classroom. White boards lined one wall. Rows of tea-ring stained MDF tables, with yet more grey plastic chairs, all faced the teacher at the front: DCI Moast. It reminded Freddie a bit too much of her and Nas's old maths Portakabin classroom. The only door – a blue-painted one, dirty fingermarks smudged on it – was closed. The noise of the rest of the station, outside in the corridor, spiralling off the metal staircase, was blocked out. A photo of Alun Mardling's brutalised body was pinned to a board. Freddie didn't look at it. Instead she focused on the words from @Apollyon's tweet that were written next to it.

The door opened and a copper came in: another plain-clothes guy, his tall, gangly frame barely fitting into his black suit. Paisley tie dangling down too long. Muddy brown hair flopping onto his face. Freddie watched him report straight to Moast. 'Sir.'

'Sergeant Cudmore, you know Sergeant Tibbsy,' Moast sounded angry. 'I don't know what impression you've been given by Gray, but Tibbsy here is my number two. As usual.'

'Sir,' Nas nodded. 'Nice to see you again, Kevin.' She shook the gangly guy's hand. 'You know PC Thomas?'

'Jamie,' Tibbsy nodded at the pale copper who was sat in the corner.

'Sir, good to be part of the team.' Jamie stood, beaming.

'All right, lad,' Moast said.

'And I'm Freddie.' She held her palm up.

'We've met a couple of times now.' Jamie nodded at her. 'At Blackbird Road.'

She raised her eyebrows at him. *Probably best not to bring that up!* He dropped his eyes from hers, his Adam's apple bobbing in his skinny, pale neck as he swallowed. *Superbrain this one.*

Nas stared at the incident board. Tibbsy gave Freddie a half smile, before standing next to Moast. 'This is the message then?' he said.

'I found it on Twitter. Again,' Freddie said to their backs. Why the hell did she keep spotting these things before them? It was as if they were all looking the other way while things were starting to unfold online. Nobody responded. *Fine, whatever.*

'Have the IT bods turned anything up on the owner of this account?' Moast asked Tibbsy.

'They've drawn a blank, sir,' Nasreen said. 'Whoever's done it knows what they're up to. They're using Tor.'

'The encryption software that bounces your signal through a series of computers around the world?' Freddie asked.

'Yes.' Nas turned to look at her. 'How do you know that?'

Freddie shrugged. 'I use it to watch American TV shows before they're released over here.'

Nas tutted. 'Well, it means we're unable to locate who and where the photo was posted from. We can't find them that way.'

'Can we get anything from the photo itself?' said Moast. 'Get it blown up: I want to identify that knife – the suspected murder weapon. Find out where it's from.'

'Yes, sir,' said Nas.

You might make some ground if you actually followed the account, thought Freddie.

'What does it mean – *for whom the bell trolls*?' Tibbsy ran his finger under the words on the board.

'My guess is nothing. Just a nutjob spouting crap,' Moast said.

'It's a pun on "for whom the bell tolls", a line used in a John Donne poem.' Freddie couldn't help herself. 'It's also the title of an Ernest Hemingway book.'

They turned and looked at her.

'Don't you people read?' Freddie said.

'No one's got time for that,' Moast said.

'Better to wait till the movie comes out,' Tibbsy added, and he and Moast snickered.

'It was a film.' Freddie approached the board. 'It's a phrase that portends to death. "Never send to know for whom the bell tolls; it tolls for thee."' Moast's brow was furrowed. Tibbsy's mouth hung open. 'It's about solidarity in humanity, right? We're all in this together,' she continued. 'We're all going to die. Alun Mardling the troll dies and a bit of us all dies.'

'This is a murder investigation not a sodding book club.' Moast stood between her and the board.

Freddie gritted her teeth. She hadn't asked to be here, and so far she was the only one who seemed to have a clue as to what was going on. 'Really? Because this "nutjob",' she made quotation marks in the air, though only Jamie could see her, 'has just made an awesome pun, which feels very much like a threat. Or as if they're laughing at you.'

Moast's shoulders tensed. 'I don't take profiling advice from the tea girl.'

'Tea girl! Good one, guv,' Tibbsy guffawed.

Idiots. Freddie eyed Nas. 'You're quiet, Nas, what do you reckon?'

Nasreen's eyes flicked between the tweet and the photo of Mardling. 'We should talk to Paige Klinger, sir. She has motive after Mardling sent those threatening messages. She's the strongest current lead.'

Were they just going to ignore this message?

The door opened and Superintendent Gray appeared, his uniform a black exclamation point in the doorway. 'Progress report, DCI Moast?'

They all stood up straight, Jamie smacking his legs into a desk in his haste. This was like being in school again. She looked at

Nasreen, upright, prim, a look of what was that – pride? – in her eyes. Just like she used to stand in assembly every morning.

'I'm going to interview Paige Klinger, guv. As so much of the abuse was aimed at her, it's conceivable there's a link. This could be a possible revenge attack,' Moast said.

The dirty bastard's shafting Nas! He's pinching her idea, thought Freddie. Taking the credit. The conniving little...

'Good plan. Take the team with you.' Superintendent Gray nodded round the room.

'Tibbsy and I can manage, sir,' Moast said. Bristling like his cropped hair.

'And Sergeant Cudmore and Ms Venton, they may be of help with the technical side of things,' said the Superintendent. 'My daughters are obsessed with Paige Klinger. A model, I believe. There could be paparazzi. So far this case has been a PR disaster, I think it's best if any photos taken reflect a well-rounded and concerted-looking unit.'

'Sir, with all due respect, I don't think it's wise to take a civilian to an interview. We don't want to draw undue attention to ourselves, and she doesn't have the required training,' Moast wheedled.

'That's an order, DCI.' The Superintendent walked out.

Freddie smiled. She couldn't give two figs about attending an interview, but meeting Paige Klinger was another deal all together. *The Model Killer.* Even if she didn't do it, it'd be a great contact. She could get an article out of this, possibly a book. *Paige Turner: The true story of Paige Klinger's rise to fame.*

Moast looked furious. Freddie almost laughed. It was good to get one over on him as well, after that stunt he just pulled with Nas's idea. Moast grabbed his jacket and stormed out. Tibbsy, desperate to keep up, caught the edge of the table and nearly went flying. Freddie looked at Jamie as he squashed one toe of his shiny shoe under the other. *Britain's finest.* Nas was still looking at the board.

'Well, that was awkward. Is he always such a prick?' Freddie asked.

76

'DCI Moast is a professional. We're all finding this situation difficult,' she said, before also striding out the room.

'Come on then, Jamie, looks like you're giving me a lift.' Freddie looked at her phone. *'For whom the bell'* was now trending in the UK. The smile fell from her face. Trepidation spread from the touch screen through her fingers, chill and juddering into her bloodstream. Trending? How big was this freak's audience? She clicked through to @Apollyon's account: he was up to nearly 17,000 followers. *Jesus.* That's a lot of people watching what he's doing. His audience was growing. How far would his message spread? Was this a performance? An act? What was he trying to do? There were no good answers to any of the questions raging through Freddie's mind. And the biggest one yet, the one question she didn't want to voice, hung over them all: what would happen next? Freddie wasn't sure she was ready for the answer.

Chapter 11

FWP – First World Problems

Paige Klinger opens her eyes. Everything is white. The colourama paper backdrop that lolls down and away from the wall like a tongue is white. She stands on it, a large white inflatable banana between her legs. Her skin is white. Her hair is white blonde. The pair of briefs she has on are white. The only colour comes from her Mexican skull bracelet tattoo – her *calavera*. Her trademark. Its toothy grin all over Instagram. Her brand, part of what the fashion bloggers call 'Klinger's kookiness'. *A modern-day Cinderella, and Twitter is her fairy godmother* (as described by *Vogue*). She makes Twitter, and Twitter makes her. She had been doing all right: one or two campaigns. But the Internet changed everything. Posting off-duty snaps of her and her hot friends catapulted her to the top in a volley of likes, heart emojis, and retweets. Thanks to her fans – the affectionately named Klingys – she gorges on campaigns,

78

rolls in money, parties like she can't believe this is her life: on yachts, in mansions, aboard private jets. They're having to shoot on the weekend just to cram it all in. And she Instagrams it all. Her Klingys gave her this lifestyle, she will live it to the full for them. Fulfil their hopes and dreams with each bottle of champagne. With each diamond-studded grill. With each shopping marathon. With each tattoo. She lives for them and she shares it all online.

The lights are hot and white, and round the edges are dark shadows within which the team move. Hair, that stupid make-up artist, the one she doesn't like, the stylist, the magazine editor, and Kenny. Kenny occasionally steps into the white, his characteristic black T-shirt, jeans and glasses silhouetted against the light. He doesn't remember the first time they met. When she was no one. When she was still getting used to her new name: no longer plain old Paige Williams, now she was Paige Klinger – model. Her first VIP room. Taken by her booker to meet the iconic photographer Kenny Reynolds. There were girls with their tits out jumping up and down on the sofas, molehills of coke on the glass tables. Kenny and the only other man in the room were drinking beer in their Y-fronts, their trainers and socks still on.

'Kenny this is Paige, new girl,' her booker said.

'Nice titties,' he'd replied and licked his beer bottle.

She'd averted her eyes, only to find them resting on his hand, which was slowly stroking the bulge in his pants. She'd never seen an erection before. She must have jumped, or made a noise. They all laughed.

Someone handed her a drink. It burnt her throat. She didn't want to be the young kid everyone laughed at. She wanted to be cool.

Her booker spoke to another booker who'd just arrived. Another model. She'd seen her at castings. Long brunette hair, skinny jeans. Anya was her name. Kenny beckoned Anya over.

'Let's see your nips then.' He mimed for her to take off her top.

With a slow blush creeping up her face, Anya took off her top and folded her arms over her bare chest.

Kenny shouted something at the girl's booker, but it was lost as the other guy sprayed a bottle of champagne over four topless screaming girls on the couch. They opened their mouths to the spray. Poured champagne over their naked breasts. Everyone was looking in their direction, apart from Paige. She saw Kenny beckon Anya closer. He said something. She bent to hear him, and in that moment he put his hand on the back of her head and forced her face down into his lap. Anya struggled, his cock came free and he ejaculated into her face.

The other guy began to whoop and the girls and the bookers clapped and cheered. Anya staggered back, clawing her face, wiping spunk from her eyes.

Paige ran. She was fourteen.

Older now, she can barely remember what it was like to have never tasted alcohol. To have felt shock – was it cold? 'I need more! I'm coming down,' she shouted into the darkness.

The photographic assistant brought a white dinner plate with pre-chopped lines. Paige inhaled the white powder. The lights grew brighter still. The dark edges disappeared.

Kenny grinned at her. He licked his fingers and tweaked her nipples. 'You hot slut, let's do this!'

She shrieked and jumped, her arm up, her tattoo aloft, riding the inflatable banana like it was a rodeo bull. Her hair flared up and around her face. White light shone from her skin. They would make the cover.

A prefab photographic studio squatting under the Hammersmith flyover didn't strike Freddie as a particularly glamorous place for a fashion shoot.

Nasreen and Tibbsy were stood either side of Moast, and Jamie was bringing up the rear. A unit. A team. All dressed in suits, and Jamie in his PC Plod uniform, they looked ridiculous in this urban setting as trance music blared from every speaker.

'We're looking for Miss Paige Klinger – we understand she's working here today?' Moast asked a cute boy with pink quiffed hair and bolt earrings behind the desk.

Freddie caught the look of disdain Moast gave the boy. It was the same look he gave her charity shop checked jumper. What the hell was she doing here?

Moast knocked on the studio door, but she heard nothing over the pulsating music. He opened it and the big white space illuminated the concrete corridor they were in. Against the back wall, Paige Klinger was posing.

'Oh my God,' breathed Nas. Tibbsy started to giggle.

'Never seen breasts before, Tibbsy?' Freddie said, but it was lost in the noise. They edged into the room. A group of people clad in what passed as achingly cool clothes gathered round a camera connected to a laptop. Looking intently at the images of Paige that flashed up on screen, none of them noticed their arrival. Moast, Nasreen, Tibbsy and Jamie stood transfixed in the doorway. Pills, powder and bottles of Scotch were easily visible. Freddie knew there'd be no chance of her securing a Paige exclusive if this got ugly. She sidestepped Tibbsy, who was now furiously blushing and looking anywhere but at Paige Klinger's tits, and stood in an empty open-plan kitchen area. Obscene amounts of sushi sat on the work surface. She popped a tuna sashimi in her mouth. She was bloody starving. Besides, these fashion clowns were too high to eat.

Moast gave up waiting for someone to notice them and approached Paige Klinger. 'Excuse me, Miss.'

'What the fuck! Get out of my shot! Who are you! This is a closed set! Stefan! Stefan!' the photographer, who Freddie now recognised as Kenny Reynolds, started shouting.

Paige looked wide-eyed. An inflatable banana fell from between her legs. A young hipster kid in a flannel-neck shirt, who Freddie assumed was Stefan, ran at Moast in a rugby tackle move. Moast swung his leg and arm round. Stefan went up into the air, a flailing flannel bird, and landed on his back with a sickening thud.

Shit!

Paige Klinger screamed. Hands in front of her face. She was shaking. Her tiny rose-pink breasts bobbing. *Jesus!* Freddie's heart was beating in time with the frenetic music. Nas sprinted to grab Kenny Reynolds' upper body in a bear hug as he swung his camera down at Moast's gelled head. Freddie took a photo on her phone. *This is insane!*

Moast, pinning the whimpering Stefan down with one knee and one hand, wrenched his identification from his pocket. 'I'm DCI Moast, with the Metropolitan Police. Stop struggling.'

Stefan went limp.

'Christ,' said Kenny, still held tight in Nas's grip.

'Someone get my agent on the phone!'

'Ma'am, please calm down.' Nas locked onto Paige's eyes. 'You're safe. No one is going to hurt you.'

Paige's mouth clamped shut. Her arms fell down by her side. Her tiny frame shook. 'Is this about the gak?'

'No, ma'am, this isn't about the drugs.' Nas spoke as if only she and Paige were here, and not as if she had one of the world's most famous photographers in a vice grip. Freddie was impressed. She took another photo.

'Okay, sir?' Nas said to Kenny. He slackened. Nodded. Nas released him.

Moast relinquished his pressure on Stefan. 'You okay, son? Need an ambulance?'

Stefan struggled onto his elbows, dazed. 'I'm 'kay.'

'Good lad.' Moast clapped him on his shoulder and Stefan winced.

Moast stood up, his face momentarily level with Paige's naked breasts. He had the decency to avert his eyes. Tibbsy and Jamie stood in the doorway like two useless, gangly bouncers. Freddie shoved the phone back in her pocket.

'Miss, we need to talk to you about a police matter. I would suggest we do this privately.' Moast aimed the last comment in the direction of Kenny, who looked like he was trying to edge away.

'Fine by me,' Kenny said. 'Pub!' he shouted to the others.

There was a flurry of movement, and Freddie noticed several baggies being shoved into pockets as the fashion people filed out, heads down. The music stopped, her ears reverberated in the silence.

'What the hell is this about?' Paige reached into a bag. 'Want one?' She offered a pack of cigarettes to Nas and Moast, before lighting her own. Freddie twitched as the smoke reached her nostrils. Nas and Moast shook their heads.

'I'll have one!' Freddie said.

'It's illegal to smoke inside, Venton,' Moast said.

Knob. 'You want me to take my top off too, will that make it better?'

Paige smirked and offered her the packet. Freddie took one. She should have asked for some coke as well.

'You cronuts scared the bejeezus outta me. What do you want?' Paige exhaled toward Moast, managing to make the evil blue smoke look sexy.

'Miss Klinger, do you know anyone by the name of Alun Mardling?' Nas asked.

'Is he a stylist?'

'No, a bank manager. You may recognise him as @Maddening Alun23?'

Paige shook her head. 'Should I know him? What's this about?'

'Have you not seen the papers?' Freddie asked. She could get some recognition here, work her way into Paige's press team's good books after all. *Model's Bullying Troll Hell.* Moast shot her a warning look.

'Never read them. Full of lies. Total cronuts those hacks,' Paige exhaled.

Maybe not then. Moast smirked. Freddie blew her smoke at him.

'Alun Mardling has been found dead in suspicious circumstances, and it seemed he was trolling you.' Moast batted the smoke away. 'On Twitter.'

'Was he?' Paige said.

'Ma'am, the messages he sent were graphic and threatening, anyone would be understandably frightened by them,' said Nas.

'It would be understandable that someone might get so desperate they might seek to stop the messages,' Moast prodded.

Paige's eye were glassy, she stared at them blankly.

'Did you bump him off for threatening to rape you?' Freddie snapped.

'Freddie,' hissed Nas.

Paige blinked and her head jerked back. 'The dirty sod. I could see how that would get to someone, like, sounds really mental. But thing is, I don't really go on Twitter. Well rarely.'

Moast looked at Freddie accusingly.

'But you've got over two million followers? You tweet all the time? You're always in those top Twitter lists?' *Was this her defence: pretending she didn't have a huge Twitter account?*

'I's got someone who does all that shizz for me. Marni. Follows me round, like, sharing titbits with my fans. I rarely go on the thing myself.'

'You pay someone to impersonate you on Twitter?' Moast's forehead crinkled. 'Why?'

'Because it's part of her brand,' Freddie smiled. All those crazed Klingys who thought Paige was replying to their 'my cat's died please follow me Paige' tweets were actually tweeting a nobody.

'Exactly.' Paige jabbed toward her with the cigarette. 'And Marni's an intern.'

'So you had no idea about the abusive messages you've been receiving?' Moast put his hands on his hips.

'No, and I'm glad. Sounds right screwed up. These losers've got nothing better to do with their lives.'

Nas coughed. 'And where is Marni now, Miss Klinger?'

'You guys just sent her to the pub.' Paige lit another cigarette. Freddie's grin grew even wider. *Revenge of the Intern.*

The door swung open, banging against the wall. 'And what do you think you're doing?' A thin woman in her forties, with a stretched face and leather trousers, marched in.

'Magda!' Paige cantered toward her.

'This girl is underage.' Magda drew level with Moast and Nas.

'You what?' Moast's eyebrows shot up.

'She's a minor. Sixteen.'

Nas staggered backwards.

'Didn't you guys know?' Freddie exhaled her smoke. *These people knew nothing about real life.*

'I'm her agent. I called my lawyer as soon as I heard you were here. How dare you interrogate her without a legal guardian or responsible adult present,' Magda raged.

'Now hang on.' Moast put his hands up as if Magda was pointing a gun at him. 'We just wanted to ask Paige a few questions. She hasn't been arrested.'

'Am I going to be arrested?' Paige wailed and clung to the hem of Magda's cashmere cardigan.

'I'm her legal guardian.'

Of course you are, thought Freddie.

'Anything she has said without me present is not admissible in court. I shall be filing a complaint with the police commission. This is harassment.'

'This is a murder investigation, ma'am, we just wanted to ask Miss Klinger some questions,' Nas recovered herself.

'Well, I think that's quite enough for one day. You've frightened this poor child.' Magda put an arm round Paige. *Her biggest asset.* 'It's outrageous. Questioning a minor. Alone. In her underwear.'

Moast winced. 'Yes, ma'am. Out!' He turned to the rest of them.

Lagging behind everyone else, Freddie saw Magda smooth Paige's hair and hand her a small pill. Paige popped it into her mouth and pulled another cigarette from the pack tucked in the back of her knickers.

'What do you think?' Nas asked Moast, as she and Tibbsy bunched behind him.

'She's so pretty,' Tibbsy sighed.

'She's not as innocent as they're making out. She's completely high,' Moast said.

'We could arrest them for drugs possession and bring her in?' Nas offered.

'Better to talk to her assistant.' Moast flicked through his notepad, 'Marni, wasn't it? I bet she won't be ring-fenced by a load of expensive lawyers.'

The pink-haired cutie behind the desk pointed them in the direction of the local pub. Freddie was thinking about Twitter. Paige's account was verified, and it was *her*, but it wasn't her. Freddie wasn't naive, she knew people pretended to be other people online all the time, but the ease with which one person conned over two million had her thinking. Freddie knew how social media worked. Prided herself on trying out each new trend, each new development, each new app. She would never think she could get tricked so easily. People did – all the time. Idiots giving their bank account details to fabricated Nigerian Princes who promised them a cut of the twenty-six million quid they just needed to transfer into the UK. Or getting cloned after posting their birthdate on Facebook. She thought about Moast and Tibbsy, they seemed clueless about the whole online world. But she too had thought Paige *was* Paige online. Bought into the myth. If she could be tricked by some work experience kid, then what else could she be tricked about? And what about the other people, the ones already disadvantaged by lack of experience or lack of brain cells? Something shifted inside of Freddie: she'd always been cynical, but now she felt out and out paranoid. What was real and what was phoney? Just who could you trust? Who could she trust? *No Matter How Internet Savvy You Think You Are, You Can Still Get Fooled.*

Chapter 12

BTW – By The Way

12:06
Sunday 1 November
1 FOLLOWING   39,435 FOLLOWERS

The Rusty Needle, the height of kitsch cool, was modelled on a classic 1970s pub. Harking back to a golden age of drinking – with racist, homophobic and sexist undertones – the fashion waifs simply adored the ironic styling. They chuckled to themselves over the witty mouldy pork scratchings on the bar and the rat bait boxes in the toilets. (All of which bore a striking resemblance to its former incarnation, The Nelson, which landlord Jimmy had bought at a knock-down price from a bankrupt brewery.)

Freddie eased herself into the carpeted main bar, behind Nas, Moast and Tibbsy. They looked incongruous in their crow-dark suits. Jamie, in his uniform, had been told to wait outside. Perched on faux-leather stools and leaning against walls covered in decorative brass wall plaques, the studio crew seemed to have doubled in size.

'Which ones are girls and which ones are boys?' Moast pushed the front of his jacket back and rested his tanned hands on his belted hips.

'Is Marni a girl or a boy's name?' Tibbsy looked especially ridiculous stooping under the low plaster rose-covered ceiling.

'Er...not sure.' Nas scanned the room of fashion peacocks. She was the only one who pulled off the smart attire they wore, Freddie thought. Her legs looked long and slim in those trousers and her tailored jacket flattered her waist.

Freddie undid the zipper on her blue duffel coat and called up Paige's Twitter account on her phone. The last post was of Paige with her arm round Kenny, both raising their eyebrows at the camera in a goofy smile. The caption merely read, 'Oh yes!' It had been retweeted 4,227 times and liked 6,543 times. Freddie replied to the tweet. A phone buzzed. A small girl with glossy dark hair cut into 1990s-style curtains picked it up off the lacquered table. 'That's her.' Freddie pointed with a chewed fingernail.

'Marni?' Nasreen stepped toward the girl.

The rest of the room ceased talking and turned to look.

'Sup?' Marni shook her hair from her eyes.

'Could we have a word?' Nas signalled over her shoulder.

As they stepped out, Freddie heard the urgent gossipy whispers of those left in the pub. *Can You Ever Be Friends With Your Work Colleagues?*

Outside, leaning against the wall of a urine-spritzed side alley, alternating between smoking and pushing her hair out of her eyes, Marni talked. 'I seen those messages. Proper messed up. She gets loads. I block 'em. Sometimes I miss 'em. It's constant, all them fans talking at once.'

Fascinated that this unknown twenty-four-year-old with bags under her eyes *was* Paige Klinger online, Freddie couldn't help butting in. 'Who do you decide to follow back?'

Moast sucked in his breath. 'I don't see how that's relevant.'

'It's random. Every week or so I just go in and follow a couple. You've got to be careful: crazy fans can bombard you with DMs.' She scrubbed one cigarette under her leopard print trainer and lit another.

'You don't recognise the name Alun Mardling at all? Freddie, could you show her the account?' Nas said. Freddie turned her phone to show Marni. It glowed in the gloom.

'Oh yeah. Now I seen his profile picture, I know who you mean.' She tapped the side of her head, her fag still between her fingers. 'Visual I am. That's why I'm in this job. Utilises my creativity. That's one crazy dude. The volume of crap he was sending. I'd block him and he'd just open up a new account.'

'Did Miss Klinger know?' Moast tapped Freddie's phone, causing it to zoom in on the nostril of the skull profile picture.

Marni looked worried. 'God, hope not. She don't have a clue what's going on. I only tell her if it's important, like, when Madonna tweeted her.'

Was it really Madonna, or just another intern?

'So she didn't know Mardling was threatening her?' Moast tugged at his white shirt collar.

'It's not possible she went into her account at all?' Nasreen added.

Marni took a drag on her cigarette. Her nails were painted in different rainbow colours. 'I suppose it's possible. It is on her phone. She does go on sometimes – she could have seen it. But I wouldn't like to say.'

'Thank you, Marni. Could you give your full name and contact details to PC Thomas in case we need to ask you any further questions.' Moast took a card from inside his jacket. 'And if you think of anything that could be relevant at all, don't hesitate to call me.'

'There is one thing,' Marni ground the butt under her trainer, next to her previous one. 'I'm sure it doesn't matter but...' she trailed off.

Nasreen fixed her with a warm and welcoming smile. 'Often it's the things that don't seem important that turn out to be leads.'

'Well, there are a number of, well, mental cases.'

'Other trolls?' said Freddie.

'Yeah, but the opposite too, you know?'

'What?' Moast's forehead creased.

Freddie remembered the time she'd called Justin Bieber a pouting melted Walnut Whip in basketball shorts. 'Of course! The fans! I once wrote a joke about Justin Bieber in a feature, and I was seriously trolled. Hundreds of teen girls threatening to kill me for slagging off their idol,' Freddie said.

'That's it,' Marni pointed at her. 'The Klingys are just as bad. They really go for anyone who lays into Paige. You wouldn't believe some of the stuff these young kids say.'

'Could you give us a list of these Klingys?' asked Nasreen.

'There's hundreds of them. I wouldn't know where to start. But I could screenshot them? I mean, if I spot any. They often @name Paige. I guess so she knows they've got her back or something.'

'Thank you, Marni, you've been very helpful.' Moast held out his hand for her to shake.

Freddie walked with the others back to the car, while Jamie took Marni's details outside the pub.

'Can you spell Marni, as it's listed on your passport and iden-tification please?' she heard him say.

'S. U. S. A. N,' Marni said. 'Marni's for work. Better, like.'

Freddie smiled: an intern called Susan, pretending to be Marni, pretending to be Paige. *Classic.*

'You thinking what I'm thinking, sir?' Tibbsy said to Moast.

'We're all thinking it,' said Freddie. 'Was Alun Mardling bumped off by a crazed fan of poor sweet little Paige?'

'Surely fourteen-year-old schoolgirls aren't capable of killing forty-eight-year-old men?' Moast put his hands in his pocket, stretching his jacket tight over his broad shoulders.

'You'd be surprised by what fourteen-year-old girls can do, sir,' Nasreen said. Moast and Tibbsy didn't seem to notice, but

Freddie felt it like a slap. As Nasreen spoke, she looked directly and unswervingly at Freddie.

Back in the incident room at the Jubilee, Jamie handed Freddie a cup of coffee. 'Cheers,' she said, looking at the brown water. Better than nothing.

'Black, two sugars, just as you like it, Nasreen,' Jamie handed a cup to Nas who was sat on the desk next to her.

'Thank you, Jamie. Perfect.' Nas didn't take her eyes from the words Moast was writing up on the whiteboard. A spotty PC in uniform walked past and Nas reached out a hand toward him. 'PC Malcolm, did you get my email?'

He rolled his eyes and walked away from her. Someone hissed 'Traitor!' behind them, Freddie spun round to see several uniformed cops barely disguising their sneers. *What was going on?* Nas's cheeks flamed and she busied herself with her notebook. Moast didn't look up.

Jamie looked agitated. Tibbsy had the good grace to look abashed. 'We should've grabbed a pint when we were questioning Marni, hey, guv?' Tibbsy said, gulping the tea Jamie had got him. Moast chuckled in return.

'Are you going to come to the pub after work, Sergeant?' Jamie's eyes were wide and hopeful as he spoke to Nas.

'We'll see.' Nasreen was still staring at her notepad. 'Will you be going, guv?'

Moast shrugged without turning around. Freddie noticed Nasreen's shoulders drop. She couldn't possibly care what this lug thought, could she? Freddie blew on her coffee.

'I'm in, Jamie lad.' Tibbsy clapped Jamie on the back and almost sent him flying.

Jamie grinned at Tibbsy and then turned back to Nas. 'Perhaps next Friday then?' He tugged at his uniform collar. 'Sergeant Cudmore's not been out with the whole team?'

You've not asked me, thought Freddie. *Or do I not count as part of the team?*

Nasreen put her notes down next to her on the desk and grinned at Tibbsy and Jamie. 'Have they got any decent red in this pub?'

'Right,' Moast took his suit jacket off and draped it over a chair back. 'Can we focus on the case please?'

'Yes, guv.' Jamie stood up straight as if he were about to salute. Nas blushed again and scooped her notes back up. *Dick*, thought Freddie.

Tibbsy took his place at Moast's side. Moast rolled his shirt-sleeves up as he spoke, revealing striated muscly forearms: 'If it is a revenge-obsessed fan, then how did they find Mardling, that's what I want to know?' Tibbsy nodded. 'I'm not convinced this has anything to do with Twitter,' Moast continued.

Freddie picked at the lip of her plastic cup. If there wasn't a link to Twitter, then why did they need a Social Media Adviser? Surely she could go home and get on with her life if this was nothing to do with the Internet?

'Has anything shown in his personal life?' Moast said. 'Have we built up a clear picture of his regular movements, his habits? Did he do anything out of the ordinary in the last few weeks or months? Any irregularities in his bank accounts? Any unknown numbers he suddenly started to call?'

Nas checked her notepad. 'Single. He lived in Manchester until he and his wife divorced, then he came back down and moved in with his mother. Last long-term relationship – according to her – was eight months ago: he took an estate agent out for a few dates. Apparently she broke it off. There was an incident in 2003, when the ex-wife reported him for harassment after he sat outside her house crying for four days when she broke it off. But no charges were brought. The matter seemed resolved.'

Freddie took a sip of her bitter coffee. 'Yeah, he just took all that hurt and anger and turned it on anyone with a vagina.' Tibbsy choked on his coffee. Nasreen tutted. 'Dude needed a counsellor, that's all I'm saying.' She held her hands up.

'Much as your insights are *fascinating*, Venton, I think it's best you leave the police work to us. What you got, Tibbsy?'

'His bank accounts show no unusual activity. Logs from his Oyster card, and use of credit and debit cards, show a fairly familiar pattern: he went to work at his branch in Canary Wharf Monday to Friday 8.30am to 7pm, and every second Saturday 10am to 5pm. He had the occasional drink in The Cat and The Canary after work with colleagues. Bought microwave meals and beer from Tesco most days on his way home. And ordered takeaway – pizza seems to have been his favourite – most Friday nights. He often paid for streamed movies, which I'm guessing he watched on his computer. No sign of online dating or otherwise. Everything we've got from his mum and staff supports all of this. He didn't have mates outside of work, and no one remembers him talking about anyone new in his life in the last few months.'

Freddie wondered where else Alun Mardling might pop up online. She took her phone out and Googled him.

Moast took a step closer to the board. 'Right let's go over what we've got again. Victim Alun Mardling. Linked to Paige Klinger – who may or may not have been aware of the abuse he was sending her. Who links to unknown fans – who may or may not have acted in revenge on behalf of Miss Klinger. Apart from a historic incident of harassment – committed by the victim – there's nothing else that flags in his personal life. Anything unusual happen at work recently?'

'I spoke to the branch deputy at the bank Mardling worked at.' Nas read from her notebook, 'A Mrs Rose Attwood, she said there was a woman a few weeks ago who got very upset when Mardling didn't agree her overdraft. Apparently she had a young kid and she couldn't afford her rent, ended up getting evicted.'

'What a charmer,' Freddie muttered. You'd think the banks'd be a bit more lenient to the little people, after they had to be bailed out of their own screw-up.

'The woman, called Charlene Beeson, had to be removed by security after she dumped a bag of used nappies on Mardling's desk,' Nas said.

Freddie laughed. *You go, girl!*

'Alibi?' said Moast.

'She and her daughter were staying in the Women's Refuge Shelter on Barnard Street, sir. They lock the door at night and the CCTV confirms she never left.'

Freddie scrolled through Google. Alun Mardling's Twitter feed came up first. Then a link to his Facebook. After that there was a mention in a write-up about a charity fundraiser in the local E14 paper, *The Wharf*, and then other Alun Mardlings. Not the one they were interested in. She clicked onto iBooks and selected a John Donne poetry collection and Hemingway's *For Whom the Bell Tolls* to download. Jesus: £5.99? She thought dead authors were supposed to be cheap! No harm brushing up anyway, they might provide further illumination on these weird tweets. She clicked through to Twitter. The politician Charles Vass had tweeted his own name – Charles Vass. That was all. It flickered through her timeline. Then her breath caught in her throat. *The Times* columnist Victoria Ducane was the first, but soon everyone was sharing it. 'He's tweeted.'

'Apollyon?' Nasreen turned.

'What does it say?' said Tibbsy.

'Read it out,' Moast said, pen poised over the whiteboard.

Freddie swallowed. 'It says: Who's next? #murderer.' She watched the colour drain from Nasreen's face.

'What, what does it mean?' Tibbsy tripped over his words.

Freddie put her phone down on the table in front of her. She didn't want to touch it. 'It means there's a serial killer on Twitter.'

Chapter 13

SMH – Shake My Head

12: 50
Sunday 1 November
1 FOLLOWING   47,001 FOLLOWERS

'We have no proof of that,' Moast snapped.

'We have @Apollyon's tweets.' Freddie was pacing, watching the message waterfall through her Twitter feed.

'We don't even know if this Apollyon is responsible for Alun Mardling's death,' said Nas.

'Then how do you explain the knife in his profile photo? The one right next to the dead bloody body?' She couldn't believe they were so calm.

'Circumstantial,' said Tibbsy.

'Can you just stop jumping about and show me that message, Venton.' Moast held out his palm.

'Here take mine, sir,' Nasreen produced her phone from her pocket.

'Cudmore?' Moast stared at her.

Nasreen blushed. 'I know we're heavily dissuaded from using social media – that the Superintendent doesn't like it, sir – but I thought it was relevant to the case. I can delete the app if you think it's best?'

'No. Good initiative,' said Moast. He bent over Nas's mobile.

'So you accept this is playing out on Twitter then!' Freddie waved her phone in front of them.

'It's an avenue of enquiry – that's all, Freddie.' Nasreen tapped her screen. 'I haven't posted anything and I have no intention of doing that, sir. I just follow @Apollyon. See, here's his tweet.'

'The tweet of a serial killer!' Freddie said.

'Freddie, we don't use that phrase, it makes people panic,' Nasreen said.

'Too bloody right, I'm panicked!' Mardling's butchered body flashed in front of her eyes. 'Can't you just ask Twitter who owns the account?'

'Requesting information from Twitter pretty much counts as communications interception, we'd have to apply for a court order under the Regulation of Investigatory Powers Act. It'd take a lot of paperwork,' Nasreen said.

'Even then there's not much hope,' added Moast.

'What do you mean there's not much hope?' Freddie's palms were wet with sweat – she nearly dropped her phone.

'I spoke to the boys in the Gremlin Taskforce – they've experience of this,' Moast said. 'Twitter is an American-owned company, they don't have to comply with a UK court order.'

'We're talking about a murderer – surely they'll just hand it over!' Freddie rubbed her hand against her jeans.

'There've been other cases: bomb threats, people boasting online about sexual assaults.' Moast clenched and released his fists. 'Because of a treaty that exists between us and the US, Twitter can easily decline to answer our questions. In fact they often don't reply at all. Typical Yanks.'

They all stared at Moast. A drop of sweat fell from Freddie's hand onto the floor. 'That's globalisation for you,' said Freddie.

'What?' Nas asked.

'The technique by which companies or organisations develop international influence to fuck us all,' she snapped. From what she'd seen of the police's involvement with technology, she wouldn't be surprised if they'd just emailed it to info@Twitter.com.

'This is no time for loony left-wing crap.' Moast leant against the desk.

'It could just be a hoax, sir.' Tibbsy folded his lanky frame next to him.

'Not sure Alun Mardling would find it funny.' Freddie was pacing again. It was getting really hot in here.

'I mean an empty threat. Toying with us,' Tibbsy said.

'Sit down, Venton.' Moast's voice was firm.

Freddie wiped her forehead. The air was heavy. She sat on a chair. Tugged at her jumper's collar.

'Or plausibly an accomplice?' Tibbsy said.

'Try to breathe slowly, Freddie.' Nasreen crouched in front of her.

Sweat trickled down her neck. It was Mardling's blood. She was breathing it in. She was drowning.

'I knew this would happen – a civilian shouldn't be anywhere near this investigation.' Moast placed his hand on her head. 'Head between your knees. Tibbsy, get her a sugary tea – she's having a panic attack.'

Freddie's face was pressed into her phone. Twitter filled her eyes. There were more.

Sandra Barnes @SandyBitch • 2m
Anyone else creeped out by this? >>> RT @Apollyon Who's next? #murderer

Flash Heart @Flasheart • 1m
F**cked up. RT @Apollyon Who's next? #murderer

Will Horton @Willy67 • 50s

NOT for whom the bell lolz. *hides under bed*
#murderer

She fought to get her breathing under control. 'They all think
it – everyone on Twitter – there's going to be another murder!'
'You're just panicking, Freddie,' Nasreen said.
'So is everyone else! Look!'
Moast held her hand still so he could see the screen. Nasreen
fiddled with her mobile. 'She may be right, sir.'
'Shit.' Moast ran his hand up and over his face and through
his hair. 'This is all we need. Call a press briefing – three o'clock
this afternoon. We need to get this under control. We don't want
the public anxious.'
'Sir.' Nasreen disappeared out the door. Freddie's body shook
as it forced oxygen round.
Tibbsy crouched to give her a tea. 'All right?' His eyes were wide
and shiny with worry.
She smiled weakly at him. As she took a sickly gulp, the words
serial killer spread like mould across her feed. It was breaking news
on BuzzFeed, *The Metro*. It was a virus. There was no getting this
under control. There was no damage limitation. Freddie thought
grimly, *The Meany is Out of the Bottle.*

14:55
Sunday 1 November
1 FOLLOWING   49,341 FOLLOWERS

Nasreen tried to smile confidently at Moast. She'd pick a one-
to-one with a violent perp any day over this. A press conference.
Cameras. Microphones. Questions. She felt sick to her stomach.
She had to pull herself together. If she wanted to get promoted to
a DCI, then she'd have to get over this babyish fear. She cleared
her throat. Again. She looked at Freddie: she was picking at a
bit of skin on her fingernail. She hadn't even brushed her hair.

This stuff had never bothered her, even when they were little. Nasreen remembered the humiliation of the school nativity play. Her parents were so proud she'd been given the starring role. 'First Indian Mary there's ever been,' her mum would say. She had one line. *The* line. 'And lo, the baby Jesus is born.' When it came to say it, Nasreen was dumbstruck from all the expectant faces. Everyone was staring at her. Mrs Allen, their teacher, hissing prompts from the sidelines. She opened her mouth but nothing happened. People started to laugh in the audience and she'd looked around desperately for help. And then up jumped Freddie, dressed as a sheep, and shouted, 'Lo, the baby Jesus is born. Baaa!' Everyone cheered. Nasreen nearly ran across the stage and hugged her, she was so thankful. But things changed. By the time they were teenagers Freddie would do anything to be centre of attention. *Anything*, she thought bitterly.

'If they ask you a direct question, let me answer.' Moast took a sip of water from the glasses provided in the Premier Inn's side room.

Nasreen nodded. And tried again to smile confidently. The conference room next door had been prepped. Interest in the Hashtag Murderer case was fevered. She could hear the journalists gathering: a threatening hum of voices.

'I don't understand why I have to do this if I can't say anything?' Freddie picked up a Premier Inn pencil from the small table that held the water glasses and put it in her pocket.

'Put that back,' Moast said. 'Me neither. But the Superintendent feels it's good for community relations if you – an Internet person or whatever – are visible at the media briefing. He insisted both you and Cudmore were here. Orders are orders. And as we've got nothing concrete, I don't want you revealing anything to *those* people.'

'*Those* people are me, mate. I'm a journalist. Maybe if you were a bit more transparent.'

'Please, Freddie,' Nas's voice came out more desperate than she wanted it to. 'Not now.'

Freddie looked at her peculiarly. 'Not still frightened of public speaking, Nas?'

'This isn't the time for a bleeding chinwag, will you both shut up. Neither of you are to say a word. Let's just get in there, read the statement and get back out.'

Nas felt the sting of Moast's words. He'd completely cooled toward her since Freddie had been foisted onto his investigation team. Nothing in her training had prepared her for this level of internal politics. She wished she'd never gone upstairs at 39 Blackbird Road, then none of this would have happened. She was being frozen out. The rest of the team stopped talking as soon as she walked in the room. There were pointed whispers as she passed groups in the corridor. And that humiliating stunt from PC Malcolm at this morning's briefing. She needed to get the situation under control. She'd stayed up all night learning how to use Twitter, going back over what they knew about Alun Mardling. He was a bank manager who'd had a messy divorce and now lived with his mother. His social life was non-existent. There were no significant others, and apart from his penchant for trolling and the one accusation of harassment in 2003, there was nothing unusual in his life. Then she'd read everything she could find on Paige Klinger, seemingly endless pointless articles about what she wore and ate. There was nothing new there either. Then she'd ploughed through everything they had on Mardling's colleagues, his former wife, his mother, there had to be something somewhere, some link that they had missed, some hairline crack that would open the whole case up. If she could just find that then she could prove to Moast she was on his side. Not Freddie's.

'Sir,' she said.

'Right, let's do this.' Moast straightened his navy tie, picked up the statement from the table and opened the door. The flashbulbs started immediately. Nasreen forced herself to follow him, willing herself to relax. How did Paige Klinger cope with this every day of her life? Maybe she didn't? *Maybe she'd cracked?*

'Detective Inspector, can you tell us if the Hashtag Murderer is going to kill again?'

'Can you confirm that @Apollyon is the murderer?' The questions came fast. 'Is Paige Klinger's PA responsible for this death?'

Where did they get their information from? Nasreen ignored the shouts. Moast took the middle seat in front of the boards bearing posters of a smiling Alun Mardling. Nasreen squeezed past to the chair the other side. They were so close her left knee was touching Moast's under the table. Freddie dragged the remaining chair out, causing the microphones to squeal in feedback. 'Hey!' a few people shouted good-naturedly.

'Sorry, guys.' Freddie leant into the mics. People laughed. Moast signalled at Freddie to zip it. Nasreen kept her eyes down, fixed on the bouquet of microphones in front of her. A mass of suited individuals in her peripheral vision. She took a gulp of the water glass in front of her, wishing it was wine.

Moast gripped his script in both hands, 'Gentleman, thank...'

'And ladies,' said Freddie, her voice overpowering the room.

'Hear, hear!' yelled a female from the crowd. They laughed.

Moast gripped his speech tighter and swallowed. 'Ladies and gentleman, thank you for joining us here. My name is DCI Edwin Moast and I am leading the investigation into Alun Mardling's death.'

Nasreen was aware of phones being held up, cameras, her stomach fell away. *Don't think about it.*

'We would like to speak to anyone who was in the vicinity of Blackbird Road, E14, in the early hours of October 31st.' Moast coughed. The audience bridled. 'We would also ask that the press exercise professional restraint when mentioning the Twitter account known as @Apollyon.' A murmur went through the crowd. 'We would like to assure the public that there is no need for alarm regarding this case. We have no reason at this stage to suspect that we are dealing with anything more than an isolated incident. If anyone has any information on @Apollyon, then please call the incident room in confidence. Thank you for your attendance today.'

A roar rose as the crowd surged forwards. Nasreen gripped the table.

'Your press statement claims Miss Venton has been hired as a consultant on this case. We've read her work for *The Post* – was Miss Venton hired because she uncovered the @Apollyon Twitter account?' cried a blonde woman at the back.

'Don't you think the public have a right to know if there's a serial killer on Twitter?' Another woman with a sleek black bob stepped forward.

'DCI, I'm with the BBC: are you doing enough to tackle online abuse?' A guy in a navy blazer stood up.

'Can you confirm the photo used in @Apollyon's Twitter account is of the crime scene?' A female voice – somewhere. Nasreen's eyes darted between the bobbing heads of the press.

'That's all, thank you. No questions.' Moast could barely be heard.

'Sergeant Cudmore, is it true that you used to go to school with Miss Venton?' A journalist with side-swept brown wavy hair and loosely knotted red tie pointed his phone at Nasreen.

'How do you know that?' Nasreen gasped.

'Google, ma'am,' the guy said, his pen hovering. 'You left though – Pendrick High. I can't find any mention of you at another school – were you homeschooled? Why was that? Are you and Miss Venton still close?'

What else do they know? Nasreen's voice caught. They couldn't know about what they'd done – back then, at school. When her life had changed forever. *Their secret.* They couldn't. No one knew. Except she and Freddie. And one more person. Nasreen looked at Freddie who was staring at the guy with the pen. Panic bubbled up Nasreen's throat. 'I…I…'

Moast glared at her and pushed his chair back to stand.

'Miss Venton, was your coverage of this case designed to smoke the culprit out, or is this just a case of nepotism?' A man with rimless glasses thrust a Dictaphone forwards.

'Hey, I got that splash fair and square,' Freddie said. 'You're at *The Family Paper*, aren't you?'

'Miss Venton,' hissed Moast.

'An unknown journalist.' The man's glasses glinted. 'Seems unlikely.'

Freddie pointed at herself. 'I'm the one who found @Apollyon and his photo of Mardling in the first place!'

The guy with the glasses twisted, so he was pushed closer by the crowd, jousting his Dictaphone at Moast. 'Detective Inspector, is this your case or are you relying on a twenty-four-year-old girl to run it for you?'

'I'm not a girl, buddy, and I'm only twenty-three!' Freddie shouted.

Moast bent toward the table. 'No further comment. Turn the mics off. Off!'

'Do the police have any clue who @Apollyon is?' shouted a woman with a ginger bob.

Nasreen forced herself up.

'What are you trying to hide, Moast?' a man shouted.

Moast grabbed Freddie by the arm. 'Out,' he hissed.

'Oww!' Freddie glared up at him. The cameras flashed.

'Sergeant Cudmore!'

'Nasreen!'

Nasreen willed her legs to work. Moast and Freddie made it through the door. She forced her way, pushing the journalists back, closing the door behind her, leaning against it as the three of them stood in the small bright purple-painted room.

'What the hell was that?' Moast swiped his hand in the air in front of Freddie. Freddie, hair springing round her head.

'Don't you ever touch me again!'

'Touch you! You're lucky I didn't arrest you!' Moast clenched his fists at his sides.

'Oh yeah, how'd that go for you last time?' Freddie's head wobbled.

'You disobeyed a direct order. I told you not to say a word.'

Only Freddie could make people this angry. Nasreen stepped toward them.

'You're endangering people's lives because you're too stubborn or too stupid to accept this is about @Apollyon – it's all there on Twitter!' Freddie shouted.

Nasreen put a hand onto Freddie's shoulder. 'Freddie there's a set process we have to…'

'Oh now you stop her, Cudmore!' Moast turned. A vein on his neck throbbed.

'I…I…' she said.

Freddie shook her hand off, shouting: 'Why am I the only one who gets this? He said, "Who's next?" He hashtagged "murderer". You need to wake the hell up. It's a threat! The tweets, the stuff he's posted: that's all you've got to go on.'

'You need to be quiet.' Moast's eyes narrowed.

'Don't patronise me,' Freddie said. 'You've got nothing. No one's safe till you catch this freak, and you're standing here lecturing me.'

'Enough!' Moast screwed his statement up and threw it against the wall. 'Back to the station. Now!'

'Jackass!' Freddie screamed at the door Moast had just walked through.

'There are procedures to follow, Freddie, you must understand…' Nasreen tried to order things in her mind.

'Give it a rest, Nas.' Freddie grabbed her coat, upsetting one of the glasses of water, and followed Moast out.

Nasreen took a moment to compose herself, then righted the glass, picked up the balled up statement and followed them. A disaster. An unmitigated disaster.

Chapter 14

NSFW – Not Safe For Work

15:37
Sunday 1 November
1 FOLLOWING   54,619 FOLLOWERS

Freddie had read Twitter on the silent drive back to the station. There were screenshots of her being pushed by Moast. Comedy stills of Nasreen with her mouth open like a fish. Looping Vine videos filmed straight from the national news. She slid her headphones in her ears: the voice of a journalist saying 'there's a serial killer on Twitter' played repeatedly. She shuddered. Articles sprang up, to be expanded, dissected and reworked from a different angle as the day progressed. Freddie knew the score: *Hashtag Murder Briefing Descends Into Chaos. Police refuse to confirm there's a serial killer on Twitter*. Moast had been summoned to the Superintendent's office, and shortly afterwards Tibbsy had told her she was to go home for the day.

Slamming into the station's ladies' loo, Freddie tried to stay calm. She pressed play on the Vine video again. *There's a serial killer on Twitter. There's a serial killer on Twitter*. Apollyon's tweet swam in

105

front of her eyes: *who's next?* She couldn't believe this was happening. And Moast and the others were all dicking around with meetings and paperwork. They should be out there. *Looking.* What if there was another way to trace the tweets? Hadn't those convicted of trolling the woman-on-a-banknote campaigner been traced through other devices? She was sure the trolls had been identified by using the same moniker they had on Twitter on traceable online accounts, like those for games consoles. Nas would know. If she could just speak to her alone, away from that bonehead Moast, she could make her understand. She'd know what to do, where to look.

Freddie scrolled through her recent calls till her finger hovered over Nas's number, but the sound of footsteps and a familiar voice approaching stopped her. She ducked into a cubicle as the bathroom doors swung open and Nas and someone else in squeaky police shoes entered.

'The whole canteen's talking about it, Nasreen,' said the other woman.

Freddie sat on the toilet and tucked her knees under her chin so they wouldn't see her feet. They must be talking about Apollyon. This could be useful.

'It's a disaster. I don't like to speak out of turn, but I think Superintendent Gray's made the wrong call with *that* girl,' said Nas.

Freddie froze. *That* girl? She heard a squeak of shoes and a cubicle door lock.

'I thought she was a friend of yours?' The woman spoke up over the rattling of the loo roll holder.

'God no,' said Nas. 'She's a liability. We're bashing our heads against a brick wall with this one: we've got no DNA, no witnesses, nothing but those bloody tweets to go on. This is a trying case already, without us having to act as babysitters to some girl.'

Freddie stared hard at a scratch on the melamine of the cubicle door. Nas couldn't mean her? There was a flush and the other woman stepped out of the cubicle. 'I heard she worked at Espress-oh's,' said the woman as she washed her hands.

'Yes, and the sooner she's back there the better,' said Nas.

'No wonder the DCI's pissed,' said the woman. 'Try not to worry, she's not your responsibility.'

Nas sighed. 'I was talking to Sergeant Tibbsy – weighing up if we went en masse to the Superintendent, if he'd take her off the case?' Nas said.

Tears pricked Freddie's eyes. *My Best Frenemy.*

'It's ludicrous she's even here in the first place,' said the woman.

'Least I can focus without distractions this afternoon. I'm going back through the vic's phone records – seeing if anything jumps out.'

Freddie listened to the door swing open and their receding footsteps. She held on tight to her knees. What an idiot she'd been. She was, and always would be, just an Espress-oh's waitress to Nas. She wiped her nose on her sleeve. She was just slowing them down. She didn't belong here. Letting her hair fall down over her face, she left the station. Tomorrow she'd resign.

Freddie easily got a seat on the Ginger Line. She didn't want to look at her phone. She was sick of rereading @Apollyon's words. They bounced round her head with every shunt of the train. She should've been on the other side of that interview table. She should've been the guy with the Dictaphone and the difficult questions. She should've known better than to take the bait. She squeaked her foot along the floor, the rubber heel of her trainer was coming away. Her original flatmate, Vic, the one she'd moved in with before she'd disappeared off to her boyfriend's Wandsworth houseboat, had described Freddie as 95% rage and 5% Converse. It was funny at the time. Now it just felt crushingly true. There were no outlets: that was the problem. There'd been a shift when she graduated. It was subtle at first, the ebb and flow of one social set into another, but now she saw less of her actual mates and more of possible contacts, people like Neil who'd take her to Wagamamas for lunch, or people she'd met on Twitter who she'd buy eye-wateringly expensive cocktails for before emailing them her CV. There wasn't much time or money for anything else: the odd shared packet of fags and laughs with Milena and Kath, and hook-ups when she could fit them in. Work and the black hole that was her bank balance swallowed everything else. *Help! I Don't Have Time For Friends.* She used to think her generation had missed out on all the fun of uni, swapping the drunken antics for part-time jobs to pay fees, continuous work experience and caning it on coursework to ensure they got the grades they needed for the big bad world. Now she looked back on the occasional drunken fancy dress party and shared pot noodles in front of the telly with nostalgia. The last time she'd seen Vic was when they'd bumped into each other on the tube: Vic on the way to a job interview, Freddie on her way home from work. The promise of drinks was always there but neither of them really had the time. Thinking back, Freddie realised the only period in her life where she was truly happy, relaxed, chilled, was back at school. Walking home from the small red-brick junior school she and Nas attended, along the common, and either stopping at Nas's parents' Victorian terrace for Mrs Cudmore's freshly cooked *balushahi* doughnuts, or on to her own 1970s cul-de-sac home for Jaffa Cakes and Diet Coke. They played hopscotch and It in the concrete playground, or hid round the back of the wood-covered portakabin that housed the school's sports equipment and swapped secrets. Her dad hadn't been so bad then. Mum would still go out with him of an evening, smelling of flowery perfume. Freddie liked to watch her put her make-up on. They would return singing, and joking, and laughing. When had it tipped over? When she was at Pendrick High. There was an incident at Dad's work. Her parents never spoke of it. It was then that the singing stopped. That dad started going out all the time. That her mum would sneak into her room and hold her in bed while he crashed and swore downstairs. Until he passed out. Freddie remembered pouring the entire contents of the drinks cupboard down the sink one day. And getting a swift hiding after. She shook the sting of the memory off.

She and Nas would stop for sweets at a stall under the yellow and blue striped awning of the town market on Wednesdays. They used to cram as many fizzy sherbet-filled flying saucer sweets as they could into their mouths. She used to laugh hysterically, so sherbet sprayed everywhere. Not the knowing chuckle she gave now. She used to dance round her room. Throw her bag from her shoulders and run into the holidays. Those endless weeks of pleasure. She was free. Before the exams started. Before the constant need to build your CV. Before dad. Before everything became hard and real and insurmountable. With Nas. She weighed the thought in her head: you have only been happy with Nas. Only with Nas. And then obliterated it by tapping her phone screen into life.

16:07. She needed distracting. Occupying. Shame to waste the rest of the day. Opening up WhatsApp, she typed:

'Hey Ajay,
Fancy a drink this arvo? Freddie x'

Freddie did up her duffel toggles as she left Dalston Junction. The sun was starting its descent, the brittle November light climbing up the front of the mini-cab office and the Co-Op. The sky, a bright blue with Pixar clouds, felt far above the cool shadows that hugged the street and the 277 double-decker, as it swept past, leaving fumes hanging in the crisp air. A girl in a hijab, and her uncovered friend, sidestepped Freddie, laughing. She plodded behind a man clutching a takeaway coffee cup and wondered what Milena and Dan were up to now. Asleep probably, or studying in Milena's case. She thought about the ridiculous faces Milena pulled behind Dan's back. Their shared toasties at 3am. Milena had sent a few pics of her and Kathy via WhatsApp since Freddie had left Espress-oh's that day. Freddie bent her foot round and took a photo of her broken shoe, dropped it into an app, and drew eyes on the image so the split leather became a mouth. She messaged it to Milena. It'd make her smile. She stared at her phone. Waiting. It was too cold to hang about. Perhaps she'd be online later.

People were sat on the stone benches of Dalston Square, huddled against the wind, smoking, also looking at phones. She could hear the tinny base from someone's headphones, a man talking into his mobile, the girls laughing. *Is London the Loneliest City in the World?* You could be anyone in London, anonymity came with the postcode. Apollyon could be anyone, and anyone could be the next victim. Freddie tried to shake the thought from her mind. Nasreen, Tibbsy and Moast didn't seem convinced Apollyon was the murderer: she had to trust them. *When to Back Down and When to Stand Up For What You Believe At Work.*

Freddie pulled her phone from her pocket, her fingers pinched and stretched by the chill air. A message from Ajay:

'Sorry, busy today. Another time. A.'

Disappointing. Freddie flicked through her Tinder messages. No one of particular interest at the moment, or rather no one who wouldn't already be busy on a Sunday afternoon. Quick shower, change and head to The Bearded Mole then? Her flatmates would be out: Anton cycling, Pete with his mates at the pub. She didn't want to be in the flat alone. Thinking.

The pub was busy. Freddie dropped her bag from her shoulder and squeezed past an animated group of blunt-fringed men and women, resting their ciders and gin and tonics on the dark wood bar. Freddie scanned the room for a free table. Two girls with rockabilly flowers in their hair had snagged her favourite spot by the fire. Four men with hair pushed behind their ears nursed pints at the adjacent table. A group of what looked like students sat along the wall that was overwhelmed with taxidermy animal heads. Freddie watched their laboured 'I'm having fun!' smiles, as their eyes and fingers nervously fluttered toward and over their phones. She recognised the anxious looks of those who thought they should be somewhere else: working? Blogging? Applying for jobs? *How Generation Y Squandered Their Student Days Worrying.* She headed to one of the red velvet stools at the bar.

'Shoreditch Blonde, please mate, don't worry 'bout the glass,' Freddie said to the cute lad with the geeky glasses behind the bar. He gave her a gap-toothed smile. *Potential.*

She hung her bag off the hook under the bar and updated her Facebook and Twitter status: I'm in The Bearded Mole, if anyone fancies a drink? Then clicked onto Happn, just in case. She was halfway through her second bottle and fiddling with her Kindle app when he came to the bar.

'Hey.'

Freddie looked up at the lanky guy in the battered Ghostbusters T-shirt and skinny black jeans next to her. 'Hey yourself.'

He leant his elbow on the bar and turned toward her. His hair had been buzz cut, leaving a curly brown quiff on the top, like a 99 ice cream with no flake. With concave cheeks and blinking eyes, he had a nervous energy she liked immediately. 'Drink?'

'Sure, same again, ta,' Freddie winked at the barman.

He pulled coins out of his pocket to pay. 'What's your name?'

'Freddie.'

'What's that short for?' His T-shirt rucked as he reached for his bottle, revealing olive hipbones.

'Freddie,' she said. His hazel eyes didn't react. He took a sip of his beer. *Don't blow it, Freddie, keep talking:* 'My dad was a big Queen fan.'

'Like royal. I get ya,' he nodded.

'No, like Mercury. Freddie Mercury.' She stared at him. He stared back. 'Freddie Mercury. Lead singer of Queen. Gay. Died of Aids?'

'Whoa. Tragic,' he said.

Freddie took a gulp of her beer. Surely no one's this void of pop culture references? Was he one of those mythical people who tweeted 'Who's this Neil Armstrong dude everyone's talkin bout?'

when prominent figures passed away? He had the air of an obsessive about him, maybe his mind was consumed by whatever his specialist subject was: parkour, Berlin graffiti artists of the late 80s – she'd met his type before. *The Twelve Fanboys You'll Meet In East London.* She smiled. He smiled back. Or perhaps he was just dim? *Are We Too Smart For Our Own Good?: Why Being Stupid Makes You Happy.*

He took another sip from his beer. Ah what the hell, she deserved a treat. 'Want to go some place else, like yours? My flatmates tend to walk through my bedroom,' Freddie said.

'Sure.' He put the bottle down. 'I'll grab my jacket.' She watched him walk to an empty table and collect his bag. Perhaps his friends had left, or was he, too, out alone looking for a little company? She pulled her coat on and made her way through the pub, the roar of alcohol growing more audible with each shriek and laugh. She was already feeling better.

'We'll have to take the 149. It's only five minutes from here.' He took her hand as he led her outside. The streets were busier as people walked through the dusk, clutching bags of ready meals, and gathering outside restaurants and bars, their cigarette smoke mingling with the condensation from their chattering mouths. His skin was smooth and warm, like it could heat her from inside. Excitement and desire tingled in Freddie.

'So, Freddie,' he said as they climbed onto the bus and squashed themselves between gobby kids in pimped trainers and weary shoppers reading the Sunday papers. Freddie caught sight of the words Hashtag Murderer on the front page. 'Do you want to know my name?'

Shit. She'd been so distracted by his hipbones she hadn't even thought of that. 'Sure.' *Apollyon could be anyone, and anyone could be the next victim.* She shook the thought from her head. Let the police work on the case; they didn't want her around anyway.

'Brian,' he said.

'Like May?' she said, as someone pressed the bell and the bus lurched.

'Who?' He caught hold of her two shoulders, keeping her upright.

'Doesn't matter,' she said, standing on tiptoe to push her mouth against his. He tasted of balsamic vinegar Kettle crisps and chewing gum.

Freddie woke up on Brian's sheet-free mattress on the floor. Shit, she hadn't meant to fall asleep. He seemed a nice guy, but she didn't want to give him the wrong idea by staying over: she wasn't interested in a relationship right now, just a bit of fun. He seemed to share a flat with two other guys who'd come in pissed in the early hours of the morning. His room was empty apart from a pile of clothes in the corner and mugs with fag butts squashed into them. Still, least he had a door that people didn't open. He was sat on the sash windowsill, a sheet hung crudely across it like a curtain. In just his jeans, he'd braced his bare bony feet against the wall so he could exhale the smoke from his fag through a narrow gap in the window. The duvet over Freddie's naked body also had no cover. She reached an arm out and along the floor until she found her scrunched knickers. 'Can I have a puff?'

'Hey,' he smiled and passed his baggy roll-up to her. Doomed to failure, she thought: I could never be with someone who can't roll a decent fag. 'Want to get some breakfast? There's a good cafe with decent coffee close?' He took the rollie back from her.

Freddie checked the time. The thought of returning to the Jubilee, of seeing Moast, of seeing Nasreen again, filled her with dread. 'Sorry, got to get to work.'

'Sure, don't want to keep The Fuzz waiting.' He stubbed out the remainder of his fag in a chipped red mug. 'So can I get your number?'

'Look, Brian.' She pulled her tights on under the duvet, wiggling them up. 'Last night was cracking.' Well, it was okay: he wasn't about to knock Ajay off the current top spot. She found her skirt at the end of the bed and fastened her black bra with her back to him. 'But I'm kind of focusing on work right now. You on Twitter? Want to hook up there?'

'Snapchat?' He passed her her black shirt.

She bent over the tiny Keep Calm and Smoke Weed mirror she kept in her bag and swiped the mascara smudges from under her eyes. 'Sure. Let's do that.' She had a great angle of her in her neon blue knickers she'd got for Christmas on her computer. It'd taken several goes, and her tits looked too good in it to send to just one person.

'Cool.' He rolled another cigarette.

Brian walked with her to the bus stop, pausing to grab Freddie a couple of cans of Coke and a packet of Quavers from a corner shop with crates of pumpkins, potatoes and frozen-looking apples outside. Freddie checked her phone as people clicked past her in suits, presumably on the way to The City. Where was she? Stokie. Cool. It wouldn't take too long to get to the station. She'd feel better after her Coke. They ran the last bit as the bus approached through cars and cyclists as the roads delivered the workers of London to their jobs. This whole rush hour thing was a real pain, thought Freddie.

'I'll message you, Frankie!' Brian called as she got on the bus.

'See you later, Brain!' she laughed. It was only as the bus pulled away that it hit her. *Don't want to be late for The Fuzz?* She had no recollection of telling Brian she worked with the police. Trepidation sprang up like spores across her bathroom ceiling. Something didn't feel right. She pulled her phone out and typed Brian's name into Snapchat. *User unknown.* She Googled him. Nothing but some accountant in Texas came up. There was no Twitter account. No Facebook account. No blog. Nothing. He was a ghost. Freddie swallowed. He'd put his number in her phone last night: she pressed dial. *This number has not been recognised. Please try again.* She tried to breathe. It must just be a simple mistake. He'd written the number down wrong. Or misspelled his name.

He could be Apollyon. The thought exploded into her head. He could be the killer. She'd posted online the pub she was in. He could have deliberately found her. Tracked her down. Hunted her. Crouching to look out the juddering bus window, she saw Brian was no longer there. He'd melted into London's anonymous canvas.

Chapter 15

ICYMI – In Case You Missed It

Tibbsy was waiting for her in reception, his tall rangy frame stuffed into an ill-fitting navy suit. The scuffed wooden doors and the indeterminate-grey squeaky floor reminded her again of school. 'Head boy looking after detention today, then?' Freddie's voice sounded shaky. She had to get this stupid idea about Brian out of her head. She thought over the night before: there were no possessions in his room. *Where was all his stuff?* And he hadn't said much about himself, just asked her loads of questions. She must have mentioned working with the police last night. *Must have.* She was being paranoid. This whole situation was getting to her. Just like when she'd panicked that Apollyon, the killer, was somehow on the same DLR carriage as her on the way back from the crime scene. It was ridiculous to think Brian might be Apollyon. For a start why would the killer be in Dalston? Mardling was murdered in E14. And why would the killer be interested in her? She'd only written that article and appeared at the press conference. Freddie ticked herself off for being self-obsessed. Or anxious. She was just spooked. She reminded herself that there was no firm evidence to suggest Apollyon even was Mardling's killer. It could just be a kid who'd hacked the police Cloud and stole that crime scene photo, or a sicko hoax. She really needed to try and get a better night's sleep tonight. She needed to get a grip. 'Here, I brought you a Coke,' she said, passing Tibbsy the can.

'Cheers,' he smiled. 'The guv wants me to bring you straight to the incident room,' Tibbsy said.

'Course he does.' She leant on the front desk, between the two raised shelves that towered up either side of it like a fortress, and signed in on the clipboard. 'Don't see why I've got to go through this palaver every day – I've got my lanyard, haven't I?'

'Them's the rules.' Tibbsy opened the push-button door behind him.

'Seems to me you guys have got too many rules.' She held her black denim bag up so the Duty Sergeant could riffle through it with his pen. Surely all these procedures were just wasting time they could be using to find the real culprit. 'I could've walked by myself to the incident room, you know. I don't see why I need a babysitter,' Freddie said.

Tibbsy turned to face her in the empty corridor. 'Because you pissed the guv off.' His voice echoed flatly off the blue metal stairs that cornered their way up to the other floors.

'Yeah, well, he pissed me off too.' All she needed now was Nasreen to come and have a go at her for copying her homework and this nightmarish rehash of school would be complete.

'Look, Freddie,' Tibbsy said. 'None of us are too thrilled about the way this case is developing, but trust me, things will be a lot easier if you just learn to give the guv what he wants.'

Tibbsy's slack-jawed face seemed to be genuine. Was his whole suck-up buddy act just a means to get on? 'I don't know how you lot do it: all this yes sir this, yes sir that!' Why couldn't Nas have come and got her? Least *she* sulked quietly. 'Urgh,' she said, flapping her arms up and letting them slap against last night's purple cord miniskirt. 'Look I'm sorry about the whole press conference thing. I'm not great at controlling my temper.' *Generation Rage: How I Learned to Manage My Anger.*

Tibbsy laughed, his navy tie, which had a dribble of milk down it, bounced.

Freddie smiled. 'I do think Moast's making a mistake over this Twitter thing though – aren't you worried about the last message?' *Or that the guy I just fucked might be Apollyon?* She had to stop this. She was being paranoid.

'We're all worried, mate, but panicking won't solve anything. We'll get there.'

They started walking again, side by side this time.

'Moast just wants to do his job well,' Tibbsy started up again. 'He's a good cop. Knows what he's doing.'

Freddie scrubbed at a small stain on her skirt with her fingernail. She wasn't so sure. 'So what happens now?'

'Team brief. Regroup. Go through what we know. See if the appeal's turned up any leads.'

Two dark-haired uniformed policemen stopped chatting as they passed them in the corridor. Freddie heard the guffaw and whispered words as they walked away. She was struggling to know what to wear. She had her black Espress-oh's clothes or the stuff she went out in. She wasn't convinced that by putting tights with this skirt she'd made it look work-suitable. She tugged the hem down. She didn't belong here. After the press conference yesterday, perhaps she'd be able to bargain with Superintendent Gray: get him to let her go? She'd speak to him straight after the meeting.

Tibbsy paused as he rested his hand on the handle of the blue-painted incident room door. 'Ready?'

'Let's get this over with,' she said.

Even though the room was painted white and lit by fluorescent tubes, the volume of PCs in their black uniforms grouped at chairs and desks lent a distinct grey hue to everything. Tibbsy took a seat at the front next to Nasreen, who looked professionally perfect in her black trouser suit. Freddie tried to meet her eye, but she was reading her notes, or avoiding her. Behind Nasreen sat Jamie, pale-faced. He gave her a weak smile and a nod. She patted his shoulder on the way past. Freddie headed to the back, weaving past the coppers who sat with plastic cups of coffee and their notebooks out. She had no idea this many people worked on a murder case. *An Insight Into Britain's Largest Institution.* Pulling a plastic grey chair out, she dropped her bag on the table in front of her, resting her arms and chin, respectively, on top. She kept her coat on – she had no intention of staying any longer than she needed to.

Moast entered, his white shirtsleeves already pushed up. The room hushed. He put his notes down on the table in front of the incident board and his mug of coffee on top of it. 'Morning all, thanks for getting here on time.' He met her eyes, she pretended to busy herself with a loose thread on her bag. 'Update on the door-to-door questioning, PC Thomas?' he continued.

'So far nothing, sir. Nobody saw or heard anything unusual at all,' Jamie said. 'We'll keep trying.'

'Good, people forget stuff or they don't realise something's important till later. Tibbsy, anything turn up on surveillance?'

'No cameras on Blackbird Road, sir. There's a community arts centre with a fixed camera that catches the end of the alleyway that cuts through from Blackbird to the DLR. We're getting those tapes now.'

'Good,' said Moast. 'Look back over the week leading up to the 31st as well, there were no signs of forced entry, which implies Mardling let his killer in. And how are we doing on the knife analysis from the photo that was posted online, Tibbsy?'

'We've blown up the image and it's a pretty standard kitchen knife. A brand called Kitchen Devil,' said Tibbsy.

119

'Killing someone with a knife called "Devil" – how fitting for someone who named themselves after a New Testament word for devil,' Freddie said. This was eerily symbolic.

Tibbsy glanced at her quickly. 'It's a popular brand available in most high-street stores, and it's Amazon's number one bestselling kitchen knife.'

Prime crime delivery, thought Freddie. Does the killer have a sick sense of humour?

'Unfortunately that makes it hard to trace. There's probably hundreds, if not thousands, of these knives in circulation,' said Tibbsy.

'Fine. Check with the mother to see if she recognises the knife – was it there already or did the killer bring it with them? What about the photograph itself – any luck with analysing what type of camera took it?'

'Based on the clarity and file size, we're fairly certain it was taken on an Android phone, sir,' said Nas. 'Unfortunately the IT lads said the metadata that embeds the GPS coordinates of where and when a digital photo is taken and posted had been successfully stripped out.'

Freddie was impressed. And she made a mental note to disable her own GPS coordinates. This made her think of Brian again. Had he *tracked* her? This case was making her paranoid.

Moast was still talking: 'I want you to cross-reference everyone on our list of Mardling's colleagues, family, friends, everyone he's ever met, with the purchase or ownership of Kitchen Devil knives and Android phones.'

'A lot of people have Androids, guv,' said Tibbsy.

'Yes, and I want to know where each and every one of them who owns one on that list was at the time of Mardling's death. I want to know if they know how to disable their bloody GPS coordinates. I want to know if they've purchased any kitchen knives recently. Go back over it until we find a link.'

'Sir,' said Tibbsy.

Nasreen raised her hand. *First to ask a question. Sucking up. Just like school.*

'Yes, Cudmore?' If Moast was still angry with her after the press briefing he hid it from his voice.

'Sir, the victim was partially dressed, ready for bed, and on his computer, for some hours, based on his online activity.' Freddie leant forwards. Where was Nas going with this? Moast nodded for Nas to continue. 'Well, it's odd isn't it? I mean, that's the actions of someone on their own, not someone who's got company at that time of night?'

One of the uniformed PCs wolf-whistled. Laughter rippled across the room. How did Nasreen put up with these dicks? Freddie gritted her teeth.

'Calm down, please,' Moast silenced them. 'Good point, Cudmore. What did the mother say – we're sure he has no girlfriend? Given he was knocking one off at the time he was killed, we could be looking at sexual motive: possibly a sex game gone wrong?'

A uniformed cop raised his hand at the front. 'Sir. The mother confirms there were no significant others she knew of. Said Mardling didn't socialise since he came back down from Manchester. Seems the ex-wife got the friends as well as the house.'

Another peal of laughter.

'So who else would he let into the house?' Nasreen said. 'At that time of night? And why would he leave them to play on his computer? And…er…pleasure himself.'

'Could have been a prostitute?' said Tibbsy.

'There's no evidence of him using sex workers before,' said Nas. 'I've looked through his bank, phone and the Internet browser records retrieved by the IT team. He wasn't very sophisticated at hiding his online porn use: just deleted the browser history. They said within a few minutes they had access to a record of every site he'd ever viewed. The way he was dressed, the time of night, being on Twitter and, you know, doing *that*, it seems unlikely anyone else was there. So it had to be someone who could let themselves in undetected.'

Nasreen was right: it didn't add up. How did the attacker get into the house?

'Whoever was there must have either been in the house already or let themselves in – Mrs Mardling said no one had a spare key to the property,' Nas said.

'Cudmore, look into your hunch some more. Forensics are fairly confident the perpetrator came at him from behind: one swift movement and it was all over,' Moast said. Freddie felt her Coke shift in her stomach. 'The attacker didn't need long. Go back to the mother and double-check no one had a key: an old cleaner? Friend? Mardling's ex-wife? And ask if they kept a spare outside. Take a look at the windows again: someone could have crawled in. His mother said they were closed when she came home.' Moast perched on the edge of the table and folded his arms. 'If it was a Tom – a sex game gone wrong – they left no trace,' said Moast. 'So far Forensics haven't turned up any DNA samples that can't be traced to either Mardling or his mother in the room.'

'It was clean?' Nas asked.

Moast nodded. 'There were trace elements of hydrogen peroxide on the desk.'

'They bleached it, sir?' Tibbsy asked.

'It's inconclusive, but certainly a possibility.'

'They knew what they were doing then?' Tibbsy tapped his pen against the desk.

Freddie thought about Apollyon's threat: who's next? *They knew what they were doing.*

'Sir,' Nasreen again, raising her hand.

Moast nodded.

'I noticed Ecover products in the bathroom,' Nas said.

'Typical woman!' one of the uniforms shouted through cupped hands. They all laughed.

'Dick,' Freddie said under her breath.

'Quiet down. And your point, Cudmore?' Moast sounded dubious.

'They're bleach-free,' Freddie said.

A couple of officers turned to stare at her, their faces sneering at the cheek of her speaking up. *Whatevs.* She'd had worse in the newsroom on work experience.

"There was a Greenpeace sticker on the window next to the front door, too.' For a second Freddie caught and held Nas's gaze. It was still there: that silent communication. When they were at school they used to do it all the time – clock something someone had said. Exchange glances. As if they knew what the other was thinking. *I'm not just an Espress-oh's waitress.* Freddie willed her to understand: *you're right. I believe you. Go on.*

Nas turned back to Moast. 'Solar panels on the roof, sir. Why would a household that's that concerned about the environment have bleach?'

'Thomas, have uniform check back with the mother to see if she kept bleach in the house.' Moast nodded. 'Have the door-to-door teams check local bins. If someone's ditched bleach I want to find it.'

Chairs scraped back, voices raised. Freddie jumped up, squeezing past the men gathering up their papers and jackets. Nas was already with Moast, studying the incident board. Freddie tapped Tibbsy's arm. 'What Nas said about the bleach – what does it mean?'

'If the killer brought it with him, this was premeditated,' Tibbsy said.

'Planned?' said Freddie. She swallowed.

'Yup,' Tibbsy said. 'And if she's right about them gaining access to the house with a spare key, then we know they've likely scoped it out. Could have been planning this for a while.'

Premeditated. Did that mean it was more or less likely to be a serial killer? She needed to Google this. *Now.* Freddie edged forward. Tibbsy was now standing with Moast and Nas. All thoughts of speaking to the Superintendent were gone. 'What do you want me to do?'

'Ah, Ms Venton, I've got these for you.' Moast turned and lifted two box files off the desk and held them out to her.

'What are they?' she asked.

'A copy of Alun Mardling's sent and received emails from the last two years,' Moast smiled. 'The boys in IT have scanned them quickly, but I want you to go through them all again and see if anything odd jumps out.' He put them on the table in front of him and pushed them toward her. 'That should keep you busy.'

Freddie stared at them. Was he joking? Then she thought back to when she'd joined Twitter, before she'd changed her notification settings. When the online service would send her an email with a copy of each private Direct Message she received. She'd over-heard Nas saying that Mardling hadn't encrypted or hidden his trolling messages in any way, what were the chances these emails contained copies of his private messages? Perhaps she would find something useful in there? 'Sure, great,' she smiled at Moast. Her phone vibrated in her back pocket, and the smile fell from her face. The noise of the incident room fell away. As if moving through water, she dragged it from her skirt pocket. It was set to vibrate if one particular account tweeted. 'DCI...'

'I've told you what to get on with already, Venton.'

'They've tweeted.' Freddie turned the phone over in her hand, slid her shaking finger across it to unlock it.

'What does it say?' Moast asked.

Nasreen answered, holding her own mobile in front of the incident board. 'It says: Hope is rearranging her name.'

Chapter 16

RTFM – Read The Fucking Manual

10:18
Monday 2 November
1 FOLLOWING   61,548 FOLLOWERS

'What?' Moast picked up Freddie's phone, his mouth a questioning curl.

'Hope is rearranging her name,' Nas repeated.

'What does that mean?' Tibbsy pushed his hand into his temple.

'Another pun? A distraction?' Moast held the phone in front of Freddie.

Freddie stared at the words. The dull shape of Moast, Tibbsy and Nasreen swam in the windowless room, framing the phone. She blinked, tried to focus. Her Coke sloshed from side to side in her stomach.

'Doesn't make sense. Someone's playing silly buggers,' Tibbsy said.

Freddie tried to still the Coke tide. 'It's a cryptic clue.'

Nasreen wrote the words from the tweet onto the whiteboard in red pen.

'Rearranging is often a clue that you need to reorder some letters to make a new word. An anagram. See. Hope is rearranging her name,' Freddie said. Nasreen underlined rearranging. 'Give me a pen, I used to do these with my gran. I need to write it down.' Tibbsy handed her a biro.

'Rearranging what?' said Nasreen.

'Shhhh I'm thinking.' She scrawled the words across her hand: hope is rearranging her name. '*Her* implies it's a girl, a woman's name.'

Moast and Nas ran their fingers underneath the words. Jumping from one letter to the next.

'Mary! Katie! Sarah!' Tibbsy said.

'Shut up!' Moast snapped.

'Hope is rearranging her name,' said Nas. 'Rearranging her name is hope.'

The letters peeled away from her skin, floated in the air, became the paper on her gran's knee. Freddie saw it. 'Sophie! The answer's Sophie.' She showed Moast her hand. 'Rearrange the letters in "Hope is" and you get Sophie. The answer's Sophie! Her name is Sophie and now we have hope.'

'But who's Sophie?' asked Tibbsy.

The pen fell from Freddie's hand and clattered onto the floor. 'There's going to be another murder.'

'And the victim is called Sophie,' Nas wrote the name on the board.

'Get the team back in here now!' Moast said.

'It could be a hoax, sir,' Tibbsy said.

'You want to take that risk? Unless we track the IP address of the account, we can't rule it out.' Moast took the marker from Nas's hand and drew a line down the incident board, a new column: at the top of which he wrote Sophie.

Tibbsy shook his head, his whole body vibrating with the movement. Freddie's breath was coming in short sharp bursts. She felt a pain in her side.

'I want to know if Alun Mardling knew anyone called Sophie. Or came in contact with anyone called Sophie. What's the name of his ex-wife?'

'Lorraine, sir,' said Nas.

'Right, and what about Paige Klinger: anyone called Sophie in her life?'

Freddie watched as the black inked name on her hand seeped into the feather cracks of her skin. She couldn't just stand here. She flicked onto Twitter. The cryptic clue was being retweeted, shared, and they weren't the only ones who'd worked out the answer was Sophie:

Tim Bryant @Timmo17 • 1s
@Apollyon: Sophie! Do I win? Do I get to keep her?

Sophie S @SweetlyPie • 5s
Shit.
fetches baseball bat *hides under the bed*

Ant Boyd @FallowlandsSwamp • 5s
Hope its Sophie Ellis-Bextor. Murder on the dance floor. #Murderer #toosoon

Hashtag too soon – are you kidding me? Freddie shook her head. Someone named @PrincessDee67 had posted 'Now we know who the #Murderer is' above a gif of Jim Carrey in the garish green question mark covered suit of The Riddler in *Batman*. This was not a fucking game. The drink fizzed in her stomach. She thought about the blood dripping from Mardling's desk, how she'd heard his mother crying in the kitchen. Those sobs from behind the obscure glass panel. The pain. The loss. There was a girl at school whose name was Sophie. Bobbed hair. Joined the army. Mum was a lesbian. What the fuck was her surname? Was she on Facebook? Should she try and…what? Warn her?

She typed into Google: 'How many people…' Google auto-suggested '…died in ww2'. Death. More death. Her oesophagus burned. She kept typing: '…are called Sophie in the UK?' She skim-read the links:

'impossible to say'
'80,134'
'Sophia is the Greek goddess of wisdom'

She flicked between screens. Sophie and #Murderer was now trending on Twitter. Fuck. Fuck. Fuck. Gassy burps forced their way out of her mouth. She had to calm down. In her head she pictured Sophie from school's mum crying. The sobbing in Alun Mardling's kitchen merging into the woman who came to sports day.

Moast was still issuing instructions. 'Tibbsy, get on to Missing Persons, I want to know if any Sophies have been reported missing. Start in the E14 area where Mardling's crime scene was and then work outwards.'

'Yes, guv,' said Tibbsy.

Officers were coming into and out of the room – carrying boxes, files, piles of paper. Nas was on her mobile with her laptop in front of her. Another whiteboard had been wheeled in, and Moast was writing Paige Klinger, Alun Mardling, Marni Pepper/Susan Pepper along the top of the columns.

Freddie left the incident room. The corridor buzzed with activity. She passed a uniformed woman – the word 'hashtag' crackling through the static of her radio. A man in a shirt and tie carrying a box of printed papers. The Duty Sergeant who'd made her unlace her boots hurried past carrying four cups of coffee as if they were pints in a bar. The taste of last night's beer nipped at her tongue. *What if it was Brian?* She pushed the door of the ladies' loo open, banged into a cubicle and vomited.

Tibbsy had said it might be a hoax, but she knew it wasn't. She could feel it. In her gut. Swimming in the toilet bowl. Too much effort had gone into writing that tweet. Desperation set in. Out there was a woman, a girl, someone named Sophie, whose life hung in the balance. All thoughts of journalism, of school, of getting out, left Freddie's head. She had to stay. She had to save Sophie. Whoever she was.

Scooping water from the limescaled tap, Freddie washed around her mouth and face, spitting into the cracked white sink. The ladies' loos were dingy, painted what had once been green, now a dirty smudge of colour punctuated by biro graffiti on the walls. She guessed those who'd been arrested used the same bathroom as they did. *They.* She was part of the police now. Part of the team. Part of those who stood in the way of Apollyon. She had chosen which side she stood on.

Her phone vibrated in her back pocket. She braced against the sink, saw the look of horror on her face reflected in the filmy shatterproof mirror. Another post from @Apollyon: The game is on.

The bathroom door swung open. Nasreen stood, her dark hair pulled back into a hasty ponytail, her face defiant, her foot propped against the metal kick guard of the blue door. 'Seen it?'

'Yes,' Freddie said. They could be in the maths block. Back in Pendrick. Away from all this.

'It's a Sherlock Holmes quote, isn't it?' Nas said.

'No shit, Sherlock.' Freddie scraped the water from her face. If Nasreen noticed the smudged mascara and the smell of bile she didn't mention it.

'Does it mean anything else?' Nas asked.

Freddie allowed Nasreen to hold the door for her. The Jubilee hummed with activity, the blue doors of the rooms and offices winking like eyes as they were opened and closed in the white corridor. Freddie felt the panic. 'I don't know.'

'Is it anything to do with Sophie? Are there any Sophies within the books or the TV series?' Nasreen's hand was on the small of her back, guiding her.

'I don't know.' She'd read some of the books, but a long time ago. *The Hound of the Baskervilles. A Study in Scarlet.* But there

129

were more. 'There are stories. Short stories. Lots of them. I don't know.'

Nasreen pushed the door of the incident room open with her free hand. Laptops, phones and files now covered every surface. Groups of officers gathered round each table, reading, typing, phones propped under their ears.

'It could be a hoax, right?' Freddie asked. 'Tibbsy said so.' Someone had written 'The game is on' on the whiteboard.

'How many stories? Think. Anything to do with Sophie and Holmes? Does anyone know of any Sophies in the Sherlock Holmes stories?' Nas called. 'Or in the films, or the TV series.'

'There have been so many adaptations,' Freddie held her phone in her shaking hand, her throat burning from the stomach acid. She Googled 'Sherlock Holmes Sophie': an actress, an author, nothing that popped. 'Maybe it's nothing to do with Holmes, maybe it's something else?'

'Like what?' Nasreen stood next to Moast. They both stared at the whiteboard, scanning the photos of Mardling, the names of Paige Klinger, Marni Pepper, the tweet, trying to link it all.

'I don't know,' said Freddie. Tears pricked her eyes. She could scream in frustration. Her phone vibrated in her hand. 'Again! He's tweeted again!'

'13 to the dozen. Unlucky for some.' Nasreen wrote the words on the board. The tweets lined up, a column of clues:

Hope is rearranging her name – Sophie
The game is on – Sherlock? Holmes? Arthur Conan Doyle?
13 to the dozen. Unlucky for some –

Freddie felt the room pause, as if they all took a breath in as one. All eyes were trained on the words.

'There's 12 in a dozen?' Moast tapped the bottom of his marker against the wall.

'There's thirteen in a…' As the words formed in Freddie's

mouth, her synapses flared. 'Baker's dozen. Thirteen in a baker's dozen. Sherlock Holmes lived on Baker Street.'

'Baker Street,' Nasreen wrote onto the board.

Freddie flicked onto Twitter:

SandeepFrog @SandyDip24 • 1s
@Apollyon Baker Street: The game is on. #Sherlock #murderer

MrBOONtastic @BoonyBaby • 2s
Baker Street. Elementary Dr @Apollyon

'Can you find out if there are any Sophies who live on Baker Street? Is that possible?' Freddie scrolled down. Everyone was saying Baker Street. It had to be that. That would make them a step closer to saving this girl. Her heart thumped in time with the Twitter updates pouring in.

Moast puffed air out of his cheeks. 'Are there any Baker Streets in East London? We believe the perp has operated in this area. If not, how many in London, including the famous one? Cross-reference with the voters registered at each address. Get on the phone to each of the local station forces.'

The sound in the room surged. Tibbsy weaved among the officers, both uniform and plain clothes, assigning, directing.

'Do you think it's right, sir?' Nasreen was still facing the board.

'I don't know,' Moast said. 'This could all be a wild goose chase. Has he replied to any of the tweets?'

Freddie clicked onto @Apollyon's profile – her heart seeming to stutter as the photo of Mardling jumped afresh into her view. She couldn't do this again. Couldn't see another body. Couldn't bear it. 'No. I don't think so. No replies. Just the clues.'

'And is he following anyone?' Nas said.

'No. Just Alun. From before. That's it.'

'How many Baker Streets in East London – anyone?' Moast was flicking through his notepad.

A uniformed PC with a round face and blonde spiky hair tapped on a laptop at the desk next to her. Freddie reached over and spun it to face her: this would be quicker. 'Hey!' he said.

'Just a second.' She clicked onto Streetmap. Typed in 'Baker Street'. The screen went blue, white writing, addresses, suggested streets. She ran her finger down the screen, counting in her head: 'None in East London. One – the Holmes one – in London.' She kept counting. 'Eighty-nine in the country.'

'Christ,' said Moast. Freddie saw the vein pop out on his neck. She'd seen it before, when he lost his cool after the press briefing. 'Start with the London one and expand out to near areas first. Focus on those near East London, as we have reason to believe this may be our perp's patch. Any in Essex?' He looked at Freddie.

She scanned the list again. 'There's a Baker Street in Chelmsford, and somewhere called Orsett, Grays, in Essex. And one in Kent – that's on that side of London isn't it?'

'It'll take us time to cross-reference with the voter registration, sir.' Nasreen had collared a laptop from someone else.

Freddie's phone vibrated in her hand. She let out a yelp. 'Again. He's tweeted again.'

Moast, who was still in front of the incident board, grabbed a marker from the desk. 'Read it out.'

Freddie looked at her phone. Stay calm. 'I Rafferty-fi. That's it.'

'What? Show me.' Moast held his hand out for her phone. 'What the hell does that mean?'

'It looks like nonsense,' Nas peered over his shoulder. 'Maybe he didn't mean to send it?'

Moast started to write the words onto the board.

'It's a capital. The R. It's a capital,' said Freddie. 'That must be important. Unless it's a typo?'

Moast was studying Freddie's phone, his hand gripping it tightly, his eyebrows almost meeting in the middle with the exertion.

'I Rafferty-fi. I Rafferty. I...I...Rafferty...Rafferty...' Freddie rolled the words round in her mouth. What if it was a simple typing mistake? They were wasting precious time. 'Rafferty. Wait: Rafferty. What's that guy's name? That song with the saxophone at the start – Nas you know, your dad used to play it all the time.'

Nas looked up. Their eyes met. 'George Rafferty! Baker Street.'

'Yes!' Freddie pointed at her as if they'd just won a game of charades. 'Baker Street. It's definitely Baker Street.'

'Are you sure? I don't see it.' Moast stared at the words he'd written on the whiteboard, her phone in his hand at his side. Nasreen pulled her own mobile from her pocket.

'Look at Twitter. See if Twitter agrees.' Freddie grabbed Nas's phone and tapped it. 'There, see?' The first tweet that came up read:

George Rafferty famously performed Baker Street. I Rafferty – fi. Like sci-fi. Say it quickly: I ratify. I agree. #murderer

'It's a bit clumsy?' Moast said.

'I guess he's doing them at speed.'

'Consensus seems to be Baker Street, sir.' Nasreen peered over her shoulder.

There was a muted buzzing sound. 'It's shaking!' Moast startled at the phone in his hand.

'It's him! It means he's tweeted!' Freddie clicked, her heart thrashing. 'There! Meow you doing? It says Meow you doing?'

'Meow? Meow Meow? Is this about drugs?' Moast was writing the words on the board. 'Tibbsy, get me someone from drugs squad on the phone. I want to know if they know anything about this. And Trident – there could be a gang link. This could be code.' He put Freddie's phone down.

'Yes, guv,' said Tibbsy.

'You think Sophie is a gang name? It might mean something else,' Freddie said.

'No. More likely Sophie's wrong: hope is gang slang for cannabis. Hope is rearranging her: sounds like a change to a drop to me. I should have clocked it before.' Moast was adding more words to the board. Drugs. Gang crime. Gang link. 'Focus on urban centres. Look for Baker Streets in places we know there's a problem. Drug hotspots,' Moast said to an officer unfurling maps.

'This doesn't feel right,' said Freddie. They didn't turn around.

'Meow meow. Mephedrone. M-cat. Drone.' Moast was writing more words on the board.

Freddie closed her eyes. This was wrong. Meow you doing? Mardling had been an Internet troll. Apollyon had posted a photo of Mardling's dead body and tweeted: *For whom the bell trolls.* Reinforcing the notion Mardling was killed for trolling. Now Apollyon was posting a meow? What meowed? Kittens. She opened her eyes. Bob the Street Cat. Grumpy cat. Cat videos. Cat gifs. *Cat lover. Sophie was a cat lover.* 'It could be another Internet stereotype: the troll and now the cat lover?'

But nobody was listening.

Chapter 17

IKR – I Know, Right?

10:46
Monday 2 November
1 FOLLOWING   67,080 FOLLOWERS

Freddie looked again at her phone, scanning her Twitter feed:

Meow you're talking. #murderer
Hello Shitty: the #murderer's going after cat fans.
Someone's been on the catnip. #murderer
First a troll and now a cat? I don't get the #murderer
Are you a cat that lives on Baker Street, do you have a human
called Sophie? Run! #Murderer
I thought Meow Meow made you less hostile, not more likely
to bump people off?
'Meow you doing?'<<< Curiosity killed the cat :/

The incident room purred around her.
'Drugs squad are sending someone over, guv.' Tibbsy had his

hand over his phone to talk to Moast. Maps were being unfurled and Blu-Tacked to the wall, red pins and highlighters used to mark known drug dealers located in and around the E14 area.

'Sir.' A bald plain-clothes policeman with glasses and a tie that came up short of his waistband was stood with Moast in front of the maps. 'The Bow Boys are known to operate in this vicinity. Blackbird Road borders onto the area belonging to the Lewisham Snake Gang who import and distribute drugs. We could be looking at a turf war. Your first vic was in banking, right?'

'Yes, manager of a retail bank in Canary Wharf,' Moast said.

'He could have been a money launderer, or perhaps someone who said no to laundering,' the bald man said.

Freddie shook her head. They were looking in the wrong place. Nasreen perched on the edge of the table in front of the incident board, studying the crime scene photos: dotted with yellow markers to denote removed evidence. 'Nas,' Freddie edged up to her.

'I'm busy.' Nasreen's gaze flicked from the photos to a file in her hand.

'Nas, listen.' Freddie glanced over her shoulder at Moast and the bald guy who were drawing dotted lines onto one of the maps. She felt her elbow bump Nas's arm.

'Careful.' Nas held tighter to her papers.

We used to hold hands and spin each other round till we fell over laughing by the swings on the common, and now you freak out if I accidentally touch you? Freddie swallowed her anger: this was more important. 'This is urgent.'

'Speak to DCI Moast if you have a problem, but wait until the investigation's finished. We're all busy on this at the moment.' Nas spoke in the voice she used to disparage her younger sisters with.

You know all too well he won't listen to me. Freddie scanned the file in Nas's hand, catching the words Pathology Report. 'What's that? What are you looking at?'

Nasreen closed the file. 'If you must know, I was looking to see if the vic had any tattoos.'

136

'That would link him to the gangs?'

Nasreen raised her eyebrows and turned to look at her. 'Yes, actually.'

'There aren't any are there?' Freddie spoke quietly so Moast couldn't hear her.

'No, but that doesn't mean anything for sure.'

'Nas, it's like the Ecover and the Greenpeace sticker: you and I notice stuff,' she said. 'Remember that time we both clocked Richard Jenkins nicked those sweets from the newsagent?' Freddie had been in favour of forcing Richard to share his loot, but Nas, ever the goody two shoes, even at ten, had forced them all to return it.

The inkling of a smile appeared on Nasreen's lips, before she spoke: her voice cold and dismissive. 'That was years ago. It's hardly relevant. I've had specialised training now to spot discrepancies, I look at things differently. There are procedures to follow.'

'Will you shut up for one minute about training and procedure and listen to your gut. I know you still see this stuff. It's the Sherbet Dib Dabs all over again. I know you still see people for what they are.' Freddie glanced at Moast. Nas's face was colouring, her chin jutted out, she was losing her.

'I don't have time for this,' Nas said.

'It's not drugs, Nas. And I don't think this Meow post is to do with gangs. You know that, you know it doesn't feel right. That's why you're trying to prove it with tattoos and shit,' she stabbed at the file.

'It's standard practice to methodically work through all known leads.'

Freddie felt panic mix with her anger. 'It's about cats.'

'Cats?' Nasreen's chin dropped and a loose strand of hair fell over her face.

'Meow you doing? It's about cats. First a troll and now a cat lover – it's like all those mad cat people on the Internet: videos, memes.' Freddie held her phone out to show her. 'It's an Internet stereotype: first he went after a troll and now he is going after a cat lover. Sophie is a cat lover. Or maybe Sophie is the cat.'

'You aren't making any sense. These messages are clearly ambiguous. Besides, it's just talk online.' Nas tucked the loose strand of hair back behind her ear and opened her file again.

She used to be able to persuade Nas to do loads of things – jump into the river that ran behind her house, lick a snail for a bet, wear her school blazer backwards in the playground. She remembered the screams of laughter, the snorts of lemonade coming out their noses, the hands gripped tightly together, but once you lost her, once Nas decided she didn't want to be part of whatever it was, you couldn't budge her. Freddie saw that stubbornness again now. 'Why won't you listen to me?'

'Listen to what,' Moast said. The bald guy was gone. Moast and Tibbsy stood directly behind her.

'Nothing, sir,' Nasreen stood from the table.

'Nothing? You clearly doubt this is gang-related,' Freddie snapped.

'I didn't say that,' Nasreen said.

'Then why are you looking for tattoos?' Freddie gripped her phone. *Why wouldn't they listen to her?*

'It's called police work, Venton.' Moast looked tired. 'Something you wouldn't understand.'

Someone's…Sophie's life was in danger. She had to make them realise. 'I don't think this tweet is about gangs or drugs.'

Moast snorted. Tibbsy closed his eyes and shook his head. 'And where's your evidence?' Moast said.

'On Twitter! Look, they also think it's about a cat. It could be Internet stereotypes: a troll and now a cat lady?'

'Ha! Great, now I don't just have to deal with one amateur detective, I have to put up with a whole Internet of them! Enough! You've wasted enough time, Venton. I've given you those email printouts: take them home and get out the way of my investigation.'

Freddie planted both feet firmly on the ground, facing him. 'The Superintendent hired me for social media advice – I would listen if I were you.'

Moast leant in so close she could smell the stale coffee on his breath. 'Don't kid yourself, darling, he only wants you on board because of that stunt you pulled with *The Post.*'

'What?' Freddie said.

'It's like you say: you're one of them. *Those people.* It's all a distraction, innit?' Moast said. 'We shove you out there in front of the cameras and reassure the masses, the keyboard warriors, that we're taking the Twitter angle seriously. Keep all that nonsense at bay while we do the real police work. You're a jumped-up media stooge. Nothing more.'

Freddie stood with her mouth open. Moast turned back to Tibbsy and took a folder from his hands. Tibbsy gave her a shrug as if to say 'tough break'. She looked at Nas who was intently studying the ground next to her shoe. Why the hell hadn't she spoken up? 'I…'

'Out!' Moast flicked his hand toward the door. 'I don't want to hear another word. Leave the police work to those of us who know what we're doing.'

Her cheeks burning, Freddie retrieved her bag from under a desk, where two uniformed coppers were going through bank statements.

'Hey, watch it, love, if you want to cop a feel you just have to ask!' A red puffy face grinned at her. The one next to him, with small rat features and big lips, laughed. She pulled at the bag. Tears pricked her eyes. She had to get out of here. Tugging, the bag came free.

'Meoooow!' someone mimicked a cat. More laughter.

Freddie swallowed, grabbed the box files of emails from the desk by Moast, and held her head up. She made it to the empty corridor before the tears fell. Wiping her eyes with her sleeve, she heard Moast as the door closed behind her. 'Quit it with the animal noises, PC Stringer, this is a police station, not a zoo!'

How could Nas not have stuck up for her? She let that tosser speak to her like that. Freddie took a steadying breath: she didn't know Nasreen at all anymore. There was nothing she recognised. The fact they'd both noticed the Ecover products was coincidence. They didn't think the same way. They didn't silently communicate

139

like when they were kids. Maybe they never had. This Nasreen was a stranger. Freddie wiped her nose on the back of her hand.

Apollyon's tweet, the clue, whatever it was, was too ambiguous. Maybe Moast was right: it *was* about gangs and drugs. What *did* she know? She hadn't had any of their precious training. She was just a wannabe journalist who'd found herself in the wrong place at the wrong time. Freddie admonished herself for using tired clichés. She was just knackered. She was as smart as any of them. She thought of the juvenile, mewing PCs: smarter than a lot of them. And she knew she could hold her own with Nas. Nasreen Cudmore may be great at swotting up, but it was always Freddie who'd had the quick-fire quips. Who could get a reaction from people: good or bad. She could tie verbal rings round this lot. *More clichés. Arrrgh.* Freddie clenched her fists and squashed the box files into her chest. This whole experience was warping her mind. Despite her pathetic attempts at self-reassurance that the police knew what they were doing, doubt gnawed at her. Freddie couldn't help but ask questions. To challenge. It *was* her job. And this wasn't just a pitch that may or may not get commissioned. What if the police were wrong?

'Er, Ms Venton?'

Freddie wiped under her eyes and turned to Jamie who was stood behind her, his pale eyes concerned, shifting his weight from one foot to the other. 'What do you want?' she said.

'DCI Moast said I had to escort you home.' Jamie looked at the floor.

'Did he now?' He really didn't want her anywhere near them. Was this Nas's idea?

'Just to make sure you get home safe, and like,' he said.

'Yeah, I'm sure. Come on then, let's get this over with.' Freddie shifted the weight of the box files and pulled her bag over her shoulder. It'd be better than getting the Tube.

'The car's out the back.' Jamie extended one of his skinny arms and fell in alongside her as they walked through the echoing white hallway, his hands clasped behind his back.

Freddie's ears pricked each time they passed a blue-painted door. Were they looking into Apollyon in there? Had anyone drawn the same conclusions as her? Was anybody fighting to stop it?

'You've known Sergeant Cudmore a long time then?' Jamie asked.

Freddie kept her head cocked toward the doors, straining to hear as they passed. 'Yeah, haven't seen her for a while though. Drifted apart.' *She won't even look at me now.* She swallowed.

'How'd you meet?'

'School. Usual, you know. Nas was real quiet as a kid, she needed someone who'd stick up for her.' Freddie thought of fat Ryan Crouch pulling Nas's red and white polka dot rucksack from her chair and waving it above his head like a trophy. The other kids were whooping and laughing as he jumped from desk to desk out of her reach. It was funny at first, but then she'd seen how upset Nasreen was getting. As Ryan cantered toward her, she'd jumped up onto her desk and blocked his path. She didn't remember hitting Ryan, but she did remember him concertinaing onto the chairs below. Back to the headmaster's office that overlooked the leafy road the school was on. Looking back on it, Ryan probably fancied Nasreen: hair pulling, etc. Basic school psychology 101.

. Freddie looked up at Jamie. He was staring off into the distance, a soppy smile on his face. 'You got a soft spot for Nasreen then, Jamie?' Another one. Just like at school.

'Oh no,' Jamie's cheeks flamed red and he dipped his chin as if he wanted to curl into his chest. 'I'd never...I mean, not that she isn't very attractive...I...'

Freddie laughed despite herself. *Typical.* 'It's all right, mate, I won't tell anyone.'

He looked grateful.

Nasreen had a way of appealing to people that Freddie had always lacked. Her mum described her as a 'gentle soul'. Freddie wondered what her churchgoing mum, with her knitting, charity fundraisers and her belief that everyone is good at heart, would make of this new tougher, cold Nasreen. Freddie wasn't the only one who stood up to the Ryans of this world now. Jamie pushed open the opaque glass door into the car park. The ivory sun did nothing to heat the cold, crisp air. A sheet of newspaper blew across the potholed ground, dodging the puddles and wrapping itself around the wheels of an unmarked car. Jamie was still burbling away as they walked toward a squad car: 'I learned round the lanes of Brighton. If you can drive there, you can drive anywhere.'

'Hmmm,' she nodded. Podgy Ryan and his ilk were no match for the young Nasreen and her, but they were no longer children. Now the bullies were bigger – she thought of an innocent faceless woman called Sophie – and the stakes were much higher.

Chapter 18

EOT – End Of Thread

12:46
Monday 2 November
1 FOLLOWING   69,987 FOLLOWERS

Freddie slammed into her flat and flung her bag and the box files onto her bed. She wanted to help. Wrenching her phone from her pocket, she tapped onto Twitter. Maybe someone had worked out who Sophie was and warned her?

BuzzFeed were running an article: *23 Reasons You Might Be The Next #Murder Victim*. Last week she might have read the piece and laughed at the absurd suggestion. Heck, she might even have written it: a wry take on the news. But clickbait now carried a much darker meaning for Freddie. Things didn't work out well for bait. She'd seen and smelt a dead body. A metallic taste pricked across her tongue and she swallowed. She didn't want anyone else to die. What if the intended victim was reading the BuzzFeed piece, unaware this was no joke? Freddie tapped it open:

143

23 Reasons You Might Be the Next #Murder Victim:

1. Your name is Sophie.

A gif of one of the Real Housewives of Beverly Hills, all stretched perma-tanned skin and industrial hair, repeatedly screamed, Edvard Munch style. Her plastic surgery features comically grotesque. Freddie had seen this episode on YouTube – wasn't she wailing because one of the other women was wearing polyester? Or was it reacting to a broken nail? What did it matter anyway? All this was trivial. Over in America the reality star was safe from the murderer. Probably. Surely this wouldn't go international? A world wide web of danger. A jet-set murderer using up their air miles. How many roads were called Baker Street in the world? How many people were called Sophie? It was impossible. They needed more. She read on:

2. You have a Twitter account.

(Gif of Beyoncé, hair blowing in wind machine, hand on chest singing 'me!')

3. You post cat videos.

(Gif of startled cat falling off a sofa).

She knew it: meow you doing? She wasn't the only one who thought this might be about cat obsessives. BuzzFeed agreed with her! But why was Apollyon doing this? Why would someone want to kill Internet stereotypes? It didn't make sense. Was it a twisted form of terrorism? No. Some group would have claimed it if that was the case. Freddie thought of Apollyon's growing number of followers – there were over 69,000 now – would someone do all this for fame? She shuddered at the thought. She opened Google to search 'online killers'. If the person behind the Apollyon account had killed Mardling, photographed it and posted it online, was he the first person to announce a crime in this way?

The first search result was a Wikipedia article on **Internet Homicide**, which the article described as referring to 'a killing in which victim and perpetrator met online, in some cases having known each other previously only through the Internet'. As they didn't know who Apollyon was, they didn't know if he'd met Mardling online, though if Mardling was selected for being a troll, then he was *sourced* online, Freddie reasoned. She read on: 'Also **Internet Killer** is an appellation found in media reports for a person who broadcasts the crime of murder online or who murders a victim met through the Internet.' Again, assuming Apollyon was responsible for Mardling's murder then he was definitely an Internet Killer. She scrolled and clicked through examples of Internet Homicides: the cannibal who advertised for a victim online before fricasseeing and eating him; several militant extremist groups who'd planned murders in encrypted chat rooms; a guy who sent a pipe bomb through the post to a Craigslist con artist. Nothing suggested there'd ever been an Internet serial killer before. Freddie wasn't surprised. That was the kind of thing you'd notice: a killer posting photos of murder victims, a killer posting threats and clues to who his next victim would be. That was what everyone was noticing now. Apollyon was sick.

She closed the article and continued to scroll through her timeline. Outraged tweeters were circulating a link to a *Family Paper* online op-ed piece: *Is the Troll Hunter a Working Mother?* Good old Sandra, thought Freddie of her Typical Student column editor, this had all the hallmarks of her usual style: incendiary statements wrapped in the cloak of moral concern. She skim-read the article, which was liberally sprinkled with stock images of exasperated women in 90s suits holding a baby in one hand and a mobile phone in the other. The first commenter on the story had written, in terrible English:

145

woudn't Be surprised if the Hashtag Murderer was a Feminazi!!!!

The comment had been liked 567 times. Freddie had to write her own *Family Paper* column in a few days. How was she going to concentrate on writing when she should be trying to prevent a murder? How could she write a deliberately provocative piece about binge drinking or some other student stereotype at a time like this? Freddie wondered if she'd ever stop thinking about Mardling's dead body. Then, like all good pitches, an idea crystallised in her mind. Swiping between screens, she scrolled through recents on her phone and pressed dial. Neil answered.

Freddie could hear the whir of the newsroom in the background. It sounded alien. She'd forgotten life was still normal for other people. 'Neil, it's Freddie. I've got a story for you.' *Why I'm Convinced the Hashtag Murderer Will Kill Again.* First-person. Insider info. The personal story behind the murder investigation. *One reporter's battle to save a life.* She could get her warning direct to the public: *Called Sophie? Own a cat? Then you could be in danger.* They'd bite. She couldn't stand by and do nothing while Moast and the others were off chasing drug barons. If she hurried, they'd make the evening editions.

07:50
Tuesday 3 November
1 FOLLOWING   83,245 FOLLOWERS

Classic FM's Hall of Fame album evened out the sounds of early morning London in Nasreen's headphones. The volume low, so if anyone approached her from behind she'd hear. It didn't happen often, but occasionally she'd be recognised by someone in the street. An acquaintance of a criminal she'd given evidence against in court. They sat in the gallery, watching you, the faces: press, family, friends of both the victim (if there was one) and the perpetrator. You couldn't remember them all. But they remembered her. It was like a spotlight shining on you: taking the witness stand. She'd lived in Hackney for a while, but had had to move house when a man had blocked her flat front door one night, threatening her with a knife, for doing over his mate. She was cool and calm. Like usual. But the other residents didn't like it.

Always better to talk your way out of a situation than let it escalate. She moved shortly after: back to the town she and Freddie were from. Back to Pendrick in Hertfordshire. She liked being close to her parents, and enough time had passed that she'd found new places to visit as an adult. She liked the farmers' market on the first Sunday of every month, the family-run Italian down by the medieval clock tower, the way the older streets tapered into narrow car-free cobbles, the way the sun set across the open sky of the common. There was a new sports complex and a cinema, and she was careful not to walk past her and Freddie's old school. She couldn't deal with the memories that flooded through her if she strayed near their old haunts. The commute was longer, but the distance helped her switch off. Reading classic novels on the train. *Great Expectations* had taken weeks, *Pride and Prejudice* mere days. She'd seen Freddie's mum one day in the library above the new shopping mall, and to her shame had ducked behind some shelves and hid. She didn't want the past to rear up and bite her. Her home was in her parents' name, she booked restaurants and holidays in her mum's maiden name. She'd grown used to hiding. Keeping her head down. She didn't want anyone to recognise her, to work out who she was, to know what she and Freddie had done. It was almost second nature. She didn't have any friends from back then. From school. She'd been careful to limit socialising to work colleagues, or those who'd moved to Pendrick recently: Sarah from spinning class, Claire at the pottery course she'd taken but only made one session of. Nasreen worked nights, weekends, whenever the case demanded it. Friends had to be flexible, tolerant, close. But no matter how close she was with the girls, no matter how many glasses of wine they drank, no matter how much they cried over broken hearts or raged over career frustrations, she never told them

147

the secret only she and Freddie knew. It could never come out. She imagined the look of shock and disgust on Sarah and Claire's faces if they knew the truth. She'd be disowned. Everything would be ripped apart. Again. Nasreen had carefully pieced her life back together in the last eight years, but she knew it was bound with secrecy, and held together by silence. She moved in the shadows, where she could hide. How could Freddie put so much of herself online? She was exposed. She threatened *both* of them.

The concerto changed from string to piano music. Freddie would take the micky out of her for listening to something so mundane. She remembered her excitedly thrusting Ramones vinyls at her from Mr Venton's collection when they were ten. Nasreen liked music with no lyrics; it helped her order her thoughts. She hadn't slept well last night and her bag, heavy with files from gang cases, dug into the soft shoulder of her black wool coat. Her heels clicked along the pavement of the tree-lined street of Victorian terraces that ran between the railway station and the Jubilee. She'd found nothing in the files that tied Alun Mardling to any gang. She couldn't help but feel Freddie was right: they were looking in the wrong place. Would DCI Moast listen to Nasreen though? Freddie had hardly made the best impression so far, but beneath her disruptive behaviour Nasreen recognised she'd made some sound points. She sidestepped a woman and a small girl on a bright red scooter wending their way along the path.

But Freddie's presence made Nasreen doubt her own logic. Was she being played? Of course not. She was a grown woman now, not an impressionable teen. Yet each time she saw Freddie's face – those joking eyes, that curly hair – she was flung back to that awful night eight years ago. The terror. The pain. The guilt. It muddied her thoughts. For years she'd fought it back: the overwhelming desire to collapse, fold, break. Freddie wouldn't understand. Nothing touched her. Nasreen had battled to get this far. Each day she'd buttoned up her police uniform she'd felt a hypocrite. Each step she took was to atone for the past. With Freddie here, the truth was so close she could feel it pressing on her – how long before it came out? And that journalist – the one who knew she and Freddie had gone to school together – how long before they unearthed it? Put two and two together with the local paper report at the time? It was unimaginable. Her colleagues could never know. Nobody could know. Nasreen summoned up all her control: she had to keep acting normal.

Not for the first time, Nasreen wondered if Freddie's involvement in the Mardling case wasn't an accident. The one person in the world who knew her darkest secret reappearing like this – it seemed unlikely. Was Freddie back to punish Nasreen? Was that her motive? Nasreen had seen crimes committed for far less. This Twitter stuff was so theatrical, as if whoever was doing it wanted a big audience. And Freddie seemed so keen for them all to take the tweets seriously. So convinced she'd worked out every riddle. Was it just bravado? Had she manufactured the whole Apollyon thing to stay close to the case? To get a story for her newspaper?

The Freddie who'd taught her to stand up to her older cousins wouldn't hurt anyone. The Freddie who'd once fed an injured bird with honey and seed until it was fit to fly again couldn't be a criminal. Nasreen thought of that soft bird, Queenie, tucked under a blanket in a box in Freddie's parents' garage. How Freddie had cried when her dad had threatened to put Queenie down. She'd cried again the day they let Queenie fly free from the common. But that girl was gone, replaced with this angry, shouting young woman. Nasreen didn't know what this Freddie was capable of. She'd alibied out for the murder, but was it possible she was behind the Apollyon tweets? Was this Freddie's revenge? Again she chided herself for letting her thoughts run away with themselves: everything wasn't all about Freddie, she thought wryly.

As the road widened into the shop-lined street that led to the station, Nasreen passed workers rolling up security screens and placing tubs of £1 cleaning products in front of their premises. She took her headphones out and pushed her phone into the woolly pocket of her coat. Frost-covered leaves crunched and slid under her feet. Her morning commute was increasingly dark. Even within the Jubilee – a place she'd always felt she belonged – Nasreen now felt the chill. She was being frozen out. The team had already decided she couldn't be trusted, following the Freddie debacle at Blackbird Road. So what difference did it make if she went against DCI Moast? If she sided with Freddie? As she pushed open the door of the station and nodded to Charlie on the desk, Nasreen made a decision. She'd found no evidence of gang links to the case. She would tell DCI Moast she too thought they should look for anyone called Sophie (with a potential cat), who was linked to Mardling.

Nasreen's footsteps echoed down the Jubilee corridor. In the distance she could hear phones ringing. The hum of those on the overnight shift handing over to the day team over coffee in the canteen. The small perforation in the rubberised grey floor halfway down the hall. This was still her station. She knew it and it knew her. She wasn't out yet. Pushing open the door of the incident room, she was surprised to see Freddie bent over some papers on a table in the back of the otherwise empty room. 'What are you doing here so early?'

Freddie looked up, her brown frizzy hair half flattened against one side of her face, ridiculous thick-rimmed glasses perched on the end of her nose, dressed in a wholly unsuitable holey black jumper, through which you could see flashes of a red top she had on underneath. 'Couldn't sleep,' she said. 'Thinking 'bout all this. I spent half the night trawling the Internet for any sign of a link between Alun Mardling and a Sophie. All I found was an online review our good friend Alun had left on a porn site. He gave *Rammers Revenge* four dildos, and logged it under his home email address, the tool. Looking up Apollyon proved equally futile, unless you happen to be particularly interested in bad demon fan art. There's nothing in those emails either, just a load of Amazon receipts for action DVDs, and two-for-one offers at his local pizza joint. Our boy liked a meat feast with extra barbecue sauce.'

Nasreen was about to ask Freddie if she'd seen anything else relevant on Twitter, when the door opened behind her. DCI Moast, his navy blue puffa jacket still on over his suit, a green scarf wound round his neck, stormed into the room.

'You!' He pointed at Freddie. 'I heard you were here. Waiting to gloat?' He strode past Nas and stood over Freddie.

'Good morning to you too.' Freddie leant back in her chair. Nasreen felt her stomach drop away.

'Don't give me that. What the hell do you call this?' Moast slammed a newspaper down onto the desk. Nasreen's teeth clenched as she stepped forward to read over his shoulder. It was *The Post – Undercover Reporter Cracks Open Hashtag Murderer Case – Are You the Sophie She's Looking For?* – emblazoned across the front page.

'Oh, Freddie,' Nasreen said.

'Did you know about this, Cudmore?' DCI Moast twisted to look at her, his face drawn, tired, and now angry.

'No, sir, I didn't…'

'Are you deliberately trying to undermine me, Venton?' He spun back to Freddie.

'You didn't give me any choice,' Freddie was saying.

Nasreen picked up the paper. *Hashtag Murderer, Alun Mardling, cat woman, Sophie, Baker Street, DCI Moast, Sergeant Cudmore, Flagship East End Jubilee Police Station.* The whole case was in here. What the hell was she playing at?

Freddie hadn't anticipated the photo. Neil must have lifted it from her Facebook page. It was from a fancy dress party. She'd gone as an 80s power bitch in a grey shoulder-pad suit she'd found in the charity store. He'd cropped it so you couldn't see where she'd ripped the pencil skirt.

'That's it. I'm taking this to the Superintendent. You've gone too far this time, you've given confidential case details to the hacks. You've deliberately disobeyed my orders.' Moast virtually frothed at the mouth. 'Once we've sorted this mess out I'm pushing for charges. Again.'

'You wouldn't listen. I don't think this is about drugs.' She wasn't doing this for a laugh.

'You don't think it's about drugs? Who cares what you think!' Moast wrestled his jacket off and flung it at a chair. 'Cudmore, don't just stand there, round the team up. I want everyone in here now. We need to contain this.'

Nasreen looked straight at Freddie.

Freddie stared back: *well you wouldn't help.* She couldn't just sit twiddling her thumbs while some poor woman was butchered by this hashtag psycho. Nasreen shook her head and walked off.

Tibbsy in his suit and with bloodshot eyes, and Jamie in his uniform, twitching nervously, appeared shortly after. Nasreen came back in with a gaggle of excitable PCs.

'Guv, it seems the phones have been going crazy,' Tibbsy said. 'The night sergeant said it started after the article appeared online,' he muttered into his mug of coffee.

No one made eye contact with Freddie. 'What do you want me to do?' she asked.

'Do?' Moast looked up from the pile of phone messages he was reading. 'I want you to *do* nothing. Which is what I wanted you to *do* yesterday. Have you gone through those emails I gave you?'

'Yes, there was nothing odd in them.' She stared at him. 'Unless you count Alun Mardling's fascination with Steven Seagal movies as odd.'

'Fine. Sit there where I can keep an eye on you until we've got this under control. Then someone can take you to meet the tech team. I'm sure they'll have lots of work to keep a Social Media Advisor busy.'

'The public have a right to know if they're in danger,' *you patronising git.* Freddie stood resting her fingers on the table in front of her. He didn't frighten her. Not compared to @Apollyon. Out of the corner of her eye she caught Nasreen looking at the floor. *You do agree with me then!* 'This could help save the target.'

'Save the target?' Moast snapped. 'This isn't a Hollywood bloody film. This is real life. Thanks to your vigilante media turn I've got hundreds of hysterical women on the phones thinking they're going to be murdered in their sleep. This is a massive waste of time and resources.'

'How many of those live on Baker Street?' Freddie asked. *There couldn't be hundreds?*

'This is what you media types fail to understand about the general public, they panic.' Moast picked up a wedge of papers. 'The paperwork for this will take weeks to get through. Every man, woman and sodding cat is calling in claiming they're in danger. I've got half the Home Counties demanding police protection for their kids because they're called Sophie!'

There was a knock at the door. A young Asian police constable poked his head nervously round. 'DCI Moast, sir,' he said.

'What now?' Moast glared at the lad.

Freddie felt sorry for him. Moast was just a jumped-up red-faced bully. Getting out of here couldn't happen fast enough.

'I…er…sir…I…' said the lad.

'Spit it out, Constable!' Moast said. Someone's chair scraped along the floor. It was as if the whole room was holding their breath.

'We've had a call from a woman in Leighton Buzzard. Her employee, a Sophie Phillips, who lives on Baker Street, didn't show up at work yesterday. And she's not answering her phone.'

Chapter 19

SITD – Still In The Dark

Freddie felt as if she'd been slapped.

'Cudmore, get on the phone to the Leighton Buzzard station and have them check it out,' Moast's voice cut through the silent room.

'No.' The word fell out of Freddie's mouth. She tried to stuff it back in with her hands. This wasn't really happening. It couldn't be. Not again. Every time she blinked, bloody bodies swam in front of her eyes: Alun Mardling's corpse laughing; Paige Klinger in a blood-splattered white studio. Freddie moved in slow motion as the room sped up around her. Voices, bodies, phone calls and words flew past in a blur. She was too late. The front page. The gamble. It wasn't enough. *She didn't show up at work yesterday.*

She forced herself back online. Searching for any mention of Sophie Phillips and Leighton Buzzard. It hadn't broken on Twitter and there was nothing on the news. There was no mention of a

154

Sophie Phillips in Leighton Buzzard at all. She checked the electoral register. She checked Yell.com. Facebook. LinkedIn. Nothing. Perhaps it was a mistake? A hoax call? *Oh please let it be that.* Everyone was busy, heads down. Checking phone records, bank statements, cross-checking friends' and family statements. A timeline of Mardling's uneventful last twenty-four hours had been put up on the white-board. Alongside it, the more glamorous timeline of Paige Klinger detailed photoshoots, breakfast at The Dorchester, a flight in from New York. There was no feasible overlap or meeting between the two. Everyone was studiously trying to move the case forward, trying to ignore the question mark that hung over the room: why hadn't Sophie Phillips of Baker Street, Leighton Buzzard, arrived at work?

Freddie watched Nasreen come back into the room; at some point she'd removed her coat. Nasreen bent to speak to Moast. Freddie saw the colour drain from his cheeks. His head dropped into his hands. She was shaking again. Moast stood, straightened his tie, and cleared his throat. Everyone looked up, and the weight of expectation crushed down on Freddie.

'I'm sorry to announce the Bedfordshire Police Force have found the body of a young woman, believed to be that of Sophie Phillips, age twenty-seven, an administrative assistant at Leighton Linslade Town Council, in suspicious circumstances at her flat in Baker Street, Leighton Buzzard.'

'No,' whispered Freddie. Her voice lost in the sighs, shuffles and swear words of those gathered in the room.

'As of yet there is no firm evidence to suggest this death is linked to that of Alun Mardling, apart from the coincidental tweets of the suspect known as Apollyon,' Moast said.

All the tweets, all the clues hinting at a cat lover called Sophie who lived on Baker Street, the photo Apollyon posted of Mardling's body: it felt linked to Freddie. Otherwise it was one hell of a coincidence.

'However,' Moast continued, 'as we have yet to trace the device used to both take and post the photo of the Mardling crime scene, and the source of the tweets by the suspect known as Apollyon, we will now be exploring the possibility that this latest murder and the murder of Alun Mardling are linked.'

Freddie expected to feel relief; finally Moast was listening to her. But she felt nothing but sadness. She couldn't meet his eyes.

'We are waiting for the preliminary forensic reports,' Moast continued, 'and I will be putting together a team to visit the crime scene. Sergeant Cudmore will be assigning new tasks in line with the investigation by the Bedfordshire force. If this does turn out to be linked to the Alun Mardling case, then we will take full control of the investigation.' Moast's voice was void of emotion: just doing his job. But Freddie could see it. The pain etched across his taut face. There was no victory in her being right about the tweets and him being wrong. Sophie Phillips lost. They all lost.

A lump formed in Freddie's throat. She blinked repeatedly. She looked round the room. The guy who'd delivered the news was slumped in a chair near the front – his tie and shirt collar loosened. Jamie sat next to him, hands clasped in his lap, head nodded forward, almost in prayer. The faces of the older uniformed officers grouped to the right of her were set in grim determination. She guessed they'd been here before. The moment when all hope has gone.

Nasreen stood quietly at the front, to the side of Moast, her hands clasped behind her back and her head dipped. To everyone else she looked respectful, but Freddie saw something glint in her eyes: anger. Freddie wanted to tell her it was all right. That they would get the sicko who'd done this. But she realised her words would be hollow. These officers, these people, Nas, they did this day in and day out. They faced the darkest parts of society and they kept going. These weren't institutional bullies; they weren't jumped-up security guards drunk on the power of a uniform. They were on the front line of humanity. And she knew, no matter what, that she could never be one of them. She wasn't strong enough. *How I Came To Change My Mind About The Police.*

Moast sounded composed: 'Look at Sophie Phillips' friends and family, her work colleagues. I want to know her habits, her routines, how she spent her free time. Cross-reference with everything we know about Alun Mardling. If there is anything that links the two, I want to know about it. For now all leave is cancelled. I want everyone on this until we turn something up. Don't eat, don't sleep, don't breathe, till we've got this bastard.'

Freddie found herself nodding to his words. People started to stand. Chairs were scraped back along the floor. Groups formed. Nasreen instructed the officers: 'Speak to the local force and get a list of all Sophie's acquaintances. PC Boulson, keep on at forensics. Particularly anything that might link the two murders.'

Jamie was stood to her right, frantically scribbling down notes. 'We have to get this guy. Have to,' he said over and over.

The room emptied out. Freddie stood. She wanted to help but she didn't know what to do. Instinctively she took out her phone: nothing. Nothing from @Apollyon. No apparent mentions of Sophie Phillips or the #Murderer. Nothing but the jokes and frightened retweets of before. Twitter didn't know about the body. The dark secret was contained. For now.

'Put that down, Venton.' Moast sounded tired. 'You do not speak to the press about this, and you do not post anything online.' Moast ran his hands over his hair, puffing resignation out of his mouth.

Freddie stared at him. 'I wouldn't. Not about this. I was just…'

'Put the phone down, Freddie.' Nas sounded detached.

Freddie looked at Tibbsy, grey shadows hung under his impassive eyes. 'Seriously, guys, I wouldn't do that. I wouldn't post about Sophie. That's fucked up.'

'Shut up, Venton.' Moast's hand had run all the way over his scalp and was gripping the back of his neck, as if he was holding himself up.

'What's your thinking, sir? On the team, I mean,' asked Nas.

It was like Freddie wasn't there.

'I've asked one of the lads to place a couple of squad cars on standby,' said Tibbsy. 'We could get there within the hour, if the traffic's all right. The morning rush hour's almost over.'

Freddie looked at the time on her phone: 9:17am. So much had happened already.

'You,' Moast pointed at Tibbsy, 'Cudmore and I are going. Thomas to drive.'

'Guv,' nodded Tibbsy. 'What about Miss Venton?'

Nasreen looked like she was going to add something, then covered her mouth and coughed.

Did Tibbsy just ask about her going to the crime scene? She wanted to help.

Moast seemed startled by Tibbsy's suggestion. 'We don't know for sure Apollyon – this social media stuff – is a link between these two cases. Yet. Besides, she's a liability. This newspaper stunt is in complete violation of procedure.'

'Yes, but the paper article did, well, it led to the tip-off phone call and the discovery of the body.' Tibbsy looked at Freddie, as if asking for her help. She stared back. 'And she did…' he stopped again. The room quiet, Freddie could hear a phone ringing down the hallway.

'Miss Venton does seem to interpret the tweets in an effective way,' said Nas. 'Assuming they're relevant, I mean.'

'Have you two been talking?' Moast looked between Nas and Tibbsy.

'No, sir.' The tops of Nasreen's ears coloured.

There was a knock at the door. They all turned: Jamie entered. 'Sorry to interrupt, sir. Superintendent Gray has asked to see you and Fred…I mean Miss Venton.'

'Looks like the decision's already been made.' Moast pushed himself up from the table. 'Bring all your crap, Venton. You'll not be back after this.'

Freddie glanced at *The Post* still on the table beside her. It was only two years ago, but Freddie knew she'd never feel the same as the carefree girl in that photo again. She closed her eyes and willed herself back there: drunk, hooting, singing along to Bucks Fizz with Vic. It felt like a film. Not her. Not real. As if she could only be a spectator to that world now. Death had come near before, but this time it struck home. She was marked. Inside. Somewhere it'd never fade. Was she going to be arrested? Charged? It no longer mattered. Somewhere, in a flat in Leighton Buzzard, lay the body of a young woman. Sophie Phillips. Cold. Dead. Gone. Despite everything Freddie had done and tried, she was too late to save her.

Chapter 20

FOMO – Fear Of Missing Out

Freddie struggled to keep up with the taller Moast, who was walking at speed along the corridor. 'I didn't want this, you know?' she said. He didn't react. 'I mean, I really didn't want what happened to the Sophie lady to happen.' She couldn't make herself clear. 'I mean, I'm sorry if I got you in trouble or anything over the newspaper thing. You guys do a…very hard job. I just wanted to…'

Moast stopped at the Superintendent's door. He looked at her, his eyes narrowing slightly. Then he tightened his navy tie, buttoned his jacket, and pulled it down. 'Ready?'

Had he heard what she'd said? 'I just didn't want anyone to get hurt.' Moast rapped his knuckles on the door.

'Come!' said the Superintendent's voice. Freddie took a deep breath in. *Here goes.* She looked down at her wool jumper. *Lamb to the slaughter.*

160

Freddie hadn't noticed the first time she'd visited this room how neat it was compared to the rest of the station. The desk, the cabinets, the certificates framed on the wall: everything was sharp-edged and gleaming. Even the rubber plant in the corner looked as if it was polished. There was something about the Superintendent's neatly manicured hands resting on the desk that hinted toward the anal. It unnerved Freddie. Everything was the same as before, apart from the latest edition of *The Post* in front of him. She swallowed. *How To Cope When You're Sacked.*

'DCI Moast. Miss Venton.' The Superintendent did not stand to shake her hand this time. Freddie stood next to Moast. He with his hands clasped behind his back, she shifting her weight from one leg to the other. She needed a wee.

'I think we need to have a little chat,' said the Superintendent, looking down his nose at Freddie. 'DCI Moast,' he turned his attention to Moast. Freddie kept her eyes forward. 'I understand another victim has been found.'

'Yes, sir.' Moast's voice was void of emotion. Freddie doubted she'd sound so calm. *Did she want out or in?* 'A young woman believed to be one Sophie Phillips of,' he faltered slightly, 'Baker Street, Leighton Buzzard.'

'I see.' The Superintendent dropped his eyes to *The Post* and leant back in his chair. 'And do we know if there is a link to the Mardling case?'

'Circumstantial evidence at this stage, sir, but yes, I do suspect the two cases are linked,' Moast said.

'Based on Miss Venton's analysis of the tweets from the person calling themselves @Apollyon,' Gray said.

Analysis? She hadn't analysed anything. Could you tell if the same person sent a number of tweets? Were there patterns, like with handwriting? *Your Online Fingerprint: How Your Posts Can Identify You.* Freddie cursed herself for not thinking of it sooner. There must be someone online who could give them an insight into if the tweets were from the same person. How would they look if you compared them to Paige Klinger's? She resolved to do it the moment she got out of this room.

'Partially, yes, sir,' said Moast.

'And can you explain to me how Ms Venton, who is part of your team,' the Superintendent's voice hardened, 'came to write an unsanctioned article revealing intimate case details?' Freddie heard Moast swallow.

Moast wetted his lips. 'With all due respect, sir, Ms Venton is a civilian with no training or experience in standard procedures. In my opinion she is ill-equipped for active casework: she's impulsive, confrontational...'

'Hey!' Freddie snapped.

'Do you have something to add, Ms Venton?' The Superintendent locked her in his sight.

Bugger. 'I...well...I just didn't want anyone to get hurt.' She looked at the floor.

The Superintendent sighed. 'This case is not progressing as I had anticipated. As I understand it, we received the tip-off about the second possible victim in response to Ms Venton's article – is that right, Moast?'

Moast cleared his throat. 'Along with the countless time-wasting calls we received in response to Ms Venton's little stunt, yes, we did take a call that led to the discovery of a body. It could be circumstantial, though.' He rocked forward and back on his feet.

Freddie felt no victory. How had she ended up embroiled in a murder investigation? No one had said the words yet but she sensed them hovering between the three of them: serial killer. There couldn't be more. They had to stop it.

'I see,' said the Superintendent. 'DCI, how confident are you that this second victim, this Sophie Phillips, is the responsibility of the first perpetrator? Leighton Buzzard is a fair distance from the Docklands.'

Was it someone who travelled? Freddie thought. Wasn't there an infamous murderer who was a lorry driver, or was that a film?

Was the Hashtag Murderer trying to recreate that celebrity? Was that a motive? She tried to think of what she'd read in the papers. What she knew about other crimes. Nothing. Flickers. Images. But she knew the Internet: a vast sprawling online world full of trolls, cat lovers. The Internet didn't need a motorway or a train link. The Internet was everywhere.

'I'll hope to know more once I've visited the crime scene, sir. It may be the Apollyon online thing is some kind of hoax or that this is a copycat of the first murder. Because of the publicity, sir.' Moast looked at Freddie.

Freddie felt her cheeks colour: was she responsible for the second death? She felt sick at the prospect. Guilt washed over her like dirty rainwater, clinging to every fibre of her being. Traces of it here and there she knew she wouldn't be able to shake. She'd felt like this once before. She thought of Nasreen's stoic approach to this job – was she seeking absolution for their past actions?

Superintendent Gray sat up straight, his voice clipped. 'I want a line drawn under this quickly, Moast. Now, Ms Venton. I cannot condone your going to the press outside of the parameters we had previously agreed, but it seems to me that this case is progressing in a number of unexpected ways,' Gray said. 'I would like to make some alterations to our existing partnership.'

This was it: she was going to be charged. She imagined her mum being pulled out from teaching her class of eight-year-olds to take the call about her wayward daughter. *No good, just like her father*, people would whisper. *She'd be humiliated afresh.*

'Your flagrant disregard for the terms under which we agreed you could publish articles relating to this case has demonstrated you can't be trusted in that area.' The Superintendent sounded like her old headmaster. *Detention. Suspension. Exclusion.* 'For the duration of this case you will no longer write or publish anything in your name or under another.'

'Duration of the case, sir?' Moast voiced the same words that were swimming round Freddie's head.

'Whether I approve of her methods or not, it does seem that Ms Venton's insights into this case have proven to be useful.' The Superintendent rested his hands palm down on *The Post* in front of him. *Someone must have spoken to him. Tibbsy? Nas? Who was an ally and who was an enemy?*

Moast's hands flew out from behind his back. 'But, sir, she…'

'This is not up for debate, DCI. Ms Venton's understanding of the online community means she is a valuable asset,' the Superintendent continued.

Did this mean she wasn't going to get charged with wasting police time, impersonating a forensics officer, and everything else they'd threatened her with?

'As the officer in charge of this investigation, Moast, it is your responsibility to ensure Ms Venton stays within the parameters of her role.'

Freddie looked from Gray to Moast, the latter's eyes bulging.

The Superintendent folded his hands onto the desk again. 'I don't want any more cock-ups on this. I assume that as of yet the press are unaware of this latest victim?'

'Yes. I mean no. I haven't told anyone. It hasn't broken on Twitter yet,' Freddie managed.

Moast quietly snorted.

'DCI Moast, let us not underestimate again the apparent power of the Internet on this case. Take your team, including Miss Venton, to Leighton Buzzard, and for God's sake get this case wrapped up.'

'Yes, sir!' Moast turned on his heel and opened the door, standing in the hall waiting for her, his face clouded with undisguised anger.

Freddie stared at the Superintendent. 'I'm worried about seeing another…' – she whispered the last word, frightened by its very significance – '…body.' Mardling's dripping neck blinked in front of her eyes. She reached a hand out to steady herself against Gray's desk.

'I appreciate this must be very traumatic for you, Miss Venton,' the Superintendent's voice softening to somewhere near fatherly.

'Where possible, DCI Moast and the team will shield you from the more unpleasant elements of the investigation.'

Freddie swallowed. How could Nasreen go through this repeatedly? 'Thank you,' she managed.

'I would like you to stay with the team though, on this one. You may spot something on the victim's computer, for example, that we would otherwise have to wait for the IT boys to pick up.'

More likely on Sophie Phillips' phone, she thought. Most people fired off quick updates while they were waiting for the kettle to boil. Or while they were feeding the cat. She nodded.

'Good,' Gray said. 'DCI Moast will ensure you have a few sessions booked with the counsellor associated with the station. She will ensure you are coping with all this.'

Freddie padded out the room in a daze. Moast shut the door on the Superintendent's office. She followed him along the hall. Halfway back to the incident room he stopped and lowered his face to hers. 'Look, Venton, stay in my sight, but stay out of my way and we might just get through this. No more games. No more of your hack tricks. I'll catch this bugger and then you and I need never see each other again. Capiche?'

Freddie nodded. She watched Moast walk to the incident room, the noise of the team inside dying down as their Chief Officer opened the door. Part of Freddie wanted to run back to the Superintendent: crying, fling herself on his desk, beg to be released from the case. Part of her wanted to rip through Twitter, computer files, phone records, whatever it took to find this maniac and stop him. Standing in the empty corridor of Jubilee police station, she didn't know which would win.

As she closed her eyes her mobile vibrated with a new notification.

Apollyon had decided for her.

She couldn't leave now.

Chapter 21

L8R – Later

In the *Family Paper* offices, Freddie's Typical Student column editor Sandra swiped *The Post* off her desk and into the bin. She was still shaken from this morning's meeting. Arthur Decimus, the editor, had torn her apart for dropping the ball on this. The biggest scoop of the year: inside the #Murderer case, and Freddie-bloody-Venton had given it to *The Post*. After everything Sandra had done for her.

Sandra poured the remnants of her coffee over the paper, watching it obliterate Freddie's face. *The Family Paper* was the biggest-selling newspaper in the country. The most read newspaper online in the English-speaking world. Sandra's feature about the woman who'd only hire obese au pairs had got 128,000 hits in one hour this morning. How the hell had Freddie done it? The one time they'd met in person there was dirt under the girl's fingernails. That fat little cow did not deserve the splash.

She'd had Freddie in mind for a piece about loving your body like Lena Dunham, complete with photos of Freddie in her – no doubt – shabby underwear. The fugly ones who said they were happy with their looks always generated the most comments. Poor girl. She'd missed out on the wake-up call she needed: join a gym, get a decent haircut, ditch the unflattering clothes. Never mind. Plenty more fat fish in the sea. Sandra squeezed her pelvic floor, centred herself. She could work with this. She took a sip of her coconut water and looked up Freddie Venton's Facebook account: *welcome to the nationals, my dear.*

Freddie watched as Nas wrote Apollyon's latest words, tweeted three minutes ago, on the board in the incident room at the Jubilee station:

How you feline @SophieCat111?

'He followed her. Her account. Almost immediately after we received the tip-off about the body,' she said. Sophie Phillips' Twitter account was littered with cat gifs, videos of cats, even her own profile picture was a cat on – presumably – her lap. Freddie tried not to think of those legs. The pale white feet with red-painted toenails on the sofa. What did those legs look like now?

'Apollyon was following only Alun Mardling's account and now Sophie Phillips' account,' said Nasreen.

'Surely Twitter must shut it down now? Apollyon. No one can condone this,' Freddie said.

'At this moment in time, it's the only solid link we have between Alun Mardling and Sophie Phillips,' Tibbsy said.

'Have there been any more photos posted? Of the victim's body or the scene?' Moast slid his pad and pen into his back pocket.

'Not yet, sir,' Nasreen said.

Not yet, Freddie thought.

'Venton, make yourself useful: find out what you can about this Sophie Phillips online,' Moast said. 'How long has she been using

Twitter for? Has she ever interacted with Mardling? Are there any patterns to her online behaviour? You got that?'

She nodded. *Anything to help.*

'How long before you can build me a basic picture of her online habits?' Moast grabbed his body warmer from the back of his chair.

'Erm,' Freddie stuttered. 'I can see how long she's been on Twitter for, see if she's on Facebook, stuff like that, and, er, have a basic overview in ten to fifteen minutes.'

'Good. You can do it on the way.' Moast slipped his body warmer on. 'Right. Let's take a look then. Dorant, keep me updated. I want to know as soon as forensics are done. Tibbsy, Cudmore, Venton, Thomas: road trip.' Moast and the team filed out. Freddie, gripping her phone, followed.

Freddie sat in the back of the unmarked police car, squashed against the window as they drove along the North Circular. The promised bright winter sun of this morning had failed to materialise. Heavy grey clouds closed in, and Freddie watched as lights blinked on in the windows of tower blocks, houses, offices, like thousands of tweet alerts flickering on a phone. Then they gave way to the surrounding fields of the motorway. They were hurtling toward Sophie Phillips. Or what was left of her. Her phone rested on her lap.

Nasreen was in the middle, Tibbsy the other side of her – his knees folded up toward his chest to fit his long legs in. Moast was in the front passenger seat, talking on his phone intermittently as updates came through from the station. Freddie could see Jamie's sandy hair bordering the headrest. His eyes reflected in the rear-view mirror – snatching glances at Nasreen, who had her eyes closed from motion sickness. She shouldn't really ride in the back, Freddie thought. She remembered the time her mum had had to pull over on the way to her ninth birthday party at Chessington World of Adventures so Nas could be sick at the side of the road. She could hear Nas rhythmically breathing: fighting it. Inhale, one, two, three, exhale, one, two, three. It was making Freddie feel sleepy. She looked at her phone, her 3G reception was patchy. News of Apollyon following Sophie on Twitter had travelled quickly. Someone must have leaked it to the press, because 'breaking news' of 'unconfirmed' reports of a woman called Sophie Phillips being found dead in Leighton Buzzard were circulating. Freddie was relieved she hadn't stopped to use the bathroom on the way out. She hadn't once been alone. There was no way they could think this one was on her.

'What can you tell me, Venton?' Moast didn't turn round to face her.

'Sophie Phillips, or @SophieCat111 as she's known on Twitter, has had an account for a few months,' Freddie's mouth was dry. 'It was activated in June. She doesn't post much. Cat gifs. Cat memes. A few photos of what I guess could be her tabby cat. She posts about once a month.'

'Any photos of the suspected victim?' asked Moast.

'No, no selfies. She hasn't liked or retweeted any other Twitter users, and there's no visible interaction between her and Mardling. Or with Apollyon,' Freddie tried to stay clinical. Sophie must be an observer on Twitter, mostly watching others. She followed a few cat-themed tweeters, Stephen Fry and the BBC news. Only 19 people followed her, most were spambots, and of course Apollyon. 'There are loads of Sophie Phillips coming up on Facebook, but without a photo I can't really tell if any are her. It's the same with Instagram. I've searched for blogs by Sophie Phillips, using cats and Leighton Buzzard in the search, but nothing's cropped up.' Freddie sighed. 'I'm not sure that's much help.' Once she knew what Sophie Phillips looked like she might be able to get somewhere.

'Least the traffic's not bad.' Jamie sounded like he was trying to cheer everyone up. 'The motorway can be a nightmare. We've all been there, right? Stuck at the wrong moment. My gran used to say it was sod's law. When I joined up she called me the law's sod. As a joke, like,' he laughed. 'She was so proud when I told her I was working with the best in the force.'

'Can't you get there any quicker, Thomas?' Moast interrupted.

'Yes, sir. Sorry, sir. I'll try the back route,' Jamie squeaked. The car lurched to the left as they abruptly changed lane. Nas steadied herself with her hand against Freddie's arm. Instinctively Freddie placed her hand on hers to comfort her.

Moast, almost to himself, said, 'Everyone makes mistakes. Sooner or later he'll trip up. And then we'll get him.'

Freddie wasn't convinced. With no further tweets from @Apollyon they had nothing. She looked at Nasreen: inhale one, two, three. They may as well all have their eyes closed, they were as good as blind.

Off the motorway, over roundabouts, the roads led to houses. Estates of red 1960s and 1970s squat brick homes. Indiscriminate. Ugly. Handkerchiefs of grass etched between them. It reminded Freddie of her childhood home: three-bed, link attached, her room over the driveway. Before they'd had to move to somewhere more remote, her mum tired of facing the constant snipes from the neighbours about Dad's drinking. About what had happened at Pendrick High. Did these houses remind Nas of then too? She often dreamt she was back there, desperately late for exams she'd inexplicably not studied for. In reality, their old house had been sold to a man and his mother. She'd heard the man had grown so obese that when he had a heart attack in bed, they had to crane him out the top window. She'd written an op-ed piece about it. *£70: thank you.*

The car slowed, pulling into a concrete bay alongside some anaemic yellow-bricked 1970s flats. White wooden slat fronts made a sad attempt at what once must have been thought of as Scandinavian. Or cheap. Nas started, as if she'd been asleep, pulling her hand away from Freddie. Freddie swallowed; she would have liked to have held on for this bit. A clutch of officers in yellow high-vis jackets, their breath coming out like slow smoke as the evening set in, signalled they'd arrived. Jamie cut the engine. Moast and Tibbsy opened their doors. Freddie stepped out, pulling her duffel coat tight around her. She took in the 'no ball games' sign screwed to the wall. A group of kids in hoodies loitered on the corner, a volley of shouts and laughter erupting from them.

'Clear off or I'll have you arrested!' Moast shouted in their direction. *Strutting, marking his territory,* Freddie thought.

'Bit nippy isn't it? No clouds. Nothing to insulate us. You cold?' Jamie asked, his own nose pink from the chill air.

'Bit.'

'Might be shock. Took me ages to get used to…well, this.' He pointed at the police incident tape. 'I've got a fleece in the car if you want it?'

She nodded gratefully. Shock already? She hadn't seen the body yet. *Yet.* She thought about Gray's assurances. Looking up at the darkening sky, the empty space, where the towers and constant light of London hung, stretched on forever here. Jubilee station felt a long way away. The car boot slammed. Jamie walked toward her, his skinny frame barely filling his uniform, a dark black fleece in his hand. 'Here,' he held it out. 'Want me to see if I can rustle up a cup of tea? Perhaps the guv'll let me do a coffee run or something? We passed a petrol station not too far back. They might have a machine. Might make you feel a bit better?'

'Thanks, mate. But don't worry, I'll be all right.' Freddie slipped her duffel off, holding it between her knees, pulling the jumper on, holding the ends of the soft fabric between her fingers and palm as she pulled her coat back over the top. Her arms felt restricted, but she felt warmer; a barrier had been erected between her and the night. 'Cheers though, Jamie.' He gave her one of his watery smiles and looked at the ground while he scuffed a stone with his shoe.

Nas and Moast were talking to some men she assumed were local cops, as they pulled on the same forensic suits Freddie had worn that first day at Alun Mardling's house. She felt sick at the memory. She stepped closer to listen to their conversation.

'Lived alone. Went to work. Came home. Fifteen minutes on the bus. Worked in the finance department at the local council. Kept herself to herself. Not one for socialising. Moved to the area a couple of years ago. No apparent family. No real friends,' one of them said.

A loner, then. Like Mardling. Was the Hashtag Murderer a loner too? Picking off his kind to – what? To make himself feel better? Did Mardling and Sophie represent something about himself that the Hashtag Murderer needed to snub out? Or did he get a kick from it? Freddie's mind fizzed with awful possibilities, but nothing seemed to click into place. She looked up at the blank face of the flats. Poor Sophie. She wondered if she was lonely. Perhaps there was a wealth of friends away from work her colleagues didn't know about. It made it easier to think Sophie's life had been happy.

'Venton,' Moast turned. 'DCI Bradbury says the crime scene is largely contained to the bedroom.' He means *the body*, she thought. 'Are you up to looking at the rest of the flat?'

She nodded. Either Moast had taken Superintendent Gray's order on board, or he was less cocky about just how much this was, or wasn't, to do with the Internet.

'You sure you're up to this?' Nas handed her a jumpsuit. Freddie struggled to pull it over her layers. The smell of the plastic transported her back to Mardling's bedroom. To the sight of his mangled body. Nas's eyes were straight ahead. This wasn't friendly concern, thought Freddie: this was business. She nodded, pulled her hood up, positioned the face mask Nas had given her over her nose and mouth and followed Nas toward the flats. Nas lifted the police incident tape with her gloved hands for Freddie to pass under.

'What was it like the first time you saw a body?' This'd make a good feature, she thought. Then reminded herself she was banned from writing. For now. It was comforting to think of a time after this. Of things being normal again. Perhaps she could get a book out of it? *A Civilian In The Line Of Fire*. Civilians: jeez, now she was thinking like them.

'It wasn't on the job. It was before that,' Nas said. 'Jogging at university. There was a tramp in the bushes. Don't quote me on that,' she added coldly.

172

'I wouldn't,' Freddie was stung. 'Not without your permission, anyway.'

Nas nodded to the uniformed PC on the door, his face enfolded in a black scarf to keep the cold out. The white PVC door was heavy. Inside, the hallway smelt of boiled cabbage and disinfectant. Council accommodation.

'I heard you went to York uni,' said Freddie. 'I was at Loughborough. Lots of sports nuts, but it gave me a break from dad's antics, you know?'

'It's the next floor up.' Nas headed to the stairs.

Freddie bunched her fists into her sleeves. She could see the white powder used to dust for fingerprints along the painted banister. 'Did you know he was dead – the tramp in the bushes?' Freddie asked.

'Yes.' Nasreen was a step ahead of her.

'How?' Freddie's plastic shoe covers suctioned to the sticky floor.

'You just know.'

Freddie felt a flash of irritation. Was she patronising her?

A policeman with clipped red hair, his high-vis vest clashing with the green front door he was guarding, held it open for them. 'Ma'am,' he nodded at Nasreen.

Freddie soon forgot her anger at him ignoring her when she stepped into the flat. She'd let Nasreen lead. She tried to prepare for the smell this time. But it wasn't meaty like before. It was sickly, syrupy: vanilla. 'It's cold,' Freddie said.

'The windows?' said Nas to the policeman holding the door behind them.

'They were all open when we got here, ma'am,' he said.

Nasreen nodded. *What did that mean?*

'It's colder in here than it is on the staircase.' Freddie shivered. The saccharine smell wafted around them. She tried to breathe through her mouth only. They stood in a short hallway, with a mottled dark grey carpet and a coarse doormat. Silver square markers had been left by the forensics team. Freddie tried to remember if she'd seen them at Mardling's house, but this just reminded her of his blood dripping from his body.

To the left was a bathroom. Window open. A handheld chrome shower tap attachment and a net sponge looped over the taps. Ahead looked like the lounge. She followed Nasreen into it. There was a small kitchen to the left, a blue and white striped mug on the draining board – a sad reminder of domesticity. Another open window. The grey-carpeted living room contained a small table and chairs, pushed against the radiator, a couple of high-backed chairs in front of a small television. A bowl of fruit going mouldy on the side. Brown curtains twitched in front of another open window. She thought of the bright red toenails. 'How old is Sophie? Was Sophie.'

'Twenty-seven.' Nas took in the brown, carved, varnish-coated furniture.

Only four years older than me, thought Freddie. 'Funny stuff for a twenty-something. Old-fashioned.' Perhaps it came with the flat? No photos or pictures hung on the wall. Like Mardling's room. As if she'd only moved in the week before. Or wasn't planning on staying long. Least she had a whole flat, Freddie thought of her own lounge bedroom. Then felt guilty.

Moast was standing in the doorway. 'Body's in here, Cudmore.' Freddie's hood clung to her forehead. Nas left the lounge.

'It isn't that bad, this one.' Moast's top button of his white shirt was undone and his blue tie loosened under his forensic suit. A look of what – resignation? – on his square face. His forehead puckered. 'The body, I mean. Nothing like the last. No blood.'

Freddie looked at him, 'Do you want me to…to look at it?'

'Well, not *it* as such, but her room. It's more personal than this.' He shrugged at the lounge. 'It's got her computer in as well.'

Freddie nodded. 'Do you think it would help?' She owed it to the dead girl for begrudging her all this space. She deserved justice.

'You might recognise something from those cat pictures you saw on Twitter. Something that concretely links the @SophieCat111 account with the victim.' Moast snapped one glove off and adjusted his hood.

The door opened behind them and Tibbsy came in, almost having to duck under the door frame. His protective suit was stretched over his long body, his face half obscured under his mask. He took in the lounge and leant into the kitchen area. 'Where's the body, guv?'

'Bedroom.' Moast's hooded eyes held Freddie's gaze.

Freddie gave herself a pep talk. *God she hated that word: a baloney Americanism she must have picked up from teen films.* She looked round the bare room: *did Sophie watch Mean Girls here?* Phone in hand, talking to the world. She *had* to see the computer. That's what she was here for. For poor quiet lonely Sophie. 'Okay,' she said.

Freddie's throat felt as if it were corrugated, the very air she was breathing tripping down it. Moast's plastic back – material pulled tight across the shoulders – disappeared into the bedroom. Tibbsy pulled his mask down and mouthed 'Okay?' at her. She nodded. But she didn't mean it. Inside her own head Freddie was screaming: *Run! Get out! Don't go in there!* Fighting her growing panic, Freddie followed Moast. *For Sophie.*

Chapter 22

IRL – In Real Life

The walls of Sophie Phillips' bedroom were painted lavender. A dressing table, with a mirror and a small wicker basket of cosmetics on it, had a plastic purple stool tucked underneath. Stencilled dark purple butterflies flew round the headboard of the double bed. Resting on top of the lilac duvet, her hands in the lap of her white dress, her blonde hair splayed out on the matching lilac pillow, her delicate pixie face almost smiling, her ginger eyelashes dusting her cheeks, was Sophie Phillips; she looked like she could be sleeping. The white arrow of her chin jutted slightly up, as if a lover had tilted her head to kiss her. Freddie took in the tinge to the girl's skin, spreading up as if from the duvet, wrapping round her neck, like an amethyst necklace of bruises. Instinctively Freddie put her hand to her own throat.

'The pathologist says it's likely she was drugged first. Then strangled. No sign of a struggle,' Tibbsy was saying. Freddie thought of the mug on the draining board.

'Is this how she was found?' Nas crouched next to the bed. Her chocolate eyes peering over her mask at the body.

'Yes.' Moast crouched the other side of the bed. The knees of his suit pulling tight. Had he been comfort eating?

'Very summery dress, for November,' Nas said. 'Purple-painted toenails. Matching fingernails. It was obviously a favourite colour. What do you think, Freddie, would you wear a dress like this at this time of year?' She looked up at her, her face almost absurdly beautiful given the setting.

Freddie swallowed, tried to tear her eyes away from the bruises on Sophie's neck. Her suit rustled. 'It's cold in here, especially with all these windows open, so, no.' She looked round the room, forcing herself to concentrate. 'Purple dressing gown on the back of the door. Slipper socks under the bed. Is that a hot-water bottle propped against the wardrobe? It's cold.'

'Are you thinking he could have dressed her in it after?' Moast said, resting a gloved hand on the floor to peer under the bed.

'Possible. It does feel very ritualistic,' Nas said.

Freddie shuddered. Closing her eyes, she could already see the body of Sophie Phillips floating there before her.

'Do we have a time of death, guv?' Tibbsy was poking the end of his biro into the basket of Sophie's make-up on the dresser.

'They'll confirm after the post-mortem, but the pathologist reckons somewhere in the last 24-48 hours based on rigor,' Moast said. 'If it'd been any warmer, she would have started to decompose.'

Freddie felt the floor buckle. *Oh, Sophie.*

'Okay, Venton?' Moast looked at her, his stance steadfast.

'Yes. Sorry. It's just...'

'Need a minute?' He stepped toward her, hands by his side.

She wouldn't pass out. 'No.' Freddie concentrated on slowing her breath. If they could all stand there then so could she. She *would* show Moast she really cared. She would help. 'If it was yesterday morning, I mean if that's when it happened, then it can't have been long after the first few tweets. He tweeted Hope is rearranging her name at 10:17am.'

'Interesting point, that'd rule out a killing inspired by the tweets and the fuss around them, sir?' Nas said. 'Unless of course someone knew of a Sophie who happened to live on Baker Street. Bit of a gamble though. She didn't show up to work. Someone could have come looking for her. They would have had a small window of time, say two or three hours max, until her work called her. And then, if they were worried, they might have come over. The council offices aren't far from here, one of her mates could've popped over on their lunch break. The perpetrator's been so meticulous with everything else – like the planning at Mardling's, how they got in the house, the bleach, knowing he'd be awake and online then. Presumably.' She stood up. 'It's the same again here. It feels like planning's gone into this. Someone that's this specific isn't going to want to take any chances, they'd want to get in and out before there was any risk of being discovered.'

'Okay,' Moast said. 'Confirm with the pathology lab when the girl was killed. If we can narrow that time window then we can start to work out just who would have known where and when Sophie would normally have been expected to be. Anything to add, Venton? There's the computer. You can take a look at what the IT guys find on it when they get it back to the station.'

To the right of Freddie, backed into a corner next to a white Ikea wardrobe, was a small grey metal computer stand. On it rested a cream plastic hulk of a monitor. 'Christ, I haven't seen one of these since school. Remember, Nas?' Computer Sciences in the tech block of Pendrick High, or Computasaurus Studies as they'd called it. The processor column was shunted underneath the desk with barely any room for the user's legs. Something tugged at Freddie's mind, but she couldn't quite get to it. 'Where's her phone? She can't just use this?'

Nasreen walked round the bed. 'I've not seen one. Let me check with the local DCI if they've taken it in as evidence.'

Freddie stood aside for her to pass, turning back she tried not to look at the soles of Sophie's feet, which danced in the corner of her vision. She stood next to Tibbsy at the dressing table. Three neat towers of shiny fifty pence pieces and pound coins were stacked next to the make-up.

'There's something behind here, guv.' Tibbsy crouched and peered round the back of the unit.

'Where?' Freddie leant forward.

'Don't touch!' Moast said. 'Stand back, Venton. I don't want your DNA turning up in my forensic reports.'

'I wasn't going to, I'm not an idiot.' *Bloody hell, he blew hot and cold.* She shivered at her accidental pun. 'You've all got your gloves on,' she nodded at Tibbsy's ones. 'Least you could do is give me some?'

Moast snorted. 'Fine.' He fished a spare pair of disposable gloves from his pocket and passed them to her. 'Tibbsy,' he said, handing him a pair of plastic tweezers.

She stretched the latex over her cold fingers as Tibbsy stuck the tweezers down the back of the unit and pulled out a photo.

'Who have we here then?' A smiling lady with tightly curled grey hair beamed out at them.

'Turn it over.' Freddie's hand hovered near the photo, impatient.

'I said don't touch, Venton,' Moast growled.

'I've got gloves on now, I'm fine!' *Idiot.*

Tibbsy turned the photo over. Written on the back was: Auntie Em, Brighton Pier, 2003.

'Family,' said Moast. 'See if the boys can trace her, Tibbsy.'

'Yes, guv.' Tibbsy produced a role of plastic baggies from his back pocket and tore one off, dropping the photo into it.

Someone's niece. Someone's loved one. The sobbing in Mardling's kitchen. The smiling face from the photo. Freddie couldn't bear to think of it. Of this woman, this girl, being ripped from life. Imagine if someone knocked on the door while her mum was having a cup of tea in front of Coronation Street, before Dad

179

got back from the pub, to tell her Freddie had been killed? Pain tore through her heart. Her vision misted with tears.

'That's enough now, Venton. Take a break. Go outside. Wait in the car.' Moast's tone was perfunctory.

She nodded, relieved. She was glad Nas was out of the room. Genuine concern would have tipped her over the edge. She sniffed. Walking back through the lounge, past the kitchen, the tiny bathroom. This was someone's world. A purple-painted inner sanctum for Sophie. The Internet wasn't fazed by that, it trespassed everywhere. Through wires, through walls, permeating our machines, our fingers, our thoughts.

'You okay?' Nas was stood in the doorway of the flat.

'Yes,' Freddie croaked. Pleaded with her eyes for Nas not to say anything else.

'Okay.' Nas opted to play along. *Or perhaps she just missed it.* She held up a small baggy. 'Got the phone – it was in her handbag.'

Freddie nodded at the brick of a Nokia. 'Good.' For a second she thought Nas might reach out and touch her. She couldn't cope with that. 'I'm going to wait in the car.' Nas nodded. Freddie passed the cop on the door, took the stairs at speed. She pushed the heavy door to the block, it opened like a seal: as if she were being spat out by the building. Taking in the clear night sky, she looked up and away from all this. The stars were bright. It wasn't until she was halfway to the car that it hit her. That nagging thought that had played round the edges of her mind. She saw it clearly. She ran back, ducking under the tape.

'Hey, all right there?' The uniform on the door tried to steady her.

Freddie shook him off, wrenched the door, took the stairs two at a time. 'Nas! Moast!' The words screamed out of her. The red-haired cop raised his eyebrows but held the door for her. 'Nas!'

Moast and Nas appeared at the entrance to the lounge. 'What's wrong?' Worry dripped from Nas's mouth. Tibbsy appeared in the kitchen doorway.

The words tumbled out: 'No lead. There's no modem lead.'

'Slow down. What?' Moast said.

'Shit.' Nas pulled Sophie's phone from her pocket.

'Show me?' Freddie held out her hand, closed it around the bag, felt the sturdiness of the bulky plastic, looked at the small screen. 'Analogue. Not a smartphone.'

The colour drained from Moast's face. He shot into the bedroom, they hurried behind him. Freddie still fighting for her breath. Moast was down on his hands and knees.

'What are we looking for?' Tibbsy was behind them.

Freddie dropped down, squinted behind the wardrobe. There wasn't enough room: it was too close to the wall.

'Nothing,' Moast said, still crouching.

Freddie leant against the cool wall, Sophie's toes at her eye level. 'There's no modem. No way this is wireless.'

'Am I missing something?' Tibbsy asked.

Nasreen held up the phone.

'That's not on the Internet.' Freddie pointed at it. 'This isn't on the Internet.' She gestured at the ancient PC.

'So how the hell does she tweet?' asked Moast. Nasreen turned and walked out of the room. 'Cudmore?' Moast called.

'Hang on, sir, just checking...'

Freddie stood up, taking in the length of Sophie. *As if she were sleeping.*

Tibbsy's steadying hand had her by the shoulder. 'Okay, I think you need some air.'

She let herself be steered into the lounge. Nasreen appeared in the kitchen doorway. 'There aren't any. No server. No hub,' Nasreen said. 'And there's something else, sir.' Freddie was aware of the bulk of Moast behind her, she was gliding, leaving, over the grey carpet, the red-haired cop held the door, Tibbsy at her side. 'Where's the cat?' Nas said.

'It's not her then,' Moast said. 'This SophieCat111 or whatever it is. Her name, the street name: that's all circumstantial. Just another distraction. Let's focus on the victim's life, the facts, what we do know about her: known associates, work colleagues, did she have a boyfriend?' As the door to the flat closed behind them, Freddie caught the last of Moast's words: 'Until we have proof to the contrary, let's assume this has nothing to do with this Apollyon character.'

Gasping to get enough air, to stay lucid, Freddie wanted to object. This didn't feel right. Why would Apollyon follow only Alun Mardling and now @SophieCat111? It had to be the same person. There couldn't be another Sophie who lived on Baker Street who'd been murdered. There had to be a link. But why would Sophie, Apollyon's selected online cat-lover stereotype, not have Internet access or a cat at home? Something wasn't adding up.

Chapter 23

GR8 – Great

07:30
Wednesday 4 November
2 FOLLOWING   115,280 FOLLOWERS

Freddie stood at the front of the Jubilee station's incident room with Nas, Tibbsy and Moast. She'd been unable to sleep last night: images of Sophie Phillips' dead body seemed to levitate in her bedroom. She'd given up around 2am and got up to research syntax similarities and if you could identify two seemingly different writers as the same person through semantics and dialectical quirks. She compared Paige Klinger and Apollyon's tweets but found nothing analogous between their spelling, cadence, tone or sentence structure. It wasn't until around 6am, when the sound of one of her flatmates, Anton, stirring, and commuters could be heard bustling outside, that she let go and slept. Less than an hour later and her alarm had gone off. Now 7.30am, she was attending the pre-meeting arranged by Moast. He looked like he'd shaved in the dark. Tibbsy's eyes were barely visible in hollowed-out sockets.

Even Nas seemed edgy. All three were pulled into suits that were comically at odds with their knackered faces. Freddie hugged a coffee and her phone. She was in her jeans and a purple hoodie.

She'd gone back over the clues from Apollyon – was it possible they'd got the wrong answers? 'I've tried looking at it from every different angle, and I still think Sophie Phillips must be @SophieCat111,' she said.

'But then where did she tweet from?' Tibbsy's tiny eyes blinked.

'We don't know that there's a link between the victim and the person tweeting as Apollyon,' said Moast. 'There's nothing conclusive to link the two. Have the IT bods been able to link the victim with the Twitter address @SophieCat111?' Freddie saw a grey smudge on his white shirt cuff, the kind you got from walking down the Tube station escalator resting your hand on the moving rail.

'No.' Nas looked taut, as if her skin was stretched so tightly she might split. 'Nothing's shown on either the phone or the home computer, but the IP address for the device sending messages from @SophieCat111 has been traced to the Leighton Buzzard area. We're speaking to her work colleagues this morning to request access to her computer there.'

'Fine,' said Moast. 'Then as of yet we've no confirmation that @SophieCat111 and Sophie Phillips are the same person. I don't want to waste valuable time on this. We need to focus our resources on identifying possible suspects, starting with those known to the victim.'

'But what if it is Apollyon?' Freddie couldn't drop it.

Moast sighed. 'Okay. Venton, you can look again at everything this @SophieCat111 posted: look for any identifying details that would link it concretely to Sophie Phillips. Have you gone to see the IT lads yet?'

'No,' she shook her head guiltily. There hadn't been time. Everything had happened so quickly.

'Okay, get down there today and see what else they've got on the SophieCat Twitter account.'

She nodded dumbly.

'I want the rest of us to stay focused on the facts. There were similarities between the Mardling crime scene and this one. As with the scene at Blackbird Road, Sophie Phillips' bedroom was clean; forensics have only found traces of the victim's DNA in the flat. In addition to this, there was evidence of bleach found in the victim's bedroom and on her computer. The SOCO team have confirmed it was the same brand of supermarket bleach that had been used at Mardling's, albeit more liberally.'

Freddie remembered the overwhelming sickly smell at Sophie's flat. 'Was it vanilla-scented?'

'Yes,' said Moast.

Why would the killer use more at Sophie's flat? 'Were Alun Mardling's computer and keyboard bleached?' Freddie thought of the blood splatters.

'No, there were traces of bleach on the door handles, on the back of the chair – presumably where he braced the victim before cutting him – and at other points in the room and leading to it,' said Moast.

'So why did he bleach Sophie's computer?' Freddie said.

'It implies he touched it, sir,' said Nas.

'Possibly, or he had more time to clear up after himself. Sophie's flat is discretely located,' said Moast. 'Perhaps the perp didn't fear being seen. As such, we can assume our killer wore gloves and is very meticulous. Time of death has been narrowed to sometime between 4am and 9am on Monday 2nd November. Dr Fisher has yet to complete Sophie Phillips' autopsy report, but traces of Temazepam and Flunitrazepam –' he looked at Freddie – 'what you might know as roofies, the date rape drug that's used to render victims unconscious – were found in her bloodstream and also in the sugar bowl in the kitchen. Whoever did this knew Sophie Phillips took sugar with her tea. That indicates this was someone who knew the victim and her habits and perhaps not someone who was selected because they watched cat videos.'

'Was she interfered with?' Freddie tailed off. *Rape*? This was too horrific.

'There's no evidence she was sexually assaulted before or after she was strangled,' said Nas.

Freddie thought of the blue and white striped mug. *Did Sophie unwittingly feed herself the drugs that sedated her while she was killed? Awful.*

Moast continued: 'Her colleagues indicated she didn't have much of a social life, but perhaps she just didn't share it with them. If someone new came into her life, someone who knew how she drank her tea, someone with potential access to her flat, I want to know about it. Go back over it with the neighbours. Do they remember anyone visiting her in the last few months: a new friend, a lover, had she started acting out of character? Look at her bank balance, where's she been?'

'Yes, guv,' said Nas.

'Have the local team canvas cafes, bars, restaurants and shops in the area. Does anyone remember seeing Sophie with anyone? Have we found any recent photos of her we can use to jog people's memories?'

Tibbsy dropped his blue eyes from Freddie. 'No, sir. Nothing in the house so far, and Freddie found none on the @SophieCat111 account, which as you say, may not be hers anyway.' Freddie tried to piece all the information together; she had a nagging feeling she was missing something obvious.

'I can ask the employers, sir, when I speak to them this morning,' Nas added.

'Good. Do that. I want a copy of all the door-to-door enquiries from the Bedford force. The local team have gone in to speak to the vic's manager and colleagues in person. Cudmore, you and I will follow it up.' Moast was flicking through his notepad. 'See if anything pops. Keep me up to date with any developments, and we'll reconvene after lunch to run through where we are. This concludes this morning's briefing. I just want to say I'm sure I speak for you all when I say the sooner we catch this creep the better.'

Nas and Tibbsy nodded and gathered up their notes.

'So you're just going to ignore @Apollyon?' In the corner of her eye, Freddie saw a message alert flash across her locked phone. And another. And another.

'It's not a question of ignoring,' Moast said.

There was another, flickering across her screen: what the hell was going on?

'It's a question of process,' Nas was saying.

'Hang on,' Freddie held her palm up. 'Something's happening.' She heard Nasreen's hands close round the file she was holding.

'What?' asked Tibbsy. 'Is it another clue?'

Freddie slid her thumb across her phone and clicked onto Twitter. She had 57 messages. *What the hell?* Clicking into her notifications, her screen scrolled with mentions.

Roger Morris @RogerMorris1954 • 1s
@ReadyFreddieGo You've tarnished the name of The Family Paper. Your actions shame you.

Feelin Groovy @KevinMastetron • 34s
@ReadyFreddieGo Dirty slag – I'll teach you a lesson. Over my knee girl! #FamilyPaper

What the hell was going on? She was being tagged into a *Family Paper* link. She clicked. The screen widened into the newspaper article. Freddie's mouth hung open. There, on the homepage of *The Family Paper*, was a photo of her in a bikini, taken when she was fifteen at a friend's barbecue birthday party. She was straddling a bottle of Cider White and pulling what she'd thought then was her best sexy duck face. They'd pixelated her right breast to make it look like the original image flashed a nipple. It didn't. Emblazoned across it was the headline: *The Truth About The #Murder Journalist.* 'Son of a bitch!'

'What's he said?' Tibbsy asked.

'Is it another tweet, Freddie, I can't see it.' Nasreen had her own mobile out now.

'They've outed me!' Furiously, Freddie skimmed the article:

The Family Paper can reveal the infamous Typical Student columnist is none other than the same Freddie Venton who has been lauded in some newspapers for her undercover work on the #Murderer case. Single Venton, 23, who has no problem sharing photos of herself in revealing clothing online, has defended her promiscuous lifestyle in this very paper. Just how much do the police know about their new recruit? The Family Paper can reveal, though Freddie Venton seems to come from a respectable middle-class family, a quick look at her Facebook page shows she has squandered her privileged upbringing on years of drunken antics.

'What are you talking about?' Moast snatched the phone from her hand.

'No!' Freddie watched as his eyebrows travelled up his forehead.

'What the fuck is this?' Moast turned the phone toward them all, revealing a photo of Freddie in a police jacket and suspenders and the word 'pigs' on a sticky label on the fancy dress helmet.

'Whoa! Nice pins, Venton,' Tibbsy whistled.

'It was a joke. Fancy dress party. Uni. Years ago. They've been on my site. They must have pulled it from there.' Rage and embarrassment burned through Freddie.

'Oh, this is just perfect.' Moast was scrolling through the article. *'DCI Moast, who appeared flummoxed by the presence of Miss Venton in a recent press conference...'*

'Sir, I'm sure it's not that bad.' Nas's eyebrows threatened to meet.

'You're in here too, Cudmore.' Moast tapped at the phone.

'What?' Nasreen's hand flew to her mouth.

'There, see? They've even got a photo of you.' Moast waved the phone around. *'Sergeant Nasreen Cudmore, who poured her curves into a fetching two-piece suit for the press conference, is known to have attended a well-respected school with the unlikely consultant, Miss Venton.'*

'Hey! Why haven't I got a mention?' Tibbsy asked, peering over Moast's shoulder. 'You look good though, Cudmore. They've even told people where you can buy that suit. Karen Millen. Very nice.'

'Shut up, Tibbsy!' Nasreen smacked his arm with the back of her hand. 'Are they allowed to do this?'

'Christ.' Freddie sat back on the table behind her and let her face fall into her hands. No wonder the troll army were out for her this morning. How could Sandra do a number on her? How could she expose her like this? She'd written for them for free for years. She'd never seen her as an equal, had she? Never considered her to be a colleague. Just a bloody content driver.

'What the hell did you say to them?' Moast was still waving the phone in front of her. His cheeks inflamed, his eyes bulging.

'Nothing. I swear. Why the hell would I give them photos like that?' Freddie's anger at Sandra seethed round every word she spoke.

'You were told: no more talking to the press.' Moast slammed her phone face first down onto the table to his side.

'Hey! Watch it!' Freddie grabbed the phone, checking the screen wasn't damaged. 'This is not my fault. I haven't done anything wrong.'

'I don't want to hear it, Venton.'

Freddie's phone vibrated in her hand. 'It's him.'

'I said shut it.' Moast swiped at his hair. 'Cudmore go get me a fucking coffee, I can't think with all this going on.'

'Don't pour your curves in the cup, hey Sarg?' Tibbsy said.

'Put a lid on it, Tibbsy,' Moast snapped.

Freddie stared at her phone. At the link to the photo she'd opened. 'Will someone please listen to me! @Apollyon has tweeted.'

'Shit,' Tibbsy said.

'Show me.' Moast's voice was calm.

Nas held out her own phone, like an offering. 'It's Sophie Phillips' room.' Moast put the phone down on the table and they all looked.

'Lilac walls, purple duvet, butterfly stencils above the bed. Sophie Phillips' room,' Freddie said. There was no hiding it.

'But no body?' said Nasreen.

Tibbsy whistled through his teeth. 'I wonder when he took it?'

'What does it mean?' asked Freddie. There were no words with the tweet, just the photo.

Moast rubbed at the uneven stubble on his chin. 'It means whoever is tweeting from that account is either the killer or has one hell of a coincidental access to both crime scenes before and after the murders.'

'It's a message,' said Nas. 'Only those close to Sophie Phillips and us would know that's the crime scene, sir.'

Moast blew air through his teeth. 'He's taunting us.'

'Freddie's right: @Apollyon is our killer,' Nas said. 'And the tweets, these clues, they're from him. He's toying with us.'

Moast looked grim. 'It would seem so.'

Finally they were agreeing with her, but Freddie felt no satisfaction. The hairs on the back of her neck bristled. 'Apollyon's conducting the whole thing online. All in front of an audience.'

'Yes,' said Moast. He gathered himself. 'We need to double back over what we've done and align it with what Venton has compiled on the online usage of Apollyon, Mardling and Sophie Phillips. Get the IT bods up to speed with this latest development, and have everything they've found compared with the results of our door-to-door enquiries and canvassing of friends and family. I want two timelines: one of the victims' movements in reality, and one of their, and Apollyon's, activity online.'

'Yes, sir,' said Nas.

'Sir,' Tibbsy nodded.

Freddie felt the air compress around her as she watched the team realise what they were up against. This was a sick, gruesome performance, and the anonymous Apollyon was calling the shots.

The incident room door opened as the rest of the officers working on the case began to arrive. Clutching coffees, files, laptops and printouts. Freddie watched them talk to each other and report in to Moast. Working alone and in groups. Surely this many police could find whoever @Apollyon was before…She didn't want to finish her thought: *before he kills again.*

She couldn't just sit here. Following directions from Jamie, she took the back stairs of the station and looked for room 01.203, which housed the tech team. She knocked on the door and waited.

'Come in!' called a cheerful voice from inside.

Freddie opened the door into what she thought at first was a cupboard. The small, dark, windowless room smelt like a teen boy's bedroom. Sat in front of two computers were two men.

'Hullo,' said the guy nearest to her. He was tubby with a nice open face, his black tie bouncing on the white shirt that was stretched over his belly as he turned his wheelie chair toward her.

'Oh, sorry,' she said. 'I was looking for the tech team.' She started to back out of the room.

'That's us,' said the jovial guy. 'I'm Sergeant Griffiths and this is Sergeant Patel,' he jerked his thumb at the slight man who sat behind him. Sergeant Patel smiled shyly, and the moustache that looked as soft as a feather on his top lip turned up at the ends.

'No need to ask who you are, we've seen you on Twitter,' said Sergeant Griffiths.

'You're actually on Twitter?' said Freddie. 'I thought the whole station was banned from it?'

'Different rules down here, isn't that right, Patel?' Griffiths turned his swivel chair back toward his screen. Sergeant Patel nodded and smiled again.

'You guys are the tech team?' Freddie looked at the hard drives, phones in plastic bags and laptops that were stacked in the windowless room.

'Ack, we may not be your e-crime super geeks, like them digital forensics they have on the top cases.' Griffiths grabbed a can of Coke from his desk. 'This isn't yours is it, mate?' he asked Sergeant Patel, who smiled and shook his head. 'But we do a mighty fine job with what we've got.' He took a swig from the can. 'Who do you think cracked the metadata on your Hashtag Murderer photo your suspect posted online?'

Freddie nodded. 'Okay, fair point. And they keep you in a dark room because?'

Griffiths took a swig from his drinks can. Sergeant Patel opened a drawer and took a napkin and held it out for his colleague. 'Cheers, mate,' said Griffiths. 'All the rooms on this side of the station are artificially lit.' He wiped his chin with the napkin.

'Oh,' said Freddie. 'I thought maybe it was a darkroom, like for photos and stuff.'

'We tend to digitally print all photographs now,' Sergeant Patel spoke so softly she just caught his words.

'Of course,' Freddie felt dumb. 'So have you had any luck tracing the device that posted on @SophieCat111's account?'

'The posts can all be linked to a mobile phone mast in the Leighton Buzzard area,' said Patel.

'And it looks like the phone was turned off in that area. The last post was transmitted by the same mast,' said Griffiths.

'Do you know where it was when it was switched off?' Freddie asked.

'Ah, come now, as our very own Social Media Advisor you should know that without the phone's number or a GPS-encoded metadata file we cannae do that,' Griffiths said, quite friendly.

'I have traced the GPS coordinates that were embedded in some of the images the @SophieCat111 account posted.' Sergeant Patel lifted a pile of photographic prints from on top of a nearby laptop. 'From the time range and spread of locations – across the globe – I would suggest that @SophieCat111 only shared images that were taken by others,' he said.

'Maybe she didn't have a camera phone?' Freddie said.

'Possible, but most smartphones have cameras these days, and her online posts would indicate they were from a smartphone.'

Then where was Sophie Phillips' smartphone? It wasn't in her flat, or her office, she had no car, or other place she frequented that they knew of. Perhaps she lost it, or it was taken by the killer? 'Can I have those photographs?'

'Sure,' said Sergeant Patel. 'I've written the date, time and location on the back of those I've identified.'

Perhaps there was a pattern to where Sophie pulled her images from? A Reddit thread or specialist website? If Freddie could compare the images and locate a common source, she might build a better picture of Sophie's online life. 'Thanks.' She took the pile of photos.

'Ms Venton?' Griffiths said, as she turned to go. 'If things continue down this road, with this Apollyon guy, then do feel free to tell DCI Moast he might want to call in the big boys.'

'The big boys?' she asked.

'Yup. Me and Sergeant Patel here do a mighty fine job with what we've got, but a Digital Forensic Analyst, a specialist, might be able to glean more.'

'But the posts on Twitter? The clues online? Apollyon?' Freddie couldn't believe this. Surely that was enough of a motivator? 'Why hasn't Moast called a Digital Forensic in already?'

'Ah,' said Griffiths. 'They're in short supply and take up an awful lot of the budget. We tend to use them to corroborate existing evidence, but I think they might be useful on this case. If it continues to develop in this way.'

'We saw the photo of the victim's room that was posted,' said Sergeant Patel. 'I can find no GPS coordinates hidden in that one. It was probably taken on a pay-as-you-go phone.'

Freddie was trying to process all this: Moast seemed to finally acknowledge Apollyon might be the killer. 'Do you think he'll call in a Digital Forensic now?'

'Ack, don't you go getting worried about it, pet,' said Griffiths. 'You know your stuff surely, else the Superintendent wouldn't have hired you. You may cost less than a Digital Analyst, but I bet you're twice as smart aren't you!' Griffiths beamed at her. Sergeant Patel looked down at the floor. Freddie managed to nod and backed out of the room. 'Tell your DCI we'll have the results on Sophie Phillips' hard drive soon,' Griffiths called as she closed the door behind her.

She couldn't compare to a digital specialist. *Had Gray used all his budget on her?* No wonder Moast was pissed. She looked down at the photos in her hands, what was it her mum used to say? *If you can't get round something then you've got to go through it.* She had to get on with this. People were relying on her.

She took the photos to the canteen and spread them across one of the long tables. She began to group together photos or memes of what looked like the same cat, or memes that used the same text font, or had what looked like the same background. Occasionally she checked Twitter in case there were any further updates. Blocking the idiots who hurled abuse at her online. And ignoring those she'd previously thought of as friends, asking with undisguised glee how she was holding up following *The Family Paper*'s smear attack on her this morning. Plenty were too eager to feast on her humiliation. What could she say? She felt sick all the time, but not because of her photos in *The Family Paper*, but because there were two people dead and she felt like nothing she did helped. She was divorced from her previous life of quick-fire cynical puns. No more hilariously inappropriate Cards Against Humanity games; the reality of death had altered her very idea of life. It wasn't so much that she'd tasted death but that it had tasted her. And now it had that taste, it kept coming back.

Again, she thought about Brian's strong hands snaking round her. It was madness to imagine they were the same hands that closed round Sophie's neck. And yet she couldn't shake the thought. There was no trace of him online. It was as if he never existed. She'd geotagged herself that night. She'd let it be known online where she was. Was he in the bar already or did he arrive after? Did @Apollyon know who she was? Her face had been all over the newspapers. Had he come close enough to taste her? No. She was going crazy. This wasn't about her. It was about Sophie. She picked up the pile of cat photos: a change of scene might help.

Walking back to the incident room, Nas stepped out of the ladies' room in front of her, shaking the last drops of water from her hands. Her hair scraped back into a practical ponytail. She nodded. They stood, awkwardly for a moment. 'I'm sorry about the shitty *Family Paper*,' Freddie tried. How did every communication between them sour so quickly?

Nasreen's lip twitched. 'Forget about it. Can't be helped.'

Freddie felt herself exhale. It was okay. She didn't hate her. Well, no more than normal. They both moved to walk back toward the incident room in unison. Like they were strolling the pinboard-covered halls of Pendrick High again, they fell into step beside each other. Nas, tall and streamlined, each click of her heels on the floor a flag planted, ground gained. Freddie, sloping, hunched into her baggy hoodie, her DMs squeaking. 'Any further news on Sophie's Internet devices?'

'We're still waiting for access to be granted to the work machine. The hard drive on the computer in her flat was wiped clean.' Nas swept an imaginary hair from her forehead. Her nails rounded pink petals against her cappuccino skin.

'Why would he wipe her hard drive?' asked Freddie.

'Presumably there was something on it that linked Sophie to him. Whoever did this not only knew what they were doing, they also took their time.'

Freddie felt a wave of nausea. How long had Sophie hung between life and death? Drugged, but potentially still saveable. 'If we'd worked a bit quicker...'

'We didn't have enough to go on. It's not worth thinking about,' Nas said flatly.

'But if we'd worked out the clues quicker?'

'Then what? There are thousands of Sophies, hundreds of cat lovers. He knew that,' Nas said.

'So why do it, why tweet clues?'

'Attention. Theatrics. To create panic. To prove how clever he is. I don't know.' Nas looked tired. 'The DCI has requested a profiler for this case, but the paperwork will take time to process.'

Freddie couldn't escape the feeling she could have done more. And now there was another dead body. Another victim. It was different than Mardling though. 'It's not just the missing cat is it?' she said out loud.

'What is?' Nasreen stopped and turned to her. A black-haired constable came towards them. They stepped aside to let him pass.

'I mean, it was different. The murder.'

'Constable.' Nasreen nodded as the copper passed. 'You mean the method?'

'Yeah.' Freddie thought of Mardling's butchered dripping body. 'No blood.'

Nasreen chewed the side of her cheek. 'I thought that, it felt less... angry. The spiked sugar implies they knew her routine. And the way she was laid out. Sacrificial. The attention to detail: that white dress. Virginal. Bridal perhaps. It felt like there was love there. Or at least care.'

'Yeah, certainly none of that with Mardling.' Freddie tried to focus her thoughts. Keep on the details. Stay away from the face of Sophie.

'Apollyon and the same bleach being used at each crime scene are the only definitive links between the victims we've found so far,' said Nas.

'The clues, and the photos posted by Apollyon of Mardling and now Sophie's empty bedroom, must mean the killer is the same person,' said Freddie. 'Or at least using the same account. Could it be more than one person?'

'How do you mean?' asked Nas.

'Sophie and Mardling, it doesn't feel the same. There've been a lot of suicide groups and pacts drawn up over the Internet. I read a report about it on xoJane. Could this be something similar? A murder group? A killing pact?'

Nas's lips puckered in thought. 'I don't know any more. It sounds so extreme. But then a week ago so did the idea of a serial killer posting on Twitter.'

'You're the first one, apart from me, to say that: serial killer,' Freddie said quietly.

Nasreen seemed to shake herself. 'We shouldn't get ahead of ourselves. DCI Moast is correct. We need to concentrate on the evidence in hand: relook at the door-to-door enquiries, speak to locals, and stay focused on the facts. The IT guys haven't turned anything up based on the photo of Sophie's room that was posted. No time or date log.'

'I know,' said Freddie.

'We need to be careful not to get distracted by silly Internet games.'

'Distracted?' Freddie couldn't believe she just said that. 'First a troll and now a cat lover is murdered. It screams online stereotypes! Who's next? A YouTuber? Some Instagram star? This is all about the bloody Internet. He must be doing it for fame. Or fear. Or…I don't know.' Freddie was gripping the photos so tightly she felt one cut into her finger.

Nasreen sighed. 'I'm as frustrated as you are, Freddie, but we can't just make up random theories. Technically it's not a pattern until there are three instances.'

Freddie's blood ran cold at the thought of a third murder: they couldn't let that happen.

'We have to look at the evidence,' Nas continued.

Freddie stared at her. *Why can't you bring yourself to agree with me?* Deep inside, Freddie knew it was because of what she'd done back then. Their past secret burned in the air between them. The incident room door opened, flooding the hallway with noise. Jamie peered out, caught site of Nasreen and his face lit up in a huge smile. *Great. Just what we need now.* Freddie rolled her eyes.

'Sergeant Cudmore, I was looking for you.' He lolloped toward them.

Nasreen stretched a falsely jolly smile across her face. 'What is it, Jamie?'

Jamie was clutching some printed pages. 'Well, it might be nothing, but I think I found something.'

'What?' Nasreen turned and gave him her full attention. Freddie felt her heart quicken.

'I thought I'd look to see if Sophie's Twitter name appeared anywhere else. Online, like. And the same name, SophieCat111, crops up in this Internet chat room.' Jamie started spreading papers out across the wall with his hands. How did I miss that? thought Freddie. Jamie must have added in something else: the separate word cat, or similar, to get the hit. Or waded back further than the fifth page of Google search results. She resolved to search again for Mardling's Twitter handle too.

Freddie squinted at them. SophieCat111 was posting in a chat room titled The Best Internet Cat Memes EVA!!! 'Is that her?'

'Yes, I'm pretty sure. I called Sergeant Patel in IT – I usually get him a coffee on the way in – and he said it's traced to the same phone mast that's registered the Twitter account activity.' Jamie was trying to point with his finger and hold the pages wide across the wall at once. One was sliding down.

Freddie pinned it with her hand and turned her head to read it. 'Who's this? This Mark Hamlin she's talking to about cat breeding? It's getting a bit heated.' Freddie skimmed the words as the conversation descended into an argument.

I think we should agree to disagree. Peace out.
~ *SophieCat111*

No, you deluded bitch: when are you going to get it into your thick head that you can't fight nature. Nature is bigger than you. Nature'll rain down like a mighty destroyer and cast you out. I will call her upon you. I will destroy you!!!
I AM VENGEANCE
~ *MarkHamlin*

'Okay,' said Freddie. 'He sounds well adjusted.'

'He threatens to shut her up with his gun, here.' Nasreen had taken one of the pages from Jamie.

'Yes, and I thought that rang a bell. I went back over the interviews with Mr Mardling's colleagues at his bank and, well, there it is: Mark Hamlin's name again.' Jamie passed the pages to Nas.

Nas read aloud. 'DGC Bank, Canary Wharf Branch Incident report: dated Saturday 26 May 2014. Mr Mark Hamlin, a customer, was asked to leave by store manager Mr Alun Mardling, when his unusual behaviour was upsetting other customers. Mr Mark Hamlin…' Nasreen broke off and exhaled.

'What? What does it say?' Freddie's heart was in her throat.

Nasreen continued. 'Mr Mark Hamlin threatened to kill Mr Alun Mardling. Brilliant work, Jamie.'

Jamie beamed. 'I wanted to bring it to you, Sergeant Cudmore,' he mumbled, looking down at his feet.

Freddie's hand started to shake: Mark Hamlin. Was that *his* name? Was he the Hashtag Murderer? Was Mark Hamlin @Apollyon? Was all this terror, this horror, finally going to stop?

Nasreen was already at the incident room's door: 'Guv, Jamie's turned up a link between Alun Mardling and Sophie Phillips. I think we might just have got him.'

Chapter 24

RT – Retweet

'Mark Hamlin. Previous for disrupting the peace when he kicked off after a neighbour complained about him firing a shotgun at a fox in his now deceased mother's garden. And he has been formerly detained under section 136, so he's got a history of mental health issues.' Moast held up a mugshot of a wide-eyed skinny white guy, with long wispy brown hair and hollow cheeks; he resembled a frightened skull. 'As we've reason to believe this nut…'

Freddie tutted. *That was hardly fair if he was mentally unwell?* Then she thought of innocent Sophie Phillips and remembered all the names she'd called Apollyon.

Moast rolled his eyes at her. He continued, 'As we've reason to believe Hamlin might still have access to firearms, and that he may have already killed two people, I have requested Special Ops on this. We'll be going in with two officers from the firearms team.'

Freddie had speed-read the bank report Jamie had found: the odd behaviour Hamlin had displayed seemed to be largely that he smelt and he was muttering to himself. The bank security team had logged a copy with the Canary Wharf police, but the decision was taken not to press charges as Hamlin wasn't thought to be a genuine threat. Had they missed it at the time? Had something happened to tip him over the edge? But she'd seen the chat room rant at Sophie, going from friendly to abusive in a few short sentences. But the words were crazed, more like the trolling Mardling and his lot enjoyed, nothing like the considered tweet clues. Or was she just upset that she'd understood the clues? That she'd got what this guy was talking about. Did that make her unhinged? *For whom the bell trolls.* It was easier to imagine some faceless monster than some skinny, mentally unwell guy. Did he even know what he was doing if he was sick? Everything was moving so fast. And now Moast was talking about firearms.

Freddie shifted in her seat as Moast finished his rallying call. 'He is registered at Flat 467b on the Shadwell estate. Let's bring him in. Let's end this.'

A few of the officers at the back whooped. Freddie caught Nas's eye. She looked worried. Freddie's phone vibrated. @Apollyon – or was it Mark Hamlin – had tweeted: Here's Johnny! 'Er, guys?' Freddie spoke quietly enough so only Moast, Nas and Tibbsy would hear.

'I haven't got time for a bleeding-heart liberal lecture about how I should describe headcases, Venton.' Moast was handing notes over to a waiting nervous-looking constable.

Freddie flinched, then decided to let it go. 'It's not that. He's tweeted.' She held her phone up.

'What does it say, Vents?' Tibbsy pulled his coat over his jacket. Freddie watched as Nas pulled on her black gloves. Had she heard her?

'"Here's Johnny!" Like in The Shining, I guess.' The wild-eyed skeleton in the photo did sort of resemble a crazed Jack Nicholson.

'What do you think it means?' Tibbsy asked, buttoning his coat with his long bony fingers.

Moast glanced quickly at the phone. 'Who knows what these loons think.'

Nas, hands in her coat pockets, chewing her bottom lip, looked like she was thinking. 'I'm not sure, guv. Shouldn't we at least compare it to the other tweets?'

'And miss the chance to catch this guy before he knows we're on to him? For the first time we have the advantage in this case. So if you're done, I suggest we get on with it, Cudmore,' Moast said. Tibbsy stood aside and Moast walked out.

'Sir.' Nas shrugged at Freddie.

Freddie stared at Tibbsy.

'I guess he means you're coming too,' Tibbsy said, opening his arm as if showing her to the door.

'But I...' Freddie glanced down at her phone. *Here's Johnny!* She thought of the film scene. *Come out, come out, wherever you are.* 'I don't know if I...' *want to.*

'Best not keep him waiting, hey?' Tibbsy pursed his lips in a squashed smile.

Freddie nodded dumbly and followed him out of the room, while the phones rang and radios crackled, and there were shouts and surges of movement. It was as if the whole building were gearing up. It was tangible in the air. Fear? Excitement? *Firearms.* She wasn't sure she wanted to know which.

Freddie had seen the concrete towers of the Shadwell estate looming as they drove toward them. In the back of a squad car driven by Jamie, she could only watch as Nas and the team filed out the back of an unmarked police van. In her flat, thick-soled boots and with her stab vest over her shirt, Nas looked like she'd stepped from a film set. Moast was talking to another uniformed officer, behind whom stood a group of four cops with guns. The team would split into two groups, one led by Moast, one by Nas, as they made their way to separate entrances at either end of one tower. Freddie's breath juddered out in mist against the closed window.

'What's going on, Jamie?' She looked up at the tower blocks, scored with walkways exposed to the elements. From afar the towers had an urban charm, especially lit up at night, but now, on a cloudy afternoon, among them, they felt oppressive. Like giant poisonous mushrooms.

'The DCI'll be briefing the team, I guess.' Jamie twisted to look out his window too. 'Don't worry. It'll all be over soon. This is a routine op. Nothing to worry about.'

'Can we at least get out and see what's going on?' Freddie wiped her misted breath from the window. She thought she could make out Tibbsy's rangy shape in a stab vest in the group behind Nas.

'Sorry, the guv gave me strict instructions you had to stay in the car. It's not safe,' Jamie said.

'What about all the people who live here?' Freddie watched as Nas's team passed a group of lads in Los Angeles style sweatshirts and baggy jeans, sitting on a car bonnet near the left-hand entrance to the tower.

'The building's too populated to evacuate and risk alerting the target to our presence. Residents have been told to stay inside their flats away from doors and windows,' Jamie said.

As Freddie watched, Nas disappeared into the tower's left-hand column. 'I can't see them anymore, open the window, Jamie.' Freddie rattled the door. Jamie looked pensive, the key clicked in the ignition. The window wound down. Kneeling onto the back seat, she pushed herself half out the window, the glass edge digging into her hands. 'Where are they?'

'Oi! Oi!' shouted one of the lads, jumping up onto the car bonnet. 'It's hashtag ho!'

Freddie twisted to stare at them. *Sandra, you cow, this is your fault.* 'Fuck off!' she shouted.

'Fancy some White Lightning, ho?' a boy with a red beanie shouted. They whooped and laughed. Freddie's cheeks flamed.

She wanted to scream. She wanted to hide, but she had to see that they were safe. That Nas was okay.

'Perhaps you should sit down,' Jamie said, his hand resting on his door handle.

'Fat lot of good you are.' Freddie dropped back into the seat as one of boys held their phone aloft and she heard the familiar sound of a camera shutter closing. Photographed. More laughter. Then it hit her. Her phone! Resting her feet on the edge of the seat, she tipped her hips toward the car's ceiling.

'You all right?' Jamie asked.

'Getting my phone. Chances are the people in that tower will be on the Internet.'

'Not much else to do round here, I guess.' Jamie's voice was quick and unnerved.

Freddie typed in #murderer. The column loaded. There it was: a photo of her half out the police vehicle, mouth open, with the caption #Murderer ho! *Whatever*. She kept watching. Inside the tower she saw Nas and Moast coming from opposite ends of the fourth floor walkway, hunched, moving fast, getting into position.

Yo Mumma @RudeBoyz • 45s
Shit be going down. Pigs all over the place talkin hashtag murder. #murderer

Charlene B @SharleneBlings • 27s
@Apollyon they be coming to get you, bitch. #murderer

Viv Dee @VivDee1986 • 20s
OMG! We been told to keep inside wile police goes next door. They look like the fucking military. Not even jokin #murderer

A couple of shaky photos taken through windows and partially opened doors appeared. The online momentum was building as more residents realised there was a live #murderer event going on in their block. Freddie could see Moast, jaw set. One of the armed force holding his gun up. Guns were never good. Images she'd seen on the telly and on social media flashed through Freddie's eyes: massacres, mass shootings, the news, films, TV shows.

News of the police raid was spreading fast through Twitter. Freddie flicked her eyes between the tower block outside and the words on the screen: 'Here's Johnny @Apollyon!'

Little pigs, little pigs, let me come in. The dialogue from The Shining thrust itself into Freddie's mind.

She looked up as the team converged on the open walkway.

A figure – which one? – stood in front of the door. There were shouts. A banging sound. Then a pop and grey smoke streamed out from the fourth floor. 'What the fuck was that?' She tried the door handle. Locked.

'Stay in the car, Freddie. It's okay, they're using a smoke grenade,' Jamie said.

Screaming came from the fourth floor balcony. A woman clutching a child was heading toward the fire exit. 'What's happening? Why is she running?'

'I don't know. Panicking, I guess. Don't worry, the ground team'll escort her out,' Jamie said.

Freddie watched figures, in jeans and hoodies, moving through the smoke toward Hamlin's flat, crouching, arms out, holding their phones up. There were shouts. The journalist in her wanted to bear witness. To see. It wasn't fair that these civilians were getting so close when she, who was working on this case, was kept at an overly cautious safe distance. 'Jamie let me out.' She shook the window with her hand. Jamie looked stunned, his watery eyes swimming in their whites. More smoke teemed from the balcony. 'You sure this is just grenades?' Freddie asked. Tens of people were streaming down the stairs now, pouring out onto the car park, turning back, photographing the grey smoke that spiralled up into the November afternoon sky. 'Shouldn't we get out and check?'

'I...I...' Jamie's hand was hovering over the handle.

A couple of children were crying. The driver of the police van was herding them away from the building.

Freddie desperately wanted to see what was going on. A video link appeared on Twitter, the first still clearly taken on the walkway in the smoke. Freddie clicked play.

The camera was shaky, she could hear breathing, the holder was running toward the door, smoke was all around. There was shouting. It sounded like Moast. 'Down! Down on the floor! Hands up!'

'No!' screamed a male voice.

'Sir, remain calm, please get down on the ground,' Nas's voice.

Freddie expanded the screen.

It was all hissing smoke and coughing.

The video went dead.

Chapter 25

ISO – In Search Of

14:09
Wednesday 4 November
2 FOLLOWING   123,223 FOLLOWERS

Freddie wasn't going to miss this. She twisted, pulling herself round so she was sat on the car's window edge. She pushed her feet against the slippery seat, finding the armrest, pushing down and herself up. One leg down. Two. She was out of the car. Running.

'Freddie, wait!' Jamie shouted. She'd tell them she was worried something had gone wrong. *Was she worried something had gone wrong? Yes.* No. Her heart hammered in her chest. She told herself Nas was a pro, she'd be fine. She was just here to see. She clutched her phone tightly in her hand and panted. She should have gone to the gym more.

Freddie heard Jamie's car door slam. Smoke was being blown down toward the car park. People were shouting. Freddie's breath was loud and hard. She heard the crackle of Jamie's radio. The thud of footsteps. Then it was obliterated as she penetrated the grey cloud and hit a wall of people. Twenty of them. Freddie dodged the scared faces, mouths open yelling, small babies in nappies clutched in the arms of young girls. At the bottom of the tower, uniformed officers gathered, trying to feed people out. 'Please keep calm. Please exit the building calmly!' a large copper boomed up the stairs.

'What's going on?' Jamie shouted at him from behind her.

'We've lost radio contact,' the large copper said. Freddie pushed past him. 'Madam, please don't run! Hey! You can't go up there!'

'Freddie!' yelled Jaime.

She was getting a stitch. *What if something has gone wrong?* She thrust the thought aside. She was here to bear witness. You always wanted to be a war correspondent, well this is as close as you're going to get to Kate Adie, she told herself. *Shadwell's War.*

Freddie pushed through the people flowing out of the tower. Clinging to the metal railing, pulling herself up the stairs.

'Our father who art in heaven,' a woman with her hair in a bright silk scarf was muttering as she passed. There's nothing to worry about, Freddie told herself. But her legs pumped a little harder.

'Freddie!' Jamie's voice, somewhere below. She looked up. The wind was blowing the smoke back into the building. Wisps swirled down the staircase.

'Out my way!' Someone pushed her. A blur of denim. Freddie's head smacked into the concrete wall.

'Remain calm! Please walk in an orderly fashion.' Jamie again. She looked down as a man in a blue hoodie took a swing at him.

'It's terrorists!' a woman shrieked, her red lips a startled O, barrelling toward her.

Freddie dodged her.

Clutching her head, she drove her feet down onto the concrete steps, her hamstrings and calves screaming as they pumped. Keep running. Alarms sounded. More sirens. Police. Was that an ambulance? As she rounded another corner, the yelling strangers grew further away. Her heart was punching against her chest: the fourth floor.

Open to the elements, the walkway to all the flats on the fourth floor was cold, clear and empty. Lazy wisps of smoke were drifting out of what she guessed was Mark Hamlin's gaping front door. Freddie slowed. A door cracked open to her left, making her jump. A pair of eyes peered out. The other doors were closed, with metal gates bolted over them. She juddered to a halt as Moast and Tibbsy stepped out of Hamlin's flat. A bedraggled man, his hair and beard overgrown, was strung between them, like Jesus. It was *him*.

'Mark Hamlin, I'm arresting you on suspicion of...' Moast said. Tibbsy looked up as if to say 'what the hell are you doing here?'

Hamlin, his head hanging down from his shoulders, emitted a low moan. Where was Nas? Hamlin looked like he hadn't eaten in some time.

Tibbsy signalled with his head for Freddie to flatten herself against the wall as they passed. The smell coming from Hamlin was rancid.

Moast turned toward her, 'We'll speak about this later. Cudmore, make sure she gets downstairs.'

'Yes, sir!' Nas stepped out from the smoke.

Freddie clutched her chest and exhaled. She hadn't realised she'd been holding her breath.

'What the hell are you doing, Freddie?' Nas stood with her feet hip-width apart, and Freddie saw it wasn't a gun in her belt but a can of CS spray.

'You're not armed? You went in without a gun?' She couldn't believe this.

'I'm a trained professional, Freddie, I know what I'm doing. You shouldn't be up here.'

Relief unexpectedly undulated over Freddie. 'I just...I just wanted to see what was happening. Other people, residents, they were taking photos. They were running out of the building.' Now she was here she felt foolish. What had she been planning to do? She could hardly help detain the suspect. She hadn't documented anything. She'd just got in the way. 'I...I don't know what I thought.'

Nas coughed, as one of the firearms team stepped out of Hamlin's flat, his face squashed like a raisin between his helmet and chinstrap. He gave Freddie a funny look. 'Forensics'll be up in a few minutes, ma'am, want me to secure the area?'

Nasreen smiled, a huge disarming slice of white teeth against the smoke wisps billowing around them. 'Don't worry, I'll do it.'

The raisin-faced guy looked faintly startled, nodded and headed past Freddie. Freddie stared at Nas.

'Well, now you're here let's take a look.' Nas pulled a pair of latex gloves from her pocket and threw them at her.

Freddie pulled the gloves on. This was her third crime scene. *There wouldn't be another body would there?* She followed Nas into the flat. Orange curtains glowed, pulled across windows, casting everything in an eerie tangerine light. Like peering through a Quality Street wrapper. Her eyes took a second to adjust. The stench of piss and shit made her gag. She put her hand over her nose. Freddie's skin crawled. Piles of newspapers and boxes filled the room. Had he done it here? Killed someone? Killed Sophie? No, that made no sense. Something moved and caught the corner of her eye. She jumped.

'Cats,' said Nas. 'I've counted four so far.'

'That accounts for the smell then.' She hoped. *And possibly why Hamlin had ended up on the cat chat room talking to Sophie?*

She followed Nas into the kitchen. Festering piles of plates and food containers were stacked like towers. A tabby was eating something from one of the bowls. Freddie didn't look too closely. This man was clearly very unwell. She tried to breathe through her jumper sleeve. 'There aren't any…bodies, are there?'

'No,' said Nas. 'Come look at this though.' She led her into a bedroom.

A bed, strangely neat compared to the rest of the flat, was bathed in a dusty plume of light pouring through the gap in yet more orange curtains. 'Shit,' said Freddie. Piles of coins, hundreds of them, sorted into denomination, covered the white veneer bedside table and marched in from the walls, covering the floor.

'Remind you of anything?' asked Nas.

'There was a stack on Sophie's dresser.'

210

'Yup. Fifty pence pieces, and two towers of pound coins. Piled up just like these.'

Had Hamlin left them in Sophie's bedroom? Had he found them and sorted them while he was there?

'Why would he pile them up like this? They're like religious columns. Totems. It's fanatical.' Freddie surveyed the room – were these an indicator of a mentally unsound mind? She took some photos of the piles of coins with her phone.

'The coins are only circumstantial,' said Nas. 'But there's that too.' She pointed at the bed.

And then Freddie saw it: the Mac Air, just the corner, shiny, clean, poking out from under the bed. Internet access. Despite the cloying musty closeness of the room, Freddie shivered.

'It could be him then? Despite all this,' she signalled at the decaying flat. 'He has a device. He could be Apollyon?'

'Everyone has computers. It doesn't mean anything. The IT boys will have to check it. So far I haven't seen a phone, but hopefully the SOCOs will turn one up. Look, we haven't got long. Forensics'll be up any second and the DCI will go nuts if he knew I'd let you in.'

For a second Freddie felt like they were together again. Like at junior school. Her and Nas versus Moast. Her and Nas versus the world. The overwhelming feeling of gratitude nearly made her cry. She had to hold it together. She followed the line of Nas's hand as she pointed at the wall. That was odd. The plug sockets had been removed and covered with silver foil. 'Why would you do that?'

'I don't know,' said Nas. 'It's the same in each room, look.'

She followed Nas back into the kitchen. The sockets looked like they'd been chipped out. Crumbled plaster lay around them. More silver foil covered the hole. Through the lounge, the hallway, all the sockets were the same: removed and covered over. Freddie bent down, using the light from her phone to look at one. She took a couple of photos. She was just peering closer when they heard a high-pitched scream. Freddie stood bolt upright. It was coming from outside. Nas started toward the front door. She raced after her.

Chapter 26

VBD – Very Bad Date

14:17
Wednesday 4 November
2 FOLLOWING   123,402 FOLLOWING

Nas powered down the steps, Freddie tried to keep up. Turning round the corners, peering down the staircase she caught flashes of Moast and Tibbsy and Hamlin. What was going on? Was there another victim? No, the sound was coming from Hamlin. Moast had him by the arms. He was kicking his legs, flailing up and away from him. Moast was trying to balance them. They were dangerously close to the edge of the stairs.

Nas was below her. Closer to them. She heard her shout, 'What happened, Jamie?'

Freddie saw flashes of the top of Jamie's sandy head as she turned down the stairs, trying to catch up. 'I…I…don't know!' he said.

Nas was past him. 'We need backup now, all units, the north stairwell in Tower B.' Nas's radio crackled as she called it in.

'Try to calm down, Mark!' Moast shouted.

Hamlin was still screaming. The sound cut through her; it was pure terror. Freddie stopped running and hung over the rail, watching the scene below. Jamie was one floor below her. Moast had Hamlin in a corner, the floor below that. A monster of arms and legs and flailing cloth. It was hard to see who was who.

'I can't hold him!' Moast shouted as Hamlin broke free and bolted toward the balcony.

Tibbsy made a grab for him and was thrown off. Hamlin careened into the railings. 'Jesus, he's going to fall.' Tibbsy sounded panicked.

'Mr Hamlin, if you do not calm down I will be forced to taser you.' Moast's voice could just be heard over Hamlin's screaming. Tibbsy scrambled and got Hamlin round the waist. Hamlin's head ricocheted back into Tibbsy's face, sending him stumbling backwards. Freddie winced. Hamlin bolted for the railings. 'Clear!' shouted Moast.

The wire hummed and shot out. The prongs stuck into Hamlin and he fell rigid to the ground. His body convulsed. Freddie clamped her hand over her mouth and turned away.

'Sir! He's foaming at the mouth.' Nas's voice had an unaccustomed note of alarm. 'Switch it off!'

Twisting back, Freddie saw Nas on the floor next to Hamlin's body, checking his pulse.

'Shit,' she heard Jamie say.

'We need paramedics on north stairwell of Shadwell estate Tower B.' Nas spoke into her radio as she moved Hamlin into the recovery position. 'Repeat: suspect unconscious, we need medical support north stairwell Tower B, Shadwell estate.'

'Did he bang his head?' Moast asked. 'What happened?'

'Ambulance on standby. Paramedics on the way up, ma'am,' Nas's radio crackled in response.

Freddie turned away, took a step back. She closed her eyes and pressed her forehead against the cold concrete wall, listening to the pitter-patter of the paramedics' shoes on the concrete steps below getting closer.

The ambulance was long gone by the time the team took their vests off and loaded them into the van. Freddie watched as a number of uniformed officers took witness statements from neighbours, and yet more officers loaded up evidence, including Hamlin's laptop. The forensics had set up a cordon, and the public clumped around it wondering when they'd be allowed back into their home for dinner. *The public.* Freddie was no longer one of them. She looked at Nas and Moast and Tibbsy, calmly talking in a huddle. But not one of them either. Who was she? She knew it must be cold: it was growing dark, and people were bundled up in scarves and hats and blankets, but she couldn't feel it. She leant against Jamie's car trying to make sense of everything. She'd seen a man tasered. She'd felt sorry for him. But he might be the Hashtag Murderer. She thought of the coins stacked up in Sophie's bedroom and the link they'd established between the two victims. He *could* be the Hashtag Murderer. If Mark Hamlin was @Apollyon, then she'd felt sorry for @Apollyon. He was clearly mentally unwell. It looked like no one – family, the state – cared for him. He lived in filth and squalor. And the terror, the fear in his eyes. The sounds of his screams. But what had he possibly done to Mardling and Sophie? What about their screams? That couldn't be excused. Explained, yes: he was not well. But not forgiven. How do you deal with a man like Mark Hamlin? How do you find justice in a situation like this?

Nas and Moast walked toward her. She stood up and off the car. Like she was at school and had been caught slouching. They were the teachers: grown-up, responsible, weary. 'Will he be okay?'

'Probably. Doctor said it was a seizure. Probably caught his head on the way down.' Nas had her hands in the pockets of her long black coat. 'There's an officer with him now. He was only out for a few minutes. They've given him a sedative. He's on the observation ward. We'll be able to question him in the morning.'

214

Moast was unstrapping his stab vest and pulling a fleece on.

Freddie thought of Hamlin curled up in the stairwell. 'He seemed so...pathetic.'

'Can't count on anything, Venton.' Moast pulled his puffa jacket over his top and rested his stab vest on the car. 'He could be a psychopath acting up. Different persona. They can do that.'

'Or schizophrenic,' said Nas. 'If he's had a breakdown, it might have triggered an episode. He could be suffering from delusions.'

'We don't know what we're dealing with yet.' Moast picked up his vest and went back to the van.

Freddie watched him go. 'Do you think he feels any remorse?'

'We don't know for sure if he did it yet,' said Nas, undoing her ponytail and retightening it.

'I meant Moast,' Freddie said.

'He just did his job. The suspect was in danger of hurting himself. This is what it's like. You have to make decisions in the heat of the moment.' Nas cupped her hands and blew warm air onto them.

'Would you have done it? Tasered him?' Moast's bravado reminded Freddie of American cop shows, but then she'd pushed people aside to get up there. Who was to say what was right and what was wrong from all this? *How I Lost Myself In A Tower Block in East London.*

'DCI Moast took the best decision he could based on his assessment of the situation.' Nas sounded like she'd been briefed.

Freddie looked at her. 'You don't reckon he harbours secret fantasies about being Bruce Willis in Die Hard then? I saw that tight white T-shirt he was wearing on the night of Mardling's murder.'

Half a smile trickled across Nasreen's lips.

She could *still* make her laugh. 'Today's been nuts. I'm not sure I believe it all myself, and I was here to watch it.' The feelings she'd had for Nas, their friendship, that bond, she was too raw to hide it now. It had flooded through her. Their den in the meadow behind Nas's house. Scary stories and stupid torch faces at Brownie camp. Lounging on the old blue sofa cushions in the garden. Covering everything with glue and glitter at Christmas. Nas giving her her ice cream when Freddie dropped hers. Their first taste of alcohol – gin and lemonade pilfered from her parents' drinks cabinet. Friendship bracelets. The first swell of their teenage years, of who they would grow up to be. She still wanted Nas in her life. She wanted to be her friend. They shared something. Something that wasn't easily found. She didn't want this moment to end. She floundered for something to say. 'So you still living out in Pendrick? I heard Jamie ask about your commute in.'

'Yeah, helps keep it separate. Plus I like being close to mum and dad.' Nasreen buttoned her coat up.

Freddie nodded. She'd often thought about Nas's mum, Afnan: small, petite, a temper as fiery as her cooking. Nas had her eyes and hair. And soppy Don Cudmore, who worshipped the ground on which his daughters walked. 'Got a flat?'

'No, a Victorian terrace. Just off the high street. It's still got the original fireplace.' Nas's face softened as she spoke of her home, morphing briefly into the girl Freddie used to know.

'Nice,' Freddie nodded. She felt no jealousy. Nasreen deserved somewhere nice to go back to after all this every day. She watched Moast who had stopped by a young mother and a small dark-haired girl, who looked bewildered, clinging to the edge of her mum's cardigan. Barely up to her mother's knee. What had that little girl seen, living somewhere like this? She watched as Moast bent down and produced a coin from the little girl's ear and held it out to her. A huge smile cracked across the girl's face as she turned her new-found treasure over in her fingers.

Nasreen followed her eyeline. 'He's not as bad as you think,' she said.

Freddie didn't know what she thought anymore. Who was good and who was bad? Whose side was she supposed to be on. 'What happens now?'

'Debrief. Back at the station. We won't be able to question Hamlin till tomorrow. They may opt to keep him in hospital.' Nasreen opened the back door for Freddie. Unlike a few days ago, when the world was very different and she was angry about things that didn't seem to matter anymore, Freddie got gratefully into the back of the car.

Chapter 27

BTDT – Been There Done That

Nasreen had always disliked hospitals, and now the sickly smell of bleach reminded her of the morgue. Never a good association. The long, spongy grey and blue corridors of the hospital could be a police station, were it not for the nurses and doctors in their scrubs coming and going. Blank-faced visitors clogged up the place, unsure of what to do. Who to pray to. The DCI and Tibbsy had come straight in when Hamlin had come round. She knew the drill, he'd be kept in for observation for 24 hours following head trauma. Even if it was slight. She glanced at the signs screwed to the wall, turned down another corridor. The hospital, a huge glass monolith from outside, like Duplo blocks constructed by a child, inside was like a maze. She hoped Hamlin wouldn't be a bolter. Nightmare running anyone down in here.

She rounded another corner and the high-vis jacket of the officer standing guard outside Hamlin's room informed her she'd finally arrived. Six foot two, Caucasian, neat, clipped brown hair, mouth that turned down. She'd encountered him a few times. He was from the Whitechapel force. It was PC Slade, she thought. Must have been brought in. The manpower was increasing on this one. The whole force itching to get the perp locked up.

'Morning, ma'am, the guv's through there.' Slade pointed at a door across from him.

'With the suspect?' she asked.

'No, he's in here.' He signalled with his thumb behind him. 'Nurses gave them that room. Family liaison usually, I think. Bit of privacy, eh?' Slade's lips bounced up and down as he spoke. A face like rubber.

Nas knocked on the door, before opening and going in. The DCI and Tibbsy were sat on low, square, foam chairs, both leaning forward resting their forearms on their knees, gathered round a low table. 'Morning, sir.'

'We made the papers again.' DCI Moast flicked a copy of The Mirror over on top of the table. A grainy photo, presumably taken by a witness, showed one of special ops, gun up, edging toward Hamlin's flat. Nasreen could just make out another newspaper under that, the words Hashtag Murderer visible above a photo of smoke pouring from the Shadwell estate tower.

'What did Hamlin have to say?' Nasreen could sense the tension in the room. She guessed other things had upset the DCI this morning.

'Gibberish, mostly,' said Tibbsy, reaching forward for a mug of coffee and downing the dregs. 'He's either putting on one hell of a show or something's spooked him.'

'Do you reckon it's shock?' Nasreen took the chair opposite the DCI.

'Hard to say,' said Tibbsy.

'I want to talk to his doctor. See if they think he's faking. You saw the coins in the flat?' Moast looked tired.

Nasreen nodded. 'Just like the ones in Sophie Phillips' flat.'

'I like him for this. The stuff on the Internet, the verbal assault of Mardling. It's starting to add up.' He met her eyes. 'Have IT turned up anything?'

'It's definitely the computer from which the chat room messages to Sophie Phillips were sent, guv,' she said.

'I knew it!' Moast clenched his fist. His skin whitening over his knuckles.

'It's not all good news, sir.' She took her notepad from her pocket. She wanted to make sure she got this right. 'There's nothing that the lads have found so far that links it to the @Apollyon account.'

'He could have used another machine though, a phone or something. Have they found anything at the flat?' Moast rested both his palms on his knees.

'Not so far. And there's something else, sir. The laptop.' She paused.

'Yes?' Moast said.

'The outside of it was also bleached clean. No DNA. No fingerprints. The same generic supermarket brand of bleach as before,' she said.

Tibbsy put his mug down. 'Surely that confirms it – this is our guy?'

Nasreen was unsure. Why would you wipe down your own machine? Unless he'd heard them coming. Done it at the last minute. But then where was the bleach? Hardly the sort of place you'd expect to find cleaning products. Hardly the kind of man you'd expect to act so coolly. 'Do you think it's an act, sir – all this?' She thought about the screaming. He *could* have staged it. To throw them off.

'It's possible,' Moast said. 'Let's see if we can get any sense out of his doctor.'

All three of them stood, Nasreen waited for Tibbsy to pass her. 'It's not enough is it though, to hold him, I mean?'

Moast paused, his hand on the silver nickel door handle. He looked up, as if at the posters offering help for those who wanted to quit smoking. 'No. It's circumstantial. Unless we can get him to confess or we turn up anything else, like a murder weapon, or evidence he took those photos of the crime scenes, we can't hold him. We'll have to let him go. We need to find his phone.'

Nasreen nodded. She already knew this was the case, but she needed the DCI to say it. The man she'd put in recovery yesterday didn't strike her as strong enough, physically nor mentally, to restrain someone. Let alone kill anyone. She felt DCI Moast and Tibbsy pulling in the other direction. DCI Moast had years of experience. Hard graft had built his reputation. He knew what he was doing. As she followed him and Tibbsy out the room, Nasreen was reminded of the joke Freddie had made about Bruce Willis. With his name and team all over the papers, just how desperately did the DCI want to close this case?

'Dr Powell? DCI Moast. Could we have a quick word?' Moast asked as the doctor came out of Hamlin's room.

Dr Powell, a tall pinched brunette of possibly Spanish descent, held Hamlin's clipboard to her chest and gave them a tight smile. Thick-framed square glasses rested on her nose. Nasreen wondered how many times they got knocked off dealing with patients like Hamlin.

'This is Sergeant Tibbsy and Sergeant Cudmore, we're conducting a murder enquiry and would like to ask you some questions about Mark Hamlin.' Moast signalled for PC Slade to wait inside Hamlin's room. The officer obliged, disappearing into the room, where beeping could be heard.

'DCI Moast, I have a lot of very sick people needing my attention, and as you know full well, patients have complete confidentiality. I am not at liberty to discuss Mr Hamlin's health with you.' Dr Powell had the world-weary look of someone who'd faced down tougher people than them.

'I just want to know if you've treated Mr Hamlin before, Dr Powell?' DCI Moast opened his arms wide as if welcoming her confession.

'I believe the patient was in the Community Care programme but they lost contact with him a number of years ago. Today is my first day on the ward,' Dr Powell said.

221

'New job?' The DCI was going for the small talk approach.

'I'm on rotation, DCI.' Dr Powell's eyes narrowed.

'Is it possible to speak to his previous doctor then? I understand the suspect, I mean the patient, was previously detained under section 136 of the Mental Health Act. Some officers brought him in for his own safety?'

'He is unlikely to have been seen by the former Senior House Doctor if that was the case, anyway.' Dr Powell tapped the toe of her kitten heel against the floor. Nas tried to smile at her warmly. Communicate that she understood: it was tough making it in a male-dominated world.

DCI Moast tried again. 'Well perhaps I could have a quick word with that doctor just to check?'

'If you insist, I can have someone find out where their rotation sent them next. Though you do understand that may very well be another hospital?' Dr Powell gave Nasreen an empty stare.

'I thought you got a job and stayed within the same hospital?' DCI Moast was floundering. Tibbsy shifted his weight back against the wall.

'That would be nice. It would certainly make things easier. No, we belong to a district that can cover several hospitals, several hours apart.'

'You mean the last person who saw Mark Hamlin isn't even in this building?' Moast's eyebrows stretched up toward his new grey patch.

'It seems I am not the only one who has had my time wasted, DCI. If you're done I have many pressing things to be getting on with,' Dr Powell snapped.

They were losing her. 'Just one last quick thing, Dr Powell.' Nasreen put a hand out onto her arm. Reassuring. Looked into her eyes. Trusting. *We're trying to help.* 'In your opinion, with cases like Mark Hamlin, is he likely to be violent? Hypothetically speaking.'

Dr Powell sighed and pushed her glasses back up the bridge of her nose. 'Hypothetically speaking, I would say the chances are slim. Patients like Mr Hamlin are more at risk of self-harm. But, of course, you can never be one hundred per cent sure.'

'Thank you, doctor,' Nasreen said. 'You've been very helpful.'

They watched as Dr Powell walked down the corridor, the soles of her kitten heels flapping up against her feet.

'Nicely done, Cudmore,' DCI Moast said. 'Though I don't know how relevant it'll prove. I get the feeling Dr Powell doesn't like us very much.'

'Another one who thinks we're the enemy, hey boss?' Tibbsy said. But Nas wasn't listening, she was enjoying the warm glow of praise. The DCI hadn't said anything positive about her since Freddie crashed back into her life. But perhaps she could still get her standing at the Jubilee back; it was salvageable.

'Back to the station. Let's see what else we can get on this bugger,' said Moast.

Chapter 28

MT – Modified Tweet

08:30
Thursday 5 November
2 FOLLOWING   124,666 FOLLOWERS

Freddie stared at the photo of Sophie Phillips on the front page of *The Family Paper*. She looked different. Her wavy bobbed blonde hair looked like sunshine glowing round her face. She was pale, yes, but apples of red bloomed on her cheeks. She was laughing. Her green eyes sparkling. Behind her, the glass of an office window smudged the bright blue sky. It was like a toothpaste ad. She looked so…alive. 'I don't understand how they got a photo before us?' She looked at Nasreen, sat across from her in the echoing canteen, folding her Marmite toast in half before tearing it into triangles, like she'd done when they were little.

'Apparently they got it from a work colleague. They had it on their Facebook account and they *forgot*.' Nasreen bit into the toast.

'More like they turned it over for a hefty fee. Bloodsuckers,' she said, only the faint edge of her bristling at her hypocritical words.

But *The Family Paper* had turned against her. She was outside again. Journalists were supposed to be on the front page because of their stories, not because they *were* the story. Freddie dropped the paper onto the wipe-clean table and flicked through the pile of newspapers that were next to her. She skimmed the headlines: *Hashtag Murderer Strikes Again. Fears of a Serial Killer Grow.* She held up a tabloid: *No One Online is Safe Warn Crime Experts.* 'Just so you know, they didn't get that from me.'

Nas gave a little laugh. 'There's growing alarm. The guv wants this case resolved and closed as soon as possible. Understandably.'

Around them, those coming in from the night shift were getting one more caffeine hit for the road or a bacon bap to help block out the memories of last night. Freddie was beginning to adjust to the rhythms of the station.

'You getting any sleep?' Nasreen wiped her fingers with one of the small plasticky napkins the dinner lady handed over with your grub.

'Not much.' *Not at all.* She shrugged.

'It gets worse I'm afraid,' Nas said. She'd come straight from the hospital this morning. Hamlin had been kept in overnight. And now here was a heartbreakingly intimate photo of Sophie Phillips to greet her: no wonder she'd decided to take five, Freddie thought. 'Hamlin's been discharged,' Nas said.

'You're bringing him in?' Freddie watched Nasreen run her tongue over her teeth for stray crumbs, poke between the front two with her nail. It was as if all her barriers had come down. Had she felt it yesterday? Their connection sparking again?

'No,' said Nas.

'What?' Freddie was momentarily confused. Had she spoken out loud?

'We can't hold him for longer than twenty-four hours without charge. We haven't got enough evidence. The police guard at the hospital puts us in a grey area. We can't really claim we were protecting *him*.' Nas's eyes fell onto the photo of smiling Sophie.

Freddie tried to make all the pieces fit in the puzzle. 'Do you think he did it? I mean, the coins, and the chat room, and…I don't know. He seemed so incapable.' *How did you tell who was guilty and who was not?* Surely there was a way. A way to know for sure. Freddie thought about all the guys she thought were cool when she first met them. She thought about Brian.

'We've got a tail on him. We're looking into him further. I'm not sure. I agree he doesn't seem *the type*.' Nas scrunched her napkin onto her paper plate. 'Ready?'

Freddie took a deep breath. Were they any closer to the truth? 'Sure.' As they left the canteen Nas's phone began to ring.

'Sergeant Cudmore,' she answered. Freddie strained to hear the other voice: small, tinny, far away. It sounded like a woman. 'Mrs Crabtree, thank you for calling me back. I understand you've already spoken to one of the Leighton Buzzard force – PC Grigg?'

Freddie raised her eyebrows at her.

Nas pointed at the phone and mouthed 'Sophie's work colleague.'

Was she going to rip Mrs Crabtree a new one for giving that photo to the police? Nas continued into her phone: 'Yes, I understand you told PC Grigg that Twitter and the other social media sites are blocked on your office computers?' Freddie stopped walking, her shoe squeaking to a halt on the rubberised floor.

Social media sites were blocked on Sophie's office computers? With no smartphone, no Internet access at home and none in the office, how the hell did Sophie tweet about her cat or message Hamlin in that chat room?

'Do you know if she had an iPad, a tablet of some sort, something she could have left at work?' Nasreen was saying. 'Sophie posted a number of things online, and we'd just like to know from where and when – to help us build up a picture of her last few days.' Nasreen paused about a metre in front of Freddie. As she spoke she gestured with her free hand and nodded and shook her head as if Mrs Crabtree were in front of her. 'I see. Yes. Thank you. That's very helpful. If you remember anything else you think might be relevant, anything out of character, anything Sophie might have been upset about, anything at all, please give me a call.' Nasreen hung up.

'Social media sites are blocked on her office computers?' Freddie said.

'I wondered,' said Nas, still staring at her phone. 'She worked for the local council; public services often ban Twitter and that from their computers. Like they do here.'

'So, did she have a tablet?' Freddie's mind was trying to connect the dots. The chat room messages Mark Hamlin sent to Sophie could be traced to the laptop found at his flat. The IP address of the messages sent from Sophie were traced to Leighton Buzzard, but as of yet they hadn't found the device.

'No,' said Nas. She started to walk again, Freddie kept stride. 'And more than that, Mrs Crabtree said Sophie was anti-social media.'

'What – that makes no sense?'

'Apparently she said more than once that she didn't trust sites like Facebook.' Nas was looking ahead, her forehead scrunched in thought.

'Why would she say that to her friend and then join Twitter? Were they close, Sophie and this woman? I suppose she could've changed her mind. My mum was well reluctant to join Twitter.'

'Your mum's on Twitter?' Nas stared at her. 'I can't imagine your mum doing that. Remember when we tried to teach her to email?'

Freddie laughed. They'd spent a whole afternoon during one Easter holiday eating chocolate eggs and trying to explain that email addresses weren't case-sensitive to her mum. 'God, when was that?'

'We must've been, what, eleven?' Nasreen smiled.

'Yeah, everything she sent was in capitals. Do you remember?' Freddie thought of how she and Nas threw screwed up foil wrappers at each other behind her mum's back. They were in the lounge, all sat on the tan sofa, her mum squinting through her glasses at the laptop screen in front of her.

'Yes! It was like she was permanently shouting at us!' Nas steadied herself on Freddie's arm as she laughed.

Freddie felt the contact like electricity. Should she pull her in for a hug? Place her hand over hers? She looked at Nas's warm open face.

'It can't have been long after we started at Pendrick High.' Nas stopped laughing. She let go of Freddie's arm. An empty feeling washed over Freddie. She wondered for a moment if she'd imagined it. That warmth. That connection. Somehow willed it into being. They walked in silence.

As they neared the incident room, Freddie heard the noise. Too many voices could be heard. 'What's happened?'

Nasreen's face had now hardened into that of the purposeful grown woman. They could hear Moast shouting. 'What the fuck? How did you manage to lose him? He's been out for what, twenty fucking minutes?'

Freddie let Nasreen go in first, a deep unease gathering in her stomach. 'Cudmore!' Moast threw the papers in his hand up into the air. 'Have a nice breakfast?' Tibbsy looked pale behind him.

'Sir,' said Nas. Her hands dangling at her side, fingers flexing: ready.

'Great! 'Cause I've got some great news. Fucking constable Slade managed to lose Hamlin.' Moast slammed his hand down onto the desk, shaking the paper on it and the people around him. 'Twenty minutes. Twenty fucking minutes and he shakes him. Our prime fucking suspect. I want all teams out looking for him. I want to know everything we've got on him. Where he goes. Where he gets money from. Any known accomplices. Where he gets his drugs from. Do any of his doctors know where he is? I don't give a fuck about confidentiality. Get a warrant. Get onto the Superintendent. I want this fucker traced.'

Freddie steadied herself against the door frame. How could they lose him? How could a person just disappear? And then she thought of laughing Sophie Phillips on the front of the newspaper. She disappeared. She vanished.

'Where did they lose him?' Nas was asking.

The phone in the pocket of Freddie's denim shorts vibrated against the wood of the door frame.

Nasreen spun to look at her. 'That's him, isn't it?' Freddie squeezed it from her jeans. 'What does it say?' Nas fired at her. Moast and Tibbsy hovering over her shoulders, like a scowling Greek chorus.

Freddie blinked and looked at the screen. 'Apollyon says: stay tuned there's more to come folks!'

'Ha!' Tibbsy ran his hand back through his limp hair, the other resting on his hip.

A terrible thought formed in Freddie's mind. Where once her brain was wired to filter the news, the headlines, television shows, trends, fads, waves of interest, into the essence of the zeitgeist, into a pitch, now it pulled together the threads of Sophie and Mardling's story. The front pages, the online jokes, the photos, the hashtags, the foreboding clues. 'It's the first time he's tweeted since he said, "Here's Johnny!"' Tibbsy was shaking his head, looking away, but Moast and Nas had her locked. She saw it register on their faces. Freddie forced the words out: 'Apollyon didn't tweet all the while Mark Hamlin was detained.' *They'd had the Hashtag Murderer and they'd let him slip through their fingers.*

'Go back over all known Internet communication from Hamlin,' Moast said. 'I want it cross-referenced with everything that's been tweeted by Apollyon. Cudmore, get onto the IT lads. Get them to look again at Mardling's, Phillips', and Hamlin's devices. If there is anything they have missed, I want to know about it. Get them to try and trace Apollyon again. He's got to trip up sooner or later.' Freddie watched as Moast turned his face away from the room and ground his palms into his eye sockets. 'Everyone makes mistakes,' he said. Freddie couldn't tell if he was talking to himself or the rest of them.

She let her eyes drop to her phone and watched as Apollyon's latest message spread. Retweeted across Twitter. Reproduced on Facebook. Quoted on newspaper sites. Dissected on blogs. Another clump of tweets uploaded. She sat down at a free chair and pulled her charger from her bag, automatically connecting her phone. Keeping the battery going. Keeping the story alive. Around her the room pulsated with energy.

She borrowed a laptop from a nearby desk and started to research Mark Hamlin. He'd attended a grammar school in Kent. Then gone on to Bristol University. There was a piece he'd written for the university's student newspaper on ornithology, the face of the man Freddie had seen pulled from the tower block – young, plump, healthy – in his byline photo. His name cropped up on a few birdwatching blogs. An obituary for his late father, Rupert Hamlin, in the *Kent Messenger*, mentioned he was survived by his wife Lillian, and son Mark. Another life before his current desolate one. Blips started to appear. Recorded episodes of mental unrest. A university log of a complaint from a room mate. A research paper by a psychiatrist at Bristol Royal Infirmary contained a reference to an M. Hamlin, but she could only see the Google search result and couldn't find the correct paragraph in the verbose PDF file. A touching blog by a local birdwatching charity talked of a Lillian Hamlin who had been struck down by Alzheimer's. Freddie caught snatches of information being fed back around her.

'He was registered as living with his mother, a Mrs Lillian Hamlin,' said Jamie. 'Until he was in his twenties, sir.'

As Lillian Hamlin faded so had Mark's apparent last connection with reality. Somewhere in the last ten years he'd vanished from the system. With one ear on what was going on around her, Freddie scanned her Twitter timeline: a pattern was emerging. 'Er…DCI?' *What was she supposed to call him?* Definitely not sir. *Never sir.*

'What?' Moast looked up from the papers he had spread over his desk, something close to fear on his face.

'I think there's a Twitter-storm brewing.' Her eyes flickered over the tweets.

'A what?' Nasreen was sat behind her; Freddie hadn't noticed her there.

230

'It's like a reaction. A mob. They're responding to Sophie's death, or the photo of her.' Freddie's updates were coming so quickly she could barely read them before the screen refreshed. Freddie began to read the messages aloud: 'Dan The Man says, "This is not funny anymore @Apollyon. This is fucked up." Cary Frome says, "This is outrageous. Shut 'Apollyon' down." Colin Banks says, "Stop tweeting about A******n you're just giving him what he wants."'

'Who are these people?' Tibbsy was at Moast's shoulder, his face sagged like he couldn't hold it up anymore.

'I don't know,' said Freddie. 'Just people online, but it's gathering pace. They're sharing the photo of Sophie.' Her generous smile spilled like sunlit raindrops over her timeline. 'Gerry Hedel says: "What the hell is this?! This girl's been murdered." He's hashtagged it: For Sophie.' #ForSophie trickled through Freddie's timeline, first the odd drip, then a torrent. 'Someone called Justified Amy has set up a Change petition online calling for @Apollyon to be blocked from Twitter.' Freddie's screen was painfully slow updating... moving between the two. 'There's already a few thousand signatures on there. They're suggesting people report him for spam.'

'What does that mean?' Moast said.

'If enough people do it, Twitter are likely to suspend the account. I think it's based on a logarithm or something. Like an automatic default.' Freddie's screen flickered. *Tweets cannot load right now.* 'Bugger, I've lost signal.'

Moast twisted the other way. 'Tibbsy, get on the phone to press liaison. I want a statement out there right now telling people not to report the account.'

Freddie held her phone up, switched airplane mode on and off. 'The system must be overloaded. Got it! Shit. Paige Klinger's tweeted!'

'Has she?' Moast sounded surprised.

'What's she said?' Nasreen pushed her chair back, joining Moast in hovering above her.

'She says: "#RIP @SophieCat111. @Apollyon go fuck yourself."'

'Punchy,' said Nas.

231

'No.' Freddie exhaled. Blinked. 'She's tweeted the link to the petition. She's hashtagged it "For Sophie". She's asked them all to report Apollyon. It's going crazy. It's going viral.'

'Jackie, this is Sergeant Tibbsy, I need to get a message onto our Twitter account urgently,' Tibbsy was saying into his phone.

'I've lost signal, again.' Freddie's fingers flickered over her phone. *Come on.* 'Get out my way, you might be blocking it.' She stood and raised her phone up.

'Someone get me Twitter on a laptop right now?' Moast shouted.

'The station server must be down. I can't get Wi-Fi.' Nas had her phone out.

Freddie closed Wi-Fi. The tiny 3G symbol appeared on her phone. 'Got it!'

She slid between screens. 'It's up! @JubileePolice has tweeted: "Pls do not report @Apollyon. It's part of an ongoing police investigation. If you have concerns, contact your local station on 101."'

'The guys on the switchboards are going to love that,' Tibbsy said

Freddie felt her shoulders drop. 'It's not working.' *Twitter was responding as she would have just last week.* 'They don't trust you guys.'

'Now what?' Moast pulled Nas's phone toward him.

'I can't see it,' said Nas.

Stupid idiots. 'They're saying things like: "Oh yeah coz you're all over it @JubileePolice? #ForSophie (David Frome @DavidBigBae). Erm, and: "We got to sort this shit. Pigs doing nothing. Let's take this mo fo down. #ForSophie" (Big Girlz @BigGirrrl).'

'Great!' Moast threw his hands in the air.

Freddie tapped between streams. 'It's trending: #ForSophie.' She clicked on the first message that mentioned @Apollyon, clicking on the link. 'Shit. It's gone. "This user is currently unavailable." Fuck. Guys, Twitter have taken it down. Apollyon's been suspended.'

'Slower, Freddie,' Nas placed a hand on her arm, looked directly at her eyes. 'What does that mean – suspended?'

Freddie swallowed. 'It means they can't tweet. We can't see Apollyon's account or their tweets.'

'Our only lead.' Moast collapsed onto a chair and kicked the desk leg in front of him. 'I want a photo of Hamlin circulated to all units. We need eyes on him.'

Freddie stared at her phone. As tweeters celebrated suspending @Apollyon's account. As if erasing him from Twitter erased him from the world. Just because you couldn't see him, didn't mean he wasn't there. There, or where? In the space of an hour they'd lost sight of both Hamlin and Apollyon. Or maybe just one person: the Hashtag Murderer. Moast's elbows rested on his knees, his head in his hands. Tibbsy was pacing. Freddie looked to Nas. For the first time since she'd walked back into her life after eight years, Freddie saw panic in Nasreen's eyes.

Chapter 29

C&B – Crash and Burn

11:30
Thursday 5 November
Account Suspended

Freddie had gone for a walk under the pretence of getting some air. She'd watched as Moast, Tibbsy, Nas and the team went into lockdown. Everyone was head down, working. Searching. Hunting. Looking for anything that would lead them to Apollyon. It all spun round her head. Was it a coincidence that Paige Klinger had cropped up again, her tweet arguably leading to the suspension of the Apollyon account? She had a beef with Mardling, but nothing that they could ascertain with poor quiet Sophie Phillips. She'd paced up and down the parade of shops that flanked the 1970s monstrosity that was Jubilee police station. But the clutter and sounds of London, which had always soothed her in the past, offered no relief now.

With the pile of coins and his timely disappearance, Hamlin *could* be Apollyon. But Freddie couldn't shake the image of the petrified frail man she'd seen forcibly arrested. Could that person be the same one who'd slashed Mardling and closed his hands round Sophie's neck? Their dead faces looked at Freddie accusingly. She heard the voices of all those who'd ever taunted her online. *What gives you the right to comment on this? Call yourself a journalist: my three-year-old could do this. Who is Freddie Venton and why should I care what she thinks? Stupid whore. Idiot slut.*

This wasn't helping anything. She pushed back into the warmth of the station, squeezing a half-smile for the fat Duty Sergeant who'd processed her when she'd been arrested. He released the door for her. *Process.* That word again. They were obsessed with it. It had got them about as far as her instinct had.

The incident room was unnervingly quiet. Half-empty as calls were made, house calls, follow-ups, favours, forensics. All process. She sat back down at an empty computer. There must be something she was missing. Again she typed in Mark Hamlin. Then added Bristol. Then Kent to his name. The mention of Sevenoaks Grammar School caught her eye. She clicked through to a page that announced it was the password-protected records of Sevenoaks Grammar School, available for ex-students and teachers to view. She clicked password and typed: Password. Worth a try. *Password incorrect.* She tried again: Password1. *Password incorrect.* Come on, think, Freddie. She typed: 7evenoaks. Bingo! The file directory opened. She typed in Mark Hamlin. Mark Hamlin: Year 1 to 7 appeared. She opened it. The first years were very standard and sweet: 'Mark plays well with others in class.' 'Mark is good at sharing.' But then they shifted. 'Despite being diagnosed with dyspraxia, Mark has sought to remain a hard-working and happy boy.' Freddie looked up and waved at Nas. 'Look at this.' She beckoned her over.

Nas read over her shoulder. 'How'd you get into this? On second thoughts, don't tell me,' she said. 'Google dyspraxia.'

Freddie pulled up the first result, running her finger under the text: *Children with dyspraxia may present with difficulties with self-care.* 'Well that fits, think of the state of Hamlin and his flat,' she said.

'What else does it say?' Freddie continued running her finger under the text. *Children with dyspraxia may also present with difficulties with typing and writing. These difficulties may continue into adulthood.*

'Wait.' Freddie's fingers flew over the keyboard. 'Let me Google that.' She typed in: Mark Hamlin Dyspraxia Bristol Uni, and scanned the results. 'There, look.' She clicked through to a student newspaper article about a yearly Summersby Prize:

Shortlisted Mark Hamlin, a gifted student and sufferer of dyspraxia, wished to make a special note of thanks to Leonie Parsons, his full-time Learning Support Officer, who types up Mark's research and assignments.

'Could someone who was that dyspractic have typed up those clues?' Freddie said.

'I'm not sure, but I'm thinking there's a strong chance the answer is no.' Nasreen leant forward and read the computer screen again.

'But that would mean Hamlin isn't the Hashtag Murderer?' Freddie said.

'Possibly. It's not conclusive proof, but a reasonable doubt,' said Nasreen.

'You've got to tell Moast.' Freddie gripped her arm. 'Seriously, Nas, if this is right then we're looking in the wrong place.'

'We need more. Could we, I don't know, search Twitter for any mentions of Mark Hamlin. I don't know what we're looking for, but maybe something will pop?'

Freddie didn't want to break it to her that she'd already done that. *Yesterday*. Before they'd even got to the Shadwell estate. There was nothing on Mark Hamlin; just some guy in Ohio who'd tweeted once in 2006. 'Sure.' No harm trying again. So far Twitter was the only thing that had turned up solid leads.

The white Twitter bird paused and then lunged toward her, opening up into the white background of her account. The photo

236

caught her like a left hook. That all too familiar photo of Mardling's dead body. Apollyon's profile picture. But it wasn't Apollyon. Couldn't be, the account was suspended. A yelp escaped her mouth; she clamped her hand over it.

'What's wrong?' Nasreen's hands steadied her as she rocked back in her chair.

'He's back,' her voice came out loud.

Moast looked up. Tibbsy turned.

'@Apollyon?' Nas said.

Freddie stared at the profile picture, the words 'guess who's back?' *A new account. A replacement.* 'No. @Apollyon2.'

'Is it them?' Moast was coming toward them.

'Could be an impersonator?' said Nas.

Tibbsy was grabbing his phone. How many of the police force were now on Twitter?

'Same photo. Same bio. Same name. Almost. Could be Apollyon. Looks like it.' Freddie watched as @Apollyon2's tweet spread through Twitter.

'What have they said?' Moast asked.

'Just: "guess who's back?"' *Did it mean anything?* thought Freddie.

'Is it a clue?' Nas said.

'I…I don't know.' Freddie scrolled through the replies. Other Twitter users were asking the same question. *Guessing. Is 'back' a place? Perhaps it's to do with a chiropractor?* 'Could be. I'm not sure.'

'Tibbsy, get onto IT, get them to get a trace on this new account,' Moast said. Tibbsy disappeared out of the room.

Freddie set her phone to vibrate if Apollyon2 tweeted. Maybe it wasn't the real Hashtag Murderer? It could be a spoof account. A tasteless joke. Her mobile vibrated.

Apollyon2 had posted an Instagram photo. Freddie opened the image: a close-up of a pair of young blue eyes, wide with fear, the edge of tape could just be seen cutting into the skin over the mouth. Freddie dropped her phone.

'What is it? Show me.' Moast grabbed it from the floor.

Freddie was shaking. She couldn't get her words out. Couldn't get enough air.

'Jesus Christ!' Moast said.

'What is it, guv?' Nas rested her hand on Freddie's shoulder.

Freddie watched as all the colour drained from Moast's face. Silently he turned the phone toward them. The terrified eyes peered out at them. *Mayfair filter*.

Freddie felt Nas's grip tighten on her shoulder. 'She can only be, what, thirteen?' Nas said.

Barely a teen. An innocent. Almost the same age as she and Nas had been when it had all gone wrong. 'Is she alive?' The words gushed out of Freddie.

'When the photo was taken, yes,' said Moast.

None of them wanted to acknowledge the implication in his words. *When the photo was taken*. Was the young girl alive now? Only @Apollyon2 could answer that.

'Guv!' Tibbsy flung open the incident room. His mobile in his hand. 'We've got the bastard.'

Moast and Nas turned. Freddie gaped at him.

'IT have got him. The bastard slipped up. The metadata on the Instagram shot is still live. We've got his coordinates. We've got him.'

Nas was already halfway into her jacket. 'Where?'

'Welsh border. Near a small village: Abbey Dore.'

'What is he doing there?' Freddie said.

'Get onto the local force, tell them to stand by. Cudmore, radio in a call for the helicopter. You, me, Tibbsy and Venton are going. I want you there in case he tweets again,' Moast said to Freddie. 'You can watch the account in real time. I'll clear it with Gray. Good work, team.'

Freddie's stomach flipped. Helicopter?

'The Welsh border,' Nas was saying. 'It can't be Hamlin: he'd never have made it up there in time.'

Helicopter. Why wasn't Nas helping her? Aviophobic. A.V.I.O.P.H.O.B.I.C. Freddie's stomach contracted, threatening to fold her in half. *Always travel by train. Or boat. So much better for the environment. Too broke to go abroad.* The cheerful voice she'd used to get out of flying in the past wasn't going to wash now. The last time she'd flown it had been on a big plane. Huge. It'd had still taken three gins and a Valium her uni mate had brought back from India. Now there was no Valium. No gin. No large sturdy aircraft.

'Come on, Freddie.' Nas placed a hand on her back, shoving her forward.

Did she not remember?

Jamie drove them at speed, blue lights flashing, to the airfield. 'You'll like this, Freddie. The Met's helicopters have their own Twitter account,' he was saying. 'Over 100,000 followers.'

'Any more tweets?' Nas asked.

Freddie shook her head dumbly. She was doing this for the young girl. Those haunted blue eyes. They had to get there in time. *Had to.* She could see Moast's face set, determined, reflected in the windscreen. Did he think they were already too late?

Tibbsy, shifting in his seat, seemed to be fighting his earlier beaten posture. He was relentlessly upbeat, but she couldn't tell for whose benefit. 'All the pilots are ex-military. No need to be nervous! We'll be in good hands,' he said.

Freddie closed her hands tight round her phone. No more tweets must be a good sign, right? Unless they were busy…doing…She let the thought go. Flipped her attention back to the impending flight. Had Nas really forgotten? But then they'd never flown together. Too young for that kind of holiday before they'd been split up. This was just like her: so focused it never crossed her mind that someone else might be weaker. The car drove out onto the airstrip; she could see it. Blue and yellow, like an angry bee, its blades sharp, like knives turning.

'The mountain force have closed the signal in on a deserted farmhouse. We'll be able to get pretty close, and then do the last bit in an unmarked vehicle so as not to alert them.' Moast twisted back to them.

'I'm frightened,' she managed.

'Nothing to worry about, Venters. We've got the bastard now,' Tibbsy said. She followed him out. The downdraught whipping her hair up and away from her face. She could do this.

'Let's just hope we get there in time.' Nas was at her side.

Think of the girl. You must save the girl. Moast's hair and jacket flapped back as he leant toward the helicopter, 'Ready?' He turned back.

The other two nodded, and Freddie's feet carried her, bending into the wind and noise. Toward the helicopter. Toward Wales. Toward Apollyon.

Chapter 30

TBC – To Be Continued

16:30
Thursday 5 November
2 FOLLOWING   17,002 FOLLOWERS

Freddie was aware of a low hum. A whine. Where was it coming from? She looked around in panic. She, Nas and Tibbsy were strapped into the back. Moast was next to the helmeted pilot, up front. The nose dipped forwards. She grabbed Nasreen's hand. Nas flinched. She was saying something. She couldn't hear it. This was it. She gripped Nas's hand tighter. Closed her eyes. The helicopter hovered into the air. Oh my God. Then she realised the noise was coming from her. The low guttural moan was fear. She clamped her mouth shut. Then opened it again so she could pant furiously as if she were going to give birth. London was a blur below. The suburbs like a child's road rug rolled beneath them. Don't look down. She clamped her eyes shut. *Think of the girl.* They *must* save the girl. She thought of that smooth soft-looking skin, the crinkle-free eyes. They must save the child.

Freddie was still trembling when the helicopter landed on farm-land near where the phone signal had been traced. 'Sorry,' she mumbled to Nas. Her legs shaky as she followed Tibbsy out the door. The blades slowing overhead. Freddie's feet hit the grass mounds and she fell to her hands and knees, gripping great big handfuls of earth.

'You all right?' Nas dropped beside her. One hand on her back, the other brushing Freddie's hair away from her face. Freddie missed the feel of her. Sitting under a duvet on the sofa watching films. Falling against each other in fits of giggles. Hugs hello and goodbye. 'Still not keen on flying, then?' Nas said.

She *did* remember. Freddie nodded. 'I'm okay. We're here for a reason.' Nas helped her up and they joined Moast and Tibbsy who were talking to the barrel-chested local copper who was waiting for them next to an unmarked Land Rover. As the helicopter lights dimmed behind them, Freddie realised there were no street lights. Nothing for miles. She traced the dark outlines of mountains, looked up to see a pregnant moon hovering low in the sky. She held her hand in front of her. A grey lunar outline hugged each of her fingers. They were going in under cover of darkness.

'PC Gwillim, this is Sergeant Cudmore and Miss Venton, an adviser who's working on this case with us.' Freddie waved her glowing hand as Moast signalled at her. 'Miss Venton will be staying in the car with you.'

'We'll be wearing cameras. These are two-way mics so you'll be able to hear us and vice versa.' Tibbsy was handing out stab vests, and what looked like riot helmets.

'You boys got some good kit down in London, eh, sir?' said PC Gwillim, holding Moast's coat while the DCI pulled his stab vest on and fastened it.

'We'll ask that you and Freddie restrict communication to that which is necessary when we're in there,' Tibbsy added. He nodded at Freddie, his hair glowing by the tracing moonlight. 'Let us know if anything comes up on Twitter, Freddie. That we need to know about, yeah?'

Freddie looked at her phone, the backlit screen instantly stunning her eyes and plunging everything around it and her into soupy black. There was signal. *It was a miracle.* 'Yes, Tibbsy,' she said, holding the phone against her chest to block the glow. Her eyes adjusted and their figures, edged in silvery moonlight, came into view again.

'We've got two boys down there, sir,' PC Gwillim said as they walked to the Land Rover. 'They think there's two people inside: the suspect and the girl. The cottage belongs to the Kemble Farm. It's been uninhabited these last two generations. Just a stone shell now. It's pretty remote and you can't see it from any road. No power or water.' Freddie's trainers slipped and twisted between clumps of long clingy grass, the leaves sharp like paper cuts through her socks.

'Soz to ask a stupid question, but where are we?' The helicopter had left Freddie disorientated.

'Black Mountains, love,' said PC Gwillim. He wasn't much taller than her. 'Golden Valley to be precise. Hereford's about 45 that way, Abergavenny 45 that.'

Did he mean miles or minutes? Or something else? Did they use the metric system in Wales? 'It can't be Hamlin then, he'd never have made it up here in time,' Freddie said. 'I doubt he's got a helicopter at his disposal.'

'The pile of coins at Sophie Phillips' flat and that online rant at her seem like more than a coincidence,' said Tibbsy as he zipped up his jacket. 'Besides, Apollyon went quiet while we had Hamlin in custody, and then he started tweeting again when he was released.'

'Paige Klinger feasibly might have access to a helicopter,' said Nas. 'She's got motive for Mardling.'

'They could have teamed up?' Tibbsy suggested.

'How would they have met? I can't imagine Hamlin hanging out with Paige's fashion crowd,' said Freddie. None of this made sense.

'We could be looking at an accomplice,' said Moast. 'Someone who is working with the killer.'

Freddie shivered. Could there really be more than one person doing this?

243

'Any signs of trouble?' Moast turned to PC Gwillim. 'Any idea who the girl might be?'

'No reports of anyone missing up here, sir.' PC Gwillim opened the Land Rover back door. Freddie steadied her hand against the roof of the car and pulled herself up and in. A dim overhead light gave a gentle yellow wash to the vehicle. It smelt of dogs.

'He could have brought the vic with him, sir,' Nas said, following her in.

'We know he's travelled before.' The car rocked as Tibbsy climbed in. The front doors opened and PC Gwillim and Moast pulled the doors behind them. Freddie fastened her seatbelt.

'Any sign of transport at the scene, PC?' Moast asked.

PC Gwillim started the car, the lights dipped, he rested his hand on Moast's seat back, looked past them and reversed. 'Nothing that we've seen, sir. You'd need a car to get up here. No trains, laddie. I'll turn the lights off when we get close.'

The car rocked as they reversed. Freddie saw the crests of grass rise and fall in the dipped headlights, then they were on a road, mountains fanned away from them, bordering the view, the sky so big she felt they were floating beneath it. Tiny. Obscure. No one would find you up here. No one would hear you scream.

Her phone vibrated. 'Another one; he's tweeted,' she said.

'What does it say?' Moast asked, their voices loud against the expanse of nothing sky.

Freddie reminded herself this was why she was here. To alert them. To bear witness. To save the girl. 'It's another photo,' her voice quivered as she clicked to view the Instagram.

The car turned off the road onto a bumpy track, trees snagged at the car as it rocked over the uneven ground. 'It's down here, sir. I'll kill the lights. Best to go the last bit by foot,' PC Gwillim said.

'What is it, Freddie?' Tibbsy asked.

'It's loading. I don't have great signal.' Freddie half didn't want the image to open.

They sat in the silent car. Freddie could hear them all breathing.

Imagined what they were all thinking. The photo opened. She shored up her shaking hand with her other.

'Christ,' Nas said, peering over her shoulder.

'What is it?' Moast twisted round, leant back between the front seats.

Freddie couldn't turn the phone. Couldn't get the words to form. Couldn't move. She was locked on it like a buffering screen. A sepia Instagram showed an array of knives, pliers, claw hammers and rusty bolt cutters neatly lined up on what looked like a table. The shot was angled so in the background you could see the back of a young girl sat on a chair, her arms bound behind her, her head lolled forward. *Cut, pull, smash, snip. Were they too late?*

Chapter 31

JK – Just Kidding

18:47
Thursday 5 November
2 FOLLOWING   30,438 FOLLOWERS

Freddie stood next to the car as Moast instructed the team in whispers. 'Cudmore and I will go in, Tibbsy and you guys man the three exits to the building.'

Freddie shivered; was it cold or fear? She didn't like being outside of London at the best of times, it reminded her of Pendrick. Of what she'd left behind.

'Constable Gwillim, you and Miss Venton stay by the car. As we're aware, there are two people inside. One unknown vic: an apparent young Caucasian girl, approximately thirteen years of age. Name unknown. And the unknown perpetrator calling himself Apollyon,' Tibbsy said.

'There's been no screams or sounds of distress heard since we've been staked out here,' said PC Gwillim.

'The perpetrator has a history of sedating victims with roofies,' Nas said.

Freddie thought of Sophie Phillips lying unconscious while the killer loomed over her. For a moment nobody said anything. Trees rustled behind them, something she hoped was an owl screeched. She took a step closer to Nas. She felt like she'd lost all her bravado.

'We have the advantage: he doesn't know we're here.' Moast spoke in a hushed tone. 'Let's go in clean and quiet, and get this sorted quickly. Cudmore and I will take the perp, hopefully with minimal force.'

A twig snapped under Freddie's foot and she jumped. It took everything she had not to cry out.

Moast continued, 'Tibbsy, be ready to retrieve the victim. Gwillim, you guys have got the air ambulance on standby, you said?'

'Sir.' The dark shadow of Gwillim nodded.

'Okay. Quiet, calm, clean. Let's keep this contained.' Moast signalled with his hands for them to take their places.

Freddie climbed as noiselessly as possible back into the car. Gwillim followed, slowly and carefully closing the door after him. He sat next to her in the dark as they watched the disappearing shadows of Moast and Nas creep toward the stone farmhouse. She could smell the cigarettes Gwillim had been smoking. She really wanted a bloody fag right now. Gwillim turned on the small black and white screen. The live video feed from Moast showed his feet walking over the stony mud path.

Gwillim silently held out a headphone for her. They wore one each. Freddie watched as the rough stone-built cottage, half its roof gaping like broken wooden teeth screaming at the sky, swallowed up the shadows of Moast and Nas.

Moast's grainy black and white video feed showed they had reached the back door. Peering inside, the camera took a moment to focus. The remains of a table and chairs. A fireplace. The camera panned round, taking in plants and limbs of trees that had punctured walls and the floor, clawing back what had once been a kitchen to the wild natural land. How did people live up here? It was so dark. So hidden. She bet you couldn't get sushi.

The camera settled on a sturdy wooden door, under which the sickeningly familiar blue glow of tech could be seen through the splinted wooden planks. The camera moved toward it, flicking down as Moast's feet traversed the uneven stone floor. He caught a piece of wood – part of a bucket? There was a scrape. The camera froze. They could see it pitch up and down as Moast breathed hard, obviously trying to calm himself. Freddie caught sight of Nas, moving silently and quickly in front of Moast, standing ready to the side of the door. Freddie fought the urge to scream: *Get out! Run!* Behind the door was the victim, and the torture tools, and the man who'd slashed through Mardling's body, turning it to meat, the man who'd squeezed the life out of Sophie Phillips like she was ripe fruit. Freddie grabbed hold of PC Gwillim's arm. She could feel him shaking.

There was a sound. Movement. Moast froze, the camera not turning from the door.

'Who's there?' A muffled voice, barely picked up by the mic. *They knew they were there.*

The camera suddenly swerved, Moast took two strides to be alongside Nas; his voice came loud into Freddie's ear: 'This is the police. The property is surrounded. Come out with your hands up.'

Silence.

Freddie looked at Gwillim, his gaze fixed on the screen. The door swung toward the camera. There was a flash of light and the camera feed went white. A girl was screaming in Freddie's ear, in her head, coming from the cottage, filling up the silence. She looked up as the shadows of Tibbsy and the two local cops dashed toward the cottage. PC Gwillim wrenched open the car door and jumped down.

'Stop! Don't shoot!' Freddie heard Nas shout.

Someone ran at the camera. The camera – Moast – fell to the ground. A gunshot rang out. Echoed. Unmistakable. Birds flew up from quaking trees and bushes. Fear ripped through Freddie. She was out of the car. Pulling her headphone out. Wings beat. 'It's Nas, she's been shot!' she screamed.

PC Gwillim was sprinting toward the cottage: 'All units assist, assist!' he screamed into his radio. 'Code zero. Officer down, officer down.'

Freddie's breath hammered out of her. She heard the crackle of static. Voices. Shouts. Screaming. A woman was screaming. *Nas? Please, no.* The two cops round the front of the house vaulted what was left of the wall. *Don't leave me.* Freddie's foot slipped on the wet mud, plunging her knees and hands down. A stone gouged her palm. *Stupid trainers. Stupid urban girl.* Her heartbeat ricocheted round her ears. She forced herself back up. Running. Panting. Jumping. She had to get to Nas. She couldn't be…Had to reach her before she…She had to say sorry. Had to tell her it was all her fault. *Don't leave me.*

PC Gwillim disappeared through the door, into the kitchen. Freddie's breaths were machine gun puffs of condensation in front of her. The blood of Mardling coated her vision. The memory of the torture tools cut her. Her hand throbbed. Her heart ached. *Don't leave me.* Every molecule of her body ran toward Nas. She followed Gwillim. The chairs, the table, the fireplace…there it was: the door, the noise. Commotion.

'Get down! Down on the ground, hands up!' Tibbsy was shouting.

'Holy Mother of Mary!' Gwillim said.

Freddie ran forwards. The moon disappeared behind a cloud. There were shapes. Someone was on the floor. A torch shone in her eyes. Glinted off her glasses. She held her hands up. There was sobbing. *Please, God, please.*

The torch was coming from Moast's helmet. He was crouched down, leaning over someone. *Nas! Oh my God, no. Please, no. She can't be gone. Can't be.* Freddie ran forwards, pulled at his shoulder. His arm shot toward her face. 'What the fuck, Venton!' His light flicked in her eyes: blinded. Freddie lost her balance, stumbled, landed on her arse, her hand bent the wrong way. Agony. Her body shaking with terror. *She couldn't lose her. Not now.* Not after they'd found each other again. She tried to blink the blue dots of light

249

from the torch from her eyes. In the pool of Moast's light, resting under his large hand, was a young girl, no more than thirteen years old, her wrists handcuffed behind her back.

'Freddie!' She looked up at the voice. A strong silhouette, carved from the torchlight. Legs hip-width apart, feet firmly on the ground, the arc of her hip, hair pulled back from her cheekbones. Nas. *Alive.*

'I…I…thought you'd been shot. I thought you were…' Freddie let the words fall away as relief engulfed her. A tear collapsed from her blinking eyes. *Thank you. Thank you. Thank you.*

'Venton, Christ, what are you playing at?' Moast kept his knee and hand on the back of the girl on the floor. Lying as if it had been kicked across the floor, Freddie saw a rifle. 'This is an active crime scene! I nearly took you out. Why are you incapable of staying in the bloody car?'

Torches flicked on, beams of light from Tibbsy and Gwillim. One of the cops, bent down and fiddling on the floor, managed to turn on a small portable blue plastic lantern that was there. The room glowed blue. Nas was helping another young girl, the child from the Instagram pictures. Same dress. The girl was crying. Were there two victims? Freddie tightened her hand around her jumper in front of her chest. Holding onto reality. 'I don't understand.'

'The property's secure, guv,' Tibbsy switched his torch off as the power-saving light bulb in the lantern warmed up. 'There's no one else here. Two pedal bikes out the back. Reckon that's how they got here.'

Freddie's gaze flicked from one to the other, returning again and again to Nas as if to reassure herself she was okay. She could feel every squeeze of her heart, jettisoning emotion round her body. Her mind unable to keep up. *She's alive, she's alive,* her heart beat.

'It was just a joke! We didn't mean any harm,' snivelled the pale ginger girl being half hugged, half held up by Nas.

'Get off me,' kicked the girl on the floor. 'You're violating my human rights! This is against the Geneva Convention!'

250

'Okay, we all need to calm down,' Nas said, looking at Freddie, then bending her head to the girl in her arms. 'What's your name, sweetheart?'

'Don't tell her, Mandy!' screamed the girl on the floor. 'Take the fifth!'

'That's in America, love. Not here.' Moast pulled off his helmet, wiping his brow. Freddie felt her own: soaked in sweat.

'Mandy,' Nas said quietly to the crying young girl. 'Short for Amanda?'

The girl sniffed and nodded. 'Amanda Rose. And that's Shell. Shellena Jones. Sorry, Shell.'

'Paul Jones' girl?' Gwillim sounded shocked.

Shell, who'd still been kicking, at that point grew limp on the floor. 'You muppet.' Mandy started snivelling again.

'He's a farmer. Jones. A mechanic,' Gwillim said. 'That where you got all of them torture tools from?'

'Yeah,' Mandy managed through her sobs. 'We were gonna give them back.'

'Well this is a fine mess isn't it?' Moast sat back on his heels. Freddie steadied herself against the rough cold floor. Her breath slowing, the situation coming into focus. These girls weren't Apollyon. They were hoaxers. A dedicated spoof. Which meant the Hashtag Murderer was still out there, while they were miles away chasing a dead-end lead in the Welsh mountains.

Chapter 32

TMI – Too Much Information

03:55
Friday 6 November
Account Suspended

Freddie came to. Her head was resting on someone's shoulder. Ajay? She slipped her hand round his soft coat. That wasn't right. She sat up. She was in a car. She'd been asleep, leaning against Nas, whose head lolled to the left, a faint vibration across her lips as she, too, slept. It all flooded back. The tweets. The photos. The helicopter. The gunshot. The fear. It thrummed through her.

She rubbed her eyes. Outside, the reassuringly tall, lit buildings of East London swam by in pools of orange street light. Tibbsy was driving; the car found, rented, borrowed – she didn't know. The young girls had to be interviewed. The helicopter had to return to London. She'd slept on a row of plastic seats in the tiny Airwick-fragranced police station in Hereford. They must have left about midnight. Moast stirred in the front passenger seat: a snail trail of drool had worked down his face. Tibbsy signalled. Turned. They pulled into the car park of the Jubilee Station, the lights on inside: the ever-ready Met. Her throat was dry. 'What time is it?' she croaked.

Moast groaned and rubbed his face with both hands. Nas started next to her; half a snore caught in her throat, turned into a cough, a swallow.

'Five to four,' said Tibbsy. 'I'm knackered.' He opened his door. A blast of cold air flooded into the car, slapping her in the face.

Freddie rubbed at her neck. Rolled her shoulders. Next to her, Nas was taking the coat she'd laid over herself and hanging it over her arm. Freddie opened the door, took a gulp of air. Now what? She'd have to get the night bus. 'I still don't understand why after all that they weren't charged.' Freddie slammed the door shut behind her.

'Well done on the drive, Tibbsy,' Moast said. 'I'll see if one of the PCs is around to drop us all home.'

'Cheers, guv.' Tibbsy stretched his arms up and back. 'I could do with a cuppa, anyone else?'

'Sounds good,' said Nas.

'Seriously, guys.' Freddie balled her hands up into her sleeves to protect them from the cold. 'Are we sure there's no link?' All that work, all that time, and for nothing.

'It was just a copycat, Freddie.' Nas shook her fingers through her long dark hair as she walked. 'They're just kids. They've been cautioned. We don't want them to end up with a criminal record because of some idiotic prank.'

How could she be so forgiving? All the times she'd had a go at her for wasting police time. All that self-righteous guff about jeopardising the case on that first night at Mardling's, and now Nas was all shoulder shrugs and *they're just kids!* Oh yeah, she was so forgiving when it wasn't Freddie screwing things up.

Freddie watched them walk to the back door, stamping pins and needles from their feet, blowing warm air on their hands, like they hadn't just wasted nearly a whole day chasing kids while a serial murderer was still out there. Waiting. 'Seriously, am I the only one who is fucked off by this?'

Nas had her hand on the back door to the station, her shoulders fell. 'These things happen, Freddie.'

Freddie hated her at that moment. A few hours ago she thought she'd been shot. Dead. Gone. All her love for Nas from when they were kids had detonated through her body. She wanted to hug her, scream that she was sorry. Sorry for everything she'd ever done wrong. But for perfect Nasreen Cudmore emotions were messy. Beneath her. She didn't look like she'd had no sleep, she looked like a fucking Disney Princess. A Disney Princess with her fucking two-up-two-down house that Freddie would never be able to afford. And her suits. Those tiny nipped waists. The smart black that never looked creased or had milk spilt on it. Those disappointed looks, the patronising half-sighs at silly little Freddie with her silly little ideas. 'Not all of us are happy to roll over when Moast tells us to,' Freddie said.

Tibbsy froze. Moast turned, his eyebrows raised.

'Leave it, Freddie. You don't understand how these things work,' Nas said, her voice unaffected. Calm.

Freddie tried to stop herself, but she felt the blistering heat of emotion. She looked at Nasreen; this was her fault. She'd opened her up to death and blood and tears and she didn't even care. 'Oh, yes, I forgot, perfect little Nasreen Cudmore never puts a foot wrong.'

'Venters, I think we're all a bit tired, mate,' said Tibbsy. Nasreen opened the door and stepped inside.

Oh no you don't. Freddie walked quickly after her. 'Don't you dare walk away from me, Nasreen Cudmore. You think you can do that again.' She grabbed at the door, jerking it back, stepping into the corridor of the station. A fucking police station. She should never have been here. If Nas had stuck up for her in the first place none of this would've happened.

Nas spun on her heel and looked straight at Freddie. 'It's been an emotional night, Freddie, I can understand you're a little over-tired…'

'Don't fucking patronise me. You know what I felt tonight when that gun went off? Terrified. I thought you were dead. Lost again. For good. It broke my heart. But you felt nothing. You felt nothing then and you feel nothing now.' She was aware of Tibbsy and Moast hesitating behind her.

'Don't Freddie,' said Nas.

'Don't…don't what? Talk about what you did?' Freddie's words hissed and crackled in the air.

'What I did?' Nas threw her hands in the air. 'What you did! I was a kid. I was fourteen. I hero-worshipped you, Freddie. I'd have done anything you said.'

'Oh yeah, blame me. Like you've always done. I saw it in your eyes that night at St Pancras. I was fourteen too. We were *both* kids.'

'Guys.' Tibbsy put a hand on her shoulder.

'Fuck off!' She shrugged him off and stepped toward Nasreen. 'You know all this changes nothing. All this perfect hair. Perfect policeman crap. We're as guilty as those Welsh girls. If not more so. Both of us. *You* are as guilty as me.'

'Ha! I love it. The great Freddie Venton, the girl who works in Espress-oh's and sleeps on a fucking sofa – that's right Jamie told me. We had a good laugh at that.' Nas's eyes blazed.

Freddie's cheeks burned. 'You…'

Nasreen stepped toward her and put her face right up to Freddie. She smelt of breath mints and coconut shampoo. She spoke so quietly Freddie was sure only she heard. 'You are the one who can't get over it, Freddie. You are the one who never faced up to what we did. I can sleep at night. I am happy with my life.' She turned and walked down the corridor. Walked away.

Moast whistled through his teeth. 'Wowee. Cat fight.'

'Freddie, they were just kids back there, one's parents are going through a divorce. No point giving them a criminal record,' Tibbsy was saying.

'Gemma Strofton.' Freddie kept Nasreen in her sights, detonated the bomb that had hung between them since that first night on Blackbird Road.

Nasreen froze mid-stride.

'Has the great, *happy with her life*, Nasreen Cudmore told you about Gemma Strofton?' Freddie was aware of people gathering in the background. Heads poked round doors to see what all the noise was about. Officers stopping en route from the canteen. An audience. She felt the power of her words. She wasn't frightened of Gemma anymore. 'Oh yes, Saint Nasreen Cudmore, Miss Goody Two Shoes suck-up…' Someone giggled. '…bullied Gemma Strofton. Tell them what Gemma did, Nasreen? To escape you! Tell them what you did!' she screamed.

'Enough.' Moast had her under her arm.

'Oww, stop.' She tried to shake him off.

Everyone started talking at once. 'What the hell?' 'Bullied?' 'What happened?' 'What did she say?' 'Gemma Strofton.'

The name reverberated through Freddie. She'd not *said* Gemma's name since then. Her mouth felt bruised.

'In here.' Moast shoved her toward the door of an interview room; she twisted. Caught sight of Jamie, his mouth open. Watery eyes wide.

'That's it! Show's over,' Tibbsy was calling.

Moast kicked at the door and pushed her through. He let go of her and leant back against it. *'Bloody women.'*

Freddie was shaking. She hugged her arms around herself, gripped her coat with her fingertips. 'I don't want to do this anymore. No more.'

'Okay,' Moast was saying. 'I'll speak to Gray. I'll get you taken home. I should have got you that counsellor.'

'I can't do this any longer. I quit.' Freddie's chest shook. Mardling. Phillips. Hamlin. Paige. Troll hunter. Apollyon. The Hashtag Murderer. The eyes in the Instagram. A terrified thirteen-year-old. *They were only kids.* Poor Gemma. Poor Nas. Poor her. The tears came. And Freddie Venton broke.

Chapter 33

B/C – Because

Eight years earlier

16:35
Monday 2 July

'Gem's just such a drama queen, you know?' Nas sat on Freddie's bed, bouncing her heels against her Fame Academy duvet.

'I know, what was that turn in maths? I mean who cries in double maths? Obviously we all hate it.' Freddie picked at the blue polish on her nail.

'I quite like maths actually,' Nas giggled, tugging at her ponytail.

Freddie rolled her eyes at her. She'd been friends with Nas and Gem since Infants, but recently they'd been really getting to her. They were so immature. 'Whatever. You and Gem can be geeks all your life. I'm getting out of this dump.'

'You're fourteen, Freddie,' Nas scoffed. 'You've got no money. Where you going to go?'

'I don't mean now. I mean soon. When school's done, I'm out of here. I'm going to London.' Freddie held her hand out as if she were admiring her nails. She'd heard her cousin say that about London. If she could get a proper grown-up job, she could earn enough to get a place so Mum could come and stay while Dad was bad. She felt guilty thinking of Dad like this, but he was getting worse. If she had money then maybe he wouldn't be so stressed. Maybe he wouldn't go out so much.

Nas stopped bouncing. Freddie felt her look at her, felt the warm glow of approval. 'My aunt took me to London last year,' Nas said. 'We went on the Underground – it's like a train underground.'

'I know what the Tube is.' Freddie scraped her hair off her face and peered in the old bathroom mirror that now lived in her room. The spot on her nose was getting worse. Stupid toothpaste: it didn't work.

'Yeah, but you've never been on it, have you?' Nas said triumphantly.

Freddie thought of the time dad had promised to take her last year. He'd never made it back from the pub. She'd sat on the doorstep until it grew dark. Waiting. Mum had come out with a hot chocolate for her. Telling her dad had obviously got stuck talking about work. She wanted so hard to believe her. It hurt to think about it. 'When I'm older I'm going to live in London and take the Tube every day.'

'Maybe I'll live in London too,' said Nas.

Freddie would love that. She and Nas living together like sisters. 'Unfortunately someone's got to stay here and look after Gem. She's not cool enough for a big city.' Freddie turned her head from side to side. Did she have a best side? They both looked pretty bad.

Nas's face appeared behind her. Waggling her glasses by scrunching up her nose. 'I don't think it's Gem's fault. Perhaps she's on her you know what.' Nas mouthed *period*.

Freddie felt her face flush. She hadn't started yet. Of course she'd told Nas and Gemma she had. She'd seen them whispering, passing sanitary towels to each other in the bathroom. Freddie had always been first. First to climb the monkey bars. First to go to the shops on her own. Always been the leader. Now suddenly she was lagging behind. What if they got a boyfriend first? Because they were women now and she was still a little girl. Would they even want to be friends anymore? She'd be alone. Her and mum while dad was out drinking. Waiting up till the early hours to hear him crash in through the front door. That was when the shouting would start. She couldn't bear for this to be it. 'I think we should teach Gemma a lesson.'

'What?' Nas picked up a lip gloss from next to the mirror. Freddie could smell her vanilla Impulse body spray.

'Teach her to toughen up a bit.' Freddie snatched it out of her hand. Nas looked doubtful. She needed to win her over. Needed to make sure she was on her side. She couldn't be left behind. 'Remember what she said to you yesterday about your ribs sticking out more than your tits?' Freddie knew how hurt Nas had been; she was painfully aware of her flat chest.

Nas winced. 'Well I guess that *was* a bit mean.'

'Right. She can't say things like that and expect us to hold her hand in maths class when she's crying all over the place. She can't have it both ways,' Freddie said.

'I guess not.' Nas hugged her knees to her chest.

'First, we won't call for Gem tomorrow on the way to school,' Freddie said.

'But she might be late for class?' Nas said.

'You've got to be cruel to be kind. It's like when you train a dog. Then we won't speak to her.' She was gathering steam now.

'At all?' asked Nas.

'For the rest of this week,' said Freddie. 'That'll teach her not to take us for granted.' Her mum always said that about Dad in the mornings, when she flung the curtains open and turned the radio up loud.

'Really?' said Nas.

'It'll be good for her,' Freddie adopted her mother's tone. 'Remind her of her priorities. And we should defriend her.' That'd show Gem. Remind her what she had.

'What?' Nas said.

'On Facebook. It'll be funny. We can write on her page and then she'll be all like *waaah! I can't write back!*' Freddie pulled a funny face and waved her hands manically round her head.

Nas laughed.

'She'll be all like *oh my God what's happening? Where's my friends?* And then next week we'll be like *boom! Only joking!* She'll be mega grateful. We'll poke her and send her a friend request, like next Tuesday.'

They were both giggling now. Freddie grabbed her laptop.

'What shall we say?' asked Nas.

'We're so over it drama queenie!' Freddie said as she typed.

'We can't!' Nas was screaming with laughter now.

'Let's post that picture of her where she's pretending to scream at Seth on The OC.'

'Oh my God! Perfect!' Nas giggled.

'And tag everyone from class!' Freddie said.

03:02
Monday 9 July

The telephone woke Freddie. It was dark. Was Dad out late again? No, she heard his voice. Then her mum's. What was going on? She rolled over. Closed her eyes. The hall light went on. Her door opened.

'Love, did you hear the phone? Are you awake?' Her mum was pulling her pink dressing gown around her.

Freddie swallowed. Was it Granny May? 'Yeah.'

'Love, I'm sorry but I need to tell you something. I'm going to put the light on.'

'Okay.' Freddie's eyes burned as the light bulb snapped on. Her room, the posters, her school kit hanging over her chair, the missing patch in the curtain where her hamster had got hold of it and chewed a fluff-edged hole.

Her mum came and sat on her bed. She ran her hand through Freddie's hair like she did when she was little.

'Freddie I'm so sorry, love. But Gemma's been…found…she… Well, she got hold of some of her mum's medicine. Cut herself. They had to break the door down to get to her. That was Mr Wilkins from school.'

Freddie began to shake, as if each word were firing tiny electric shocks at her. 'No,' she said. 'I didn't mean...Is she?'

Her mum's voice caught. She put her hand over her mouth. Freddie felt her shudder. 'The poor girl. Her poor parents. She's at the hospital. Unconscious. Love, they don't know if she's going to wake up. I know you girls are all so close. We'll see if we can take you in tomorrow.'

Tears shook out of Freddie. A pain deep inside her chest felt like it was going to pull her apart. Her mum pulled her close and rocked her, resting her face on her head.

'Shush. Shush. It's okay, love. It's okay. Let it out.' Freddie's chest heaved and the tears of her mum washed over her cheeks. *What had they done?*

The telephone rang again. Freddie froze. Her mum squeezed her tight. She didn't want to let go. She didn't want to hear more. Her dad answered the phone, his gruff voice, muffled by Mum's dressing gown, raised and suddenly cut off. She closed her eyes as she heard him approach.

'Dirty bastards,' his voice sounded gravelly.

'What is it, love?' said her mum.

'That was some hack from the local paper, he says they received a tip-off that our Freddie and Nasreen were bullying that Gemma lass.' Her dad's words sliced into her like broken glass. Freddie thought she might be sick.

'No.' Her mum was still gripping her tightly. 'They're friends. There must be a mistake?'

Her dad had her by the arm and yanked her away. Her mum reached for her. Freddie let out a cry as he shook her. 'What did you do, you stupid girl? What did you do? It's going to be in the papers! Happy now!'

'Stop it!' her mum cried. 'She's just a child!'

Her dad let go and Freddie crumpled to the floor. She felt the bruise ripening where his hand had been.

'This is all I fucking need.' He slammed out of the room.

Freddie closed her eyes as she heard his receding footsteps and the familiar crystal tinkle of the drinks cabinet opening. *What had she done?*

Eight years later
06:00
Friday 6 November
Account Suspended

Freddie pulled the duvet back over her head. Closing the world out. The noise. The smell. The fear. Her phone vibrated on the windowsill above. Reaching up, she grabbed it, sliding her finger to the power button. Holding it down. Force close. Don't look. She couldn't do this anymore. Her limbs felt heavy and tired. Her insides were coated with dust. It was claggy: sticking her together, turning her into a solid block of wood. Petrification. She was frightened. Truly, deeply, madly frightened. She eyed her Mac plugged into the wall. With a burst of energy, she leapt at it and ripped the plug from the socket, panting like an animal. As if a dead battery – silence – could save her. She crawled back into bed, still in her clothes from the helicopter. She curled into a ball and cried. Fitfully she slept. Dimly aware of time and life shifting, the other side of her curtains: the rise of the sun, the darkness of night. Her flatmates coming and going. Life had no place for her. Time was nothing. Her duvet was a heavy black mass upon her. The air thick as treacle. There was no rising for her. Only the darkness of the night.

There was a bumbling, muttering at the door. Her flatmate, P-something, Pete, whispered: 'Sorry, milk.'

She dug herself further into her duvet. Closed her hands over her ears as a spoon scraped against a teacup. Freddie screwed her eyes and mouth shut. Dust. She was turning to dust. Pete passed back out, crunching silver foil over leftovers. Gradually, her hands, her toes, her calves, her arms, her back, her stomach, her neck, relaxed and she fell asleep again; dreaming of Gemma and Nasreen dancing and laughing by Pendrick's outside pool in summer.

Chapter 34

WUBU2 – What You Been Up To?

21:40
Sunday 8 November
3 FOLLOWING   124,998 FOLLOWERS

Apollyon @Apollyon • 11s
Correct me and I will correct you.
Permanently.

The ground floor of Dr Michael Grape's terraced house in Leyton was open plan. Before their split, his wife, Cynthia, had insisted they extend and relocate the bathroom upstairs. The renovations had been costly. Dr Grape often looked at his obsolete kitchen and imagined what he could have done with all that money. He could have bought a jazzy racing green MG. That would have looked grand parked up at the university. A vehicle his impressionable female students would admire. When the divorce was finalised he insisted on keeping all the trinkets Cynthia loved from their travels. He couldn't care less about the global bric-a-brac that adorned his walls but felt his ex-wife's distress at losing them was fair compensation for the MG he'd been denied. So it was with great irony that he realised the gloved hand was clutching Cynthia's ugly Portuguese chicken jug just before it rendered him unconscious. Through those final blurry moments of pain and terror, he could imagine his ex-wife laughing. And with that truly horrifying thought Dr Grape left this world.

Monday 9 November
08:30
3 FOLLOWING   125,550 FOLLOWERS

Freddie sat up in bed. *Silver foil.* Why hadn't she thought of it before: the sockets ripped out and covered over with silver foil. Irrational fear. Wanting to keep the world out. The Internet out. What did those crazies do when they thought they were being attacked by government gamma rays? Made tinfoil hats to protect themselves! She looked at her computer marooned in the middle of the room. Where the fuck was her phone? She jumped up. Kicked the duvet from the couch and swatted her pillows away. It had to be here somewhere. It was like that article she'd read – was it on *The Times* or the *New Yorker*? About that infamous hacker the Americans had finally tracked down. His whole room, all the windows, all covered in tinfoil. It stopped his signal escaping. It stopped other signals getting in. Hamlin was scared. He'd ripped the sockets out and covered them with foil to protect himself. Her phone was wedged down between two sofa cushions. She pulled it, turning over, lying on her back, looking up at the watermark on the ceiling. But what did it mean? She didn't know, but maybe someone else would. There was a brisk knock at the door. 'Fuck,' she uttered. Freddie pulled her T-shirt off and grabbed a yellow eighties-style paint-graffitied jumper from the floor. She really needed to do some laundry. Picking up her glasses on the way.

She pulled open the door. Nas was standing there, her face pale and wan. Freddie gripped the door handle.

'Hi Freddie, can I come in?' Nas said.

Gemma's name crashed over her again like an icy wave. 'Sure.' She stood to the side. Freddie scooted a towel off the bed and pushed the duvet back, kicking a pile of clothes out of the way. 'Have a seat,' she said.

Nas, in her long black cashmere coat over her work suit, stood awkwardly in her heeled boots, hands in her pockets. 'Thanks.' She perched on the edge of the sofa like it might bite.

Freddie sat on the coffee table opposite so they faced each other. 'You want a drink, tea or anything?'

Nas looked at the mug full of cigarette butts next to Freddie's bed. The empty cereal bowls, soya milk congealing into yellow tidemarks. 'No thank you, I'm okay.'

Freddie caught her eye and looked down quickly, pretending to pick a piece of fluff from her jeans. 'Look, Nas, I'm...'

'@Apollyon's account has been unlocked,' Nas interrupted. 'He's back. There's been another one.'

'Another tweet?' Freddie said. 'I switched my phone off,' she said guiltily.

'I know. I called.' Nas cleared her throat. She still had her black leather gloves on. 'Another victim.'

Freddie steadied herself against the table.

'Caucasian male, fifty-four, university literature professor, found apparently knocked unconscious, restrained and then stabbed to death, Leyton.' Nas looked up at her.

Freddie shuddered. 'I've been a bit...' she looked at the closed curtains, 'out of it. Sleeping a lot. You know. How long's it been?'

'You've been gone three days. There were tweets. Clues. Yesterday. The day before. We tried to crack the code. The call came in an hour ago. Moast sent me to get you.'

'Moast?' Freddie was surprised.

'Yes. Look I know you said to him you want off the case.'

'I'm sorry, Nas. About what I said. About...'

265

'Gemma,' Nas said quietly, her gaze down.

'Yes.' Freddie hoped her flatmates were out.

Nas flexed her fingers. 'I saw her.'

'What?' Freddie said.

'About three years ago. Found her. It wasn't hard. They hadn't moved far. I went to see her,' Nas said.

Freddie's skin prickled. 'I didn't know that.'

'She's a nurse. Midwife. Lives with her partner.'

Freddie didn't know what to say. She tried to picture Gemma with her curly mousey hair in a blue nurse's uniform.

Nas took a deep breath. Looked up. 'She was okay. Tried to tell me it wasn't about…us. That her mum was ill. Really ill. I guess that's why she was acting so strangely and kept crying. Explains the medication being in the house.'

Freddie nodded. Tried not to think of empty pill bottles, blood dripping from an arm, water overflowing. *Her mum was ill?*

Nasreen looked up, her brown eyes locked onto hers. 'She told me it wasn't our fault.'

Freddie fed each word through her mind, turning it over like a pebble from the beach. *Wasn't our fault.* 'You believe her?'

Nasreen thought for a moment. Freddie watched her eyes for relief. Found none. 'She seemed happy,' Nas said simply. Freddie had carried it around with her for years: these pebbles, these stones, these rocks. The guilt. The empathy. They were what anchored her to Nas. Could she ever let it all go?

Nas cleared her throat. Pushed her hair from her eyes. 'The latest victim: Dr Michael Grape – he had tweeted directly at Apollyon.'

'Lots of people have done that.' Freddie thought of the reams of people @naming Apollyon. Feeding his mentions, his popularity, his followers, his reach.

'Yes, but it seems Dr Grape corrected his grammar. Apollyon's.'

'A pedant.' Freddie closed her eyes.

'A quick Google search turns up several published letters from Dr Grape to national newspapers. He was campaigning for

Waterstones to reinstate the apostrophe on its trading name. And a big fan of the Oxford comma,' said Nas.

Freddie knew the type all too well. 'A troll, a cat lover, a pedant. It's another Internet stereotype.'

'Yes.' She heard Nasreen swallow. 'It looks like a pattern. DCI Moast would like you to come back. To look at the tweets. Compare the online profiles you compiled of the previous victims with Dr Grape's Internet activity. All hands on deck.'

'No trace on the IP address then?' Freddie said.

'No, nothing.'

Freddie thought about the silver foil. 'Has Mark Hamlin been found?'

'No,' said Nasreen. 'Not yet.'

'I've been thinking about his plug sockets. Silver foil has been referenced in a few things: for blocking Wi-Fi signals and stuff,' Freddie said. 'I think he may have been trying to keep the Internet out of his flat.' Freddie looked at the plug she'd ripped from the wall. 'I think he was scared.'

'Well, that would certainly fit with his behaviour,' said Nas. 'What do you think it means?'

'I don't know,' Freddie said honestly. 'But I feel like it's relevant.'

'Are you up to coming back?'

Freddie thought about everything that had changed in the last week. Everything. Right down to Gemma. The one thing she could never write about, out there in front of all those people. *Her mum had been ill?*

'We have to stop this freak, don't we? He's going to do it again otherwise, isn't he?'

'We can't say for sure,' said Nas. 'But yes, this looks like a pattern.'

'Give me two minutes to jump in the shower.' Freddie stood. 'And find my spare charger.'

The suggestion of a smile chased across Nas's lips. 'Jamie's downstairs. We'll wait for you in the car,' she said.

Chapter 35

CU – See You

09:00
Monday 9 November
3 FOLLOWING   125,550 FOLLOWERS

'Leyton: he didn't travel far this time then?' Freddie watched as they drove past newsagents and an off-licence, boxes of exotic fruit and veg piled up outside them. Groups of men, some in traditional Arab dress, stood on the corners, smoking and talking.

'It appears not.' Nas was up front next to Jamie. They passed a park, the morning gloom punctuated by trees sparkling with fairy lights, ready for Christmas. The car turned down a street, narrow Victorian terraces stretched along each side. Filled recycling boxes piled up outside, ready for collection. Is this what Nas's house looked like – two-up two-down? The car slowed and Freddie saw the all too familiar police tape fluttering in the breeze. A uniformed officer she vaguely recognised stood guard outside.

'Do the press know?' she asked.

'Not yet,' said Jamie. 'But it won't be long. The guv asked me to keep an eye on it.'

'The neighbours, a Polish couple, heard screams,' Nas said.

'Nasty business,' Jamie tutted. 'What must they think coming to our country and having this happen?'

'They thought at first it might be a row with his ex-wife. Apparently they had a few of those,' said Nas. 'They weren't sure what to do but called it in last night.'

'Poor people,' said Jamie. 'Imagine living next door to something like this. I reckon I'd want to move.'

Freddie shuddered at the thought. It was bad enough visiting crime scenes, she couldn't imagine living in one.

'The neighbours' kitchen window looks straight into the victim's kitchen but they didn't see anything,' said Nas.

The car slowed to a stop outside the house. Nas turned the collar of her dark coat up – against the cold or for fear of being recognised following the footage online of the arrest of Mark Hamlin? Afraid of being photographed again? Everyone carried a phone. Everyone carried a camera. Freddie thought about the lads shouting hashtag ho at her. Her phone battery was almost flat. She tucked her chin down and hid half her face behind her scarf, then pulled the hood of her jacket up. Stepping out into the cold air and walking toward the police tape, she remembered doing the same at 39 Blackbird Road. When it all started. 'Good luck,' she heard Jamie say.

The front door of the house was ajar, throwing out a triangle of artificial light. Moast stepped into it. He had his forensic suit on over his usual suit and tie, but Freddie was shocked by his face. He looked exhausted. His eyes shrunken, disappearing red dots into the greying folds of his skin. She must have stopped walking because he lifted the tape cordon and stepped under it to meet her.

'Venton, thanks for coming.' He gave a respectful nod to Nas who'd joined them at her side. 'Have you had a chance to look at the tweets?'

'No, I've been offline.' The sentence sounded silly. She usually said it in response to missing an opinion piece someone asked if she'd read at a party. Offline was the new super busy, but Freddie hadn't been busy, she'd been broken. Hiding. She dropped her gaze to the cracked pavement.

'I've got copies in my notes.' Nas pulled her pad from her pocket and showed the page to Freddie. Freddie flicked through the pages of Apollyon quickly:

Correct me and I will correct you. Permanently.
The pedants are revolting.
Knock, knock, who's there? Dr. Dr Who.

'It's definitely him? I mean, who the clues are about. The victim,' Freddie said.

'There was another photo: blood dripping down a wall in the victim's house,' Nas said matter of fact. A chill passed over Freddie. Nas didn't move to show her the photo on her phone, and Freddie didn't want to see. 'Plus look at this tweet here,' Nas said.

Freddie followed Nas's finger across the page: *My favourite book is Grape Expectations.* 'He actually used the victim's name?' Freddie said.

'Yes, but we didn't realise the significance until we identified the body,' said Nas.

'We thought it might have been another anagram or something,' Moast added.

'Forensics are pretty certain 9.40pm is time of death. The vic has a smashed wristwatch which corresponds with rigor mortis,' said Nas. 'Apollyon followed Dr Grape's Twitter account at 9.15pm.'

'Before he killed him?' Freddie said.

'He's getting bolder,' said Moast.

'Did the victim know he was coming for him?' Freddie couldn't imagine how terrifying that would be.

'Dr Grape only tweeted a few times a week, so he might not have been online, and his initial phone records show he made no calls, so we think not,' said Nas.

'So there was time to get here...' Freddie trailed off.

'The window of time was very small,' said Moast.

'Has he followed anyone else?' Freddie braced.

'No,' said Nas. 'He's following Mardling's, Sophie Phillips' and Grape's accounts. That's it,' she added. 'He hasn't interacted with anyone else. No replies. No retweets. Nothing. It's a pattern.'

'By the time he'd tweeted the last two clues, Grape was already dead,' said Moast.

Freddie shuddered. 'Why send them then?'

'We presume Hamlin was taunting us,' said Moast.

'So you still think it's him?' Freddie looked at Nas. 'I've been thinking about that silver foil he had covering his sockets. People use that to block signals.'

'Could he stop devices being detected with that?' said Moast. 'We never found his phone.'

'No I don't think so,' she said. 'It's more the other way round; it's what people use to block Wi-Fi signals, radio waves, disrupt phone calls, that sort of thing. Like he was trying to keep stuff out?'

Moast sighed. 'I've also seen the report you and Cudmore turned up about the dyspraxia, but I still think he's our guy. The tweets stopped while he was in custody. They started up as soon as he was released. And now he's disappeared.'

'You can pre-programme tweets,' said Freddie.

Moast stared at her.

How had she not thought of this before? 'There are various programmes: TweetDeck, Hootsuite, et cetera. You could write them at one point and set them to post at another date and time.'

Nas's brow furrowed. Moast's lips crinkled down at the ends. 'It would still have to be one hell of a coincidence. When we arrested Hamlin it was widely documented by the press, but our releasing him was less so.'

'I guess,' Freddie said. Dyspraxia, silver-foil-covered wall sockets. Was Hamlin's panic an act? Were they dealing with someone able to present two sides of themselves? It was easy to be someone else online. Catfish. Hundreds, probably thousands, of people did it

271

every day: the tiny untruths that painted a more glamorous and exciting life of smiling Instagram shots of people with cocktails, at sold-out gigs, post-sex. It was a self-branding exercise to convince the world your life was amazing. From that to those who pretended to be other people completely, sock-puppeting on Amazon to positively review their own books, on dating sites so they could cheat or find better options, on Twitter, in chat rooms. How could you tease out who was real and who wasn't? Freddie prided herself on spotting when a female tweeter was actually a Nice Guy – some crusading jerk that was angry women hadn't shagged him when he'd been 'nice' to them. She could see the impersonators. Uncover the fakes. But she couldn't see Apollyon at all. The picture was obscure. 'Is it possible it's not the same person?'

'Another copycat, you mean?' Nas said.

'Or a team,' Freddie's face fell. 'It'd explain the change in location. Multiple people can be logged into one Twitter account.' She'd read about people seeking the help of others online to help them kill themselves. Like a death club. She thought of her and Nas's conversation about suicide pacts. No one would want to go like Mardling, surely?

'Jesus,' Moast shook his head. 'It doesn't bear thinking about. But you might be onto something. This crime scene is like Mardling's.' Freddie's stomach flipped. 'Not like Sophie's.'

'It's possible the perpetrator has an issue with men,' said Nas. 'It would explain the comparative violence. Someone who is threatened by men or dismissed by them in their day-to-day life.'

Moast looked straight at Freddie. 'I've put in a request for a profiler for this case, but the weekend has delayed the paperwork from being cleared by above. In the meantime we need to pool all our resources. When forensics have finished do you think you'd be up for taking a look at the body, Venton?'

Freddie felt the earth open up in front of her.

'The gap between the tweets and the murders is lessening. We've got three bodies and we've lost our prime suspect.' Moast's eyes pleaded, desperate.

Freddie was frightened. These guys were the professionals; they weren't supposed to freak out, give up. They were supposed to keep it together. They were supposed to catch the bad guys.

Moast stuck his hands in his pockets, shrugged his shoulders, 'It'll be a while till the SOCOs are clear. You've got time to prep yourself. Jamie can get you a cup of tea.' He looked at the ground before looking up and straight into her eyes again. 'Please, Freddie,' he said.

Nas shuffled awkwardly at her side. Freddie thought of pure, beautiful Sophie, so young. And Mardling, yes he'd been a dick online, but no one deserved to be killed for it. And now Dr Michael Grape: a pedant. Yes annoying, yes patronising, and yes normally the kind of person Freddie would ridicule. More concerned with the Oxford comma than any valid point someone was making. But he didn't deserve to be murdered. Idiots on Twitter threatened violence all the time. Even she, when having a really shitty day, knew she'd mouthed off. Throwaway comments about giving someone a slap if they didn't shut up. A vicious little pool of spittle. People's bad days and bad lives spreading like an angry virus online, but it was just the Internet. Things weren't supposed to spill over into real life. They were told repeatedly that those who threatened people online didn't really mean it. That they just didn't understand context. It was a joke.

Freddie felt sick.

Three people dead was not a joke. There couldn't be any more. 'Okay,' she said. 'I'll do it.'

Chapter 36

TBA – To Be Announced

15:15
Monday 9 November
3 FOLLOWING   125,561 FOLLOWERS

Freddie saw the books lining the walls, sprayed red. The carved wooden mask on the wall speckled with blood. An overturned table, dripping, dripping, drip, drip, drip. Newspapers kicked across the floor, smeared. A smashed crystal Scotch glass, its jagged edges sparkling. The body of the doctor tied to a dining chair, slumped forward as if he were a fabric doll. Imitating the fake Instagram photo of the Welsh girl, Amanda. At first she thought he'd been tied with red ribbons, then she realised that was his skin hanging away from him. She stumbled backwards. Nasreen and Moast were behind her, voices muffled as if underwater. 'It's too much for her, sir.' The room squeezed together and bounced back, like jelly.

She was outside. Trying to exhale the word fuck, but nothing came. She felt the man's soul dripping from her. Drip. Drip. Drip. Someone said: 'Let's get you back to the station.'

274

She got in the car, listening to her own breath. Her own heart-beat. Her own life. Jamie was already in the front. Engine running.

'Rough one, huh?' he asked.

She nodded, though he couldn't see her.

'He's one sick fuck,' Jamie muttered.

One? *Multiple people can be logged into one Twitter account.* She thought she'd been ready. But you'd never be ready for that. Freddie closed her eyes. Red ribbons. She opened them again. Nas was next to her. Moast was in the front, chewing on a biro. They were all silent. The street lights pulsated above them as the car moved through London. She closed her eyes. Red. She opened them to see the Thames, sparkling and undulating, a wide open promise: it is a big world. She could go anywhere. Do anything. More than anything, she wished she was back in Espress-oh's, pulling faces at Milena after another customer ordered extra syrup.

18:49
Monday 9 November
3 FOLLOWING   126,003 FOLLOWERS

'Forensics have turned up nothing again. They must be wearing gloves, maybe a hood. They're very thorough,' Tibbsy said.

Freddie tried to focus. Tibbsy, Moast, Nas and she clustered in the front of the room. Sifting, trying to piece together all they had before Moast briefed the team. Somehow, and she couldn't quite understand it, Freddie had found herself among the chosen ones. Others were tasked to help, but it felt like it was down to them to find Apollyon. To stop him. To win. Freddie felt queasy. A photo of Dr Grape – clearly pulled from the university's website – had been added to the incident board, alongside written versions of Apollyon's clues about him. Alun Mardling, Sophie Phillips, Michael Grape. *For whom the bell trolls. Hope is rearranging her name. Grape Expectations.* Freddie stared at the photo of Grape;

275

his white-flecked brown hair was full, bordering on messy, and he had one eyebrow raised as if he were laughing, or sneering, at the photographer. He had on a tweed jacket and a button-down navy shirt. Freddie knew twenty-year-old hipsters who dressed like that, but Dr Grape was clearly void of sartorial irony. He looked solid. 'He looks strong.' Everyone turned to look at her: Moast, Tibbsy, Nas. She hadn't been listening. 'Sorry, but he does.'

'Like he wouldn't easily be overpowered,' said Nas.

'Forensics will tell us if there are any drugs found in his system. We know that's an MO Apollyon's used before, with Sophie Phillips,' said Moast. Freddie thought of the smashed Scotch glass.

'I spoke to his colleagues. Apparently there were rumours about his involvement with a number of female students,' Tibbsy said.

'The old dog,' Moast laughed.

Freddie felt her lip curl. She tried to reassure herself Moast was all right, just a bit…70s. Besides, she didn't have to like him in order to agree they had to work together to find this sicko. What was she going to do? Sit at home on Twitter until she spotted something useful?

'It didn't go down well with everyone. There were a lot of those hard-line feminists at his university,' Tibbsy continued. 'A Dr Fielding reported him for "inappropriate behaviour" to the dean.' Another Nice Guy, Freddie thought sarcastically.

'Motive for murder?' asked Moast.

'Unlikely,' Tibbsy said. 'It was last year. Besides, you don't think she could be our Hashtag Murderer?'

'Does she use Twitter?' Moast asked.

'I'll find out, guv.' Tibbsy scribbled onto his notes.

They were silent, staring at photos and notes. Freddie sighed. They had nothing. Again. 'Now what?'

'We complete our standard questioning: friends, family, the ex-wife.' Moast counted them off on his fingers. 'Unlike Mardling and Phillips, Grape appears to have been surrounded by friends and family. If anyone saw or heard anything odd, we will find it. Again there were no signs of forced entry: if he let someone in, into his house, he must have known them. If there's anyone new in his life someone must have clocked it. We should get back to the neighbours for a start. If they heard his ex and him arguing, then what else did they hear? That big kitchen window barely a foot from their own house, if someone new came to visit in the last few weeks, did they see anything?'

'Yes, sir,' said Nas.

'The first-response team are going door to door, forensics will be another few hours yet. We've got an arrest warrant out on Hamlin if he surfaces.' Moast looked at his watch. Freddie couldn't believe it was gone 7pm already. 'I want everyone in at 7.30am. We'll brief the team then. For now go home and rest.' He looked up at Freddie. 'I need you fully functioning tomorrow.'

Freddie waited till she got home before she took it out of her pocket. Cold and hard, she weighed it in her hand. There was no hiding. There was no running anymore. She turned her phone over, bending down to reach the short lead of the charger and plugged it in. The angry red battery symbol appeared, but she knew it wouldn't be long until the vibration signalled it was alive. Unlike Grape. She climbed into bed and closed her eyes. All night she dreamt of red ribbons.

07:30
Tuesday 10 November
3 FOLLOWING 126,615 FOLLOWERS

Freddie settled herself in the incident room. The police officers who'd been there earlier, or just coming in, were taking seats around her. Moast looked like he hadn't slept a wink, even given his own order last night. Freddie sipped at her coffee. She'd almost grown used to the hot brown caffeine that stripped her mouth of all feeling. Frothy milk was a distant memory.

Tibbsy came through the door, his black coat over his arm, bags under his eyes even bigger than Moast's. Then Nas appeared, coat on, collar up. Freddie felt it immediately.

Nas went straight to Moast. 'Guv, I think I've found something.' Freddie *knew* it. A hush descended over the men sat around her. She crossed her fingers that Nasreen would come through.

'What is it?' Moast asked, rolling up the sleeves of his pale blue shirt.

'It seems our Dr Grape also corrected the tweets of Paige Klinger.' Nas had an iPad in a red leather case out. *Where'd she get that from?* Nas caught her eye. 'It arrived yesterday – I thought it'd be useful for the case.' Freddie put her coffee down as Nas turned the tablet toward her.

@Paigeklinger 'You're not alone.' Not: 'your not alone.' And certainly not: 'ur not alone.' That's balderdash.

@Paigeklinger 'There' is a noun, an adverb, a pronoun, or an adjective. It doesn't indicate possession. Children grasp this.

This was another link to Paige Klinger. Mardling trolled her, and now it turned out Grape corrected her grammar.

'He even wrote an article about it for the *Guardian*.' Nas, still in her coat, swiped between screens. 'Here: *The Defilement of the English Language by Generation Y*. He cites Paige as "the illiterate leader of the millennials: void of nuance, charm, or wit, she, and the child-limbed harpies who anoint her with *likes,* reduce all human sentiment into something called emojis".'

Freddie couldn't help but smile. Grape sounded like a pompous arse; of course he was irritated a sixteen-year-old girl was adored and worshipped while he was virtually unknown.

'Interesting.' Moast was reading over his shoulder. 'What's an emoji, Venton?'

'Little pictures you can send to people. They often stand in for words. Smiley faces, dancing ladies, smiling poo,' she said. One or two officers laughed.

'Smiling poos?' Moast looked up. 'Oh, never mind. Let's focus on this.'

'There's more, sir,' said Nas. 'They had a row. Online. It got pretty nasty. Look here's a Storify of it.' Nas pointed at the screen.

'It could be Paige's intern, Marni?' Freddie stood. She had to see this.

'Possible,' said Nas, still directing her words to Moast who was squinting at the screen. 'But look here, where he calls her the whore of Babylon, she calls him a douchebag cronut.'

'Paige said that when we were in the studio,' Freddie said. 'It's a pretty weird insult. I've never heard anyone else use it. If it is her using it online then it means it's likely it was Paige arguing with Grape. Not Marni.'

'Even without that, Grape belittled her in the national press, sir,' Nas said. 'I think that's...'

'Motive,' Moast finished. He ran his open palm over his cropped hair. 'Links to two murdered men: that's reason enough to question her. Right. Let's bring her in.'

'What about the paparazzi?' Freddie asked.

'What?' said Moast irritated.

'They'll be swarming all over her, like usual.' She didn't want to go anywhere near Paige; she didn't want any chance of her photo appearing on *The Family Paper's* website again. She couldn't face the burn of betrayal and humiliation twice in the space of a week.

'Valid point, Venton. Tibbsy, send one of the uniforms to bring her in. I don't want the press guessing this is about the Hashtag Murderer. If Klinger is involved, then it's possible she paid someone else to do her dirty work. We don't want them getting wind of this. Let's keep it low-key. No one is to talk to the media.' Moast's chest was puffed, his voice commanding.

Freddie rolled a loose thread from her jumper between her fingers. Was this just a coincidence or could Paige Klinger be Apollyon? She was a small girl, she would have had to drug the victims to overpower them. But she obviously had access to some strong stuff. It was feasible. They needed more, but Freddie fizzed with excitement, and dread, but the nightmare might finally be over.

Chapter 37

AKA – Also Known As

Bringing Paige Klinger in for questioning did not go according to plan. The uniforms found her nose-deep in a bag of coke, so they arrested her for possession and intent to deal. Paige denied she had any intention of sharing the drugs, but the coppers refused to believe one person could snort that much gak. Freddie was inclined to believe Paige. Despite having shovelled great quantities up her snout, Paige was still lucid enough to deliver an impassioned speech to the waiting paparazzi.

The incident room was empty – everyone was busy elsewhere, the remnants of half-drunk cups of tea and piles of papers scattered about the hot-desking space. Freddie sat in her favourite spot at the back of the room, close to a plug socket. Tapping play on YouTube on her phone, she watched the footage again.

Paige, adopting the wide-eyed innocent expression Freddie

recognised from the day at the studio, looked virginal in a baggy white T-shirt and pale pink skinny jeans. PC Folland, the balding fat cop from outside 39 Blackbird Road, had hold of her arm. Folland, obviously intimidated by the braying mob of photographers, lost hold of Paige, and so the teen model, her hands cuffed behind her back, her long blonde hair blowing in the wind, delivered the performance of a lifetime.

'I have been wrongfully arrested and accused of murder,' Paige's voice trembled.

Not true, thought Freddie. *They've got you because you're off your tits on God knows what.*

The crowd around her fell quiet. The camera jostled to keep her in sight. Camera bulbs flashed. Freddie could see a number of phones being held up: *Klingys*.

Paige spoke clearly, her pretty little chin tilted up in defiance. 'My heart breaks for those that have lost their lives, for they are as innocent as me.'

Freddie thought of Alun Mardling and the vile bilge of abuse he'd sprayed out.

'I am but a martyr at the mercy of the justice system, and I ask my fans to pray for me. You know me better than anyone. You know I could never do such a thing. Pray for Paige.' And then, in a moment of pure genius, Paige let one solitary tear roll down her perfect cheek. Dozens of camera flashes fired, capturing the heartfelt performance.

There were murmurs in the crowd. Folland, recovering himself and no doubt sensing the bollocking he was going to get back at the station, tugged on Paige's arm to get her to the car.

It was then that a dark figure, a blur of green, flung themselves forward, screaming, 'No! Paige! No!' The camera jerked as a wave of heads appeared, trying to capture the drama. Shouts went up. Light bulbs flashed. The camera lunged forward. PC Folland was knocked backward, taking a stricken-looking Paige with him, her T-shirt fluttering up and revealing a flash of nipple as she flew through the air.

Another PC surged forward, dragging the man, who appeared to be dressed in a military-print onesie, from on top of Folland. All the time the man was screaming, 'No! Paige! No! Save yourself!' The video cut. 2.6 million views. 20,675 thumbs up on YouTube.

Freddie put her phone down on the incident room table. She'd misjudged Paige. She thought she never said anything in shampoo commercials because she couldn't act. But *that* speech was Oscar-winning.

The next day's front pages were coming up on Twitter. Paige's arrest dominated all of them. *The Post* had gone for a close-up of Paige crying. Her face beautiful, fragile, set with a look of resilience and pride: the tear all the more poignant for it. The Sun had excelled themselves. They had a shot, mid-fall, zoomed in to show the taut stomach of Paige and her bee-stung tits making their own bid for freedom. The headline was 'Paige Three Stunner!' *Classy*.

The *Family Paper* had another close-up crying shot, with the banner headline: 'Paige's Hashtag Murderer Hell'. So much for keeping it from the press. Moast had been torn a new one by the Superintendent, and a memo had been circulated saying all officers were to undergo additional press and PR training in the coming weeks. Freddie wasn't surprised when Nas told her she'd heard the external PR firm that managed the station's online presence had been given their notice. What a mess.

Freddie exhaled. Along the corridor in one room, Paige was being questioned by Moast and Nas; and in another, waiting his turn, was the military onesie guy. He'd been identified as Noel Richards. Was he Apollyon? So consumed for his love for Paige he'd murder anyone who slighted her online? A crazed fan defending her honour? He'd have a long job with the Internet. There was so much hate. And adoration. How did Paige cope? Or perhaps she didn't: started to bump her tormentors off. She was a multimillionaire so she could easily have paid someone to do it for her. But what about Sophie, what had she done to Paige? Nothing that they knew of. Perhaps Paige really fucking hated cat videos. Not for the first time Freddie feared she might actually be cracking up. *Please let it be one of them. Please let this be the end of it.*

She looked up as Tibbsy walked into the room, white shirtsleeves rolled up, pink tie flung back over his shoulder from his pace, the door reverberating off the wall behind him. The photographs on the incident board quivering. His face set in a scowl, his eye bags jiggling: 'She's out.' He turned a grey plastic chair round to face Freddie and slammed his body onto it.

'What?' Freddie said. There must be some mistake.

'Paige. She lawyered up. Real nasty ones. Alibied-out for the murders. She was in Rio for Sophie's: hundreds of people saw her in a string bikini on the catwalk. They had her out of here within an hour.' Tibbsy folded his arms across his chest and kicked his legs out. *Beaten.*

'What about the drugs?' This couldn't be right. Freddie would bet anything Paige's agent, Magda, was behind it.

'Claims they're not hers,' snorted Tibbsy, his wiry arms conducting his frustration. 'Refused a drugs test.'

'What?' Freddie couldn't believe this.

'She's a minor. We can't test her unless we charge her. And thanks to her lawyers we can't do that. Without a test, we've no proof of drug use,' Tibbsy spat.

'You found her with enough coke to revive Amy Winehouse! What about Folland and the other cop? They saw it!' Freddie heard her voice getting high. What if Paige was Apollyon? Then he... *she*...was back out there.

'That performance she gave to the press has damaged our ground. Her lawyers are pressing for charges against Folland for assault.'

'What? Can they do that?' *What if it was her? What if...?* This couldn't be happening.

'Oh they have! Claiming it's a vendetta. That he deliberately threw her to the ground.' Tibbsy rocked forward and slammed his fist on the table. 'The idiot. We should have gone and brought her in. With them pushing for charges, we can't progress with the drugs case: it's become her word against ours. Her team are saying we planted the drugs.'

'Jesus.' This was bad, thought Freddie.

'Hamlin and now Klinger – we've lost both. This case just won't cut us a break.' Tibbsy dropped his head into his hands. His dark hair a curtain to the truth.

'Where's Nas and Moast?' Freddie asked. Tibbsy losing it like this did not fill her with hope.

'They're going at Noel Richards, the guy at the arrest who jumped on PC Folland to *save* Paige. Turns out he's got form for stalking and harassment. Remember Josie and Rosie?' Tibbsy pushed his hands against his knees to straighten up, his voice calmer.

Freddie remembered some godawful pop duo when she'd been at school. Videos and songs liberally sprinkled with artificial sweets. 'The pop singers?'

'Yeah, seems he was a bit obsessed with Rosie. Broke into her house and cut himself so he left a heart shape from his own blood in her mother's room.'

'Holy crap. Why her mother's room?'

'Thought it was hers,' said Tibbsy. 'He has several restraining orders out on him.'

'Great, so he's creepy and stupid.' Is that what it took to be a serial killer? It was pretty messed up to break into someone's house and cut yourself.

'The guy's clearly unhinged,' said Tibbsy.

'Could he have done it – the murders – out of some crazy loyalty to Paige?' Freddie asked. Could he be Apollyon?

'No history of actual violence – apart from against himself. But he doesn't have an alibi for any of the three murders. He can't tell us where he was on those days at all. We're tracing his cards. His Oyster card. Seeing if anything shows. We'll hold him till then,' said Tibbsy.

'What about his phone – if he is Apollyon, the account might be on that,' said Freddie.

'It was smashed during the arrest – the tech boys are piecing it back together now. But it doesn't look like it's encrypted or blocked,' said Tibbsy. 'We're applying for a warrant to search his digs for a computer.' Tibbsy's shoulders slumped.

'It's okay,' Freddie heard herself say. She reached out and squeezed his arm. 'We'll get through this.'

They both looked up as the door to the incident room opened again. Nas stalked in. A look of thunder on her face. Moast appeared, a step behind, scowling. Freddie still had her hand held out. She felt like an hourglass, like her very self was sinking down and collapsing through a hole into her feet. *Now what?*

Tibbsy jumped up. 'What's happened?'

Nas, her eyes stony, her voice flat, stopped. Exhaled. Her shoulders mirroring Tibbsy's minutes before. 'Richards has been released.'

Chapter 38

WTF – What The Fuck?

21:29
Tuesday 10 November
3 FOLLOWING   127,392 FOLLOWERS

Freddie watched as Tibbsy grew more animated. 'What? Why? How?' he said.

'Klinger's fancy-pants lawyer just came down here and tied us in legal knots,' Moast said. 'Seems Richards has a history of mental illness, we violated some EU human rights directive in bringing him in without a guardian.'

'What? Paige's lawyer?' Freddie was trying to piece this together.

'She's just released a statement to the press praising Richards for his loyalty and love,' Nas said. 'She's paid his legal fees.' They stood, the four of them facing each other in the middle of the room. Freddie looked from Moast to Nas to Tibbsy and back again. 'Can she do that?'

'She can and she did,' said Nas. 'We can't hold him till we get more. We need to turn something up.'

'Did she actually say loyalty and love?' Freddie's head was spinning. 'That's like something off a TV show: like a Queen to a subject.'

'Yup, and all to the press,' said Nas, dropping down to sit on the edge of the nearest table. Tibbsy looked stunned.

'It's weird. That she's doing this?' Freddie was talking with her hands. Each disbelieving word accompanied by a pitch and swoop. 'Almost like she doesn't want him here in case he says something?' She thought of Paige's performance on the YouTube video. She was believable. Very believable. How many people could be won over by somebody like that? Was this all orchestrated by her? Money and fame making her invincible. Twisting her self-value to make her void of morals? Building a literal army of fans. It'd make a hell of a story.

Moast seemed to recover all of a sudden. 'Right. I want everything we've got on Richards. I want to speak to everyone who knows him. We need to pin down where he was on those three dates. If he was so much as in the same postcode as any of these victims, I want him back in.'

'Guv,' Tibbsy practically whispered. Nas had her phone out and was looking at it. Freddie was full of nervous energy, she was walking up and down on the same one-metre spot.

The door opened and they all turned at once to face a frightened-looking Jamie.

'What is it, Thomas?' Moast snapped. Freddie tried to smile reassuringly at Jamie. It wasn't his fault this was happening.

'Sorry, sir, I just, it's just…' Jamie trailed off. Looked at his big feet.

'Spit it out, man!' Moast said.

'There's been another post,' Jamie said to the carpet tiles.

'What?' Freddie's phone hadn't buzzed. 'On Twitter?'

Jamie looked up, his thin lips stretched into an almost straight line. 'On Facebook. Sergeant Patel in IT just called me.'

Freddie sat down on the table next to Nas. *Branching out. New forums. Spreading the brand.*

'It's definitely from Apollyon – they're sure?' Moast said. He had his back to Freddie but she saw his hands clench into fists.

'It's a video, sir.' Jamie's eyes swam.

'Of what?' Moast's words shuddered through Freddie. She felt Nas tense.

'It's a video of Michael Grape's murder.' Jamie's voice cut through the silence. Red ribbons.

'Oh my God,' Freddie whispered.

'Richards is out there. He could have done this,' Tibbsy said.

'It could be preloaded,' said Freddie. It was spreading. An epidemic. A virus. They couldn't control it.

'Why's he changed platform?' asked Nas.

'Or Hamlin,' said Moast. 'He could have done this too. Don't suppose Patel has got a trace on the account holder has he, Thomas?'

'No, sir, it's been rerouted, or whatever they call it, again,' said Jamie.

'Fucking hell!' Moast screwed up the papers in his hand and threw them at the wall. Freddie winced.

'Get someone from the Gremlin IT task force down here. I want the video up. I want them to run sound analysis, whatever. Look in every glass surface. Every windowpane. For a reflection. I want something, anything, that can identify who this murderer is,' Moast shouted.

Jamie bolted out of the door. Tibbsy and Nas followed. Freddie was shaking. Moast put his hands on the back of a chair, leaning into them, flexing his fingers and gripping. Flexing and gripping. 'We're not going to catch him are we?' Freddie said quietly.

Moast exhaled. 'First thing they teach you in training, Venton: never make promises you can't keep,' he said.

Sergeant Patel introduced a sour-faced woman in her thirties, with straight bobbed black hair, wearing a black wrap dress and black tights. 'This is Caroline Arnold, from Digital Forensics.'

'Caroline, I'm DCI Edwin Moast.' Moast held out his hand to shake before indicating each person in turn. 'This is Sergeant Kevin

Tibbsy and Sergeant Nasreen Cudmore from my team. And this is Freddie Venton, she's acting as a Social Media Adviser on this case.'

Caroline looked at Freddie. 'You're the one who's been translating Twitter,' she said, like it was an accusation.

'I didn't ask to be dragged into all this,' Freddie said. 'I'd much rather leave it to you lot, believe me.'

Caroline Arnold's nose crinkled.

Moast shot Freddie a warning look. 'Excuse Miss Venton, it's been a trying case.'

'I can see that,' said Caroline. 'Shall we get on with this?' She turned to the desk on which Sergeant Patel had opened a laptop. 'This footage was loaded approximately one hour and thirty-seven minutes ago.'

Approximately? Freddie could just imagine Caroline Arnold ordering all her black outfits into *approximate* tonal order.

'The name of the group flagged on the search algorithm we utilise.' Caroline's fingers flew over the keys as screens of code scrolled down.

Moast looked like he was concentrating so hard Freddie worried he might have a stroke.

'The source of the account has been rerouted and sent via Tor,' said Caroline.

Nas leant forward to look at the screen. 'The anonymity software? Like he used to block us tracing the Twitter account.'

'Precisely,' said Caroline. 'Originally launched as a tool to evade censorship, Tor has mutated and allows anyone to hide from whoever they like online.'

I said this on the first day, thought Freddie.

'So we still can't find who bloody uploaded this?' asked Moast.

'No,' said Caroline. 'Whoever has set up these accounts, both Twitter and Facebook, knows what they are doing. We've tried almost everything we can. We're unable to trace them.'

Try harder, thought Freddie. *This is life or death.*

'I've extracted the video to see if we can find any other digital footprints on it, and I understand you want copies to test for sound or caught images?' Caroline continued.

'Yes,' said Moast.

'Okay. Well here it is. I warn you, it is not easy viewing.' Caroline clicked a key and the screen was filled with a video.

Freddie gripped the back of the chair in front of her. They watched in silence. The footage was shaky. Soundless. A handheld device. Probably an iPhone. The doctor was tied to a chair in his lounge. The background was dark but you could make out a smashed jug on the floor. The camera came closer and closer. He was gagged, hands tied behind his back, his hair was matted with blood. His eyes grew wide. Panicked. He began to squirm violently. A knife appeared, held in a black-gloved hand. The doctor's attempts to free himself grew more desperate. As the hand came down and the knife flashed, Freddie instinctively closed her eyes.

'It's all there: two minutes and thirteen seconds of a man tortured to death,' said Caroline Arnold.

Freddie felt sick, she kept her eyes away from the screen. The final shot, a bloodied Michael Grape: frozen. Her insides foamed.

'I reported the video to Facebook immediately,' said Caroline. 'Unfortunately they have decided not to take it down.'

'What – how can they do that?' Nas looked incredulous.

'They sent a standardised reply stating it was not in violation of their community standards,' Caroline said.

Freddie's body shook. Silent, mirthless laughter.

'What the hell does it take to fall foul of their community standards?' Tibbsy said.

'Nipples,' Freddie gasped as the word came out, shaking like salt over chips.

'What?' Nas turned to look at her. 'Are you all right, Freddie?'

She was sick with laughter now. Hysteria rupturing her. It was absurd. There was a madman making snuff videos and circulating them online, and there was nothing they could do. 'Nipples. The American conservative equivalent of the Anti-christ.' Moast was looking at her strangely. 'Breastfeeding, mastectomy scars, they'll all get you suspended.'

'She's right,' Caroline Arnold added without turning around.

That was it: a stupid patronising woman in black was the last straw. Freddie burst out laughing. Halfway through the second peal something snapped and it turned into a sob. *Poor Michael Grape. Poor beautiful Sophie.*

'I thought Facebook was photos of kids and Candy Crush,' Moast was saying.

'Freddie, try to breathe slower.' Nas had a hand on her shoulder.

Freddie watched as a tear plummeted onto the carpet tiles. Rage erupted up through her. 'Don't you see? He's turned us all into an audience. This'll spread like wildfire.'

'Take a breath, Venters.' Tibbsy reached out to touch her.

She swatted him away. 'He's already got 16,000 Facebook followers,' she screamed. 'And there's nothing we can do.' It hurt. As if someone had reached inside her and squeezed. Ripped part of her out. Thrown it away. Freddie had only felt like this once before: when Gemma had tried to kill herself and Nasreen Cudmore disappeared from her life. A broken heart.

'You need to calm down, Freddie.' Nas was in front of her.

'Get away!' Freddie pushed past her. Past Moast. Out. She had to get out. Red ribbons. Red ribbons all over the Internet. There were faces. People. A voice. Jamie's? She kept going. Slamming into the fire escape bar released her into the car park; she felt the cold air wrap round and cup her, pain pouring out. She had her phone. Was typing. Blinking. The words blurry:

Freddie Venton @ReadyFreddieGo • 1s
@Apollyon you freaking sick fucktard. This is going to stop. I'm going to stop you.

This was bullshit. *Bullshit.* Bubbles were coming out of her nose. She wiped at her face. Anger subsided. Bigger gaps between the aftershocks. Her vision cleared. Her breathing slowed. The icy air was making her shake. Her mother always said she had to work harder to control her temper. She swallowed the remnants of tears and snot, as what she'd done settled into her stomach. *It was okay*, she told herself. *It was okay*. Other people had tweeted @Apollyon. But she knew this was different. She was the girl on the front of the newspapers. She was the hashtag ho. She closed her eyes.

Her mobile vibrated in her hand.

Apollyon had replied.

Chapter 39

DIY – Do It Yourself

Freddie read the words over and over.

Apollyon @Apollyon • 1s
@ReadyFreddieGo and what are you with your red fucking fake hair going to do about it?

Over and over. She had to get help. She managed to open the station door. Head down, walking. Reading her phone. Over and over. Wishing it was a mistake. Wishing she'd misread it.

'Hey! Watch where you're going!' a policewoman snapped at her.

Freddie veered out the way, catching site of a uniform and blonde hair. 'Sorry.' Had to get to the incident room. Had to get help. Over and over. The door was open. Caroline Arnold was gone. The room was empty apart from Nas, who looked up from the laptop Caroline Arnold had left behind.

'Freddie, are you all right? Tibbsy went to look for you.'

'I...I...'

'Can I just say, I'm sorry that you had to see that. I think we should have pre-screened it. It was...awful.' Nas was straightening folders around the laptop.

Over and over. 'I...I...'

'You should probably go home for tonight. Have some sweet tea and take a rest.' Nas was pulling Freddie's coat from the chair at the back of the room. Scooping her bag out from under the desk with her foot. 'I'll square it with the DCI. He was worried about you. I'm sure of it.'

'He tweeted me,' she forced the words out.

'What?' Nas stopped. 'The DCI?'

'No. Apollyon.' Freddie held the phone up with her shaking hand.

The colour drained from Nas's cheeks. 'Let me see?' She left Freddie's bag and coat on a table and took the phone from her outstretched hand, tapping the screen. 'Oh my God, Freddie, what have you done?'

'I...I...was angry,' Freddie said.

'Jesus, Freddie!' Nas sounded uncharacteristically frightened.

'I didn't mean it. I didn't mean for this to happen.' *Please don't look worried. Please tell me it's going to be okay.*

'We've got to tell Moast,' Nas said. 'Now.'

Freddie managed to nod and followed Nas out of the room. The floor was spongy under her feet. They found Moast in his office, a small beige rectangle of a room. No external windows, just a glass panel into the corridor covered with a lowered blind. Freddie hadn't been in here before.

'Sit down, Freddie,' Nas said, signalling at one of the two chairs that faced Moast's desk. She still had hold of her phone.

'You all right, Venton? You worried me a bit there?' Moast said. The overhead strip lighting bleached any remaining colour from Moast's cheeks. He looked dead.

'Freddie has had communication from Apollyon, sir.' Nas held the phone toward him. Freddie tried to nod.

'What? On Twitter?' Moast reached for the phone. 'What did he say?'

'Er…"and what are you with your red fucking fake hair going to do?"' Nas said.

'Wait,' Moast was tapping his biro against the desk. 'Did you tweet him?'

'Yes,' Freddie managed.

'Show me.'

'See here, sir.' Nas reached across the desk.

Moast whistled like a plumber assessing a broken boiler. He was up and pacing now. He took the phone. Read it. Handed it back to Nas. Freddie realised she was still shaking. Moast was tapping his finger against his mouth.

'Sir?' said Nas.

'I'm thinking.'

'What should we do?' asked Nas.

Moast came round to their side of the desk and leant against it. 'The way I see it, this could be good,' he said.

Freddie was surprised. Nothing about this felt good.

'If this communication is genuine we could gain something from it. Draw him out. See if we can learn more about him. What did you say to get him to respond?' Moast looked at Freddie.

'I called him a fucktard.'

'Okay. So you angered him, you've pierced his ego. This is good.' Moast shook his biro between his thumb and forefinger. Nas nodded.

How was it a good thing to piss off a serial killer?

'Yes,' said Nas. 'Display arrogance, that's what you need to do. He clearly thinks Freddie is no match for him.'

'I'm not,' Freddie's voice came out in a squeak. *One day that temper of yours will get you into real trouble.* Her mum's prophecy rang through her head. She looked at the certificates of training Moast had hanging on the wall.

'We could get her to do it again, sir. See if he bites.' said Nas.

'Now wait a minute…' said Freddie.

'If she can wind him up sufficiently, then he may reveal something, is that what you're thinking?' Moast looked at Nas intently.

'Now wait, seriously guys. The first time I was angry. I don't want to be on his radar,' Freddie said. Moast had three used mugs on his desk.

'This is the first time he's interacted with anyone…well, anyone who wasn't already dead.' Moast was still looking at Nas. The two locked in an excited conversation, caught by the idea this might be the long-awaited breakthrough. Freddie's throat slammed shut.

'Do it again, Venton,' Moast said. 'I know you know how to get on someone's nerves.'

'You do it,' Freddie wheezed.

'I haven't got a Twitter account. Besides, he's responded to you once,' Moast said. 'You're in his sights.'

'Like prey?' This couldn't be happening, Freddie thought.

'You're sitting in the middle of a police station, nothing's going to happen to you,' said Moast.

'Ha!' she scoffed. 'And what about when I go home? Or do you envisage me living in the canteen till you catch this psycho. *If* you catch this psycho.'

'Venton, there's nothing to suggest you're a target of his. It doesn't fit with his previous pattern of behaviour. He's followed people he's killed, but never tweeted anyone.' Moast held out her phone to her. 'If it makes you feel better I'll have officers escort you to your door and back again.'

She nodded. Apollyon hadn't followed her. She wasn't in danger, she told herself.

'We will get this guy,' Moast said.

'What happened to making promises you couldn't keep?' she asked.

Nas put an arm round her shoulder. 'I think it'll really help, Freddie. We could get him with this. People make mistakes when they're angry.' Her voice was soft, convincing.

'Don't I bloody know it,' she said.

'Either you do it or I will.' Moast pulled the phone back.

'Wait! Stop! I'll do it.' She had to keep control of the situation. Freddie took the phone from Moast. Closed her eyes: imagined herself in a small dark room, facing a shadowy figure. She would make him talk. She typed and showed Moast and Nas the message:

@Apollyon You think you're such a big shot? You're nothing but a dumbfuck wank smear.

They nodded and she pressed send. They all watched it go, bent over the phone, their three heads almost touching. Freddie closed Twitter and reopened it. She put the phone on standby and restarted it. She shook it. Nothing.

A beep from Moast's phone on his desk made all three of them jump. 'Fuck!' Moast grabbed it. 'Bloody pizza company text: Two for one.'

Freddie tried to slow her heartbeat. Willing it to settle. She couldn't spend every waking minute like this. Strung out. Thrumming with anxiety. 'I don't think it's worked.'

'It's sent, right?' asked Moast.

Nasreen leant back in her chair: 'Yes, but he hasn't replied. Oh well. It was worth a shot.'

They sat for another minute in silence. Freddie willing her phone to vibrate. To tell them something. Send up a tiny flare they could trace.

Moast exhaled. 'Perhaps you weren't offensive enough?'

'What would you suggest,' Freddie snapped, 'I tell him I fucked his mother?'

'Maybe,' said Moast.

'This is ridiculous. I'm not doing that. It doesn't even make sense. It was obviously a one-off. A freak occurrence.' Freddie tried to reassure herself. 'Maybe he has two phones? Or two accounts and he posted it on this one by accident?'

'No,' Nas shook her head. 'That was no accident. That was taunting. Apollyon wants us to know he's always one step ahead.'

'Well he is!' Freddie closed the screen on her phone.

'Okay, calm down. It's been a stressful day,' said Moast.

Freddie snorted.

'Let's regroup.' Moast ran his hand over his scalp. 'Do we think there's anything in Hamlin's, Klinger's or Richards' personalities that aligns with this? Any telltale signs?'

'Paige Klinger's privileged, expects special treatment – she could have a God complex?' Nas suggested.

'Richards is certainly delusional. He's obsessed with Paige,' Moast said. 'Where's Tibbsy?'

'Not sure, sir,' said Nas.

'It'd be good to get his input on this,' Moast said. 'Let's compare what Apollyon tweeted to Venton with his other tweets. See if there's any pattern.'

Freddie shook her head as if trying to dislodge it all. Paige Klinger. Noel Richards. Mark Hamlin. Moast was looking at her.

'Okay, I think you've had enough for today. Cudmore, have someone take Venton home, make sure she gets there safe. We'll pick this up again tomorrow. With Tibbsy as well. We're all tired. We all need sleep. I need to think.'

Nas smiled at Freddie as if she were a child. 'Yes, sir,' she said.

Nasreen cupped the vending machine tea in her hands. A quick five-minute break and then she'd crack on. DCI Moast was coming out of his office, pulling his coat on.

'You still here, Cudmore?' he said, zipping his puffa up.

'Just wanted to run over a few things again, guv.' There must be something they'd missed about Alun Mardling, Sophie Phillips and Dr Grape. Some thread that tied them to Paige Klinger, Noel Richards or Mark Hamlin. She could sense it, the hole in the jigsaw puzzle.

DCI Moast pulled his leather gloves on. 'Did Venton get off all right?'

'Yes, Tibbsy is giving her a lift home. She's a bit shaken up.' Nasreen was relieved Freddie had left, she was so jittery it was distracting.

'This case is getting to us all,' Moast frowned.

He looked shattered. 'We'll get there, sir,' she said. 'We have to.'

Nasreen watched Moast walk out into the car park and thought about calling it a day too. She longed to curl up on her sofa with a glass of Malbec and iPlayer. Put all this out of her mind. But she knew it didn't work like that. She wouldn't be able to let the case go until it was resolved. She was knackered, but that could work for her. Nasreen often found there was clarity when her mind was slowed by tiredness. When her rushing thoughts were stilled. That was when the truth might float to the surface.

The incident room was empty. Nasreen stood in front of the boards, reading again everything she already knew. Everything she'd read a thousand times before. Why had Paige Klinger sent her lawyers to free Richards? It did suggest she was trying to protect him. Had she instigated the attacks? Insisted Richards do it, possibly paid him? She was rich, influential and a known drug user, did she feel entitled to snub out those who got in her way? Both Mardling and Grape had publicly abused her.

But then there was Mark Hamlin. He'd seemed frightened, weak to Nasreen. But Apollyon's tweets had stopped while Hamlin was in custody. And they started up when he was released. It seemed an unlikely coincidence. Nasreen thought of the piles of fifty pence pieces and pound coins on Sophie Phillips' dresser: just like all those found in Hamlin's flat. And where was Hamlin? Since the tail had lost him he'd not resurfaced. Hamlin had met Alun Mardling. Mardling had thrown him out of the bank. But they'd found nothing to link Hamlin to Dr Grape.

Nasreen looked again at the photo of Sophie's body on her bed. It was largely unmarked compared to the violence meted out to Mardling and Grape. Nasreen had double-checked all of Sophie's work colleagues' statements: no one remembered her mentioning a cat. It didn't fit. Something wasn't right. They'd still not found the device Sophie Phillips had used to post online. Locating that might provide some answers. Alert them to someone in Sophie's life they'd missed.

There were links between Paige Klinger, and possibly Noel Richards, with Mardling and Grape, but not Sophie. There were links between Mark Hamlin and Mardling and Sophie, but not Dr Grape. Was it possible they were looking at two different culprits? Or was the perpetrator genuinely selecting victims at random from Twitter. It was an alarming thought. With no links, no patterns, and with arbitrarily selected vics, how would they narrow their search down?

There was a knock at the door. 'Come in!' Nasreen shouted. The robust figure of PC Boulson leant into the room. 'All right, constable?' she said.

'Sorry, I was looking for the guv.' Boulson's teeth shone white against his skin.

'He's left for the night. Anything I can help with?' She didn't want to get stuck here, but Boulson was a nice guy. A good cop.

'I've got this woman on the phone. Says she's a friend of your Sophie Phillips,' he said.

'From the council?' Nasreen said.

'No, before that. From university,' he said.

Nasreen tucked the pen she was holding behind her ear. 'But Sophie didn't go to university. We have no record of that.'

'That's what she says. Probably a wind-up merchant. Seen all the fuss about this in the press, like,' he shrugged.

Nasreen sighed. She could do without this. 'Yeah, all right. Put her through.'

'Hello?' said a female voice on the other end. 'I want to speak to someone about Sophie Phillips.'

'Yes, ma'am. I can help you with that.' Nas sat at the desk and slid her bag toward her with her foot. She'd get this over with and call it a day. 'I understand you claim you went to university with Sophie Phillips?'

'That's right. We were at Brighton together. Except she wasn't called Sophie then, she was called Imogen Leatherby.'

'You knew Sophie under a different name?' Why would she be using a different name?

'Yeah, I always wondered what happened to her. She's changed her hair and that, but I'd recognise that face anywhere.'

'Sorry ma'am, what did you say your name was?' Nas looked up at the smiling photo of Sophie from the newspaper that was pinned to the board.

'Mel. Melanie Cole,' she said. 'Was it him – that killed her?'

He? 'Who?' Nas asked. The woman seemed calm. The slight hint of upset when she said Imogen. She didn't sound like she was lying. Nasreen wished she could see her body language.

'I can't remember his name. It must be nearly ten years since I saw her. But I always thought it was down to him that she left,' Mel said.

'She left?' Nas was writing all this down.

'Sorry,' Mel said. 'I'm not making myself very clear. It was a bit of a shock. I've just seen the photo in the paper. In the pub. It's a few days old.'

'Yes,' said Nas. Perhaps this was a time-waster after all. Some lonely woman who wanted to talk.

'I met Imogen at university. Nice girl. Quiet. Bit of a sad home life: she was raised by her Auntie. Emma I think she was called,' Mel said.

Nasreen gripped the pen. *The photograph of the older woman they'd found in Sophie's room had said Auntie Em, Brighton Pier on it.* 'Yes,' she said.

'Imogen wasn't really up for going out drinking and it got worse after she met this guy,' Mel said. 'He worked for the university. Did the computers.' *Computers. The Internet. Twitter. Was this the breakthrough they were looking for?* 'Well I never liked him. Creepy he was,' Mel said. 'The jealous type. He didn't like Imogen seeing us. I started to notice bruises on her arms. A black eye once. She said she was clumsy...' she trailed off.

'Go on,' Nasreen said, scribbling down every word Mel said.

'I kept trying to see her. To reach her. But it got harder and harder. She dropped out of university in the end. I never saw her after that,' Mel said.

'And you can't remember the name of Imogen's partner?'

'No, sorry. I only saw him once or twice. In the computer labs. He didn't want to talk to us.'

'And do you have any proof that Imogen Leatherby is Sophie Phillips – any photos?'

'I might do. Back at my flat. I'll have to look. She had red hair back then,' Mel said.

'Great. Could you do that? Email it over to me as soon as possible. And what year was this – when Imogen was at Brighton University?' Nas typed Imogen Leatherby into the police database. Zero results. She'd never been involved with the police then. Never reported a crime.

'2005,' Mel said.

As soon as she was off the phone Nasreen Googled 'Imogen Leatherby Brighton University 2005'. An article in the Brighton & Hove newspaper was the first result: University Computer Club Receive New Equipment. A photo at the top of the page showed a group of students smiling in their new lab. Nasreen gasped. There in the front was Sophie Phillips with long red hair. Sophie Phillips *was* Imogen Leatherby. She printed the photo from the newspaper. Holding it up against the photo of Sophie Phillips on the incident board. Her hair had been cut and dyed blonde, but it was clearly the same girl. No doubt about it. It was then that Nasreen saw another face that she recognised in the photo. Toward the back. Almost hidden by the others. *It couldn't be?* 'Holy shit!' *Computer club. Imogen Leatherby.* What had Melanie Cole said? *I always wondered what happened to her. Was it him – that killed her?* Nasreen's eyes took in the whole incident board. *Auntie Em Brighton Pier 2003.* Sophie wasn't a cat lover selected at random from Twitter by Apollyon. No wonder nothing seemed to feel right or fit with Sophie's murder compared to the others. There was no cat. There was no device. She wasn't a cat lover at all. Sophie Phillips *was* Imogen Leatherby. And the missing piece clicked into place.

Freddie took two attempts to undo her seatbelt as Tibbsy stopped the car outside her flat. The pub glowed warm and inviting in the dark. It was rammed. It reminded her of meeting Brian at The Bearded Mole. Of her posting her location online. Had he sought her out that night? Was he the Hashtag Murderer? She couldn't bear the thought that the hands that had done that to Grape had been on her, inside her. No, it was nonsense. She was paranoid. Cracking up. She shivered at the thought of Apollyon's tweet again. What an idiot she'd been.

'Need me to walk you to the door?' said Tibbsy.

Freddie hesitated for a second. Apollyon hadn't replied though, had he? He wasn't genuinely interested in her. He was probably having a bad day – trouble at t' kill, she thought wryly. He'd just lashed out. Then she felt the guilt trickle through her veins. It was no laughing matter. She had to pull herself together. 'No, it's cool. I'll be fine.'

She slammed the car door behind her and gave a little wave. No sign of any of her flatmates enjoying a post-work pint in the concrete garden of the Queen Elizabeth pub. A group she didn't recognise was huddled under one of the outdoor heaters. The football was on tonight, wasn't it? Great: no early night for her. Steam rose from a mulled wine glass one of the women was cradling in her hand. Her hair was dyed with chalk like hers had been. But better. She would've liked to ask what brand it was, but she couldn't bring herself to talk to anyone. The thought of small talk mortified her. Now was not the time to think about bloody hair dye.

Freddie reached the door and put her key in the lock. As it turned, it hit her: *you with your red fucking fake hair.* How the hell did Apollyon know she'd dyed her hair a fortnight ago? The significance trickled over her like icy water. Whoever Apollyon was he must have seen her. Up close. In person.

Chapter 40

PDA – Public Display of Affection

Nasreen's heart was pounding. She was up and running. *Imogen with her red hair. Red hair.* Apollyon's tweet to Freddie had talked about her red hair dye. The hair dye she'd had on that first night. She tried Freddie's number. Straight to voicemail. She was out of the incident room now, halfway down the corridor. She called DCI Moast. Straight to voicemail. The door from the car park opened in front of her. Tibbsy came in rubbing his gloved hands together. Stamping his feet.

'Where's Freddie?' She heard the panic in her voice.

'What do you mean?' Tibbsy asked. 'I've dropped her at hers like you said?'

'We've got to get over there.' She reached for her radio and realised it was still in her handbag under her desk.

'What is it?' Tibbsy turned as she reached him. They were running together now.

She slammed through the door, sprinting to the car. 'I know who it is. The Hashtag Murderer. We've got to get to Freddie. She's in danger.'

Tibbsy unlocked the doors and Nasreen threw herself into the car. The engine sprang to life. Tibbsy fastened his seatbelt. Nasreen grabbed the radio handset. 'All units assist. All units assist: Dalston E8. We need immediate response. Suspect is potentially armed and dangerous.' She tried Freddie on her phone again. Voicemail. She had to warn her. She kept hitting redial. The siren blared and the blue lights lit the world in short sharp flashes as they sped out of Jubilee police station.

Freddie tore through her room. Her Mac, still disconnected from the wall where she'd ripped it out the other day, barely had battery. The wire had split. Dammit. She must have damaged it at the time. She prayed it would hold: buffering. Buffering. She must have made a mistake. She pulled *The Family Paper* up first: scrolling through the article about herself, checking every photo. *What about at Hamlin's arrest?* No that made no sense, that would be too late. *The Post* was easier: just the one photo, far too old, when she was back at uni. Her heart was hammering. She scrolled quickly through her Instagram. Drinks. Her in a bobble hat. Some leaves in the park. Nothing that revealed it. Finally she checked Twitter itself, searching for her name. She scanned the results for photos. *Hashtag hunter. Hashtag whore. Who the fuck is this Freddie Venton?* A photo of her running toward Hamlin's tower block. Plenty of hits, but nothing, nothing anywhere, that showed her with her red hair chalk. She'd watched it, the dye, on that first night, wash down the plughole. When she was back from Mardling's place. The realisation hit her so hard it winded her: the only people who knew she had red hair chalk were the people who'd seen her that night. She scrabbled for her phone. Climbed up onto the windowsill for signal. Called Nas: straight to voicemail. She typed the words into a text, trembling as she did:

It's someone on the team! Apollyon is on the team!

Why hadn't she seen it earlier? The careful concealing of DNA? It was obviously someone who knew the law and police methods inside out. They were always one step ahead of the team *because* they were part of the team. Part of those making the plan. She thought about everyone who had been there at Mardling's house. How many had she interacted with? How many had she seen? She tried to replay it in her mind, but things were blurred. Who was at Grape's house and who was at Mardling's? She'd seen Dan, Milena, Kathy, the drunk guy in Espress-oh's before she left. No, it couldn't be them. What possible motive would they have? It had to be someone closer to the case. Someone who was at the crime scene. Her Mac hummed as the battery died. Dammit.

Think. Think. She was pacing, running through it all again. The SOCO suit. Nasreen pulling it up to cover her hair. She froze. *No.* But it made perfect sense. How removed Nasreen had seemed about Gemma. Almost like she didn't care. *No.* How calm she was in a crisis. *No.* How quickly she'd got a Twitter account – how quickly she'd got to grips with it. *No.* And she'd known about the anonymity software Tor. *No.* It couldn't be. But then Freddie had been so quick to work out the Apollyon clues. Maybe it was nothing to do with understanding the Internet, and maybe it was about the person who was writing them understanding *her* better than anyone? *No.* Her best friend. Her ex-best friend. They'd been through something traumatic. That messed with people. She thought of Nas's shoulders hunching when she'd screamed at her about Gemma in the police station. She hadn't fought back. Nas hadn't said much of anything at all. Perhaps she didn't need to? Perhaps she already had her dialogue, her plan: her revenge. *No.* Perhaps Nas was already making Freddie pay for what she did. Was it coincidence they'd been in St Pancras station that night? Freddie had a Twitter account, Facebook, Snapchat, Google bloody +, she documented her whole life. It'd be easy to find her. Track her down. A quick search and you could

307

probably build a background picture of all of Freddie's habits, her movements, just like the police did when they investigated someone's murder. Standard procedure. A process. *No.* She felt sick. It couldn't be, but everything pointed to it. It all made sense: Nasreen Cudmore was Apollyon. Nasreen Cudmore was the Hashtag Murderer.

Her phone buzzed in her hand. Freddie jumped. *Fuck.*

Apollyon @Apollyon • 1s
@ReadyFreddieGo Boo!

She began to shake. *Everyone makes mistakes eventually* – wasn't that what Moast had said? *You with your red fucking fake hair.* She was the mistake. Horror spread over her like a stain: she'd texted Nasreen! Apollyon knew she was onto them. Nasreen knew she was onto her. Freddie shook her head. People don't change like that. They don't become serial killers. Unless…unless something happens to them. Triggers it. Like a great loss. A breakdown. A suicide attempt. Oh poor Gemma. *What had they done? What had Nasreen done?*

Her phone buzzed in her hand: '@Apollyon is following you.' She froze. Apollyon only followed Alun Mardling, Sophie Phillips and Dr Grape. The Hashtag Murderer only followed those they had killed or were about to kill. And now the Hashtag Murderer was following Freddie.

Superintendent Gray was driving when his in-car phone rang. He glanced at the screen: *Emily calling*. His daughter. He flicked the switch to turn on hands-free.

'Hi darling, I'm on my way home, I just need to run a quick errand first,' he said.

'Daddy?' Emily said. He heard the hesitation in her voice.

'What is it, darling?'

'I've got something to tell you, but you've got to promise that you won't be angry?'

'What's happened? Are you in trouble at school?' He flicked the indicator up to turn left. The traffic was even slower than normal. There must have been an accident, he thought.

'Daddy, you've got to promise. It's important.' Emily's voice crackled in and out.

'Okay, darling. I promise.'

'I've got a Twitter account,' she said.

'Emily! We've spoken about this before. I don't like those social media sites. They're dangerous.' He'd have to talk to her school. No doubt she was getting this from one of her friends.

'Yes, but listen, dad, it's not that. I follow that Hashtag Murderer, dude.'

'Emily! That person is involved in a criminal case. You should not be following him. This is exactly why I don't want you on these sites.'

'Everyone follows him at school, Daddy. But listen, I saw him tweet that girl you're working with. That Freddie one with the weird hair.'

Superintendent Gray watched the red brake lights stretch in front of him toward the next lights. 'I see.'

'No, you don't, Daddy. That's why I called. The murderer dude just started following her too.' Somewhere behind, people started beeping. 'Daddy, are you listening? He hasn't followed anyone else. Only people he's killed and stuff.'

Superintendent Gray ran his hand through his hair. This was potentially catastrophic. 'Tell your mother I'm going to be late, Emily. And that you're grounded.' He cut the phone off. And punched in the station number. Flicking on the blue lights in the grill of his unmarked car, he spun 180 degrees and sped toward the East End. 'This is Superintendent Gray. I need the address of Freddie Venton, now. And back-up. Get DCI Moast. And get him there.'

DCI Moast figured he only had a short window of time. Five minutes, ten minutes max. He'd got the message from the Superintendent, and heard the call-out on the radio. He was most of the way to Dalston now. He gripped the steering wheel so his gloves pulled tight over his hands, and swung the car round the wet backstreets of East London. He hammered the horn at a cyclist who was dawdling away from the kerb. *Fucking cyclists.* He was aware he was grinding his teeth. Every part of him contracting, winding down, tight, like a spring. He'd never liked Freddie Venton. Never. But he didn't think she'd ever cause this much trouble.

Fuck. Fuck. Freddie couldn't think. She didn't have long. Minutes. She had to get help. She scrambled up onto the windowsill. She had to get signal. The phone rang immediately in her hand. Flashing like a warning light: Nasreen calling. *Oh my God.* Freddie dropped the phone. Dashing into the hall, she knocked on Pete's bedroom door. 'Pete, you in?' She pushed it open. Empty. Anton's room too. 'Anyone!' She was alone. She heard a noise. The lights went out. A roar went up from the pub below. The power was out. Her heart was hammering in her chest. She was blinking in the darkness. There it was again, that noise. She turned. The front door. The handle was opening. She couldn't see anything. Fuck their blackout blinds. *@ReadyFreddieGo Boo!* She inched backwards. Holding her breath. Don't make a sound. The noise of a slow clap and jeering drifted from downstairs. The people in the garden. If she could get to her bedroom window she could shout. Reach her phone.

The door swung open.

Freddie ducked into the lounge. Her heart racing. Sweat dripped into her eye. The blue glow of an iPad filled the hallway, floating toward her. The drinkers downstairs were singing, 'Why are we waiting? Why are we waiting?'

She tried to back away, but she bumped into the coffee table. The blue light turned the corner, the iPad turned toward her: Twitter open, glowing. Everywhere else she looked was plunged into darkness, her eyes blinded from the screen. She could just make out the dark figure behind it.

'Wait…' Freddie grabbed at the nearest thing – a cold half-empty Espress-oh's coffee – and threw it at the iPad light. She staggered backwards as the screen batted it away. Closer. Closer.

'Why are we waiting? Why are we waiting?' The singing grew louder downstairs.

Where was the sofa? The chair? Disorientated, she crouched and felt and tried to keep moving. Blinking blue spots in front of her eyes. She got to the chair, turned, one foot on it. She could see the faint outline of the blind. The window. Launching herself, she screamed: 'Help!' Desperately slamming her palm against the window.

'Why are we waiting? Why are we waiting?'

A hand grabbed her foot. Pulled. Freddie twisted, fell between the sofa and the chair, the radiator cutting into her cheek, her glasses shattering. Her breath was all she could hear. Pain seared through her face. Her ears rang. She held her hands up. Hot and wet. Blood. 'No!'

The iPad screen swinging in a blur toward her was the last thing Freddie Venton saw.

Nasreen had the car door open before Tibbsy had stopped. Freddie's building was dark. 'He's here! He's going to kill her.' Loud singing was coming from the pub.

'Nas! Wait!' Tibbsy was shouting. 'Jesus! All units assist. Assist. Where the fuck is everyone?'

Nasreen vaulted the wall and ran at the gate. *Shit*. Each time she'd been before it was on the latch. Now it was locked. She thought of the meticulous planning. *Him*. She stepped back and kicked it. Once. Twice. Three times. The gate sprang open, smashing back against the wall. She ran forward, jumping a pile of post and newspapers. Her eyes adjusting to the darkness.

Fight or flight. Nasreen knew all the science from her training. Norepinephrine made her alert. Epinephrine shot her full of energy. She saw it all clearly now, like an out-of-body experience. Every gym session, every book she'd read, every criminal she'd tackled – it was all preparation for this moment. She was running. Kicking her high heels off.

'Cudmore!' Tibbsy was trying to keep up.

She was taking two stairs at a time. She blocked out the sound of the pub. She felt the movements above. Her body glowed with heat. Adrenaline powered through her. The door was open. A blue light from Freddie's room. The lounge.

'Freddie!' she screamed. Nasreen saw the dark figure standing over the crumpled heap of her friend. The iPad screen dripping with blood. Freddie's blood. 'Jamie, stop!' she shouted. His arm swung up and made its sickening way down toward Freddie. Her childhood friend. *BFFs*. 'James!' she shouted. Jamie faltered, looking back at her. Fear and panic gave way to something else in Nasreen. Something bigger and stronger than experience. Something greater than any other chemical reaction. She grabbed for the nearest thing, The Oxford English Dictionary, and she swung it at Jamie. It burst up through her like a geyser: love. *This is my friend and you will not take her from me.* Jamie was knocked sideways into the wall.

Nasreen took her chance; she flung herself on him, wrenching his hands back behind him.

Tibbsy appeared behind her. 'Fucking hell.' He ran to Freddie.

'We need an ambulance. Now!' Nas heard her voice crack. The screech of a car. Footsteps on the stairs. Shouts. Moast's hands on her shoulders. Constable Boulson cuffing Jamie. The lights came on. The roar of the pub. Blood. There was so much blood. 'Jamie, what have you done?'

Tibbsy was clutching Freddie to him, stroking her blood-soaked hair, rocking. 'Don't you give up on me now, Venters. Don't.' His voice cracked.

'Jesus Christ.' Moast gently pulled on Nasreen's arm as the paramedics pushed past. 'Come away.'

Chapter 41

WTAF – What The Actual Fuck?

12:30
Friday 27 November
Account Terminated

Superintendent Gray and DCI Moast insisted Nasreen take some time off to recover. The decision was forced upon her. Jamie's face was plastered across every front page. Every website. *Cop On Case Unmasked As Hashtag Murderer.* Everywhere she looked she saw photos of him being dragged, cuffed, into Moast's car. The ambulance just behind it. She couldn't escape the memory of Freddie: bloodied, crushed.

Nasreen had aimlessly wandered round her house during the last two weeks, looking at photos of her and Freddie when they were kids. Birthday parties, their faces smeared with icing, fingers orange from Wotsits. Trips to the zoo with Mr Venton when he was sober. The week Freddie had spent with Nasreen and her family in a wind-buffeted caravan in Cornwall, Freddie and Nasreen streaking far ahead of her younger sisters on a twilit beach. Running into the setting sun. What had started as a few glasses of red wine to help Nasreen sleep at night had soon turned into a bottle. The call from the station was a lifeline. She'd washed her hair, got dressed, left the house. Tibbsy was waiting in the foyer of the Jubilee police station. His hands in his pockets. Shirtsleeves rolled up. Rocking on his feet. 'You're the welcome party then?' she said.

'I guess.' He managed a brief smile. He looked like he'd been sleeping as well as she had.

'Let's get this over with.' She strode past him. Her heels sounded reassuringly familiar clicking on the floor. Back in her suit she felt stronger. Together.

'The guv wants a word first. To brief you.' Tibbsy walked alongside her. Ahead of them in the corridor, PC Boulson stopped, his smile dropping from his face; he stood aside to let her pass. His head bowed in reverence. She couldn't deal with *this*. Eyes peered out of offices as they walked. 'You're a bit of a hero. After what happened.' Tibbsy nodded at the two constables who were watching them from either side of the vending machine. 'You took down the Hashtag Murderer. Cracked the whole case wide open.'

'It was just a lucky break.' She tasted the bitter irony on her tongue.

Tibbsy opened the door of Moast's office for her.

'Ah, Cudmore. You're here.' DCI Moast stood up from behind his desk and ran his hand over his hair. The last time she'd seen him, those hands were pulling her away.

'I'll be outside if you need me, guv.' Tibbsy held up his palm to say goodbye. She smiled at him. He looked at the floor and closed the door.

'I'm sorry we've had to get you back in so early,' Moast said. They stood awkwardly either side of the desk.

'It's fine. I'd rather be busy,' she said.

'Well, that aside, I appreciate you doing this. I know it can't be easy.' Moast frowned.

'Has Jamie said anything, sir? Explained why he did it?'

'Just that he'll only talk to you. I'm afraid that when we searched his apartment we found several photos of you, Cudmore. And a number of personal items.' Moast passed her a pile of images.

Nasreen felt her chest constrict. 'That's me at the gym. And leaving Claire's house. Christ. I never saw him.'

'Well it seems he was very adept at following, hiding…'

'Tracking,' she said, looking at the photos. That was her hair tie. A scarf she'd lost last year. She'd never suspected Jamie was collecting these things. Turning her into an exhibit.

'Yes,' said Moast. 'We found the spare phone he used to post as Sophie when he was impersonating her online. The IP address is local to Leighton Buzzard because he was there. Watching her.'

Poor Sophie, she was at the heart of this case. 'How the hell did he pull all this off?'

'It seems he's been at it for years. We've had the forensic psychiatrist in. They spent three hours with him. He would talk about everything but the case.' Moast sighed. 'They say he scores highly on the psychopath spectrum. Overly developed capability for deceit, ingratiation, cool-headed, imitation. Apparently it was no surprise he fooled us.'

Nasreen sat down on the chair. She'd thought about this over and over in the last fortnight. If she hadn't have seen Jamie with her own eyes, seen him strike, then she might never have believed it.

'They call it the mask of sanity. That's what the doc said. She recommended a book on it if you want?' Moast said.

'What do you need me to do, sir?' she asked.

'We spoke to Sophie's – to Imogen's – old classmates. We've built up a pretty clear picture. Jamie, or James as he was back then, was controlling, abusive, both psychologically and physically. She never went to the police.' Moast moved the papers on his desk with the tips of his fingers. He'd clearly been working on nothing else since the night at Freddie's.

'Too scared,' Nas said. 'Too ground down.' She'd seen it before with domestic abuse cases. The victim too frightened to talk.

Sophie had done well to get away. To start a new life. Albeit a brief one.

'Yes,' Moast nodded. 'That's all alleged from her friends, years ago, no actual witnesses so we can't use it. But it gives us an insight. We found the same brand of supermarket bleach used at the crime scenes, key cutting equipment, the same plastic ties used to restrain Grape, and a knife matching the description of that featured in the Mardling photo on Twitter at his flat. He'd soaked the knife in bleach and put it through the dishwasher. The DNA sample is corrupted.'

'Thorough. Meticulous. Fits with the MO.' Nasreen shuddered. She'd chatted with Jamie. Sat next to him in the car. Hugged him goodbye at the end of the day. Thought of him as a friend. He'd driven her to Freddie's house. He knew exactly where she lived. 'He was the one who found the link between Mardling, Sophie and Mark Hamlin. Was it a set-up?' she asked. Jamie had manipulated the case from the inside and they'd never suspected a thing.

'Most likely. We still haven't been able to trace Hamlin. We found two smartphones on him, one was an Android and running Tor; this software that encrypted his Internet activity. He was able to post messages while he was here at the station and we had no way of telling. We also recovered a laptop at his flat. Digital forensics are trying to crack into it now. We'll get him. But a confession would help. The doctor reckoned he might talk to you. Want to impress you, like. You up to it?'

Nasreen thought about Freddie. She nodded. 'Yes.'

'Good. The doc said the trick is to always treat him like he's smarter.'

Nasreen thought of all the deception, all the technology, the way they'd all been looking in the wrong direction. 'He is,' she said.

Nasreen eyed Jamie opposite her. His uniform buttons shone. She knew his shoes did too. 'I'm glad you came, Nasreen. I wanted to see you again,' he said. He was still manipulating them all. She tried to keep her face impassive. 'Not frightened are you?' Jamie asked. 'I always admired your bravery.' She steadied her hands on the desk. The blinds were pulled down. The only light a strip above them. 'I admired your intelligence too.' His watery eyes narrowed conspiratorially. 'Unlike these other idiots,' he whispered.

'I came, Jamie. So let's talk,' she said. The tape machine hummed gently. Moast was just outside. 'Can you tell me about you and Sophie, or Imogen as you knew her?'

Jamie raised an eyebrow. 'Okay. Imogen would have liked you. You were very similar. She was pure: like you. Mired by those around her.'

'I spoke to Melanie Cole.' Saliva pooled in her mouth. She kept swallowing.

'That parasite,' said Jamie. 'She wanted to take Imogen away from me.'

'Melanie said you hurt Imogen. Hit her.'

'Imogen was so pure, so innocent. When I found her she knew nothing. She'd been locked away in that old house with her aunt. The only things she knew of real life were from the telly they watched: Poirot, Miss Marple, Sherlock Holmes. Her batty aunt watched them every day. Imogen knew them word for word. Thought the world was populated by 1930s toffs. I had to help her, but sometimes she could be difficult. Like a naughty child. You'd discipline a child for their own good, wouldn't you? I was like a father to Imogen. I only hit her when I had to.'

Nasreen thought of the Baker Street clue he'd tweeted, the 'game is on' reference. 'Is that why you did the clues, Jamie? Because of the shows Imogen used to watch?'

He dipped his chin forward and looked at her. His face looked different. The wide-eyed simpering Jamie was gone. This was someone else. His eyes burned bright blue. Stone cold. He drummed his fingers lightly on the table. 'You are a clever girl, Nasreen. All those old murder mysteries, that's what we talked about when Imogen and I met. It seemed fitting. To make her the star of the mystery. Once I'd decided, I couldn't let her stay out there in the real world. Not after she'd run away from me. After everything I'd done for her. I'd made her special. She was mine. She couldn't just leave. There was a debt to be paid.' He paused, his voice even, unfeeling, as if he were discussing a supermarket shopping list. 'She liked Poirot best. Do you remember The ABC Murders?'

He'd killed her because he couldn't have her. Because she ran away. Because he thought she was his property. Nasreen tried to think if she'd seen the television show. 'I'm not sure, Jamie, why don't you tell me?'

'Well the very clever murderer in The ABC Murders tricks everyone into thinking there's a serial killer on the loose, bumping victims off in alphabetical order. A distraction. From the intended victim. Of course that story's just make-believe. What I did was much harder.' Jamie's fingers were still drumming rhythmically.

Nasreen felt her blood run cold. 'A distraction? From the real motive?' His fingers drummed. 'You wanted to kill Sophie, but you knew that if it was just her then we might uncover her true identity...start tracing things back...maybe reach you? So Mardling, Grape, all this about the Hashtag Murderer was a diversion?'

'It was masterful,' he said. 'I fooled everyone. The police. The media. The whole of the Internet. I had you all in the palm of my hand.'

'Why the Internet, Jamie? Why Twitter? Was it because you and Imogen met in that computer class? I've seen DCI Moast's notes. We know you applied to university. Brighton and others. For a Computer Science degree. They didn't let you in?'

'Imbeciles.' He smashed his hand down on the desk. Nasreen's heart was racing. Moast and Tibbsy were right outside. One shout and they'd be in here.

'They were so stupid, they couldn't see real genius when it was right in front of them. Idiots obsessed with their pitiful little academic exam results. Well, I showed them. They couldn't just discard me. Couldn't put me in a little box marked reject. I was the best coder. I built a programme to remote tweet from my Mac. I stood right next to you all in the police station and pressed send, and you had no idea. I'm a master of Tor. I'm untraceable. I can orientate objects in C++ with my eyes closed. Parallel processing, I'm fucking amazing. An IPv6 guru. I am the Hashtag Murderer. I am Apollyon. I had fans – those teen girls in Wales? Imitation is the sincerest form of flattery. That's influence. That's power. I put those petty-minded fools in their little boxes. Their little pigeonholes. Their little stereotypes. I made you all dance. I made you all follow me.'

Nasreen's breath was quick. 'Is that why you picked Dr Grape, because he was an academic, Jamie? One of those who hadn't seen your real potential?'

'He was a stupid fool. Patronising Apollyon. The most feared person online. He deserved to die,' Jamie said. 'A pedant. I screwed him up and stuffed him into his pigeonhole.'

'And what about Mardling? Was he stupid too?' She had to keep him talking. Keep him boasting.

His lip curled. 'That cretin. He disgusted me. He came in all high and mighty when Mark Hamlin kicked off in his bank.' *So Jamie had taken the police report. Jamie was the link between Mardling and Hamlin.* 'I looked into him. All that filth he was spewing out. You don't talk to women like that. He was scum. I did the world a favour. Pest control,' he said. 'One less troll. They played their parts perfectly.' Jamie looked at her hand. It was shaking. He smiled. She pulled it away. Under the table. Into her lap.

'And what about the cat, Jamie? Sophie Phillips' online account, her cat posts – was that all part of the plan?'

Jamie was still smiling. 'Now I'll admit I did underestimate you on that one, Nasreen. You saw straight away there was no cat. I should have left the phone I used for her posts there. That was the plan. But I was upset. She was so beautiful. Poor Imogen. If only she'd behaved herself.'

'I remembered that when you drove us to Sophie Phillips' flat, the day her body was found, you took a back route. Avoided all the traffic.' Why had she not questioned it at the time? Why would Jamie know the back route to the victim's home? If only she'd spotted it, she could have stopped this sooner.

'Very handy of her to move so close,' Jamie smiled. 'Just a quick zip up the M1, and then along the A roads. I did it in under thirty minutes once; funny how no one will pull over a police car for speeding. It took me no time at all to get there and back.'

'And you weren't worried someone would notice the police car?' Nasreen tried not to look away. She felt stripped. Naked. As if Jamie could see her very thoughts before they formed.

'I'm not an idiot, Nasreen. I kept a van up there for when I got close.'

Nasreen dug her fingernails into her palm. 'It was a nice touch with the coins – mimicking Mark Hamlin. I guess that was you too?'

'Thank you.' His eyes looked warm, heartfelt. Nasreen felt sick. 'It's all in the details. I spent some time with Mark – not much you understand, that flat was fetid – but enough.'

'Where is Mark, Jamie?' She kept her voice even.

'Regent's Canal. Surprised he hasn't bobbed back up yet.' He looked bored. 'After his whole hissy fit when he was arrested we couldn't really work together anymore.'

'So you're the reason he was screaming when he was arrested? He saw you, didn't he – on the stairs up to his flat?' She remembered Hamlin's frantic desperation to escape.

'He wasn't very robust,' Jamie sighed. 'I'd been looking for someone I could work with, and when I met Mark after that complaint was filed against him, it was like a gift from God.'

Nasreen's stomach contracted. 'What did you do to him?'

'I spent time with him. Bought him food. Bought food for those bloody cats he was obsessed with. Got him a nice shiny new laptop. But he was fickle. I had to train him to listen. To behave. A few techniques I picked up online from the Chinese and the Americans – nothing that would leave a physical mark, obviously. He was little more than an animal himself. Did you know gorillas use intimidation to gain and maintain their hierarchical dominance? I was Mark's alpha. All he had to do was look after the laptop and look mental. I mean, that was hardly difficult for him was it?' He laughed.

Nasreen managed to nod.

Jamie continued. 'But he never really got my vision. I was trying to save him from his own pathetic existence. He'd go down in history: the Hashtag Murderer. Famous. But you can't help some people. I terminated our agreement. I couldn't risk him shouting his mouth off.'

He was deluded, she thought. No, worse than that: he seemed to see all the people he'd killed as mere pawns in his plan. Collateral damage. A means to an end. 'Why join the force, Jamie?'

'Great benefits package,' he said, and as a faint smile appeared on his lips she saw something of the old Jamie. The one she thought she knew. It was the most unnerving moment so far. 'I needed your resources,' he said. 'To keep track of everyone. It's amazing what you have on record. And it was pitifully easy. I got myself a new name. Goodbye James Wakelin, hello Jamie Thomas.'

'You joined the special forces first,' she said.

'Yes, a quick online search will tell you that's the easiest route in. Less checks. I made myself useful. Transferred across as a PC. Nobody questioned poor nervous little Jamie, did they? Daft little Jamie who was sick when he saw the terrible crime scene.' He laughed. Then stopped. 'I like it when you wear your hair down, Nasreen.' He held her in his gaze and she felt like she couldn't move. 'Aren't you going to ask about her? Ready Freddie go away?'

Nasreen felt like her whole body contracted. She owed it to Freddie. After everything. She had to get the truth. 'I...' she stuttered.

'It's okay, Nasreen,' Jamie smiled. 'Call me by my real name and I'll help you.'

Nasreen's voice shook. 'What about Freddie, James?'

'Good. I like it when you call me that. Jamie was getting a bit tiresome. Bit of a drip, don't you think?' He looked like he was feeding off her fear. Enjoying it.

321

'What about Freddie?'

'It was too good, you see, when she turned up at the door of Mardling's house. Of course, I knew she wasn't a forensics officer – with that ridiculous hair.' Nasreen felt sick replaying it in her mind. If only she'd spoken up to begin with, things might have been different. 'She was my wild card.' Jamie leant forward, lowered his voice. 'I didn't think there'd be any harm in having another ball in the air. Someone else to blame. Someone to help destroy the evidence. It was a master stroke. It was a sign: that she was a journalist. I'd set up the account already. I was hopeful it'd spread. I poured the petrol, but she lit the match.'

Bile burned the back of Nasreen's throat. 'Freddie never did anything to hurt you. She wasn't a cliché. A pigeonhole.'

'Don't you see? I stopped her for you, Nasreen. A present. That day she shouted at you in the station. What she said about Gemma – the girl who tried to kill herself.'

Nasreen's hand flew to her mouth. 'How do you know?'

'How do I know?' Jamie laughed. 'I know everything. I told you, they tried to use computers against me, and now I use computers against them. Against everyone. Everything is at my fingertips. The others were for Imogen, to give her the story she deserved. But Freddie Venton was for you, Nasreen.'

His words were twisting shards of glass cutting through her. She fought to stay calm. She owed it to Freddie. To Imogen. To everyone he had hurt. 'There's one thing I can't work out, James. How did you get inside all their houses? Did you go in your police uniform?'

'Oh, sweet Nasreen, of course not. The bobby on the beat is long gone. People would be alarmed if I came to their door like this.' He flicked one of his buttons. 'You need something far more regular, far more everyday; something that'll let you inside. Finding a key to copy or propping a window open for later is easy then.'

'What about Imogen, she'd not let you in?' Nasreen struggled to put what he was saying together.

'I asked her neighbour for her spare key. When you're wearing the uniform, carrying the bag, it's easy,' he said.

She felt him enjoying her confusion. Her discomfort. Keep it going, she told herself. Just a few more minutes and then you never have to see him again. *For Freddie*. 'What uniform, James?'

'You'll like this,' he smiled. 'BT Openreach.'

'You mean...?'

His voice shifted down an octave, his eyes cleared, his whole face seemed to take on another look: altered. 'Hello, sir, we've got reports of server issues in this area. Are you happy for me to come in and check your hub? Don't want you without Internet access do we!'

Chapter 42

BRB – Be Right Back

16:00
Friday 27 November
Account Terminated

Nasreen stood in the incident room. Tibbsy looked shocked. Moast look resigned to it. 'Thank you, Cudmore. I appreciate that can't have been easy. You did a great job,' he said.

'Sir,' Nas nodded. She was still shaking. Jamie would go down for this. 'Do you mind if I take the rest of the afternoon off?' she managed. 'There's somewhere I'd like to be.' Tibbsy looked at the floor. *Perhaps she should ask him along too?*

'Of course,' Moast said. 'Tibbsy, give us a moment please?'

'Guv,' Tibbsy nodded. 'Nasreen,' he gave her a smile. Then disappeared toward the canteen.

'Sergeant Cudmore, I want you to know that I'll be recommending you for promotion. Your actions on this case have been…' Moast paused. Seemed to search for the right word. *Failed.*

'Thank you, sir.' Being made inspector, progressing, it was all she'd wanted. Everything she'd worked for. She'd caught the Hashtag Murderer. She'd caught Jamie. The image of Freddie, blood-soaked, broken, clutched in Tibbsy's arms, flashed across her mind. It haunted her. Would any of them be the same after this? They were all tainted. They could have stopped Jamie at any time, if only they'd realised earlier. Any one of them. Her promotion, her win, had come at too high a cost.

Moast looked like he might try and hug her. That would've made Freddie laugh, she thought wryly. In the end he extended a hand for her to shake. 'Good job, Nas.'

Nasreen walked out of Jubilee station. The flagship of the East End force. The wind blew an empty takeaway chicken box across her path. She pulled her coat tight around her. Christmas shoppers and excitable kids ran past. Fairy lights and tinsel twinkled in the shop windows. She'd get to spend this year with her parents. Compassionate leave: the Superintendent didn't want her back till the New Year. All this special treatment. Nasreen shook her head. She'd just done her job. She was a policewoman. She was trained. She was supposed to take on criminals like Jamie. Everyone kept telling Nasreen she was a hero, but she knew there was only one person who'd given more than was expected. Freddie. She should never have been put in harm's way. It was Freddie who had acted selflessly, above and beyond the call of duty.

She saw the number 277 bus and ran for it. Inside, the windows were steamed from the heat of weary workers. The night was already drawing in, and it was barely 4pm. She struggled to see out past the woman with the buggy and an auburn-haired lady leaning against the window. She wasn't sure precisely where she needed to stop. Everyone staring at their phones, the pale illumination of their faces reminded her of torches under chins for ghost stories round the fire at Brownies. Her, Gemma and Freddie. She swallowed. It was here. She pressed the button.

As she walked down the side street, past Georgian windows, Nas caught glimpses of others' lives as the warm glow of electric light overpowered the growing dusk. It was cold. But she couldn't turn back now. The church was at the end of the road, a green spire rose up into the night sky. It was one of those old buildings in London that made you feel like you were insignificant, only passing, history. She wondered how many feet had trodden this path before, and for how many hundreds of years. At the gate, she turned right, down the pathway away from the front archway and into the graves. Stones rose up. The old, moss-covered and mottled. The new, shiny like slabs of kitchen granite. There was one that was more subtle. New, but made of traditional stone. Cheaper. Its white lettering growing increasingly unclear in the fading light. Nas swallowed the lump in her throat: *for what might have been.* Opposite the new grave was a bench. She sat on the damp wood. 'Why on earth would you want to meet here?'

'I find it peaceful,' said Freddie.

Nas turned and looked at her friend. Stitches grew as if from a bruised plum on her forehead. The gash on her cheek had been sewn into a Y shape. Permanent, but she'd get reconstructive surgery on the NHS. *Eventually.* Freddie's left arm in a cast, the bone crushed from the blows of Jamie's iPad. Freddie had spent days in hospital, undergone emergency surgery to relieve bleeding on the brain, but she'd been lucky. The doctors had said if Nasreen had got there just a few minutes later Jamie would've finished the job. The thought punched a hole in Nasreen's chest. 'How you feeling?'

'Fucking dreadful.' Freddie exhaled smoke rings into the evening air. 'My head's still buzzing. They say it's like tinnitus. The shock from the operation. It'll go. But I can't use any screens. No fucking phone. Nothing. Brings on headaches. They make me feel sick just sitting up.'

'Should you be smoking?' Nas asked.

Freddie rolled her eyes at her. 'What the hell else am I supposed to do with my fingers if I can't use my phone.'

Nasreen laughed gently.

'And did you see that fucker did a kiss-and-tell on me?' Freddie drew sharply on the cigarette.

Nasreen thought of the newspaper article: *My Night With Hashtag Murderer Hunter*. A lurid exposé from an undercover journalist who'd met Freddie in a bar and slept with her. Her mum had brought it over. 'I'd hoped you wouldn't see that. Who was he?'

'Brian,' Freddie said. 'He wasn't even that good. I knew something was off with him. He said something about me working with the police. I knew I never told him that. I actually thought for a while that he might be Apollyon.'

'I guess some people will do anything for a story,' Nasreen said. Freddie laughed. 'And don't I know it.'

Nasreen smiled. In some ways Freddie seemed the same: the aggressive statements, the swearing. But there was a new frailty that clung to her edges, Nasreen could sense it. As if every word she spoke had been crafted into a delicate paper doily. If you handled her too hard she might break. They sat for a moment. Quiet. Listening to the hum of the traffic in the distance. One last bird song: a desperate goodbye to the sun. Nasreen looked up into the trees, dark leaves cut against the deep blue sky.

'It's why I like it here,' Freddie said, following her gaze. 'It's quiet. Peaceful. Not many people staring at you.'

'It'll get better,' said Nas. She didn't know what to say.

'Ha!' scoffed Freddie. 'You sound like the bloody doctors.'

'Well, maybe they're right,' said Nas.

'Can't work though, can I?' Freddie stubbed her cigarette out on the metal arm of the bench. Tiny orange ashes flared in the darkening sky.

'Are you okay, do you need money?' Nas thought about her promotion. The pay increase that was coming her way. Freddie's lounge bedroom. 'Or a place to stay?'

Freddie laughed, and then winced. 'It isn't about that, Nas. Money. None of this was about that. Don't get me wrong, I'd love a place of my own, you know? Stop sleeping on a bloody couch.' She smiled. 'I've just never been any good at anything else. Writing was always it.'

Nas sat for a moment, looked at the interlaced fingers of her hands. Then spoke. 'When I was nine there was a domestic incident on my road. Mr Frans dragged his wife kicking and screaming out onto the front garden. Their kid was naked, wet, just out the bath, I guess, crying in the doorway. Another neighbour, I can't remember his name, dad of one of the kids at our school, went out with a baseball bat. Threatened Mr Frans. Mr Frans got in his car and drove straight at him. Then backed into the lamp post in front of our house. Knocked it over. I watched the whole thing. It must have been summer. It was light. I was up. The dads all took their cars and blocked the ends of the road so he couldn't drive back in. Couldn't hit one of us riding round on our bikes.'

'Hard core,' said Freddie.

'Next day it all went back to normal. Mr Frans was back at home. With his wife. With his kid.'

'That's fucked up.' Freddie lit another cigarette.

Nasreen swatted the smoke away. 'It's why I did it. Why I joined the police force. To try and help Mrs Frans. Or people like her.'

Freddie exhaled. 'I wondered if it was something to do with Gemma. With the suicide bid.'

'I guess that too,' said Nasreen. 'I want to help people. I'm good at it.' There was so much Nasreen wanted to say. So many apologies. So many thank yous.

'I do it – writing, or at least I did it – because I want to make a difference. To bear witness. I should've been a war correspondent,' Freddie said.

'You'd have been killed within two seconds!' Nas laughed.

Freddie turned the end of her fag round, twisting it into a glowing point. 'Thanks, Nas.'

'I'm only kidding.' She didn't want to upset her. Every time it felt like they were back on the same page, in the same place, they'd judder apart again.

'No, I mean for…you know…saving me.' Freddie sounded awkward.

'It was nothing.' The image of Freddie broken in Tibbsy's arms flashed across Nasreen's vision. She tucked her hair behind her ear. Blinked it away. 'What'll you do?'

'I got some money from selling my story. Enough to take a few months off. I might wait till this heals and go travelling. I quite fancy South America. Columbia's got to be safer than here.'

Nas smiled. 'Sounds good.'

'What about you?' Freddie said.

'I'm getting promoted. Sorry,' she said with a wry smile.

'Course you are! I knew you'd make it in the institutionalised bureaucracy that's the police. Congrats!' Freddie held her hand up to high-five. Like they used to.

Nasreen smiled, bringing her hand against Freddie's. They laughed. She looked up at the spire above as it merged into the dark sky. 'I better be getting on. Got to pick up a few bits. Do some paperwork and stuff.'

'Got to keep working, hey Nas? Make sure you keep Moast and Tibbsy on their toes.' Freddie looked up at the sky too.

Nasreen watched their frosted breath drift up and intertwine. 'Let's catch up again soon, yeah?' she said.

Freddie looked at Nas in her smart suit and her black coat and felt jealous for a moment of her anonymity. Of her ability to blend in. 'Definitely. It's a date.'

Nas turned and leant in, giving her half a hug. A gentle pat on the back. Freddie could smell her Coco Chanel perfume. Feel her warmth. They pulled apart. 'See you later.'

'See you soon.' Nas stood and walked away from her.

Freddie watched as Nas reached the gate and turned, giving a quick wave into the dark. Too much had changed. They were from different worlds that had briefly and catastrophically collided. But she knew they were different. She'd always be fond of Nas. Always have a place for her in her heart. But she needed to retreat. Recover. Freddie held her hand up in response to Nas. She suspected deep inside herself that they'd probably never see each other again.

Keys are pressed and code unfurls; filling the screen, multiplying, travelling through wires, air, light; reaching out in invisible waves of orange, blue, yellow from one computer to another. From one phone to another. Spreading the millions of words, the millions of images that fill up the Internet, that fill us all up. An email address is entered. A password. A date of birth. A phone number. A new account is created. Across Twitter, Facebook, Google+, Vine, Snapchat, WhatsApp, Instagram, the same message appears:

Apollyon's Revenge: Who wants to play?

Acknowledgements

Thank you to the red lipstick wearing goddess that is my agent Diana Beaumont. I'm endlessly grateful for your faith, patience, advice, encouragement, and friendship. Plus, you crack me up when you call anyone a silly arse. I'd also like to extend my thanks to Juliet Mushens and all those at United Talent, especially Sarah Manning for her unerring behind-the-scenes hard work. Next time I come to the office I'll bring a cake with no nuts in it. Promise.

To Eleanor Dryden, in whom I've found a fellow late night lover, an expert and talented editor, and someone who gets Freddie even more than I do. Eli, the support, commitment and energy you've put into Follow Me is tremendous, and the story is so much the better for it. I hope very much that this is the beginning of a long and beautiful friendship. And to Victoria Jackson, Oliver Malcolm, Kate Ellis, Helena Sheffield, Jennifer Rothwell, and all the lovely, dynamic team at Avon: thank you for welcoming me into the family. And for the chocolate biscuits. Especially the biscuits. And to Jo Marino and Sabah Khan from Light Brigade PR for spinning my mad ideas into publicity pitches.

Various people gave their expert knowledge and time to explain aspects I researched for this book. And they usually had to do it twice, as I'm a bit slow on the uptake and/or I wanted a different answer to fit with the plot. Dr Hayley King for her medical opinion, continued emotional support, and a fascinating conversation about the effect of tasering. Dr Matthew Jones, Sarah Jones, and their esteemed dinner party guests, for their pharmaceutical advice on how best to sedate someone with a cup of tea. Matt Cook for coding, and software hacks. To Rhiannon Lucy Cosslett and Holly Baxter for telling me how truly awful (and great) being a millennial is. To Deb and Bob at Retreats For You for a safe haven. Thank you to Clare Mackintosh, and Amy Jones' other half for insider police information. And I will never again mock the television idea of the stunning female cop, with the perfect hair and killer heels; I've met the real deal, and she's even more impressive: thank you to the awe-inspiring, cocktail drinking, wonder woman Amy Jones, who gave so much of her time, memories, and knowledge of the UK police force. Nas totally wants to be you when she grows up.

To Wendy, Paul, Miranda, Julie and all at Orchard Physiotherapy St Albans, who keep me ticking over, working and walking: thank you.

Thank you to Lucy Shaw, Lauren Bravo and Fleur Sinclair for bringing light, joy, writing advice, and winning outfit game into my life. You all hold a special place in my heart. And to Li Wania, Jenny Jarvis and Kate McNaughton for continued support and cheerleading. I owe you all a million drinks, and possibly some babysitting (where applicable). And to my wonderful, incomparable limes; Claire McGowan and Sarah Day, who bring it all from encouraging thumbs up, to reassuring hugs, speed reading, writerly words of wisdom, love, laughs, Taylor Swift sing-a-longs and much, much wine (not necessarily in that order). Without you guys I'd never write a word, though I would probably get up earlier.

To my mum and dad, I may be a writer, but I struggle to put into words just how much you have done and continue to do for me, and just how grateful I am. I love you. And to Chris for being an excellent brother, and very handy for reaching things off high shelves. To Hannah, Guy, Ani and Bertie, and all my family both here, in Ewyas Harold, and in America, for your love and support. And to my wonderful Sammy, thank you for everything you've done for me: for every pep talk, plot planning session, beta reading, spell checking, and emergency chocolate bar you've bought. It would take more than all the emojis in the world to convey how much I love you.

And finally thank you to all those dedicated, brave police officers who risk their lives daily to uphold justice and protect us: you guys are the real superheroes.

Want to know what inspired Angela Clarke to write *Follow Me*?

Read on to find out more...

Q: What inspired you to write *Follow Me*?

A: Like many people, I use Twitter (and Facebook and Instagram!), and I love the interesting articles, books, films, songs, and glorious creative projects social media platforms have introduced me to. I've been part of online social movements and charity campaigns I feel passionate about. I've made great friends, and if I didn't have one already, I'm quite confident I'd find a husband on Twitter too. It's a source of constant joy, which is why it's so distressing when someone does behave badly, aggressively, or offensively towards you on there. I've written a number of feminist articles in the past, and the trolls really aren't keen on that. I'm fascinated by what drives people to troll. I watched documentaries, read up on case studies, including about those who were convicted for harassing feminist activist Caroline Criado Perez, and observed friends I know in real life say dreadful things to others online.

The reason people troll is probably varied; mental health issues, disillusionment with their own lives, they get a kick from it etc. But the motivation I kept coming back to, was those who seem to simply forget there is a real person at the other end of the Internet. Would these people say the same vile threats to your face? Apparently not, I experience much less hate in real life than I do online. I thought, what would be an extreme way to illustrate people getting whipped up by online buzz, and make them forget that there's a human being on the other end of the Internet? Showing social media users retweeting, liking, and sharing a killer's clues of who would be their next victim. And so *Follow Me* was born.

Q: Are the characters based on real people?

A: I was fortunate enough to interview an ex-policewoman who had been in some pretty hairy situations, as part of my research. Her spirit and determination definitely found their way into Nas. It was important to me that Freddie and Nas were articulate, convincing, driven, compassionate, and brave (and sometimes foolhardy) women. Because those are the women who fill my life.

Those are my work colleagues. Those are my friends. Those are the women who inspire me. Those are real women. Some people have said they can see bits of me in Freddie, which makes me laugh; Freddie's way cooler than I am. I wish I was Freddie, but I am much more like the goody-two-shoes people pleaser Nas!

Q: Do you think your discussion of social media will affect what people write about in public forums?
A: If just one person thinks twice before they post something mean or cruel, then I'd take that as a win. Technology is developing so quickly, we're all having to learn what social etiquette, norms, and even laws are needed as we use each new tool. But yeah, perhaps disabling your geolocation services on your phone might not be a bad idea.

Q: How did you find writing your debut novel? What is the hardest thing about writing?
A: Writing a story is fantastic fun. I could write all day, every day and I'd be happy. It's the editing that gets to me. The moment I have to turn my tale into something that is spellchecked, drafted, and readable by someone else, is the moment the hard work starts.

Q: Where are you most comfortable writing?
A: I have a degenerative connective tissue disorder called EDS III, which means that though my mind could write anywhere, my body is best in the memory-foam-pimped chair in front of my physio approved desk at home.

Q: Have you got a writing desk, if so can you describe it?
A: I have a reclaimed teachers' school desk. It's wooden, over a metre long, and parked in front of a pin board that covers my study wall. On the notice board are things I find stimulating, or heartening. Photos of family and friends, postcards of artists' work I love, cards and notes, and a sprinkling of Moomins. Yup, you

read that right. Gotta love the Moomins. I also pin up motivating quotes. My favourite is from Hilary Mantel (New Statesman April 2014); 'The inner process, the writing life, it doesn't change at all. Every day is like the first day, it's like being a beginner. There's no time for complacency. You need to be extending your range all the time.' I try to write with that in mind.

Q: Finally, what can we expect from your next novel?
A: *Are You Awake?* is part of the Social Media Murder series. So expect to see some favourite characters, and more techy twists, turns and tension. I'll give you one hint: You have six seconds to view this suicide note and twenty-four hours to save the girl. Snapchat, I'm coming for you!

Freddie and Nas are back.

You've got six seconds to view this suicide note and
twenty four hours to save the girl's life.

Are You Awake?
By Angela Clarke

Coming soon

MISSING: 7-MONTH-OLD INFANT DISAPPEARS FROM CRIB

***Brooklyn, NY* – The New York City Police Department is asking for the public's help in locating 7-month-old Mia Connor.**

The parents and the NYPD are pleading to the public for any assistance in the investigation and are asking residents in the North Dandry neighborhood in Brooklyn to come forward if they witnessed any suspicious behavior on the night and early morning of the 26th.

Mia Connor was last seen by her mother Estelle Paradise (27) around midnight when she laid her down to sleep. The mother discovered the child was missing when she woke up the next morning. The father was out of town when the infant disappeared.

'It's very frustrating,' said Eric Rodriguez, spokesperson for NYPD, when he appeared briefly at a news conference on Friday. 'We're hoping somebody will come forward and give us the information allowing us to locate the child.'

Immediately call the TIPS hotline at 1-888-267-4880 if you have any information about the infant's whereabouts. All calls are strictly confidential.

Chapter 1

'Mrs Paradise?'

A voice sounds out of nowhere. My thoughts are sluggish, as if I'm running under water. I try and try but I'm not getting anywhere.

'Not stable. Eighty over sixty. And falling.'

Oh God, I'm still alive.

I move my legs, they respond, barely, but they respond. Light prowls its way into my eyes. I hear dogs barking, high pitched. They pant, their tags clatter.

'You've been in a car accident.'

My face is numb, my thoughts vague, like dusty boxes in obscure and dark attic spaces. I know immediately something is amiss.

'Oh my God, look at her head.'

A siren sounds, it stutters for a second, then turns into a steady torment.

I want to tell them . . . I open my mouth, my lips begin to form the words, but the burning sensation in my head becomes unbearable. My chest is on fire, and ringing in my left ear numbs the entire side of my face.

Let me die, I want to tell them. But the only sound I hear is of crude hands tearing fragile fabric.

'Step back. Clear.'

My body explodes, jerks upward.

This isn't part of the plan.

When I come to, my vision is blurred and hazy. I make out a woman in baby-blue scrubs, a nurse, slipping a plastic tube over my head and immediately two prongs hiss cold air into my nostrils.

She pumps a lever and the bed yanks upward, then another lever triggers a motor raising the headboard until my upper body is resting almost vertically.

My world becomes clearer. The nurse's hair is in a ponytail and the pockets of her cardigan sag. I watch her dispose of tubing and wrappers and the closing of the trashcan's metal lid sounds final, evoking a feeling I can't quite place, a vague sense of loss, like a pickpocket making off with my loose change, disappearing into the crowd that is my strange memory.

A male voice sounds out of nowhere.

'I need to place a central line.'

The overly gentle voice belongs to a man in a white coat. He talks to me as if I'm a child in need of comfort.

'Just relax, you won't feel a thing.'

Relax and I won't feel a thing? Easy for him to say. I feel lost somehow, as if I'm in the middle of a blizzard, unable to decide which direction to turn. I lift my arms and pain shoots from my shoulder into my neck. I tell myself not to do that again anytime soon.

The white coat wipes the back of my hand with an alcohol wipe. It leaves an icy trail and pulls me further from my lulled state. I watch the doctor insert a long needle into my vein. A forgotten cotton wipe rests in the folds of the cotton waffle weave blanket, in its center a bright red bloody mark, like a scarlet letter.

There's a spark of memory, it ignites but then fizzles, like a wet match. I refuse to be pulled away, I follow the crimson, attach myself to the memory that started out like a creak on the stairs, but then the monsters appear.

First I remember the darkness.

Then I remember the blood.

My baby. Oh God, Mia.

The blood lingers. There's flashes of crimson exploding like lightning in the sky, one moment they're illuminating everything around me, the next they are gone, bathing my world in darkness. Then the bloody images fade and vanish, leaving a black jittering line on the screen.

Squeaking rubber soles on linoleum circle me and I feel a pat on my shoulder.

This isn't real. A random vision, just a vision. It doesn't mean anything.

A nurse gently squeezes my shoulder and I open my eyes.

'Mrs Paradise,' the nurse's voice is soft, almost apologetic. 'I'm sorry, but I have orders to wake you every couple of hours.'

'Blood,' I say, and squint my eyes, attempting to force the image to return to me. 'I don't understand where all this blood's coming from.' Was that my voice? It can't be mine, it sounds nothing like me.

'Blood? What blood?' The nurse looks at my immaculately taped central line. 'Are you bleeding?'

I turn towards the window. It's dark outside. The entire room appears in the window's reflection, like an imprint, a not-quite true copy of reality.

'Oh God,' I say and my high-pitched voice sounds like a screeching microphone. 'Where's my daughter?'

She just cocks her head and then busies herself straightening the blanket. 'Let me get the doctor for you,' she says and leaves the room.